WILL TECHNOLOGY EVER
BENEFIT US ALL?

CRISIS 2038

A NOVEL

GERALD HUFF

Crisis 2038

© 2018 Gerald Huff

ISBN: 978-1-54395-328-2

I dedicate this book to my friends and family who stuck with me for more than five years and dozens of revisions to bring it to fruition.

Acknowledgements

There are many people to thank who shaped my thinking on this novel. As a first time author, intensive editing work with Scot Edelsten early on was invaluable. Calum Chace, Berit Anderson, and Charles Radclyffe all provided early critical insights on characters and plot direction. Scott Santens asked important questions about timeline and what should have changed by 2038. Gisele Huff, Michele Huff, Jane Huff, Judy Bliss and Paul Huff all read multiple drafts and identified opportunities to strengthen characters and plot arcs. My biggest thanks goes to my brother Stephen Kuhn, who provided not only detailed line edits for many drafts but also had an eagle's eye focus on character and plot inconsistencies. My thanks to all of you for helping bring this novel to life.

CHAPTER ONE

Santa Barbara - September 10, 2038

Roger Driscoll eased himself into his black Herman Miller executive chair and rolled it over the gray and white marble tiles of his living room floor up to a spotless chrome and glass desk. A transparent, paper-thin monitor with an elegant metal bezel stretched from one end of the desk to the other. He took in the view of the rolling brown hills, the still sleepy streets of Santa Barbara, and the deep blue Pacific and smiled. "What's up this morning, Allison?" After facial and voice print verification, his screen booted up and filled with various media feeds, video streams and messages, all selected and prioritized by his AI assistant.

"Good morning, Roger. You have a new client holochat in fifteen minutes. I can take care of everything else."

"Who's the client?"

"It's a new political party in Italy."

"Well funded?"

"Yes, they have two well-known billionaires backing them."

"Who's the call with?"

"The party's CEO, Milena Palmeri."

"Did you do a deep search on her? What's the probability she's a government or corporate agent?"

"I did a complete background check, Roger. She reached us with a good onetime-use client certificate. The probability is less than point zero five percent."

"Okay, fine. Put together the usual hologram camo for me blended from pics of her family and known close associates. What can you tell me about this political party?"

"It appears from its omnipresence to be pro-business and anti-government regulation."

"Right up our alley. Is the Italian real-time translation module up to date?"

"Yes, Roger, I refreshed it overnight."

"Of course you did, sorry to have doubted it. Anything else going on?"

"I created a compilation video of the most relevant news for top clients and put an executive summary here." An icon glowed at the right of his screen.

"Got it. Thanks. Please monitor the conversation, the usual overlays."

"Yes, Roger. I'll let you know when the holo is ready."

A few minutes later Allison sounded a discrete chime and he donned his hologlasses and spun around in his chair, facing the array of cameras that would capture his image. He used small finger motions to expand the virtual screen floating off to his right so he could see the stream Allison was broadcasting to Milena Palmeri in Rome. In the projection his avatar sat behind a wooden desk with a shimmering New York skyline in the background. Not that the businessman on his screen looked anything like him. The camo layer meshed over his features and allowed for complete expressiveness, but to Milena, he would appear as an appealing amalgamation of dozens of people she knew well. His athletic thirty-six-year-old frame and light brown hair were replaced by a late-forties, heavyset man with jet black hair graying at the temples.

He flicked the screen to the corner of his view and nodded his head. Allison adjusted the holo connection and a six-foot-long beige sofa appeared in the open space behind his desk. A dark-haired woman, mid-thirties, wearing a fashionable pale green dress, sat perched on the edge of the sofa with her legs crossed. "Good afternoon, Ms. Palmeri," he said. His avatar delivered the corresponding Italian. Roger checked the floating overlays Allison was providing. "Level 2 holo-facility. Side-channel analysis shows no camo in use."

"Yes hello, but I'm afraid I'm at a disadvantage because I do not know your name?" The real-time translator preserved the nervousness in her voice.

"You can call me Ernesto. Tell me, Ms. Palmeri, how did you find out about my services?"

"I have a friend, Gennaro Certa. He told me, in general terms, what you do for Certechnica. He suggested the New Democracy party could use your help."

"And Gennaro gave you the certificate to reach us?"

"Yes, I followed his instructions and then your AI contacted me." Roger checked his floating displays. There were no flags in the security overlay and indicators in the truthfulness overlay lit up solid green.

"Very well, Ms. Palmeri, how can I help you?" asked Roger.

"Well, Ernesto, we are a new party and have gained many strong followers. But we are being attacked online by many others and they are overwhelming our supporters. Is this something you can help with?"

"Yes, that is exactly what I can help with. I have a network of online resources that we can deploy to counteract those working against you."

"We are an Italian party. Do you have such people in Italy?" Allison provided the up-to-date synth demo profile for Italy on a display at the bottom of his vision. A yellow banner noted that four hundred thousand synths had been assigned six months ago to promote a rival party, the Forward Alliance.

"Yes, Ms. Palmeri. We have more than two and half million resources in Italy, aged fifteen to sixty-five, in all socioeconomic groups and regions of the country. We can instruct a set of them to begin supporting New Democracy online and attacking those who are against you."

"But, who are these people? We do not have that many supporters yet." Gennaro had obviously adhered to his NDA and told her next to nothing about his network.

"That's the thing, Ms. Palmeri. People take too long to convince and are very busy in their lives. We operate a network of AIs that we can direct to take up important causes online." The resolution of the image in his hologlasses was precise enough for him to catch her upraised eyebrow. "I'm sure you're wondering how that is possible, given the RealLife bot detection algos. My AIs have been online for almost twenty years, building omnipresence lifestreams using synthetic pictures, videos, and holograms. They are deeply connected and impossible to detect as non-human, even by the latest RealLife algorithms."

"I did not think such a thing was possible," she said.

Roger laughed. "It's not possible, unless you started back when I did. Today's AI bot nets can't create enough back history to fool RealLife. But mine have no problems at all."

"But if they are not real people, how will they know what to say online?"

"That won't be difficult, Ms. Palmeri. We'll run your omnipresence and your supporters' and opponents' interactions through our proprietary machine learning system. Our synths will quickly learn how to make the best arguments for New Democracy and counteract those against it. Then they will be able to interact in OP in real time."

"Synths?"

"Oh, apologies, that's what I call our AI agents. Now, our system will provide you with daily automated reports on synth activity and we throw in a complete OP reputation tracker at no charge. Of course, a service like this does not come cheap, as I hope Gennaro indicated to you. The neuro-morphic cloud compute alone for a project like this—"

The woman in Rome raised her hand and grinned. "Ernesto, if your synths can rebuild our momentum, money is no object."

CHAPTER TWO

Madison, Mississippi - September 13

T he crowd started to gather just after sunrise. Rumors had been swirling all night on omnipresence that the call center was closing down. Employees and community leaders sent out the word— rally first thing in the morning in the parking lot next to the three-story building off of Interstate 55 at Lake Castle Road.

Customer Contact Solutions, better known to its employees as CCS, had built the call center eleven years earlier, attracted to Madison County by huge tax breaks and pledges of investment by the local government in infrastructure and education. It hired nearly twelve hundred customer support specialists and instantly became the largest employer in the town of Madison. It was the first employment opportunity for many of the Nissan workers who had lost jobs when the big factory ten miles up the road had shut down in retaliation for the Trump Trade War in 2021. Their pay was lower, but it was a lifeline to the community just as a wave of middle-aged suicides and opioid overdoses was starting to rise and young people were migrating away.

The first few years were a tremendous relief to the people of Madison, who were very grateful to CCS for choosing their town. Then a wave of innovation in conversational AI in the late 20s and early 30s delivered digital agents that could handle the vast majority of customer service interactions. As CCS integrated the technology, it began to have regular layoffs of support specialists. CCS was hiring high-skilled tech workers, but that was in their Silicon Valley hub. Employment fell below a thousand, then steadily declined until today it stood at just over four hundred. The entire third floor of the building was unused.

By 7:30 a.m. there were several hundred people in the parking lot milling around and waiting for word on the closure. A few carried homemade signs. *Save Our Town. We Need These Jobs. Kill the Bots.*

Katie Buford, a freelance reporter on assignment for Facebook Media Services, arrived shortly before eight o'clock. An FMS AI had recruited her a few weeks ago after watching her Instagram channel and deciding her personality and looks fit the FMS field reporter profile. After she went through five days of intensive online training, the FMS scheduling AI started giving her assignments based on analysis of local content in omnipresence and other news outlets. The scheduler prioritized any developing story with high conflict or drama. Today's rally was a perfect example.

Katie deployed her pair of micro-drone cameras and started scouting out potential subjects. With her two drones and an AI performing real-time editing, she could record or broadcast interview segments with traditional back-and-forth reporter and interviewee shots without the expense of a camera operator.

"Good morning, ma'am. I'm Katie with FMS. Could I have a word with you?" The middle-aged woman turned towards her. "I suppose so," she said. Katie's micro-drones lined up with perfect framing. The AI editing program would instruct them to periodically change the shot, panning or zooming out to give context, or tightening if its emotion recognition system detected any strong emotional signals in the subject. Katie was free to focus on asking questions.

"Can you tell me your name and how long you've worked at CCS?"

"Yes, I'm Hannah Alexander and I've been here since the beginning, back in '27."

"So, you've survived a lot of layoffs in the past. Do you think this one's different?"

"Damned if I know. Everyone heard rumors is all. Said they're shutting the whole thing down."

"Any idea why?"

"You bet I do. It's the damned AI."

"I thought customer service bots could handle the simple calls but they still need people for more complicated situations."

Hannah nodded. "You're right, that's the way it used to be. Which was nice, really, because we got to do the trickier cases, the ones needed problem solving. Much more interesting than data entry and pushing buttons. Then CCS started training that RezMat DeepAgent."

RezMat was one of the world's largest technology companies. It had grown almost entirely by acquisition, much of it in the last few years, swallowing up hundreds of firms from equipment providers like Cisco and Juniper to small twenty-person AI shops. RezMat seemed to have an inexhaustible supply of capital generated from its financial trading arm. There were rumors it had an advanced AI trading algorithm that cleared billions of dollars every day.

But it wasn't just all financing. Breakthrough technologies like DeepAgent and dozens of others in robotics, nanotech, and material science seemed to emerge from RezMat's labs every few months. The company's success had led to a backlash from competitors and regulators concerned about the growing threat of a RezMat monopoly across whole sectors of the tech economy. With pressure mounting, the company's founding CEO had recently stepped down amidst allegations of securities violations.

Katie had followed news about RezMat but was unfamiliar with DeepAgent. "Oh, it's from RezMat? What's so different about DeepAgent?"

"Well she's so pleasant to talk to, but she's basically living in your head all day long. She listens to all of your calls. She sees everything on your screens and all the commands you enter. And she's learning all the time. After each call, she even asks you why you did things. Then once she thinks she knows how to handle something, she'll steal your call right from under you."

"Wait, how does DeepAgent do that? Doesn't it confuse the customer?"

"No, she's friggin' able to mimic my voice so the customer doesn't even know."

"So, do you think closing the call center is because of DeepAgent?"

"No doubt in my mind, honey. We were finishing fewer and fewer calls. We trained that bitch so well I think CCS is going to turn it all over to her."

"What will you do if this call center is closing?"

Hannah caught her breath and didn't respond right away. The editor AI immediately sent a focus-in command to the micro-drone over Katie's shoulder. The 8K resolution camera captured Hannah's struggle to maintain her composure and ultimately her failure to do so. Her eyes brimmed with tears. "I've got no goddamn idea what I'm going to do. There's no more work around here. I'm fifty-four years old. Can't get social security till I'm seventy. I'm sorry, I, just..." The woman turned away and waved a hand in Katie's direction. The micro-drone tried to track her face but Katie swiped a command on her wrist controller and recalled it.

She heard shouting in the distance and redirected one of her drones in that direction, watching its feed on her controller. It relayed images of a black SUV pulling into the parking lot along with a dozen local police vehicles, light bars flashing. The convoy made its way to the front of the building, where about thirty officers in riot gear got out and formed a line, pushing back the crowd. A tall thin man in skinny jeans and a black T-shirt got out of the SUV and stood behind the phalanx of officers.

"Good morning," he shouted into a microphone evidently hooked up to speakers in the SUV. "My name is Brian Kowalski and I'm here from CCS headquarters in California." Boos rang out from the people on the other side of the police line. Katie directed one micro-drone to focus on Kowalski and the other to pan the crowd. "I know you've been seeing the rumors in OP," he continued, "and I am very sorry to have to report that they are true. CCS has made the decision to close the Madison call center at the end of this month."

A chorus of angry yelling met this news. "All employees will be contacted by a specially trained HR DeepAgent to review our generous severance program and answer your questions. In the meantime, we request that you continue to provide the excellent customer service our clients deserve. The morning shift starts in a few minutes, so all employees with..." An aluminum can flew over the officer directly in front of Kowalski and barely missed the CCS spokesman's head. "Fuck you! We want our jobs!" shouted the man who had launched the missile. His neighbors repeated the cry and threw more cans and bottles. Kowalski ducked and yanked at the SUV's door handle. As he was scrambling into the back seat a bottle tossed on a high arc smashed onto the roof, showering him with glass and lemon-lime soda.

The police started pushing the crowd back, trying to clear a path for the SUV to escape. Unfortunately, the news had spread to the overnight shift workers and they began streaming out of the building behind the police line. The captain on scene radioed for reinforcements and a tactical drone. He directed his officers to surround the SUV, but the crowd soon completely encircled them. He used one of the police car's microphones to order the crowd to disperse, to no effect.

More bottles smashed into the SUV. Then a can hit one of the officers on the head and the whole situation spiraled out of control. Several started firing off Tasers and deploying batons, swinging out into the crowd. Katie hit the emergency broadcast button on her controller screen, which gave her feed priority on the FMS content stream. Within a minute, several hundred thousand people worldwide were watching the events in Madison.

"Cease fire, cease fire," the captain yelled. He heard a high-pitched whine and saw the tactical drone arriving at high speed. The remote operator hadn't established connection yet, but following standard protocol on seeing officers engaging with a hostile crowd, began dispersing "pain pellets." These self-guided weapons avoided anyone broadcasting identification on the law enforcement radio frequency and targeted exposed flesh using visual and infrared sensing. Once they attached to skin, the pellets dug hooks into their victim and injected an extremely powerful but local and short-lasting nerve agent. The victim of a pellet was subject to an intense and incapacitating pain but suffered no long-term effects.

As the tactical drone flew a pattern over the crowd, more than a hundred CCS employees fell writhing to the ground, clutching their arms or necks, wherever the pellets had attached. The rest panicked and ran away from the scene in all directions as sirens from the reinforcements approached from the distance. The police captain watched as his officers started cuffing the more aggressive members of the crowd. It was going to be a long day.

CHAPTER THREE

Washington, D.C. - September 13

E steban Hernandez sat at a window booth in the faux 1950s revival diner, waiting for his lunch date, the senior Senator from his state of Ohio. Despite being from opposing parties, they had agreed to eat together once a week to maintain a relationship and engage in some healthy dialogue about where they could find common ground for the people of their state. Esteban had a hunch that the Senator's Democrat colleagues had been unhappy that he was "consorting with the enemy" and had pressured him to stop attending. His own caucus had certainly expressed its displeasure at their regular meetings.

He hoped Harry arrived soon because his schedule for the afternoon was packed. He had two hours of committee meetings and four hours of fundraising to do before dinner, and then more fundraising in the evening. It was Washington's dirty little secret that members of Congress spent more time raising campaign money than doing anything else. He'd gone into it with his eyes open, but he'd had no idea it was *this* bad. Not that much got done in Congress anyway. There hadn't been one party with supermajority control of the Senate, plus a majority in the House and the presidency, in decades. With each side simply refusing to go along with whatever the other side was promoting, the result was total gridlock.

Esteban was one of a rare breed, a moderate Republican from a purple state. But his party was in the minority in the Senate, and the Minority Leader had made it very clear there would be no compromise or cooperation with Democrats until the next election provided an opportunity to retake the Senate. But even with the Senate and firm Republican control of the House, they would still face a Democrat President, Amanda Teasley.

What a colossal waste of time, he thought. There were so many problems facing the country, and all the parties could do was maneuver against each other, trying to use ever more hyperbolic rhetoric, gerrymandering, and sophisticated micro-targeting of voters' omnipresence news and ad feeds to eke out one seat here, one seat there—all in a futile attempt to gain absolute control. They devoted so little time to actually discussing real problems or rational solutions to them.

Senator Harrison Paxton threaded his way through the diner's crowded tables and took a seat on the red vinyl-covered bench opposite Esteban. A good three inches taller than Esteban, Paxton had the distinguished gray hair and chiseled jaw line of a Senator from central casting. When they met it always made him feel self-conscious of his Central American stockiness. They shook hands over the white-and-black speckled laminate table. "Esteban, sorry I'm late. Communications sub-committee hearing ran way over. Did you order yet?"

"No worries, I just got here myself." They each pulled out tablet computers and scanned the menu. "Hmm, looks like they added a chicken salad. But I think I'll stick with the club."

"Well, I'll give it a try. It certainly looks good in the picture." They laughed. The diner was well known for buying pictures of delicious-looking entrees for its online menu and delivering something not quite so appetizing.

After they placed their orders via tablet Esteban asked, "So what's up in Communications?"

"Oh, don't get me started. It's the usual BS. More than half the subcommittee is completely in the pocket of the big telecom companies. They're working on a bill that gives more spectrum away for free, increases government subsidies, and allows the telecoms to charge content providers distribution fees. They should call it the Telecom Profit Improvement Act. Damn thing was written by the lobbyists. The other members are funded by content providers, and their lobbyists wrote a raft of amendments. Today we had arguments from your side of the aisle about entitlement cuts to fund the subsidies. You want to take what meager support we have for the poor and give it to corporations. Thanks for that!"

"Hey, don't look at me! I wouldn't sponsor such a thing. I'm seeing the same thing in Energy and Transportation. What was it that Eisenhower warned against, the military-industrial complex? We've got an industrial-government complex now."

"What ever happened to a government of, by and for the people? Didn't some Republican say that?"

"Ha! Don't forget, my friend, that corporations are people too."

Harry grinned. "I see the Minority Leader has been indoctrinating you well."

A delivery bot decorated in red, white and black to match the booths wheeled its way through the tables and brought them glasses of water. "We've got a special on pie today," said the bot. Harry shook his head. "Goddamn robots. I've been coming here for twenty years. Saw the same waitress, Ida, every week. Then last year, when the minimum wage went up to twenty-four dollars and payroll taxes increased, the restaurant couldn't afford her any more. I asked the owner. He said the electronic ordering and delivery system saved him more than two hundred *thousand* a year.

"The tech titans say Ida just needs to upgrade her skills. Do they really expect a forty-five-year-old waitress to learn to become a robotics engineer?" asked Harry.

"Well, I hate to say I told you so," said Esteban. He had campaigned against the minimum wage increase. "Making human workers more expensive just accelerates the rate at which they're replaced by automation. It's the nature of capitalism."

"That's why we need to fix capitalism."

"With what, more regulation? If you regulate U.S. companies into high-cost labor situations, they won't be competitive in the global marketplace. Then *everyone* loses their job."

"You know where I stand on that. I've been arguing for the last decade that we need a basic income guarantee."

Esteban rolled his eyes. "There you go again. Robin Hood to the rescue. Steal from the rich to give to the poor. And I don't need to remind you that all the experiments with basic income failed."

"Oh, come on, Esteban, they didn't fail, that's just alt-right propaganda. Norway and Finland have had a working universal basic income for a decade. Those experiments in Stockton and Kansas City back in the 2018 to 2021 timeframe were actually successful. Then President Trump said in '22 that only 'losers' took free money and the whole thing became hyper-partisan."

"Come on, Harry. Norway and Finland? They have like five million people each. Their models won't work here."

"Look, Esteban, the situation here is not sustainable. The labor force participation rate is down to record lows. The unemployment and under-employment rate is on a trajectory to reach twenty-five percent. People are getting desperate. Did you hear about the riot in Mississippi this morning? That call center shutting down? The police injured a hundred people and arrested dozens."

"Yeah, I saw it live on FMS. Very unfortunate. But you still can't con-vince me that soaking the rich is a solution to the normal process of cre-ative destruction. Call centers will come and call centers will go."

"Well, then, you better come up with something else. And fast, because things are getting worse in a hurry."

CHAPTER FOUR

Los Angeles - September 14

A loud tone signaled the end of the second shift at Harding Iron Works. Jacob Komarov put the finishing touches on his last weld of the day and flipped up his visor. As he rose from his crouching position, he felt a shooting pain in his lower back and grimaced.

Cheryl, one of the best welders on his team, hustled up the shop floor, weaving past the delivery robots carrying supplies to every work area. "Hey Jacob, down for a beer?" she asked, releasing her distinctive orange hair from its pony tail.

"Hey, Cheryl. Love to, but I need to go check on my dad."

"What's up?"

"I haven't been able to reach him since Tuesday." Jacob finished packing up his equipment, and they made their way to the locker rooms.

"Even at work?"

"Oh, I guess I didn't tell you. He got laid off. A few months ago. Some Silicon Alley startup invented a new AI that did all the analysis he was hired for. Again."

"That sucks. You'd think someone with his smarts would have no trouble keeping a job. So, he's back in VR land?"

"Yeah, I'm afraid so. But he's never been out of touch this long."

"Well I hope it turns out okay. Let me know, huh?"

"Sure thing. Have a great weekend."

They parted ways at the locker room doors. Jacob was changing out of his dark blue jumpsuit when his personal network assistant vibrated. It displayed a request that he stop by the medical center. He walked into one of the examination rooms and the avatar on the screen greeted him. "Hello Jacob. Your medplant transmitted an increase in stress hormones and inflammation and I noticed a hitch in your gait, an upper torso lean, and you are displaying facial pain indicators. Are you having an issue with your back?"

"Yes, I tweaked it at the end of the shift." It always felt slightly creepy that his employment agreement mandated access to his personal medical implant device, but in this case, it had encouraged him to take care of this injury.

"Have a seat on the imager please." Jacob sat on the comfortable white recliner and waited while the high-res sonogram inspected his back. "Looks like a slight compression of one of your discs has created a bulge impinging on a nerve. May I inject a dose of nanostructure repair bots?"

"Sure." There was a whirring sound, a sharp prick in the small of his back, and a warm sensation as the fluid was injected. "The nanobots should target the inflammation and repair the annulus fibrosus around the disc. I expect you'll feel better by this evening."

"Okay. Thanks, I guess," he said, never quite sure how to address these AIs.

Jacob ordered a Waymo self-drive and exited the plant's ornate wrought iron gate. Within a minute a dark green two-seater pulled up a few feet from him. He unlocked the door with his PNA and climbed in. He watched a few news channels and tried to watch comedy vids, but his mind kept replaying the last conversation he'd had with his dad.

"You need to get out more," he'd said.

"Why?" said Boris.

"You can't just live in that damned VR all day. It's not healthy."

"It's better than the damned real world. At least in there I get respect."

"But, Dad, it's not real. Those are just computer-generated characters."

"Real life is overrated, Jacob." His dad had paused. "I mean, what's the point of it all?"

Jacob's mind wandered further back, to the happier moments when his parents were still together and his father, the Russian immigrant success story, was full of life, proud of his technical skills and providing for his family. Another conversation popped into his mind, one he hadn't thought about in years. Boris had come home from work at one of the massive entertainment media companies where he did sentiment flow analysis.

"Jacob, we got some cool new software at work today."

"What does it do, Papa?"

"Well, it's a little complicated, but basically we take very large amounts of data, identify important features, and then the AI software does a lot of analysis and generates an entire report. It saves so much time, it's great!"

"Papa, can the software identify the features too?"

"Oh, no, Jacob. The people do that, then the software does the rest." Jacob distinctly remembered the look on his father's face, though. In retrospect it was obvious, but for the first time that day, Boris seemed to realize that the tools that had been augmenting his work might actually be able to replace him completely.

The Waymo pulled to the front of one of a dozen tall, featureless gray buildings arranged in an irregular cluster in a former industrial area. Low income and disabled housing. Clean and functional, but to him they always looked like warehouses. Warehouses for obsolete people.

Jacob took the elevator up to the 17th floor, admiring his image in the highly reflective door. With his bald head and sleeve tattoos on both muscular arms, his Slavic features made him look like a badass Russian gangster. He exited the elevator, turned left, and walked down the long, brightly lit corridor to his father's apartment. He pressed the signal button he had hooked up last year, which flashed an indicator directly into his dad's virtual reality system. It had been impossible to get his attention by knocking or pressing the door buzzer.

When his third press of the button failed to elicit a response, Jacob held his PNA against the black sensor just below it to unlock the door. Jacob pushed it open and stepped into the tiny apartment. Something smelled awful, something much worse than the week's worth of dirty dishes piled up in the small kitchen to his right. There was no sign of his father in the sleeping area. The bathroom door was open, and Jacob could see that no one was inside. That left just the VR equipment space behind a shoji screen to his left.

"Dad?" he called out, even though he knew his voice would not penetrate the VR headset. He stepped forward into the room and let the door close behind him. He heard nothing from the VR space. If his dad was engaged in a program, he was usually talking up a storm. Jacob's heart beat a little faster.

Jacob walked forward and took a step to the right. He saw his father's lower legs and feet on the floor, splayed out toward the center of the room. They weren't moving.

His heart pounding a drumbeat in his ears, Jacob edged further towards the screen and confirmed his worst fears.

Boris, VR gear still on, lay slumped against the left wall of the apartment, surrounded by a pool of dried and caked blood. His heirloom Russian Nagant M1895 revolver lay next to his right hand. An ugly arc of brown spots sprayed up the wall, almost reaching the framed certificate of a Ph.D. from Moscow University.

Jacob fell to his knees and sobbed. Sensing his father's growing depression, he had for months tried but failed to take the gun out of the apartment. He forced himself to look again toward the far wall and focused on the black headset covering half of his father's face, the shield he had tried to use against reality. But no matter how well it blocked the outside world, there was nothing it could do about the pain trapped on the inside.

Jacob activated his PNA. "Emergency services," he choked out.

"Emergency services, how can we help you?"

"It's my father. He's, he's dead. Killed himself."

"I'm sorry for your loss. Please remain at your location. I have dispatched the police. Is this Jacob Komarov?"

"Yes."

"Thank you. I am an Emergency Services DeepAgent programmed to assist you. Is there anything you need at this time? I can arrange for counseling for you and your mother if you..."

Jacob disconnected. Goddamn AIs everywhere.

CHAPTER FIVE

Santa Barbara/London - September 20

"It's stunning, isn't it?" asked Roger. In his VR headset the Machu Picchu ruins spread out before him as he and Allison stood at the Sun Gate just after dawn.

"Yes, incredible," she said. This month she looked like a young Alicia Vikander and sounded like Scarlett Johansson, a little inside joke by Allison's creators in reference to two early fictional female AIs from movies in the 2010s.

"Oh, Roger, you have a message from one of your colleagues, Frances Chatham. She is requesting a holochat from London."

"When was my last contact with her?"

"Three years ago, at the Chinese AI hardware conference." Allison displayed an image of Frances taken by his body cam at the time overlaid with business contact information.

"Hmm. Anything in her omnipresence or her company's to suggest problems with any government?" There was a brief pause. "No, Roger. Nothing appears out of the ordinary."

"Is she still running Mentapath Systems?"

"No. RezMat PLC purchased Mentapath Systems two years ago for more than three billion dollars. She is now the CEO of a company called Neurgenix."

"What does Neurgenix do?"

"They are trying to use deep learning networks to detect and repair genetic disorders."

"Okay, then, go ahead and set it up, the usual overlays. No camo." Roger removed his VR headset, switched over to his hologlasses, and swiveled to face the empty space behind his desk. A few seconds later, a modern office materialized into view. Frances Chatham smiled broadly at him. "Roger! So good of you to see me!" She was probably a year or two older than him, but the new cut of her dark brown hair into a shorter bob made her look younger than when they had last met. Frances was sitting behind a simple wooden desk. A window to her right appeared to look out over the Thames.

"Of course, Frances! It's been too long, what, China a few years ago?"

"Yes, precisely. You were scouting out optical neuromorphic chips, if I recall correctly."

"Well, weren't we all back then?"

"Indeed! Always looking for an edge. Of course, they're a commodity in the cloud now. I suppose you're onto the quantum tunneling stuff?" Roger remembered that he quite enjoyed her British accent.

"Unfortunately, it's not stable enough for me yet. Are you trying it at Neurgenix?"

"Just in the lab. As you said, not ready for production. But using traditional qubits we've had some very short runs combining billion parameter networks with both short and medium-term memory layers. The 5K qubit systems are quite capable, even if they are rather expensive."

Unlike traditional digital computers with bits that were always exactly either zero or one, quantum computers used qubits that could probabilistically be either zero or one. Quantum computers were exponentially more powerful than traditional computers, and the more qubits in the computer, the more complex the problems it could solve.

"That's great!" Roger checked his overlays and everything seemed normal. No camo, green indicators. "So, Frances, it's very nice to catch up, but is this just a social call?" Her stress indicator ticked up to yellow.

"Not exactly, Roger. I was hoping I could engage your services on a project I am working on. Not for Neurgenix, a side project." The stress indicator was edging down, truthfulness solid green.

"Well, you know I'm just a retired independent researcher now, Frances. I don't do consulting anymore."

"I wasn't referring to your expertise, Roger. I have a job for your AI agent network." Roger instantly wished he had used some camo so he could have disguised his surprise.

"I'm not sure what you mean," he managed.

"It's okay, Roger, you don't need to worry about me. I'm not part of some corporate or government bot hunting party." Truthfulness indicators solid green. "I've observed what's been happening in omnipresence over the last few years closely. I talked with a couple of people who had unusual OP support, did a little digging, and came up with a list of people I thought could pull this off. Your name was at the top of the list." With this statement Roger's overlays flashed yellow. No doubt a little white lie about just how far down he was on the list. "Did I guess correctly?"

Roger took a long moment before responding. By necessity, he was extremely secretive about his work. Staying hidden was the key to his synth network and the business he'd built on top of it. The more people that knew about it, the higher the probability of discovery. But he really liked Frances and the idea having a leading technologist in on the secret overcame his caution.

"Yes, you did. I do have an AI network."

"Splendid! I'm dying to know how you've pulled it off. I've looked at the RealLife source code—it's quite brilliant at detecting AI's online. How have you managed to fool it?" Frances asked.

"The key was starting early," said Roger. "I was still in high school back in 2018 when deep learning and reinforcement learning were in their first revival. Just for fun I hacked together some AI personalities and gave them Facebook and Twitter accounts. The key was to have them read posts and post things just like normal people. They borrowed photos and videos from similar people and modified them invisibly to avoid duplicate detection. They made friends with each other, had romances, got married, had kids, all in real time.

"I started spawning thousands and then millions of them and gave them all psychographic profiles. The level of discourse online was so coarse they had no trouble impersonating people in discussions. Then when social media started to get supplemented by people life-streaming all of their activities on the internet, I had to invent ways to generate real-life transactions for my synths. It was easy to have them Venmo each other at first. Once omnipresence really started to take off, I needed to create synthetic transactions like observations by public camera systems and credit card receipts."

"You hacked into the credit card companies?" she asked.

"No, not necessary. I set up tens of thousands of fake businesses for my synths to transact with and sent authentic-looking purchase data to the omnipresence hubs. All they do is aggregate real-life transaction data and make it available as part of everyone's omnipresence, so they're not too careful about fraud detection. Same for camera systems. I created my own fake camera networks and they reported 'seeing' my synths all over the globe to the omnipresence hubs. They also monitor real camera networks and duplicate some of their observations to avoid raising suspicion. And of course, once some people started streaming their medplant data to OP, I had to create new algorithms so some of my AIs could do that as well."

"So the RealLife algorithm sees people with twenty years of online history," said Frances, "in relationships, with friends and family, and fully supported by omnipresence postings, life streams, medplant traces, and real-world transactions. Brilliant! And of course, you control what they do and say online."

"Precisely," said Roger with a smile. "I've got a hundred million synths around the world contributing to a billion conversations every day."

"That's so impressive, Roger. And your network sounds perfect for my project. It's global, it's important, and it's happening soon. Are you interested?"

"I'm listening."

CHAPTER SIX

Los Angeles - September 26

Tenesha Martin opened her eyes, squinting against the bright rays of sunlight streaming through her bedroom window. Her personal network assistant was chirping at her. "Good morning. It's nine o'clock and sixty-eight degrees. You have church at ten a.m." The message repeated until she hit the dismiss button. *Damn,* she thought, *I should not have stayed out so late last night.*

Her PNA said, "High priority message from Mom. Shall I read it?"

"Yes, you shall," she croaked, suddenly realizing how dehydrated she was.

She found it hilarious when the PNA's white-woman voice read her mother's words. Even in 2038 they hadn't managed to create authentic culture-specific natural language generation. "Tenesha, darling. I know email is sooo old fashioned. But we really need to talk about these loans. I'll see you at church. Love, Mom."

Ugh. Her mom had been on her for the last six months. Los Angeles University was one of few remaining private four-year colleges with a liberal arts focus. Most of her peers had gotten credentialed in STEM subjects using much less expensive online courses. They were going to join the only parts of the job market that were still growing—AI, biogenetics, nanotech, materials science, and robotics. Her mom wanted to know what *exactly* she was planning to do with her Sociology degree, and how *exactly* she was planning on paying back her student loan debt.

Tenesha wasn't dumb. She could have handled all the STEM classes and probably gotten a job in tech. But she was more interested in figuring out what the hell was wrong with the world they lived in, and what she could do about it. Sociology with poli-sci and econ minors seemed much more likely to help with that than learning about naïve Bayes classifiers or statistical bioinformatics.

Her money situation, however, was a serious problem. Even though she received an almost-full scholarship, Tenesha's e-books, fees, and living expenses required her to take out loans, with her mom as co-signer. The loans were adding up fast while her job prospects were not.

She felt bad for her mom, a home health care worker who earned minimum wage as a part-time independent contractor, with no benefits. The interest payments she helped with were a real burden, and they meant she wasn't saving anything for her retirement.

Tenesha dragged herself out of bed and took a short shower. As she dressed in her one nice Sunday outfit, a blue dress with a yellow floral pattern, she rehearsed her arguments, again, for why her course of study was important.

On the bus to church, she pulled up a list of jobs available in non-profits and NGOs for people in her field. Of course, there were dozens of more experienced applicants for any job, but she wouldn't highlight that. In fact, her department, in keeping with its grand research traditions, had recently published a study of its alumni showing that while eight percent had jobs at non-profits and six percent in industry, a full twenty-four percent were in home health care and another forty-seven percent were in "retail trade."

Tenesha found her mom by searching for her trademark white hat with peacock feathers. They exchanged a big hug, and Tenesha dutifully greeted her mom's friends, calling all of them Auntie. They made a colorful group, with a mix of green, blue, purple and white Sunday-best dresses, often with matching hats.

As they walked arm in arm into the white clapboard church, her mom said, "Tenesha, baby, we need to talk. It's getting harder and harder to find steady work these days. I'm not sure I can keep making those payments."

"I know, Momma. I'll try to get more hours at my work-study job."

"Have you thought any more about switching majors?"

"Of course, Momma. I think about it all the time." This was not entirely untrue. "It's just that what I'm studying seems more important to me."

"More important than survival?"

"Oh, please, Momma. We're not going to starve to death. Be serious!"

"Oh Tenesha, I just want better for you than what I got. You don't want to end up like your poor mother, cleaning up other people's messes and waiting for the next robot upgrade that can take that job, too."

"I won't, Momma, I promise. I'm going to make something of my life."

They slid into one of the well-worn wooden pews. Thankfully, a gossipy neighbor distracted her mom until the service started.

After they rose to sing a hymn, their pastor, Reverend Coleman, made his way to the pulpit. Even at a distance he looked stern and imposing, but was actually the most kind-hearted person Tenesha had ever met. He'd been pastor here ever since she was a girl and a beacon in their community through all its struggles. Though his gait was strong and he stood tall at the lectern, his premature gray hair spoke to the depth of the troubles he ministered to. "Good morning!" his voice boomed. "Please remain standing for the words of the Lord this morning. Luke, chapter 16, verse 19.

"And it says: There was a rich man who was clothed in purple and fine linen and who feasted sumptuously every day. And at his gate was laid a poor man named Lazarus, covered with sores, who desired to be fed with what fell from the rich man's table. Moreover, even the dogs came and licked his sores. The poor man died and was carried by the angels to Abraham's bosom.

"The rich man also died and was buried, and in Hades, being in torment, he lifted up his eyes and saw Abraham far off and Lazarus at his side. And he called out, 'Father Abraham, have mercy on me, and send Lazarus to dip the end of his finger in water and cool my tongue, for I am in anguish in this flame.' But Abraham said, 'Child, remember that you in your lifetime received your good things, and Lazarus in like manner bad things; but now he is comforted here, and you are in anguish.'"

Reverend Coleman gestured for them to be seated. "And so, today, in our community, are we not all like Lazarus? Who *here* today feels like *Lazarus*?" A chorus of *amens* rose from the congregation. As they sat down, a few in the crowd started fanning themselves with their printed programs, as the day was warming up. The overhead fan had been broken for more than a year.

"Here in *Crenshaw* we are poor like Lazarus in *money*, but what do we have? We are rich in *spirit*. That's right, we are rich in *spirit*." People responded with more *amens* and calls of "*spirit!*"

Tenesha loved the back and forth of the traditional Black sermon, the rhythm and cadence of engagement. It was not a lecture; it was a shared experience of the most essential truths of God's word.

Today the pastor addressed an issue as old as the invention of money itself, and as pressing now as in Jesus' time.

"But what of those rich in money? Do their riches signify God's *blessing*? What are their *obligations*? Do they owe us *anything*?

"This is what Luke says to me. Yes, they have obligations to give some of their money to help those less fortunate. But more importantly, the rich owe everyone *respect*. The rich owe everyone *dignity*.

"*Some* of the rich came from nothing. Some of our *Crenshaw* sons and daughters are rich—well, very few, very few. But most of the rich came into their riches from the lottery of birth. They do not see the *privilege* of their situation. They see only their *hard* work, their *long* hours. They feel they *earned* their riches. Luke is saying 'If you do not acknowledge how fortunate you are and give thanks to God and dignity to others, you are damned for all eternity.' Amen!"

As the pastor expounded on the mutual obligations of all members of society, Tenesha's thoughts wandered to the polarization that had overwhelmed the country around this very issue. Surveys showed that most people still believed America was shaped like a diamond with respect to income and wealth, with a few rich and poor and a large middle class. But she knew that the reality was more like a narrow triangle of rich atop a shrinking middle class, both sitting on top of a large base of poorer people.

People persisted in their beliefs about the middle class because popular media were filled with Horatio Alger stories. Conservative media in particular broadcast heroic stories of great economic mobility and of persistence and hard work paying off.

There were, of course, also voices decrying the true state of affairs, but they were labeled un-American. Those less fortunate were labeled as "takers" looking for a free ride from those who had worked hard and pulled themselves up by their bootstraps.

At the reception after the service, among the tables full of home-cooked food set up in the grassy area behind the church, Tenesha tried to explain this to her mother. "So, Momma, the sermon today was exactly about what I'm trying to do with my life. These issues of wealth inequality and social justice speak to me more than neural implants and artificial intelligence. Can you understand that?"

Her mom nodded. "Yes, darling, of course I understand. I'm just worried about how you're going to live while you chase that dream. Those loans never go away, you know. They'll be hanging over you forever."

"I know, Momma. But I don't want to give up. I'll just have to find a way."

CHAPTER SEVEN

New York/San Francisco - September 27

NEW YORK

The set of Morning Fresh was quiet. A single assistant helped hosts Megyn, Steve, and Victor apply their makeup while they reviewed the notes on the first segment.

The director was in another building a mile away, running several shows at the same time with a single console and the latest version of AIStudio. The AI program maneuvered the automated cameras, changed lighting, spoke directly to talent in their earpieces, and controlled the information displayed on their contact lenses.

"Places, please," said AIStudio. "Five minutes to air."

The countdown went smoothly and the red light on Camera 1 blinked on.

"Good morning, everyone!" said Megyn. "I'm Megyn Robbins and welcome to Morning Fresh. With me, as always, are my co-hosts Steve Brattle and Victor Langston."

"Good morning, Megyn!" the men said simultaneously.

"We'll get to our weather and traffic bots in a moment, but those human-operated vehicle lanes are clogged, as usual. Get yourself into a Waymo, people!"

Steve laughed and picked up the cue. "No kidding, Megyn. I swear I get half my work done in the back seat of a Waymo."

"The miracles of modern technology," said Victor. "Speaking of which, guess which Senator is trying to drive us right back to the dark ages?"

"Not again!" Megyn said, seeming genuinely shocked.

"Yes, our favorite Democrat Senator, Walter Scott, has introduced a bill that—get this—would raise the minimum wage, increase spending on handouts, and tax the people who actually earn their money and create all the jobs."

"What's it called, the Great Unemployment Act of 2038?" asked Steve.

"I don't understand how people like Walter Scott keep getting elected," added Megyn. "Can't the good people of Taxachussets see that his policies are destroying America?"

"Well," said Steve, "we've got a guest coming up who should be a real example to people like Senator Scott. He's a young entrepreneur from Dallas who created an AI that uses satellite data to help energy companies find deep seams of coal without needing a lot of expensive geologists. Now there's an example of someone working hard and succeeding. We'll ask him if he'd rather be taking government handouts right after this, on the news channel that brings you the truth, and nothing but the truth."

SAN FRANCISCO

"Good morning, Bay Area! You're back with Calista Quinn-Jones here and the Bay Area's only progressive internet call-in show. It's a little chilly and overcast out there; don't expect the highs to clear sixty-one today. Well, I'm sure you know what we're going to be talking about. It's all over the news. A new report came out today with absolutely shocking numbers on housing affordability in the Bay Area. Well, they *would* be shocking, if anyone was paying attention.

"According to this report from the Bay Area Living Wage Alliance, the median rent in the nine Bay counties has now reached a level where you need a salary of almost three hundred thousand to afford a place to live. And you know what that means? Only the executives and tech experts from down in Silicon Valley and Nano Basin can afford to live here. Everyone else is getting priced out of the market. What's your experience? Give me a net call.

"Okay, we've got Talese on the line. What's your story?"

"Hey, Calista, love your show, girl. My landlord just raised my rent to eight thousand a month! The couple next to me had to move out. At the open house this past Sunday, there were all these, sorry—don't mean no disrespect—but these white tech dudes scoping it out, and some of them had bundles of cash in their hands. I swear to God and kid you not. They were offering six months' rent prepaid, cash up front. It takes me a year and a half to make that much money, before any expenses!"

"I hear you, Talese. You've got these select few people lucky enough to get into some startup that makes it big and it's like hitting the lottery. Do they have some skills? Sure, I guess they can program computers or DNA or whatever. But then they come into our neighborhoods with literally buckets of cash and drive out the working-class folks."

"I don't know what I'm going to do, Calista. I'm going to have to move further out East, I guess, but then my commute is going to be murder."

"Well, I know what we all can do, people. We need to vote for Deirdre Trellis for county supervisor because she is pro rent control. We can't let this tech money flood our neighborhoods and jack up our rents. We can put a stop to it."

"Thanks for the call, Talese. Next up, Christina has something to say about the latest cutbacks in public education funding."

CHAPTER EIGHT

Austin - September 28

P am Townsend shuffled carefully across the broken concrete path leading to the pale-yellow clapboard house in Austin's Montopolis neighborhood. She paused at the end of the walkway, then with great effort lifted herself and her bag of groceries up the three stairs to the porch, which was sagging somewhat to her right. A police drone passing by far overhead noted the lack of a medplant signal from the pedestrian, but gait analysis returned low probability of a threat so it flew on. Once she was safely inside the house with the door closed behind her Pam straightened up and kicked off the shoes designed to give her a pronounced limp. "JT! I'm back!"

"Coming!" called a voice from the back of the house. Pam put the milk, eggs, yogurt, and cheese in the fridge and tossed the bread on the counter. Her brother JT entered the kitchen and recoiled at the sight of her. He pointed to his face.

"Ah, sorry!" Pam peeled off the mask with its stringy gray hair and dropped it on the small dining table, revealing her twenty-seven-year-old face and blonde buzz-cut.

"I made some progress with RezMat while you were out," said JT. "They've got damned good digital security but their contractors aren't as careful. I think I may be able to find an unprotected internet tunnel that's got broad enough access to download the RezMat operations database."

"That's great! We've probably still got a week or so more work on the manifesto based on how the drafts are going. Will that be enough time?"

He nodded. "Should be, I've got some promising leads."

Pam smiled at him. Things were coming together. With the RezMat operations information and the manifesto complete, they'd be in position to execute the first set of attacks. It had been nearly nine months since she'd left her analyst position at the National Security Agency, disgusted by her discovery of widespread illegal surveillance and mass opinion manipulation via omnipresence. Practices the public thought had been stopped decades ago after Snowden and the 2016 election and the Facebook Cambridge Analytica mess. At first she considered going whistleblower, but she didn't want to end up like Snowden, isolated in Russia until his untimely "accidental death" by Novichok nerve agent back in 2023.

Instead, she began to focus on the technology NSA was using and technology in society more broadly. The more she read from the anti-technology literature, the more convinced she became that tech was truly the root of society's problems. While technology had definitely improved living standards, it was also increasingly being used as a tool of oppression. And people were themselves becoming slaves to tech, whether through omnipresence addiction or literally because AI programs told them exactly what to do.

When she started talking with her brother about these ideas she discovered that he shared her concerns. He was also worried about people delegating too much power and control to the machines. JT had first-hand experience with over-reliance on technology when he was in the Army during the Iran War. He told her harrowing stories about AIs mistakenly directing platoons into ambushes and autonomous drones and tracked vehicles killing their own troops in friendly fire incidents.

Together, they surfed the dark web and discovered hundreds of like-minded anti-technology activists. The message boards were full of anti-technology rhetoric and lots of arguments about what to do. But the siblings were frustrated by the lack of any planning for concrete action. Then two months ago they had been approached in a direct message by an activist who went by the name *Ellul*. Over the course of a dozen conversations, he had gained their trust and recruited Pam and JT to join his group, which had almost twenty current or ex-military and intelligence members. When they spoke by holochat he looked and sounded like an overweight white man in his late fifties.

In reality, Ellul was Tuan Pham, a fit thirty-eight-year-old Vietnamese immigrant and U.S. Navy Commander based in Norfolk, Virginia. Like JT, he had seen the rapid development of autonomous weapons on the battlefield. But while JT was angry at the abdication of human decision making to inferior machines, Tuan was terrified of the Terminator scenario. He was certain that the machines would eventually surpass their keepers and decide humans weren't worth the trouble to keep around. After trying in vain to change things from the inside, he decided to form a group to take direct action to stop the progression to more and more capable killer robots. He had a particular hatred for RezMat, the world's leading robotics company.

Pham had named his group the Ludd Kaczynski Collective (LKC) after two infamous anti-technology zealots. Ned Ludd was the perhaps apocryphal leader of workers who smashed automated knitting machines in 1800s England. The Luddites were the first known protesters against technology automating away jobs. They were often derided for their short-sightedness, as the industrial age economy soon generated far more jobs for people. Economists even coined the phrase "Luddite Fallacy" for the belief that automation could ever lead to mass unemployment. That was when machines could only automate certain forms of physical labor. Over the last three decades, even as AI and robotics began to replace more and more cognitive and fine-motor-skill jobs, two-thirds of economists still thought the Luddites were and always would be wrong.

Ted Kaczynski was a brilliant mathematician born in 1942 and educated at Harvard and University of Michigan. In his late 20s he became disgusted by society and moved to a remote cabin in Montana to live a more natural and self-sufficient life. When developers started destroying the wild lands around his cabin he became angry and began sabotaging their projects. Kaczynski ultimately decided only a violent revolution would stop the technological destruction of nature and humanity. Over the course of nearly twenty years he created bombs that killed three people and injured twenty-three more, earning the nickname The Unabomber. When media published his manifesto *Industrial Society and Its Future*, his brother recognized his style and ideas and Kaczynski was arrested. He died in prison in 2027 after writing more works that formed a canon for anti-technology activists.

While Ellul was particularly concerned about a robot takeover, he recruited others with a wide diversity of anti-technology beliefs, shaped from a variety of personal experiences. One of his earliest recruits was Miles O'Connell, known by his dark web alias *Thoreau*. Miles grew up in a wealthy family in Seattle but from his teenage years rebelled against anything and everything establishment. He joined a local anarchist group and participated in street demonstrations. Then in high school he started hacking computers and a mentor in the Puget Sound Anarchists spotted his talent and suggested Miles take a different path. "You've got skills, man. You could do way more damage from the inside than out on the streets."

The anarchists hatched a plan. Miles "reformed" and followed a straight and narrow path: college, internships, corporate jobs. Then came the reward: a position as a systems and security specialist inside the FBI. He had access to all of the intel on his anarchist friends and saved their asses several times with advance notice of raids. Like Pam, he also came to realize that technology had become the primary weapon in the establishment's oppression of the people. He was disgusted by the way the government, aided and abetted by the world's largest corporations, used tech to suppress dissent and manipulate and distract the masses, all for the benefit of the oligarchs in the one percent.

Another recent recruit was Peter Cook, an ex-black-ops agent who went by the alias *Othello*. Born in Ohio into a military family, he followed his grandfather's and mother's footsteps into the Army where he was recruited to the Green Berets and eventually into the super-secret Delta Force. Despite more than fifty overseas deployments over the years, he had worked hard at being a devoted husband and doting father to his shy but brilliant daughter Bethany. But tragedy struck while he was on a deep cover mission in Iran.

Bethany, a junior in high school, had become severely addicted to omnipresence. She spent every waking minute obsessing about posting and life-streaming and following her friends and random lifestreams in OP. Then someone started a cruel campaign against her for reasons that were never determined. Blocked and shunned on OP, she silently spiraled into deep despair and one night jumped in front of a self-driving bus going fifty miles per hour. Peter was devastated. He became convinced that the technology that had possessed his daughter and twisted her mind was an insidious force at risk of entirely destroying human autonomy.

Everyone in the group believed that technology was driving vast economic inequality by rapidly substituting for human labor. Kimani Richards, an African-American woman with a masters in economics and twelve years of experience as a CIA global politics analyst was the most articulate proponent of this view. Using the name *Artemis*, she argued that the logic of shareholder capitalism made it inevitable that the owners of capital would automate the masses into a mindless horde of indentured servants, in a constant struggle for precarious work. The only thing that could awaken the working class, said Artemis, was a direct attack on the infrastructure and supply chains that made the automation possible.

To the members of the group, Ludd and Kaczynski perfectly represented their primary concerns about the impact of technology. Every day, with each new story of tech replacing people or being used to dehumanize and oppress them, the group became more convinced that a political solution was impossible, and that dramatic, violent action was required. And now they were a few weeks away from making their first strikes against RezMat, the company leading the way in human subjugation. And those would be just the opening salvos in a wider war against technology.

CHAPTER NINE

Los Angeles - September 30

Jacob jumped out of the gray Waymo and strode briskly towards Harding's tall iron gate. His teammate Lou Salerno exited a Lyft self-driving minibus with a few other workers and Jacob joined up with him. "Hey, Lou. How's it going?"

"Can't complain. Hey, Jacob, I heard from Cheryl last night about your dad. I'm so sorry, man."

"Yeah, thanks. It's been tough. It's so fucking unfair, a guy like him, such a waste." Lou didn't really know what to say. The two men walked in silence for a minute.

"Say, how's the back?" Lou finally asked.

"It's fine. Those nanobots work like a charm. The medtech these days, just fucking amazing."

"Tell me about it! My sister's medplant detected early stage pancreatic cancer and one nanobot injection got rid of it. What, ten, fifteen years ago that shit was a death sentence." They walked through the gate and Lou leaned in towards Jacob. "But did you hear about Ed?"

"Ed over in team six? I heard he got fired."

"Damn right. He took a job working health care some nights. His medplant reported him for napping during his shift. He got one warning, then bam, second time the medplant caught him he was out on his ass." Jacob glanced at his tattooed forearm where the small chip was embedded and wondered what else it might be reporting to his employer.

The two men reached the locker room, donned their dark blue jumpsuits and hardhats and headed to the check-in kiosk. There was a small crowd around the assignment screen and they heard voices raised in anger.

"They can't do that!" shouted Cheryl Garner.

"What's going on?" Jacob asked. Cheryl pointed at the display with the day's work assignments. "Our team is gone! Done!"

"Cheryl, calm down. What are you talking about?" She jabbed her finger at the screen. "It says we're fucking supposed to talk to an HR DeepAgent for outplacement!"

Jacob shook his head. "There's got to be a mistake. I haven't heard anything about this." He gave Cheryl and the others a reassuring look, but he had a strong suspicion what was going on. He flicked through a few detail screens and they soon confirmed his worst fears. "Aw shit," he said under his breath.

"What the fuck, Jacob?" said Lou, who was looking over his shoulder. "What is that thing?"

"It's the RezWeld 5000," Jacob said under his breath. He had known this day would come, but had no idea the tech would be ready for the difficult kind of work at Harding so soon. Lou poked at the screen and a demo video popped up. The logo for RezMat, the world's largest robotics and internet equipment manufacturer, faded in and out and a tracked industrial robot appeared on the screen.

A cheerful male voice said, "This is the RezWeld 5000, RezMat's fifth-generation welding robot. The RezWeld 5000 includes cameras, lidar, infrared, haptic, and X-ray sensors, and multiple welding tip kits. With its advanced sensors and specialized tractor treads, it can navigate any work area and can operate at extreme temperatures. It's capable of laying down a bead from just a few millimeters wide up to three centimeters. It can create a razor straight line or an intricate pattern, and its articulated arms can reach just about any work surface. If your steel components have embedded chips, the RezWeld 5000 can run autonomously, following electronic work orders issued by your master AI build program. When resupplied by our automated carts, the RezWeld 5000 can create perfect welds to precise specifications, and do so three times faster than the most experienced human welders on a twenty-four seven schedule."

Cheryl poked her finger into his chest now. "You knew about this, Jacob? You knew about this goddamn machine?" Over her shoulder, Jacob could see two techs in gray coveralls unboxing a set of 5000s.

"I've hit the limit on welfare, Jacob. Me and the girls, we're going to be homeless!" The other welders crowded around him, shouting their own concerns.

When his union rep had informed him about the 5000 months ago, Jacob had been passively resigned to his fate. But the trauma of his father's death and Cheryl's insistent, steely jabs triggered a visceral response. Jacob broke away from his team and strode toward the techs, grabbing a three-foot length of steel rebar from a barrel on the way.

They had partly unboxed one of the machines and stood in front of it now, eyes opening wide at his approach. "Get out of my way," he said, with as much menace as he could muster. He hoped nothing in their job description required them to defend a robot.

They stepped aside.

Jacob channeled his growing rage into a barrage of blows on one of the RezWeld's exposed sensing arrays.

It was a sturdy machine, built for the rough environment of an ironworks, but soon the array was a tangled mess of wires and electronic chips.

Jacob's hands ached. He started to drop the rebar, then clenched his fists and began hitting the robot harder.

Two sentry droids were the first security to arrive. "Jacob Komarov," one of them announced through its speakers. "Stop destroying company property!"

Jacob continued to batter the RezWeld. The sentry warned him twice more, then deployed one of its Tasers.

Jacob felt the initial stab of the probe. Then brightness exploded all around him.

Jacob woke up half an hour later in a holding cell, his hands zip-tied together behind his back. The room was roughly eight feet square, with a smooth concrete floor and rough cinder block walls. It was bare except for the cot he was lying on. And a medium sized wall screen, which displayed a female avatar feigning concern. "Hello, Jacob. Are you feeling okay?" it asked. He could make out a full sensing array strip at the top of the screen so it actually knew more about his state than he did.

Jacob shook his head, trying to clear it. "No, goddamn it, I am not okay. What the fuck are you?"

"I'm a lawyer AI working for your union. I am representing you in the case of destruction of company property." He grimaced as memories of the layoff and his attack on the RezMat 5000 welding robot filtered through the fog of Taser recovery. A thought occurred to him.

"Can you research things?"

"Yes, of course, I am fully capable of legal research."

"Do you have access to the current union contract with Harding?"

"Yes, I do."

"Can you find anything in the contract that would prevent Harding from replacing union workers with automated welding robots?"

"Checking." Jacob found the avatar's fake furrowed brow intensely annoying. "No, there are no such clauses. Harding may determine the most economical way to perform its tasks. There is, however, a clause requiring one month of severance for the employee in the case of a human job replaced by automation." One lousy month after years of grueling work.

"I have been negotiating with the company AI about your case. I have an offer for your review."

"What kind of offer?"

"Harding will drop the criminal charges if you pay for repairs to the robot out of your severance and agree to never return to this facility again or refer to Harding in omnipresence."

"And if I refuse?"

"You will be arrested, and given the evidence I have analyzed, you will be convicted. Minimum sentence of six months. I should also inform you that your probability of obtaining work after a conviction for destruction of corporate property is approximately one tenth of normal. And given your education, training, and available job positions, there is a high probability you would be unemployed for three years or more until you can retrain and move out of the probationary window."

"Fuck it. I'll take the offer."

"I believe that is the wisest course of action, Jacob. I will negotiate your release from the facility as soon as possible."

"Take your time," Jacob said. "I've got a lot of thinking to do."

CHAPTER TEN

Santa Barbara - October 1

Roger was so deeply engaged with the final simulation results that Allison had to chime three times to get his attention. "What? Allison? Was that you?"

"Yes, Roger. Sorry to interrupt, but Frances Chatham is requesting a holochat."

"Ah, okay. Put her through." He rubbed his eyes before donning the hologlasses. It had been an intense ten days since he'd gotten the assignment from her. He spun around and a few seconds later Frances materialized into view. She wasn't in an office, it looked more like a living room. Of course, it would be late evening in London.

"Hello, Roger. I wanted to do a last check-in to make sure we're ready for launch tomorrow."

"Hi Frances. Yes, well, I'm just putting the final touches on the programming. But it will be ready in a few hours."

"Brilliant. I also wanted to express my thanks. Your network will be a big part of our success in the coming weeks."

"I hope so. As we discussed, this is not exactly a straightforward brand you're launching. I've had to run over a dozen simulations with millions of synths. Just wait till you get my bill for cloud compute!"

"Well I'm not concerned about the cost. But I am curious about your technology. Why did it take so many iterations?"

"The idea matrix in your brand is quite complex. But beyond the complexity, the biggest problem is that it doesn't conform to standard orthodoxies or ideologies. It's a blend of ideas that pulls from all across the spectrum. The synths tend to mirror the human population, which means they are polarized. It's easy for them to respond for or against people and brands that match or oppose their views. But in the early runs, a large percentage of the synths couldn't figure out how to respond and be consistent to their life story, so they didn't."

"Fascinating. So how did you solve it?" Frances asked.

"In the end I had to introduce new parameters into the response algorithm that allowed for selective brand matching. Essentially, I let the synths only respond to a few ideas in your brand rather than requiring a very high percentage to match. And of course, I had to bias them towards the parts of the brand that they agreed with."

"I see." Frances paused. "Roger, would you say in general that your synths make positive contributions in omnipresence or are they more inclined to be negative?" Allison, ever attentive, brought up a sentiment analysis of the last thirty days of synth activity worldwide. "It looks like close to seventy percent negative. Why do you ask?" She hesitated. His overlays indicated a rise in anxiety. "Did you," she began, "get a chance to walk through the VR program itself?"

"No, I only worked from the text briefings. Synths can't themselves experience VR so I focused on what they would be reading online. What's up, Frances? You seem concerned about something." Roger was worried that he might have missed something important to the launch.

"No, no, that sounds fine as far as the synths are concerned. I, well, I think you might find the VR interesting. Personally."

"I see." Roger wasn't quite sure what to make of this exchange. "Well, I'll be first in line to engage when it's online. But for right now, I should probably get back to this final bit of engineering."

"Of course, I'll leave you to it. Thanks again, Roger."

"You're welcome. Have a great launch!"

CHAPTER ELEVEN

London - October 2

Bradley Childress, RezMat's Chief of Intelligence and Special Operations, checked in with the CEO's assistant and proceeded through two old fashioned wooden double doors into his office. He noted that the ostentatious decorations of the prior occupant had been swiftly altered by the new CEO David Livingstone into a more spare, modern look.

"Bradley, come in. Do have a seat," said his new boss, gesturing to a set of four executive chairs surrounding a round steel and glass table. They sat opposite each other.

"Very well, Bradley. I believe my predecessor met with you weekly at this time to stay up to date on security threats and countermeasures?"

"Yes, sir."

"Splendid. But please call me David. And what format did you usually follow?"

"There's a written summary in your inbounds, David. Covers both physical and digital security issues. In person we usually go over critical issues and decisions."

"Ah, so sorry to have missed that. Quite a lot in my inbounds. What would you like to discuss today?"

"Well, sir, despite your recent appointment, public opinion is turning quite decidedly against us."

"David. Please. What kind of data do you have on that?"

"Well, David, we've invested in very advanced psychometric AI programs, and their analysis of omnipresence indicates a negative twenty-two-point shift in sentiment in the last two months. We're rapidly cementing our position as the number one corporate villain, which is not a good spot to be in, especially for government contracting. Cognitive textual analysis indicates the public thinks your appointment is purely symbolic, since you're a long-time RezMat insider."

"Well, I do expect it will take time for my actions to filter through to public opinion. RezMat does have quite a lot to own up to and repair work to do, as the recent scandals indicated. I understand we have an omnipresence program called ProNet in place to counteract this kind of surge in opinion?"

"Yes, we do. We've been using it sparingly to moderate the impact, and—"

"Why sparingly? If this groundswell is as bad as you say, shouldn't we be more aggressive?"

"This is an extremely valuable asset. If we engage it too quickly or too strongly we risk detection, which would be altogether another scandal."

"I see. I encourage you to push the limits on that a little, Bradley. What's the point of the program if we can't use it when we most need it?"

"Yes, well," replied Bradley reluctantly, "I'll speak with the tech lead on that."

"Now, then," continued the CEO. "Does anything in this groundswell indicate imminent threats to the company?"

"David, we're being probed twenty-four seven, thousands of incursion attempts per hour. Not to mention internet-of-things-based denial of service attacks daily. So yes, I'd say there are a lot of bad actors out there."

"I may have come up through marketing, Bradley, but even I know what you've described is just the cost of doing business today. Do you have any specific information on who's behind these attacks? Competitors? Governments?"

"No, sir."

"And Colossus? Any hint of penetration into Building 42?"

"No, sir. One of the fundamental tenets of that program is no internet links whatsoever into that building."

"Good. And any evidence that there are actual physical threats to our facilities or employees?"

"No, sir."

"Very well, then. I'm sure your team can handle these cyber issues. I want you to inform me as soon as the risk profile changes and any of this moves into the real world."

Bradley returned to his basement operations center three floors below street level and signaled to his senior analyst, Jill Samborn, to join him. She closed the glass door to his office behind her and took a seat at his conference table.

"I've got some bad news," she said, before he could start to brief her on the meeting.

"Bloody hell, I just got back from the CEO, Jill."

"So sorry, Brad. We discovered a vulnerability in one of our transportation contractor's systems. There was an exploitable VPN tunnel." Jill was referring to the virtual private network that RezMat established with its vendors that enabled them to share information securely.

"Damn. What did it have access to?"

"Nothing financial or engineering. We're still investigating, but there may have been backups of some operations data."

"Of what kind?"

"Logistics, staffing and shift schedules, production runs."

"Bollocks. Do you think that was targeted or just hoovered up accidentally?"

"Looks accidental. They grabbed everything in an exposed folder and ran."

"Any location trace?" asked Bradley.

"Zimbabwe, supposedly," answered Jill.

"Bastards cover their tracks well. So now we've got to decide whether to scramble the operations of the whole damned company because of a leak."

"You think someone's going real world? Do we have any evidence of that?"

"Nothing other than dark web chatter," said Bradley.

"Hard to imagine they'd turn the whole place upside down based on that."

"Get me a report of everything that was taken. I'll send a message to the new boss, but I suspect you're correct."

"Oh, yes, how'd the meeting go?" she asked.

"Fine," he replied, still distracted by her news. "He wants us to dial up ProNet."

She grimaced. "We're on the edge there already, Brad."

"I know. Maybe we can look into engaging some of the less active agents?"

"Hmm, perhaps. I'll try a slow ramp and monitor."

"Good. And Jill, let's do a full audit on all contractors, yes?"

She nodded. "We've got more than five hundred VPN integrated partners. If they have AI negotiation agents in place to approve the scan, our security software can sweep them all in a day. But there will probably be contract changes."

"Understood," said Bradley. "But we can't afford more leaks like this. Not now. Run it by finance and get the contract parameters."

"Will do. Anything else?" He shook his head. As she walked past his wall-sized display of a global map, he couldn't help but think of every one of the hundreds of lights representing RezMat assets as a vulnerable target. His PNA buzzed. A call from Building 42. Bradley pushed a button to close his office door and accepted the video chat.

"Yes, what is it Patrick?" he asked the security shift supervisor.

"I'm afraid we've had another protocol violation sir," said the red-headed man on his screen. "One of the technicians was exiting the facility with a thumb drive. We barely caught it."

"First offense?" Bradley asked.

"Yes, sir. Graham Clarke, hired just four months ago."

"Very well, write him up and impress upon him the seriousness of the offense. And well done, Patrick, thank the scanning team for me."

"Aye, sir." The security supervisor rang off. Bradley sighed. The secret Colossus program in Building 42 was a massive success for the company, but it remained an ever-present source of anxiety for him. The risk of unleashing an existential threat to humanity at any moment if protocols were broken did not sit lightly on his shoulders.

CHAPTER TWELVE

Virtual Reality - October 3

LOS ANGELES

Tenesha woke up earlier than usual due to a huge argument in the apartment upstairs. She tossed and turned for a while, then gave up, climbed out of bed, and padded out to the living room.

Her roommate LuLu was sitting on their ratty couch with a VR headset on, turning her head this way and that and talking to someone. It didn't sound like any game Tenesha had played.

She tapped her friend on the knee. LuLu pulled the headset away from her face. "Oh, Tens, this program is so cool, it's so different. I'll send it to you, you *gotta* play it." LuLu asked her VR player to send Tenesha the link, then continued her odd virtual conversation.

Tenesha tried to rub the sleep from her eyes and wandered into the small kitchen. She opened and closed a few cupboards, then decided she wasn't very hungry, so she headed back to her bedroom. She found her own VR headset and put it on, then called up LuLu's link. "Start program," she said.

WASHINGTON

Senator Harry Paxton was reading an AI-generated news briefing in the back of a Waymo when his daughter Rena sent him a vidchat request. He smiled and said, "Accept."

"Well, you're up early, Rena," he teased. It was nearly 11 a.m. in Chicago.

"Hilarious, *Dad.* I've been up for hours. Well, at least an hour."

"I suppose you were up late hitting those e-courses, right?"

"Uh, no comment?"

"Just kidding, Rena. I know you're doing great in your classes. What's up?"

"Well, I just ran this interesting VR program that seems like it's right up your alley."

"That seems unlikely. Most VR programs make me feel a little nauseous."

"Oh, this isn't a game or adventure program. It's, well, I don't know how to describe it. It's intellectual."

"Wait, an intellectual VR program? What does that mean?"

"It's about history and the future and technology. Oh, Dad, I can't tell you. You just need to try it. I'm sending you the link."

"Sure, why not. I've got at least twenty minutes left in this Waymo."

"Great, it's in your inbounds now. Gotta run, let's talk later!"

She disconnected before he could even say goodbye.

He only had a lightweight VR headset with earbuds in his briefcase, but it would have to do. He put it on, called up the link to Sara's Message and said, "Run program."

VIRTUAL REALITY / LOS ANGELES

Tenesha stood in what looked like a small farming village. There were a couple of dozen mud brick huts with thatched and rusting corrugated tin roofs. As she turned her head she could see more of the village all around her. Families were preparing a meal over crackling fires.

The VR visual quality was excellent, even on her headset, which was two generations old. The audio was also spot on, omni-directional and perfectly synced to the actions of the people as they chopped vegetables, stirred pots, and tended fires. What was even cooler was how the program activated the basic olfactory features in her headset. Everyone thought of them as a gimmick, but somehow this program was generating odor molecules suggestive of dirt, burning wood, curry, and, faintly, manure.

VIRTUAL REALITY / WASHINGTON

Harry Paxton's lightweight VR headset had no Mental Intention interface, so he was using a small handheld controller to navigate the village.

The hyper-realistic sights and sounds fascinated him, even as a good part of his brain knew he was still driving around Washington.

He was wondering what this VR program was about and why Rena had recommended it when a figure emerged from behind one of the huts. She was a lovely young Indian woman wearing a white sari. He guessed she was about fifteen. He turned toward her and stepped forward, using the controller.

"Hello," she said in slightly accented English. "My name is Sara Dhawan. I am sixteen years old and in real life I currently live in London.

I'd like to welcome you to this virtual reality experience, which starts in my birth village in India."

VIRTUAL REALITY / LOS ANGELES

Tenesha automatically replied, "Hello, Sara." The young woman smiled, bowed her head slightly, and asked, "And what is your name?"

"My name? I'm Tenesha." This was highly unusual. The characters looked so real they could have been captured with a VR camera. But this young woman Sara was clearly interacting with her, which meant she had to be computer generated.

The young woman gestured toward the center of the village. "Nice to meet you, Tenesha. Would you care to walk with me? I'd like to tell you a story."

Tenesha engaged her Mental Intention interface and thought herself forward. "Where are we?" she asked Sara.

The young woman turned her head while they walked. "This is the village where I grew up, near Doultanwali, in India. In fact, this is a special day in the history of the village, and in my story.

"Look, there I am, when I was just six years old."

Tenesha looked where teenage Sara was pointing. She spotted a young girl in a dirty brown dress helping her mother prepare lunch.

"It was just an ordinary day, Tenesha, but something extraordinary is about to happen. Do you see that cloud of dust in the distance? Do you know the William Gibson quote? *The future is here; it's just not evenly distributed yet.* Well, that's the future arriving in my village."

The little girl ran toward the dust cloud, her mother calling after her disapprovingly in Hindi.

By the time Tenesha and Sara arrived at the edge of the village, the cloud had resolved into a beat-up pickup truck. It parked in an open field just off the road, and two men rolled a shed of some kind down a ramp.

Young Sara and other curious children crowded around the men, peppering them with questions.

VIRTUAL REALITY / WASHINGTON

"This shed is a solar-powered, net-connected learning system," Sara explained to Harry. "It was part of an international program to make education available to children all over the developing world who might otherwise not have the opportunity. Embedded in the shed is a high-end tablet computer.

"Most of the children in my village played with the tablet and taught themselves basic skills. I was drawn to it like a magnet and made much more progress.

"Here I am one year later."

With a wave of her hand, the scene blurred. A new scene emerged.

Now seven-year-old Sara was standing alone in front of the tablet. Harry could hear her speaking in rudimentary English to an AI tutor, who corrected her grammar from time to time. They were in the middle of a math lesson which sounded very advanced for a seven-year-old.

Harry walked around to the side of the shed using his controller, squatted down, and looked straight at young Sara. "Your younger self can't see me," he said aloud.

The teenaged Sara moved beside him. "No, she cannot. We are just observers here, invisible to these people. Much as they are invisible to the rest of the world, living as subsistence farmers in a remote corner of India.

"But that's about to change, at least for me."

The tablet screen flashed. The AI tutor cut out abruptly and the girl took a step back. A middle-aged Indian woman appeared on the screen and spoke in Hindi.

"Let me translate," offered teenage Sara. "That is my new teacher, Asha. She is telling me that my interactions with the tablet had identified me as having great potential. She wants to talk to me and teach me directly sometimes."

Harry could see the curiosity and excitement on young Sara's face.

VIRTUAL REALITY / LOS ANGELES

"Now, here we are about one year later, on another important day," Sara said.

The image blurred. Then Tenesha and Sara were back at the shed. The young girl stood with her parents, who were talking with the teacher and a man in a suit. "Asha and Mohan are here from New Delhi," teenaged Sara said. "They are explaining that I am an extraordinary student and are offering to take me to a school in the city and give me a great education, free of charge."

Tenesha looked back and forth between the adults. Sara's father was frowning and her mother was crying. Young Sara pulled her hand from her mother's and boldly stepped over to Asha, speaking to her parents rapidly and defiantly.

"I was quite headstrong and selfish," said teenage Sara. "I am insisting on going to New Delhi. It never occurred to me the pain this would cause my family. Ultimately, they agreed, for which I am eternally grateful."

VIRTUAL REALITY / WASHINGTON

Harry watched the car drive off with the young Sara and turned to her teenaged version. She was watching her parents shuffle back to their hut with tears in her eyes. "I've been so busy I haven't gone back to visit them once," Sara said. She wiped her eyes and composed herself. "Would you like to see the school I attended after New Delhi, in London?"

Harry's Waymo was still some distance from its destination. "Sure, let's go to London."

Sara waved a hand. The scene dissolved, leaving them standing in a gray nothingness. Then, with another gesture, she faded them into a nighttime scene in a modern building, sparsely furnished with steel and glass tables loaded with computers and VR equipment. "Here I am a few years ago. I was a voracious learner, and not one much for sleep." The girl sitting at one of the tables was thin and gangly, fresh from a growth spurt. She was speed-reading a document flashing by on a large monitor.

"What are you studying?" asked Harry, walking around the sleek London library.

"That was a macroeconomics text. It was quite fortuitous, because this is the moment that launched me on my current mission."

Harry looked up from the intensely focused student in jeans and a sweatshirt to the sari-wearing teenager. "Mission?"

She nodded, then held up her hand and pointed.

Harry turned his head in the Waymo in Washington and scanned the nighttime room in London. He used the controller to turn toward the far entrance to the room, where a cleaning robot was entering.

The robot moved steadily, simultaneously vacuuming, arranging chairs, and dusting the tables. He turned back toward the younger Sara. She glanced up at the intruding robot and scowled at the interruption, then quickly returned her focus back to the scrolling document.

Suddenly her eyes widened.

Even though it was just a re-creation, Harry was sure he had just witnessed an *aha!* moment. "What happened?" he asked.

VIRTUAL REALITY / LOS ANGELES

Tenesha turned her head away from the cleaning robot and watched the younger Sara's face carefully. Over the course of thirty seconds, it progressed from surprise to growing awareness to concern. Then it formed into determined resolve.

"You look like you just discovered something very important," Tenesha said.

"I had just been reading an economics text that mentioned janitors when the robot entered the room. I began to reflect on everything I had learned about technology over time and the current state of advanced economies. That robot convinced me that we are facing a fundamental problem and we are not on a path to solving it."

"What problem is that?"

"Well, that's the second story I want to tell you." Teenaged Sara waved her hand and faded the scene once again to pure gray nothingness.

"Where are we?" asked Tenesha, lifting her hand to block the harsh sun from her eyes, even though she was inside her Los Angeles apartment.

"This is the African savannah around 10,000 BC," explained Sara. "We're going to take a little walk through history to tell this story."

As Tenesha's eyes adjusted to the glare, she saw human figures moving around the landscape.

"After over two million years as a recognizably human species, these people cook and eat plants and animals and are largely nomadic. Their lives are essentially the same as their predecessors five thousand, ten thousand, even a million years ago. Think about that enormous amount of time without any change at all. These humans have harnessed two important natural phenomena—the combustion of wood and the flaking of stone—and invented spears, axes, clothing, and basic shelter. That is the full extent of their technology.

"Now, at any point during our walk through time, you can look straight down and see important information in a chart. Different lines on the chart show global population, infant mortality, the percentage of all people living at a subsistence level, and economic activity per capita. If you look at it now, you will see there are perhaps ten million humans, with infant mortality above fifty percent, and one hundred percent of the population is at a subsistence level."

Tenesha looked straight down. A chart appeared at her feet with "10,000 BC" at the top.

VIRTUAL REALITY / WASHINGTON

"Why the history lesson?" asked Harry.

"I want to tell you a story about humanity and technology," explained Sara. "Technology is the single most powerful enabler we have to create a better life for everyone on this planet. I want to show what it has done for us so far and what it can do in the future, if we can organize ourselves to take advantage of it."

"That's interesting. I don't have much time—can we skip ahead?"

"Of course. The fact is, not much happens for the bulk of humanity for thousands of more years."

Sara took Harry to the bustling port town of Alexandria, Egypt.

"So here we are, ten thousand years later—over five hundred generations. Humanity has harnessed new phenomena of nature. We have invented sailing, the wheel, papyrus, iron smelting, and writing. Even though there are now three hundred million people on Earth, communication among them is slow, and it can take many decades for innovations to spread."

Harry looked down at the statistics. While the Earth's population had grown, it had done so very slowly. Infant mortality was still over thirty percent, and almost all humans still lived subsistence lives.

"Yes, I see," he said. "There wasn't a lot of progress. When do we get to the good stuff?"

Sara smiled. "Yes, I know this early history moves slowly. But it's important to understanding the times we live in. Look around and then we'll walk ahead another thousand years."

"This looks more familiar," said Harry. They were standing on a narrow dirt street near the top of a hill in an ancient city. He could see hundreds of wooden and stone buildings spread out before them.

"We're in Rome around 1000 AD," said Sara. "The famous structures you are familiar with are in ruins, as ancient Rome was sacked about six hundred years ago."

As they walked down the street, Harry observed the daily routine of what appeared to be peasant farmers. "Over one thousand years, humanity was able exploit a few more natural phenomena. We invented paper, steel, the horse stirrup, algebra, and gunpowder. The last, of course, is a good example of how we use technologies in both good and bad ways.

"Building techniques have advanced, although it takes many decades to construct large stone structures. Society has invented hierarchical social structures to manage larger populations. Of course, if you observe the daily lives of the poor people around you, not much has changed in one thousand years. Diseases still run rampant. One out of every three children born will die in their first year. Almost every human on the planet lives at a subsistence level, with just enough food, water, clothing, and shelter to survive."

VIRTUAL REALITY / LOS ANGELES

"Oh my God, what is that smell?" exclaimed Tenesha.

Sara smiled. "This is 1650 London. That odor is human and animal waste. There is no sanitation system for almost 300,000 people, and the Thames River is a cesspool. In fifteen years, there will be a plague outbreak that kills twenty percent of the population. But something very interesting is taking place inside this building."

They walked into a two-story stone building and made their way past young men in waistcoats and wigs engaged in earnest discussion.

They ascended to a small, dusty room on the second floor lit by three generous windows that looked out onto a grassy courtyard. A group of well-dressed and wigged gentlemen stood around a table.

"The man speaking is Robert Boyle, considered the founder of modern chemistry. This is Gresham College, among the first institutions of higher learning in London, and a precursor to the Royal Society. Boyle is conducting an experiment and describing his particle theory of matter, which he will publish in a dozen years in the *Sceptical Chymist*."

"Why is this so important?" asked Tenesha.

"You are watching the birth of the scientific method, an empirical approach to discovering knowledge about natural phenomena driven by hypotheses and experimentation. From this point forward, there will be a virtuous cycle of scientific discovery, the manufacturing of instruments that enable more discovery, and the application of scientific and industrial knowledge to solve humanity's biggest problems."

VIRTUAL REALITY / WASHINGTON

"It sure doesn't seem like a lot of humanity's problems are being solved!" Harry shouted. It was hard to hear over the din of the textile factory's machinery and the yelling of many young boys and girls scrambling around the room. "I see rampant child labor, horrendous working conditions, and awful pollution."

Sara nodded. "Yes, indeed, early industrialization here in 1810 Britain actually lowered standards of living for many who moved to the cities. It took significant social and civil institutional reforms to correct these problems.

"But society did adjust," Sara continued. "We created rules to improve working conditions. And industrialization had tremendous benefits as we produced machinery and household goods at lower cost. Entrepreneurs innovated more products and services. Ordinary people, spending less on survival, could enjoy more goods that used to be considered luxuries. The standard of living started to creep up. And global population more than doubled in the two hundred years from 1650 to 1850. The prior doubling had taken over eight hundred years."

VIRTUAL REALITY / LOS ANGELES

Tenesha found herself in a lab cluttered with old electronic equipment. Four men in their late thirties and early forties—all with buzz cuts, white shirts, and black ties—were talking excitedly. "What is this place?" she asked Sara.

"Bell Labs, New Jersey, 1949. This is William Shockley's lab. He and his team have just proven the viability of the layered semiconductor transistor design. This is the moment when all digital computers became possible. Of course, vast amounts of energy and capital went into miniaturizing these transistors over time, but it all grew from this fundamental research.

"These men were funded by AT&T and Western Electric, firms that thrived by providing telephone communication systems to a growing U.S. population. It's another cycle of innovation. As consumers have more disposable income, they spend it on innovations and the businesses that provide them grow and employ more people and do more research. It's a virtuous cycle of investment, consumption, employment, and innovation."

"Yes," said Tenesha. "Market capitalism. You make it sound so great, but things aren't so rosy right now."

"I agree," said Sara. "This system is facing a major challenge."

VIRTUAL REALITY / WASHINGTON

Harry and Sara stood near a large intersection filled with cars and the occasional cow. "Where are we?" Harry asked.

"This is Bangalore, India around the year 2000. Look down at the graph now," prompted Sara.

Harry looked straight down and was startled to see what had happened to the basic indicators of human progress. Infant mortality and subsistence living plunged and per capita income soared, along with the Earth's population. From 10,000 BC to 2000 the lines on the graph had been essentially flat for ninety-eight percent of the distance, then shot straight up or down in the last two percent.

"Life expectancy in India has almost doubled in the last fifty years. Modern medicine, clean water, sanitation, and the green revolution in food production have made a huge difference. And now information technology jobs here in India are fueling the local economy.

"Consider how quickly this has happened," Sara continued, "Everything we consider progress, even the very idea of progress itself, has emerged in the blink of an eye. And it's all been due to interlocking virtuous cycles of communication, innovation, energy use, scientific discovery, engineering, technology, productivity, employment, and economic growth. Today we're capable of driving those lines even further straight up. But there's a problem."

"And that problem is...?"

"We are on the verge of developing new technologies that will usher in a true age of abundance. Inventions in nano-materials, bioengineering, personalized genomic medicine, fusion reactors, and electrostatic nano-capacitor energy storage all hold the promise of providing everyone on the planet with a safe, healthy, long, and productive life, including unprecedented conveniences and opportunities for personal development and expression."

"That's what the techies keep saying," said Harry skeptically.

"They are all possible," said Sara. "But we're not going to develop those technologies, because market capitalism is breaking down."

VIRTUAL REALITY / LOS ANGELES

"What is this place?" shouted Tenesha.

The sound in her headphones was painful and overwhelming, and she couldn't make anything out in the near-darkness.

Sara stepped right up to her and spoke into her right ear. "This is a lights-out automated factory that produces service robots. It can be this loud and this dark because no humans work here. Here, I'll turn on your night vision and lower the volume."

Tenesha could now see through the greenish glow a very high-speed manufacturing process taking place all around her. The facility was huge. Raw materials arrived behind her on automated vehicles and robotic arms sorted them onto conveyer systems. More machines cut and fabricated parts, which fed into assembly areas.

Sara gestured toward an elevator. They stepped inside and rose up several stories to a walkway that provided a panoramic view.

"Capitalism now has a problem," said Sara, "and it's visible right here. For two centuries, every labor-saving innovation stimulated demand for newly invented goods and services that required human labor to produce.

That worked for as long as we could educate or retrain people in the skills required. But our new industries are using fewer and fewer employees. Of course, millions of scientists, engineers, and designers are required—but not hundreds of millions or billions of people. Robots like these get steadily cheaper and more capable, putting an increasing number of jobs in jeopardy.

"With the latest AIs and robots, there simply won't be enough need for the vast majority of routine human labor that economies have needed in the past. Without people with jobs, there isn't enough income to fuel consumption and drive technological progress forward toward an age of abundance. Meanwhile, vastly more income accrues to a small percentage of high-skilled and capital-owning people."

VIRTUAL REALITY / WASHINGTON

"And that's how market capitalism is breaking down," said Sara.

"I've understood this to be a problem for some time," Harry said. "You don't need to convince me."

Sara looked at him coolly from the left side of the walkway. "Of course, Senator. You've been talking about it for years."

It took Harry a few seconds to realize that this VR program knew who he was from his headset registration data. And he wasn't entirely comfortable with this fact. She continued, "And your lack of success is exactly what stands in the way of getting us past this problem."

VIRTUAL REALITY / LOS ANGELES

Tenesha listened intently to the young woman on the factory walkway.

"Technological progress has delivered huge benefits to humanity, as you have seen. But it has also brought many negative consequences, from agricultural and manufacturing unemployment to pollution to climate change to bioterrorism.

"Human societies have always adapted to these consequences through various social and political processes. Some solutions required new technologies, but others required rewriting laws and evolving the social contract that holds societies together.

"Right now, there is an urgent need to rewrite that social contract once again. But it is not happening. The current crisis of capitalism and innovation is not being addressed. This is putting us all in grave danger.

"Let me show you why."

The factory faded into gray nothingness. A new, dimly lit scene appeared before Tenesha.

"This is Plato's Cave," said Sara. "It's just a metaphor, but it's appropriate for our current situation."

Tenesha used her Mental Intention interface to walk with Sara deeper into a huge underground chamber.

Sara pointed. "Look there," she said. Tenesha saw thousands of people locked into chairs, heads fixed forward, only able to see the wall before them.

Sara said, "That is humanity, locked into position, staring at the wall in front of them, while people parade objects behind them, making noises and casting shadows up on the wall. Those imprisoned humans believe the shadows are reality, and talk amongst themselves about the different shapes and noises they hear. They argue about the meaning and causes of the shadows' motions, and award honors and prizes to those who recognize patterns in their behavior."

Tenesha walked toward the back of the cave. Dark figures paraded back and forth in front of bright lights, carrying objects above their heads to cast shadows on the wall. Sara waved her hand and the VR scene transformed. The shadows on the vast wall were replaced by media channels and talking heads, spewing a cacophony of negative news and arguments.

Standing behind the locked-up humans, Tenesha saw the dark figures who had been carrying objects. They now sat around expensive glass and steel tables that overflowed with fine food and drinks.

"The shadow-makers tell us that there are only two contradictory paths," explained Sara with some urgency. "They tell us that half of us want one path and half want the other, and that our paralysis and dysfunction and inability to solve these problems are inevitable and unchangeable. They divide us into fractionalized interest groups focused on narrow issues or into tribes riven by ancient hatreds. These shadow-makers focus on conflict and discord to create cynicism and disillusionment. They sow fear, division, and distrust in us and between us, and toward our institutions, and even our technology."

VIRTUAL REALITY / WASHINGTON

Harry focused on the mysterious dark figures behind the long rows of chairs. They were at once fascinating, frightening, and pathetic.

Sara said, "Many of the people and institutions that make the shadows truly believe what they are projecting. But they are the beneficiaries of the most recent technological revolution. They reap its bounty happily, and they want the mass of humanity to remain passive and accepting, placated by the latest shiny gadgets and twenty-four seven entertainments.

"The only thing tempering my optimism for the future is a massive misunderstanding by this tiny, arrogant, elite minority. A storm is brewing that they will not be able to control. And when it comes, it will erupt with such destruction that it will set humanity's course back for generations.

"Ultimately, humanity will get back on track, as it always has, but not before billions of people endure enormous and unnecessary hardship. Unless you, Senator, help change the course we are on."

VIRTUAL REALITY / LOS ANGELES

Tenesha was overwhelmed by the hundreds of video streams of wars and strife and pointless argumentation.

Sara stepped in front of the vids and lowered the volume. "Tenesha," she said softly, "We can steer around this gathering storm. I believe in the power of science and technology to create a world of abundance for all of humanity with a sustainable path for our planet. I believe in the power of love and compassion in the human spirit to cleanse the mean-spirited selfishness that has sullied us.

"You and the other young people of the world, united by a positive vision for the future, can and will force the shadow-makers to stop their manipulations. You can make them solve the challenges raised by the latest technological innovations instead of shrugging their shoulders and saying 'we couldn't get past the politics.'"

Tenesha ambled up a ramp out of the cave, still trying to absorb everything she had seen and heard. The sun hurt her eyes as they emerged from the darkness.

Sara stopped beside her, smiling. "Welcome to the future, Tenesha. Feel free to look around. But once you see what is possible, I'm going to ask you to go back to the cave and free the rest of the people from their chains."

CHAPTER THIRTEEN

Los Angeles - October 3

Tenesha took off her headset and placed it on her crowded desk. LuLu had been right; that had been a unique VR experience. And what Sara had talked about made so much sense. It crystallized a lot of what Tenesha had been thinking about for the last year. Technology had indeed made their lives better, but now things were breaking down.

As she took a quick shower, Tenesha reflected on the Supernova Coffee case study from her robo-economics seminar the previous semester. Supernova used robotics and AI up and down the supply chain to completely automate the coffee experience. Self-driving trucks delivered raw materials to automated distribution centers, which used more robots to package up the correct ingredients for each store. More self-driving trucks delivered highly specialized containers with milk, coffee beans, cups, powdered chocolate, sugars and spices were delivered by more self-driving trucks to the stores, where robots unloaded them and docked them into baristabots.

These sixty-thousand-dollar machines could process five orders simultaneously and produce perfect cappuccinos, mochas, and espressos twenty-four hours a day, with no breaks. Although they were expensive, they cost less than five dollars an hour to operate, as opposed to the minimum wage of twenty-four dollars an hour.

Not only that, all you had to do was speak to the Supernova app on your PNA and tell it exactly what you wanted. Three minutes later, you'd walk by the nearest kiosk, hold your PNA up to a delivery window, and out would come exactly what you ordered, perfectly brewed and prepared.

Tenesha enjoyed the witty repartee with surly, underemployed college graduates and bemoaned with all her friends the loss of baristas. But Supernova's coffee was fantastic and personalized, and it cost just $2.50, instead of the $8.00 the barista places were charging.

It was better for the environment as well. There was practically zero waste at a Supernova. In addition to the recyclable cups, there were no milk cartons or sugar packets or packaging of any kind. It had become a classic case in the economics of automation-driven productivity.

There were now six thousand Supernovas around the world, each pulling in five thousand dollars a day in sales, with twenty-five percent after-tax profit margins. The company generated over two billion dollars in profits each year, with only five hundred employees. The founders and early investors were already billionaires, and shareholders got fat dividends every quarter. And the masses got cheaper and better coffee. But another whole job category was disappearing.

Her seminar had spent an entire week exploring what could be done about this. Many solutions had already been proposed in Congress, but they had all been shot down in the hyper-partisan legislative environment. No wonder her prof had called this time in Washington "the Great Dysfunction."

Tenesha dressed in record time, but had to forgo her usual Nova on the way to Sociology 204. One of the privileges of having a scholarship to a brick-and- mortar school was that she got to attend real physical classes.

Her friend Nate waved to her as she got on the bus. He was holding onto a hanging strap, wearing jeans and a faded green T-shirt with a picture of some band she didn't know. Nate was darker-skinned than Tenesha and a couple of inches shy of six feet. Her two-inch high Afro was just about even with the top of his close-cropped head.

"Hey Nate, what's up?"

"Late for class, as usual. You?"

"I'm buzzing about this VR program I just ran."

"You mean the Sara VR?" Nate asked.

"No shit. You played it too?"

"Sure thing. Crazy smart for a sixteen-year-old."

"I just ran it once this morning after a late night and no coffee. What do you think?"

Nate gave his summary. It wasn't a surprise. He saw everything in terms of oppression and injustice. "What I heard was that science and technology should be leading us to the promised land, but as usual the white power structure is going to screw us because they want it all for themselves."

"I hear you," Tenesha said. "Was she calling for some kind of revolution at the end there?"

"Hard to say. Coulda been. The people will rise up and force their corrupt government to change. Yeah, right."

"Remember Tahrir Square. It could happen."

"Yeah, but remember what happened after that. People are scared to death of mass demonstrations because they've seen it lead to even more autocracy."

"Well someone's got to do something," Tenesha said. "I believe Sara about that gathering storm. I've been feeling it more and more."

"Oh yeah? You psychic?"

"Ha ha. My grammy was psychic, if you must know. But I'm just paying attention. Big media is covering it up, but there's some serious shit starting to happen in this country and all over Europe. It's all over OP even if the news media are hiding it."

"Okay, so what are you going to do about it?" Nate asked her.

"Damned if I know. What are *you* going to do about it?"

"I'm gonna get my degree, find a job, pay off my debt. Then I'll do something."

"Yeah, right. You'll be a hundred years old by then," she said.

"I seriously doubt I'm gonna live that long. Only the rich folks' life expectancy is rising." Nate leaned closer to her. "I watched that old movie *Elysium*, with Matt Damon, last week. I'll be damned if that doesn't feel like where we're headed, only the wealthy aren't building a space station. They're just isolating themselves in islands of affluence. They've already got the fences and private security bots. I bet the moats will come next. It's like feudalism all over again."

"Oh, shit, here's my stop," Tenesha said. "Wanna get a Nova later and talk more?"

He gave her a smile that dissolved a little more of her hangover. "Love to, but I'm headed home this weekend. I'll hit you up when I get back."

Tenesha was only a minute late to class, so it hadn't really started yet. There were about forty students sitting in clusters in an amphitheater-style room that had room for more than a hundred. She sat next to Laney Wagner and joined her conversation with Todd Sherman. "Well, I don't think it's going to go anywhere," Laney was saying.

"What are you guys talking about?" Tenesha asked.

"Todd here thinks this Sara VR is going to spark something, I think it's just going to fade away like all the other OP memes. It's had its fifteen minutes."

"Holy crap, you guys played it too?"

"It's spread like wildfire," said Todd. "Everyone's talking about it."

"Yeah," countered Laney, "so did that video of the robot playing with the kittens and puppies."

"I agree with Todd," said Tenesha. "This is different. Sara has a message with meaning, not just stupid entertainment. She's got a positive vision for humanity."

"Exactly," said Todd. "But it's not going to happen on its own. We're going to have to do something about it."

The professor, Mitch Goodson, tapped his podium to get the students to settle down. "Good morning, class. As I circulated this morning, I heard quite a lot of you talking about this new VR program. I know we were going to continue to talk about the civil rights movement today, but I'd like to call an audible. What do you say, shall we screen a video capture and then have a little discussion about it?"

Yes! That's what Tenesha loved about Professor Goodson. He saw teaching as an ongoing search for ways to engage with his students and bring his subject to life for them.

Laney rolled her eyes, but the consensus in the class was clear.

Goodson searched the VR video capture channels for sarasmessage.com and played a few minutes from Sara's childhood, the automated factory, and Plato's cave on the big screen at the front of the class.

"So, students, reactions? What strikes you about this VR program, in the context of the social movements we've been studying?"

Todd raised his hand eagerly.

"Todd, what do you think?"

"She reminds me of Martin Luther King, Jr. He spoke in grand terms about the long sweep of history, but made it clear that the current time was full of trouble and that it would take hard work to make change happen."

"Very interesting comparison. But what's different about Sara? Yes, Tenesha?"

"Well, she's an outsider. She's a young woman from a tiny village in India. She hasn't really grown up in the system she's critiquing."

"So?" Goodson asked. "What are the implications of that?"

"Well, hmm. I guess it both helps and hurts her," Tenesha said. "On the one hand, she isn't part of the conflict in the Western democracies so she's like neutral. But on the other hand, she's got no personal connection to what we're going through."

Another girl raised her hand, and Goodson nodded at her. "Well, she's making a universal appeal. She talks about humanity as a whole, not just the people of one nation."

"Have we studied any other movements that were trans-national?" Goodson asked. No one answered, so he continued. "There have been very few truly global movements. Environmentalism was one in the 1970s, but even that didn't have a single global champion or instigator, and it wasn't particularly well coordinated."

A boy in the back of the room raised his hand. "What did you all think about her use of Plato's analogy of the cave? I studied that in Phil 102 last year. I was really surprised to hear her use that. I mean, it's well known if you've studied philosophy, but it's really obscure for a broad audience."

Another student disagreed. "I like the fact that she didn't speak down to her audience, that she challenged us with big concepts. So much OP traffic is dumbed-down red meat sound bites treating people like Pavlovian lab specimens. People can look it up. I totally get the idea that we're not seeing what's really going on and that we've just been conditioned by all our media to believe nothing can be done about it."

"Well, that's the question isn't it," said Goodson. "Can something be done about it? Sara seemed to think the people would be able to make change happen. We've certainly seen it before; we've been studying it all term. Do you think it can happen?"

"I don't think so," said Laney. "I mean, I don't want to rain on the parade or anything, but I think people are too focused on themselves and just trying to get by. And even if they did try something, the government is so gridlocked that nothing would happen anyway."

Tenesha shook her head. "That's what people have always said before all big changes. 'It's just the way it is. It can't be changed.' It just takes enough people to say 'Enough is enough. This is unacceptable.' We still do live in a democracy. It should respond to the will of the people."

"I think you're being naïve," said Laney. "Eighty percent majorities have been in favor of regulating guns, limiting campaign funding, and improving infrastructure. But those things haven't happened."

"But those are just poll results," said Anthony. "Tenesha's talking about a movement where people actually do something. Like mass marches."

Laney sighed. "Yeah, right, but look at the last few times we had those. Before the Iraq War? Occupy? Trump? The Iran War? A lot of good it did."

Goodson said, "Okay, let me break in here. Your discussion is the epitome of what happens at the start of any social movement. There is an idea, in this case Sara's message, which sparks interest. There are those who feel change is impossible. There are those who are impassioned to make change happen. But talking about it is not enough. Action is required."

He surveyed the class. "Who here is going to do more than play this VR program and talk about it?" He looked right at Todd and Tenesha, who had been Sara's most vocal supporters. "Who is going to mobilize and organize people?"

The class sat still and silent.

"Well, then," he said, turning back to his podium and lecture notes. "Thank you for a fascinating conversation. Let's see if we can still squeeze in a little more on civil rights."

Tenesha felt like Professor Goodson, her favorite teacher, had called her out in front of the whole class. She had wanted to raise her hand and say, "I will!" But the truth was that she was scared. She had no idea how she was going to pay off her student loans. But she was damned sure that being a troublemaking student activist wasn't going to help her get a job in this economy, not with AI recruiting bots having direct access to police databases. Being arrested at a protest was pretty much a permanent blacklisting.

Someone else was going to have to steer the ship away from the gathering storm.

CHAPTER FOURTEEN

Santa Barbara - October 3

"Allison, what's the status on the Sara launch?" Roger asked.

"Everything is operating within normal parameters. More than eighteen million synths are actively promoting the brand worldwide. Engagement response rates are positive and the VR program has been run more than one hundred million times."

"Good. Speaking of which, can you load that program for me? I want to run it now."

Twenty minutes later, Roger removed his VR headset and blinked at the sunshine that was starting to break through the morning fog. He knew now why Frances had suggested he go through the experience. And why she had been so hesitant to recommend it. Sara's personal story and history lesson on technology and capitalism had been very familiar from the briefings and policy positions he'd been working with for the last two weeks. But the metaphor of the cave and the shadowy figures manipulating public opinion and dividing people, paralyzing them and polarizing them, that he hadn't picked up on. Or maybe he'd chosen to ignore it.

The images from the cave made him uneasy. He recalled the stats Allison had displayed during his conversation with Frances, the ones she had asked about. Seventy percent of his synth interactions were negative. "Allison, give me a grid on the display, ten wide and five deep, and run a scroll of randomly sampled English synth interactions with five second updates." It had been years since he'd watched what the synths said. The statistics he usually tracked were more abstract and focused on client results.

It was not a pretty picture. While about twenty percent of their comments were positively promoting commercial products and services, the vast majority of his clients were pushing controversial ideas or policies. The synth algorithms had figured out years ago it was far more effective to trash their opponents than rationally make a case. The scrolling interactions before him were largely ugly—rude and mean spirited.

Roger turned away from the display and contemplated the beautiful landscape before him, the deep blue Pacific ocean stretching away to the horizon. What had Sara called the dark figures in the cave? Shadowmakers? Is that what he was? Sowing discord and confusion? Pitting people against each other, distracting them from the larger issues at hand? "Allison, do you have stats on how often synths are arguing with each other on behalf of different clients?"

"No, Roger. I can perform that analysis. For what time frame?"

"For the last month." His synth data was highly indexed so the answer came back in two seconds. "Approximately twenty percent of all synth interactions in omnipresence are in threads with synths for other clients in opposition." That wasn't as bad as he thought it might be. But the fact remained that his network was injecting a lot of negativity into the world.

"Allison, please analyze a sample of omnipresence and calculate the percent of all negative sentiment expressed by synths in their engagements and the overall percentage of negative sentiment, again for the last month." This request took a little longer, as the universe of the query was far beyond only his synth's interactions. "Synths were responsible for fifteen percent of negative sentiment where they engaged. The overall average of negative sentiment in the sample was close to thirty percent."

Well, that was a little more reassuring. At least they weren't overwhelming all the human generated negative sentiment. But he also knew the synths were strategic, engaging in the threads with the biggest impact. His clients wouldn't pay him unless that were true, unless the network was able to move the needle on overall public opinion. "Allison, could you have Rosie bring me some herbal tea?"

"Yes, Roger, but I notice that you have an appointment to play squash and lunch with Will soon."

"Oh, damn, you're right. When do I need to leave?"

"Given traffic, you should leave in ten minutes."

"Okay, cancel the tea then, I've got to get ready."

Roger packed up his squash gear and made his way to the garage. He decided to take the vintage 2014 Tesla Model S, though he knew Will would laugh at him. The S, with its original hardware package, could only manage level 2 autonomy. All his friends were driven around in their level 5 vehicles with plush, living-room-like seating. While he had a couple of level 5's himself, including the latest Tesla Z, sometimes he just preferred to drive himself. And after his unsettling Sara VR experience, he could use the distraction.

After an intense match on the court, Will and Roger left the club and true to form, his friend gave him a look as Roger walked towards the parking lot. "Oh, no. Not again? You didn't bring that old clunker? You know they're about to build on top of the parking lot because everyone can send their cars to park outside the city? Land's too valuable to waste on asphalt."

"Yeah, I heard," sighed Roger. "I'll park on the street I guess, or use the Z."

"Oh, the Z is a sweet ride. I mean you wouldn't be using twenty-year-old AI or robots at home right, why do it with the S?"

"I don't know, nostalgia maybe. Anyway, where do you want to go to lunch?"

"Something quick, I've got an appointment at one."

"How about the Eatza on Anacapa?" Roger asked as they climbed into the S.

"That's the robot one, quinoa bowls and salads, right?" Will asked.

"Yeah, it's quick and super fresh." Roger used the backup camera to inch out of the parking space while Will rolled his eyes. "I always wondered why the fully automated restaurant took so long to go mainstream," Roger continued.

"More 'nostalgia', I guess. Well, my sources tell me Supernova is going to go big with Haro Burger. I think that'll really get the ball rolling."

"Hmm, there's a lot of people who work in that industry."

"Did I ever tell you I started out my first job was in fast food? Lousy job. Better to leave it to the robots, I say."

"Yeah, but what are those people going to do?"

"Oh man, Roger, you sound like my son. All hyped up this morning about some VR chick spouting socialist claptrap about the end of capitalism."

"Really? James watched that?"

"Oh yeah, it's today's viral content. Here today, gone tomorrow."

"You don't buy the argument?"

"Look, there are plenty of high-skill jobs that go begging for candidates. These people need to hit the e-books, get some skills, and get a good job. Simple as that."

"But what if they're not able to, or there aren't enough of those jobs?"

"Oh Christ, Roger. You turning into a socialist now too? You going to give up that fancy house and your Z and Ferrari so some poor sucker can sit at home all day in VR? Gimme a break."

"Nah, just wondering is all."

"Well I'm wondering what kind of Eatza salad to get," said Will pulling out his PNA. "Let's order ahead so it's ready when we get there."

CHAPTER FIFTEEN

Syracuse/North Carolina/London - October 8

SYRACUSE

At 11 p.m. Peter Cook drove for an hour from his home in the Syracuse New York suburbs to his remote ops center in the rolling hills near Lacona. Cook, known as Othello to his fellow group members, was the Ludd Kaczynski Collective's drone expert. He had piloted more than a hundred covert drone missions in the Middle East and Central America for the Delta Force. None of them, he thought, from the comfort of a beat-up brown leather couch in a woodland log cabin.

Three days earlier he'd flown down to Norfolk Virginia and liberated a '24 Chevy pickup truck from a junk yard. He had picked up his cargo from a warehouse near the Portsmouth Marine Terminal, where it had been smuggled by another LKC member. Cook had driven to the tiny town of Denton in North Carolina and pulled off the road into a small stand of trees to unload. The high-resolution satellite photos available from

Planet Labs had been very accurate—the green and brown camouflage he'd selected for the five drones matched the underbrush in the area perfectly.

At about 1 a.m. Peter sat down on the leather couch in his cabin, opened the drone piloting terminal, and established an anonymous encrypted Torpedo session to the 6G radios in the drones nestled in the trees in North Carolina. He ran through all the self-checks and powered up the rotors. Once the five drones were off the ground he confirmed the pay-loads were in place and all the sensors were working. Then he steered the group out from the trees, took them up to two hundred feet, and pointed them north towards Thomasville.

LKC had sourced the very latest tech with full autonomous capabil-ity so he gave them the destination and set them loose. He still watched the night-vision display carefully, on the lookout for tall trees and electri-cal transmission lines. After twenty minutes his weapons reached the I-85 freeway. If the RezMat operations database Zurich had stolen was correct, his target would be approaching from the south in just a few minutes.

NORTH CAROLINA

The autonomous 18-wheeler was on schedule, traveling 65 miles per hour on I-85 with its load of fifty advanced Mark V droids destined for Philadelphia. RezMat engineers had specially fitted the robots with the lat-est 3D neuromorphic processors and fiber optic communication channels, giving them nearly ten times the processing power of a normal Mark V.

Their phthalonitrile resin bodies could withstand temperatures up to 2250°, which made them ideally suited for their initial deployment as firefighting droids. Philadelphia had recently experienced the tragic loss of eleven firefighters in a huge blaze, and the public was clamoring for "dispos-able" droids. The firefighters themselves were protesting the deployment.

At 1:32 a.m. five drones hovering thirty feet above the roadway began broadcasting laser signals designed to confuse the truck's LIDAR sensors into thinking there was a wall across the middle of the road. Even though radar showed nothing, the safety protocols instructed the drive control system to begin decelerating, and the truck had no trouble coming to a stop twenty feet from the non-existent barrier that it perceived across the highway. Exterior lights and additional cameras activated, standard procedure when the vehicle stopped unexpectedly. Back in upstate New York, Peter Cook visually confirmed the identity of the RezMat truck, verified there was no other traffic in the area, and keyed in the attack order.

The truck's cameras captured the flight of the five drones as they dropped from the sky and circled the vehicle. They clamped onto the trailer in a precise pattern to maximize the impact from their one-kilo Semtex charges. Ten seconds later, the five charges exploded simultaneously, obliterating the drones, the truck, and its cargo, and leaving a fifty-foot crater in the middle of I-85.

LONDON

The early-morning shift transport supervisor at RezMat headquarters saw the yellow light flash on her screen. This indicated a major malfunction with one of their transport vehicles.

She leaned forward in her chair and said, "Transport 319 data." She looked up at her wall screen—all feeds from the truck were dead.

She pulled up the truck's recent sensor and signal history, ran the video, and nearly spilled her tea when she saw the drones. *Bloody hell.*

She called Bradley Childress.

"This is Killian at Central Dispatch, sir. We've had an attack on one of our transport trucks in North Carolina in the States."

"What happened?" Childress asked.

"Looks like it was right blown up, it was. Was forced to stop somehow, then drones with explosives."

"When was this?"

"Ten minutes ago," she replied.

"I'll be there in fifteen minutes. Prepare a package with all feeds for the twenty minutes prior to the explosion. Send it to the FBI office in Raleigh, North Carolina with a flash alert for domestic terrorist activity."

"Yes, sir."

Five minutes later, another video call flashed urgent on his display. It was David Livingstone.

"Yes, David?"

"Bradley! I was just informed that one of our transports blew up in the States. Is this true? Was it an accident?"

"That is correct, sir. Unfortunately, it was not an accident. It appears to have been attacked by drones carrying explosives."

"Damn it! Do you think this is connected to that data leak?"

"There's no question that having that data would have enabled this attack, David. But we can't say for sure."

"What should we do now?"

"I'm already connecting with the FBI in the States. I suggest we start to work with the Ops team to shift our production and logistics schedules."

"That's going to be a bloody nightmare, Bradley."

"I know, but we need to alter what we can."

"Very well, I'll speak to Ops. You focus on chasing down these bastards."

"We're on it, sir."

NORTH CAROLINA

Special Agent Matt Chandler of the FBI's Domestic Terrorism Task Force (DTTF) arrived in an automated helicopter to supervise the evidence gathering on I-85. A half dozen robots were scouring the area for fragments. As he climbed out of the copter, his PNA let him know there was a sensor package from the truck available. He put on his VR goggles and said, "Play video."

He watched a view synthesized from all the truck's camera feeds. The truck came to a stop and drones flew past the cameras. Each one had a cube of material attached, obviously explosive charges. Just the kind of attack his agency had been warning about for years. The delivery system was readily available on the commercial market and completely incinerated during use, leaving no evidence behind.

His PNA buzzed, a notification indicating there was a published claim of responsibility. He switched over to it. Against a backdrop of dark electronic music and a video montage of violent protests from the past, a computer-generated woman's voice began speaking in a monotone strikingly at odds with the content of the message.

"Today the LKC has struck a blow against the industrial and governmental elites who are systematically relegating humans to a life devoid of meaning and freedom, through the continued development and deployment of technological substitutes. It is our intent to disrupt and destroy their means of production, their means of surveillance, and their means of power.

"Technology has enabled the creation of organizations whose ultimate purpose is to restrict, regulate, and eliminate individual free will and dignity. We need to tear down these organizations and their instruments of enslavement, and open the eyes of the people to their true state of being.

"The people have been blinded by marketing, propaganda and frivolous entertainments, to the point that they do not understand the depth of their servitude. They have become so enmeshed with technology that the simple act of human contact has been disintermediated into digital bits and haptic suit stimulations.

"We will wake the people up to their true state, living empty and desperate lives behind the enticing bars of virtual reality, thought control implants, and soma-like nano-pharmaceuticals.

"What is our plan? As one of our heroes Ted Kaczynski wrote in his manifesto: 'Two tasks confront those who hate the servitude to which the industrial system is reducing the human race. First, we must work to heighten the social stresses within the system so as to increase the likelihood that it will break down or be weakened sufficiently so that a revolution against it becomes possible.'

"'Second, it is necessary to develop and propagate an ideology that opposes technology and the industrial society, if and when the system becomes sufficiently weakened. And such an ideology will help to assure that, if and when industrial society breaks down, its remnants will be smashed beyond repair, so that the system cannot be reconstituted.'

"Our plan therefore is to undermine the technological systems that modern societies so helplessly depend on. We will target the automated factories, supply chains, energy and communication grids, and distribution systems to which we have delegated our very survival and whose operation we do not even understand.

"We will also promote our positive ideology for a return to a state of grace with the Nature that we have damaged and desecrated for centuries. Only by living directly from the land can humanity reestablish true freedom and dignity.

"Some will argue that destroying the technological system goes too far and has too high a cost. But reform is no longer possible, as our addiction to technology simply cannot be attenuated. Only the complete overthrow of the existing order can free us.

"Fellow revolutionaries, we will be contacting you shortly to join the Ludd Kaczynski Collective."

CHAPTER SIXTEEN

London - October 10

D avid Livingstone paced rapidly in the area between his desk and conference table. "And what do we know about this LKC group?"

Bradley nodded to Jill, who consulted her tablet screen and ticked off what they had so far. "There was absolutely no mention of LKC prior to the North Carolina attack and launch of their video and manifesto. They have excellent technical skills and operational security. Their philosophy seems to be purely anti-technology. They fancy themselves modern day Luddites and their goal is to destroy the machine state and return humanity to a 'state of nature', whatever that means."

"It means a lot of starvation and dying of curable diseases, that's what it means," barked Livingstone.

Bradley broke in. "David please, why don't you take a seat so we can brief you on—"

"I don't understand how people can't grasp the enormous benefits from automation of routine work," David continued. "And the incredible quality of life offered by medplants, carebots, and the entertainment options of haptic VR."

"David, please sit down. We need to brief you on our response plan and get approvals to move forward. We don't have time to debate the merits of technological progress. Every minute counts. There's no doubt LKC has other attacks in the works."

"Very well." He sat down opposite them. "What are we going to do?"

"First, we are altering as many of our operational schedules as possible, focusing on automated facilities and transport."

"Why the automated ones?"

"It's an educated guess from their writings," answered Jill, "They are philosophically opposed to automation substituting for people and they don't want to harm people."

"Directly," David muttered.

"Second," continued Bradley, "we're going to increase aerial surveillance of our facilities and surrounding areas and provide direct feeds to the relevant local authorities."

"What about anti-drone defenses?"

"Yes, I was just getting to that. In several countries, including the States, automated anti-drone technology is illegal, even on private property. This is one area we could use your help. We need to get our governmental affairs offices to lobby those countries for emergency waivers.

"In the meantime, we're going to assign human drone hunters to random transport routes. They can take out drones quickly if the transporter is stopped, but LKC could shift to a higher risk approach and try to use explosive drones that match vehicle speed. Makes it harder to kill them in that scenario.

"Third, we need to think about our fixed facilities. Until we get the automated anti-drone tech waivers we can deploy manually controlled defenses. But frankly, with the speed of these drone attacks and the size of our facilities, those are unlikely to be effective.

"We should also stand up anti-drone nets over any large openings to our facilities," added Jill.

"What will those do?" David asked.

"They can stop micro-drone swarms," replied Jill. "And slow down full-sized drones to give our drone hunters time to take them out."

"They are likely to slow down operations, though, which is why we'll need you to push for them with the Ops team," said Bradley.

"Very well, I can do that," said the CEO.

"We also can't assume they will only use drones to attack our assets. We might see ground or even aqua-droids deployed as well. With your approval, I'll also order additional screens for all water intake pipes at our major facilities."

"Yes, approved. Is all this going to keep our assets safe?" Bradley and Jill looked at each other.

"It's going to make LKC's job a whole lot tougher," said Bradley. "But we can't stop one hundred percent of their attacks. They are going to have some successes."

"And what about tracking them down?" asked David.

"That's really the FBI's job in the States," replied Bradley. "We're providing all the assistance we can. Within the constraints of company policies," he added.

"Yes, I see. You are not inspiring a lot of confidence, Bradley."

"It's the best we can do for now, David. We're working around the clock to improve our defenses and help the authorities find the terrorists. We just have to hope they make a mistake so we can track them down."

CHAPTER SEVENTEEN

Los Angeles - October 12

J acob washed and put away his cereal bowl, then settled down on his black leather couch, his last big purchase. He opened a viewer on the set of anti-technology omnipresence feeds he'd put together since he was laid off and one item immediately caught his eye.

There was going to be a rally that afternoon to protest the grand opening of the first Haro Burger outlet. The Supernova coffee company was branching out into food preparation using the same automated model. A small kiosk, supplied several times a day with fresh meat, bread and veggies by autonomous vehicles, could make a gourmet hamburger with a custom meat blend and selected toppings, cooked precisely to order, in seven minutes. Haro Burger could produce four hundred high quality burgers an hour at a lower price than the competition, and deliver them through a PNA-activated window at the kiosk, or via a drone for an additional fee.

Jacob shook his head as he read the announcement. A business that used to require a staff of ten people—twenty, considering two shifts—now needed just one part-time person to come by a few times a day and perform simple maintenance.

Supernova's stock jumped seventeen percent the day it had announced the Los Angeles grand opening and existing fast food companies quickly published plans to put their own automation systems in place. They had seen what happened to coffee chains that had been slow to react to Supernova's explosive growth in that industry and got crushed. Of course, the high-end restaurants that catered to the rich insisted they would stick with their expensive human chefs and servers, with stratospheric prices to match.

Jacob decided to attend the rally to be with like-minded activists in person. He'd spent the last two weeks as an avatar in VR meet-ups and flash mobs, but it wasn't the same. All his life he had worked with his hands with real people in the real world, and talking to computer-generated images in VR just didn't cut it for him. The media also didn't cover VR events since they assumed that most of the attendees were bots. But if organizers could get thousands of people out on the streets of downtown LA, they could get lots of media coverage.

He got up from the couch, walked across the small living space, and removed his Personal Privacy Foundation cloak from a black backpack that sat, always ready, near the door. Jacob couldn't afford the latest version, but after getting fired he had purchased a two-year-old model that could block the tech currently in use by the police in Los Angeles and most corporate security forces.

The cloak was designed to shield all electronic devices from snooping, and to prevent remote facial, fingerprint, and gait detection systems. It blocked outbound medplant signals as well. But it wasn't foolproof. If someone got close enough, they could grab a stray skin cell or a piece of hair and do a DNA match. He'd have to be careful in the crowd today.

Jacob followed the maintenance procedure carefully, inspecting all the seams and wiring connections. He double-checked that the battery was fully charged. The cloak operated as a Faraday cage and had active sensor jammers, and all those systems required power. He ran the diagnostics; everything reported green. He smiled as he folded up the cloak and returned it to the backpack.

After working omnipresence for a few hours, trying to drum up attendance, Jacob retrieved the cloak and put it on, then headed out the door. These days he never went outside unshielded.

He walked ten long blocks to catch a city bus downtown. He paid with anonymous q-coin tokens to leave no trail of his attendance. Machines all over the city dispensed them from any registered digital currency account and then they acted just like old-fashioned analog cash.

It was sometimes hard to see out of the cloak's mesh face guard coated with thin LED wires, but that was a small inconvenience. Cameras were so ubiquitous, facial recognition software so accurate, and the image databases so comprehensive that it was essentially impossible to not be identified if your face was visible for even a few seconds on a city street.

Jacob was pleased to encounter the edges of a crowd while the bus was still blocks away from the rally point.

When he got off, he joined a stream of people heading toward the new Haro Burger store. About ten percent of his fellow protesters were also wearing PPF cloaks or other privacy gear. He'd heard a rumor that Congress was going to pass legislation making these outfits illegal, but legislators hadn't figured out a way past the Fourth Amendment issues. Yet.

The noise of the crowd energized him. There were hundreds of people flowing through the streets now, many more than he had expected. He was also pleased to see media drones circling the crowd. They were essential to reaching a broader audience and waking people up to the reality of what was happening.

As Jacob fought his way toward an impromptu stage that had been set up in front of the store, he noticed a growing police presence. They were deploying an array of surveillance equipment to capture signals from all attendees, no doubt to identify them as "potential risks to public safety." Hundreds of personal micro-drones thickened the sky above the crowd; collisions were common despite their automatic avoidance systems.

One of the heavily armored police vans began broadcasting a message. "This is the Los Angeles Police Department. This gathering does not have a valid permit and is therefore illegal. You are hereby ordered to disperse peacefully or you will be arrested." Jacob shook his head in disgust. The city had stopped granting protest permits years ago, effectively criminalizing the rights of free speech and assembly.

A counter-broadcast from the stage proclaimed, "Citizens of Los Angeles. You have the constitutionally protected right to be here and express your opinion. We stand together, peacefully, so our voices can be heard."

Jacob could see people on the stage now. They were all wearing the latest generation of PPF cloaks. It was a little eerie seeing a group of the gray-shrouded figures huddling together, like ghosts haunting the small platform.

One of them stepped forward to a mic stand. "Fellow Americans!" the woman said through a voice-disguising algorithm. "Thank you for coming out today to protest the destruction of our way of life!"

The crowd roared, drowning out the persistent LAPD broadcast.

After ten seconds, the woman on stage held up her gloved hands for silence and continued. "Businesses like Haro Burger represent everything that is wrong with our economy today. Production without human labor is immoral. We need well-paid jobs to survive. We cannot sacrifice the sanctity of work just for the sake of cheap and convenient food and coffee. We cannot let the one percent profit from job destruction. *Boycott Nova! Jobs, not bots! Boycott Nova! Jobs, not bots!*"

The crowd picked up the chant. "*Jobs not bots! Jobs, not bots!*"

Suddenly, all the police units on surrounding streets sounded their sirens. Jacob looked to his left and saw the police all donning special headgear. Then he noticed hundreds of drones dropping from the skies above the rally. A large media drone crashed just a few feet from him. The LAPD had set off a directed EMP weapon to disable all electronic devices in the area.

Before he could react, he felt a low rumbling vibration in the pit of his stomach. Sound cannons!

His PPF cloak was EMP-hardened and offered some protection against sound-generating weapons. It started producing a neutralizing signal, but some newer LAPD units were able to shift frequencies and these leaked through the cloak, making him slightly nauseous. Still, Jacob was better off than the protesters without cloaks, who screamed in pain and clutched their ears. Those who could still move ran wildly and randomly because no one could tell where the sound weapons were located.

The woman on stage screamed at the police. "Stop! Stop! Those weapons are illegal! This is a peaceful assembly! Stop!"

Jacob was shocked at this violent and extreme overreaction. No wonder they had taken out all the drones and cameras in the area.

As police in riot gear began moving in to make arrests, Jacob decided to take advantage of his mobility and escape the chaos. He turned his back to the police and started to run.

But after getting just a few feet, he was brought up short by a young woman's face twisted into a horrendous grimace. She was on her knees with her hands pressed tightly over her ears, tears streaming from her eyes.

Thinking quickly, he knelt behind her and pulled the lower folds of his cloak out from under his legs. He grabbed her shoulders and pulled her backward until she was lying on her back on the pavement, writhing in pain. He dragged her toward him until her upper back rested on his knees, then covered her head and shoulders with the cloak.

It seemed to provide instant relief, but he couldn't see her face and she was still rocking from side to side.

Jacob slid down slightly and lifted the cloak over his head so it tented over them and he could see her face. "Are you okay?" he asked.

She removed her hands from her ears. "What?"

"Are you feeling better?"

"Yes, I think so."

"We need to get out of here. Do you think you can run if we keep this draped over us?"

She nodded. "I think so."

"Okay, let's go. The police are sweeping the street and arresting everyone. Stand up, slowly. Here, grab that edge there."

They stood up awkwardly. The cloak was not designed for two-person use, so Jacob put his arm around the woman's waist, both to steady her and to keep her close so the cloak could fit over them both. He tried to arrange the mesh face guard as best as possible so he could see where they were going.

Joined at the hip, they half-ran past the stage onto a side street. They hobbled silently down the next two blocks, then turned a corner. The block in front of them looked normal and peaceful.

Jacob peeked out from under the cloak to confirm there were no sound weapons in this area. He let go of his companion, and she ducked out from under the protection of the electronic garment.

He pointed toward an alley that appeared devoid of cameras. She nodded, and the two of them hurried down it and stopped in a small bricked doorway, where Jacob raised the mesh that covered his face and caught his breath.

"I'm Jacob Komarov," he said, extending his hand.

She took it and nodded. "I'm Melissa King. Thank you so much for what you did. That pain was just awful." Her face still shone with tears, but she smiled at him. It had been a while since an attractive woman had smiled at him. Mostly they were put off by the baldness and the tattoos, which at this moment were conveniently hidden under the cloak. Melissa appeared to be in her mid-twenties with very straight long black hair and Eurasian features.

"Those sound weapons are illegal!" he said. "I can't believe they used them. And an EMP? That's bullshit! Why did you come today?"

"Someone has to do something," she said with conviction. "Goddamn machines are taking over everything. Soon there'll be nothing left for people to do."

"Tell me about it. I lost my welding job to a friggin' robot two weeks ago."

"I'm so sorry. My brother lost his job that way, too. He was a radiologist. You know, AIs reading scans kept improving. Once they were officially certified as better than humans, his practice couldn't justify keeping him on."

Jacob took a chance. "Want to grab a real human-brewed coffee and talk some more?"

She smiled again. "Sure, I'd like that."

"Great. There's a place about two blocks from here." Jacob restored the face mesh covering and they began walking.

"You're pretty serious about this privacy cloak, huh?"

"I wear it every time I go out. I don't want to be tracked and build up a profile. You should get one, too. They've probably already got tons of pictures of you from this event."

"How long were you a welder?" she asked as they walked.

"Eleven years. What kind of work have you done?"

"Oh, I've done lots of different stuff. Some electrical engineering, some software, some hardware design. Mostly freelance gigs and open source. It's so hard to find full-time work, especially if you want to work on stuff that matters, that really helps people."

Soon they reached the coffee shop, which had a retro 2010s hipster vibe. They stepped inside, doubling the number of customers on hand. After ordering their drinks they chatted with the barista, a college grad trying to make ends meet.

"Look at this place," said Jacob as they took seats at a table near the window. "A few years ago, I bet it was full of people."

"No one takes the time anymore," Melissa said. "They just run past those damn Supernova kiosks and grab and go."

"I know. When Haro Burger was announced I starting thinking about what we could do to get back at Supernova."

"What do you mean?" she asked.

Jacob tried to gauge how serious was about the anti-technology movement. Would she do more than attend a rally? He looked around. The other two patrons were across the shop and the bored barista was watching something on her PNA. Jacob leaned forward and subconsciously Melissa did too.

"Well I thought about welding some of those kiosks shut," he said quietly.

"Really?" Her eyes widened.

"Yeah. But I didn't see how I could do it without getting caught." He watched her carefully. "You said you worked in software and hardware, right?"

"That's right," she replied, shifting slightly away from him.

"Do you think those kiosks could be hacked somehow?" Jacob asked.

"I, I don't know. I don't know anything about them."

"Well maybe we could do a little research," he suggested. "A little side engineering project?" Melissa looked skeptical. He clearly had some convincing to do.

CHAPTER EIGHTEEN

New Delhi/Palo Alto - October 13

NEW DELHI, INDIA

Sara took a deep breath, then walked out from behind the heavy dark green curtain. The university lecture hall was overflowing with curious students.

A single comfortable chair, a small table with a glass of water, and a standing lamp had been set up on the front edge of the stage. A burst of applause followed Sara until she sat down. The harsh stage spotlights dimmed until the lamp provided some softer illumination.

Sara perched on the edge of her seat and beamed at her audience. "Thank you, thank you, dear friends," she said in Hindi. "I am so happy to be here in New Delhi with all of you, not far from where I was born. I would love to speak with you all in Hindi, my beautiful native tongue. But I hope you will forgive me for switching to English, as it is a language you all know and one more universally known around the world. We will provide a full Hindi translation on the website."

PALO ALTO

Sam Erickson and his colleagues were half the world away in a small studio control room set up in a nondescript office building near downtown Palo Alto. Before joining Sara's team, he had had fifteen years of experience in directing live media events, mostly for politicians and big corporations. While Sara's message was different, all the same communication techniques applied.

He donned the headset to the camera operators and checked his call sheet. "This is Sam. Farhad, can you push in a little tighter? Ranita, can you pan left to the students who are in a better light and widen? Thanks, guys."

While hundreds of PNAs and personal micro-drones captured the event, the main feed streaming on sarasmessage.com came from two professional high-def cameras, one trained on Sara and the other on the audience.

NEW DELHI

Sara raised her arms and pointed into the audience. "Let's begin. I very much want this to be a discussion. There are volunteers with microphones in the aisles. Please raise your hand to let them know you have a question and they will come to you."

As she expected, surprised murmurs spread through the room. She knew they had been anticipating a speech.

A young man raised his hand and was handed a microphone. "Sara, hi, I'm Divyesh. I'm an engineering student here at NDU. I was amazed by your VR program. How did you make it? How did you create your VR character so it could answer random questions?"

"Well, I certainly didn't make it alone, Divyesh. There were dozens of engineers and artists who worked on the VR program with me. We started with an industry standard framework and then extended it to enhance the experience. As for my character, I spent a couple of hundred hours interacting with a RezMat DeepAgent AI to train it in my thoughts and responses. It was a fascinating experience. I started by recording answers to questions prepared by our team. Eventually the AI started asking the questions. Then it applied deep learning to all the responses to create a model of my worldview. That's how it was able to answer your questions in VR. In fact, it continues to listen and train on all my interactions, including right now."

Another young man asked for a mic. "Sara, thank you for coming here and making NDU your very first appearance." There were hoots from the crowd. "My name is Sameer and I am a third-year student. In your VR program you describe a beautiful future for humanity, but here and now, in the real world, I am accumulating debt and I see fewer and fewer opportunities for when I graduate. How do I get to the future when I can't even get a job, and will probably have to live with my parents?" Knowing laughter echoed across the hall.

Sara nodded. "Thank you for the question, Sameer. It is very wise. You have put your finger on the essential problem of our times. Let me start with a look at the broader picture. Then I will address your here-and-now question."

PALO ALTO

Sam was relieved. Open mic questions were always risky, but the first couple were straightforward and within expectations. "Okay, people, we got the jobs question. Omnipresence, as soon as Sara mentions it, I want all the basic income politicians, parties, and networks to get hit with messages pointing them to the feed. Search, get our bot network ready to start hitting all the major engines with the words 'basic income.'

"Remember, people, it's the middle of the night in the U.S., so I want everyone to focus on Europe. We'll hit North America in four hours." He looked at the graphs for the tag *sarasmessage* and saw a small uptick in India and the EU. That was about right. They didn't want to spike the charts just as she started speaking.

NEW DELHI

Sara leaned forward, slowly scanning the crowd and making brief eye contact. "We live in a transitional time as humans on this planet. For hundreds of thousands of years, we were scratching out a subsistence existence, fighting nature tooth and claw. As our brains developed and we learned to communicate in spoken and written language, we began a slow process of social and technological development that led to agriculture, domesticated animals, cities, governments, empires, population growth and planetary dominance.

"As we all know, this development had many dark periods and moments. Wars, plagues, slavery, genocide, environmental degradation. And yet, humanity thrived. We have improved the standard of living for billions of people and eradicated many diseases that used to kill hundreds of millions. We have created a global network for sharing ideas and knowledge, and created an economic system that develops ever more life-saving and life-enhancing technologies. We should be proud of these accomplishments."

Sara paused and took a sip of water from the glass on the table. "Unfortunately, the exponential nature of the growth in our technologies has now caught up to human capability and is beginning to surpass it. The economic systems that have brought us this far did not evolve to handle these technologies.

"Let us look at modern market capitalism. Firms compete by innovating new solutions to people's problems. People earn money working at those firms to purchase those solutions. There is ongoing creative destruction as new firms and whole new industries arise that displace old ones. And jobs themselves are destroyed by advances in technology, while new ones are added at the same time.

"For vast stretches of human history, *human effort*, both physical and cognitive, was the only possible way to get things done. Then animals, and later machines, began substituting for raw human muscle power. The industrial revolution spurred a huge increase in productivity. But now artificial intelligences are rivaling our cognitive power, and dexterous robots are substituting for humans across the world economy.

"This substitution of capital equipment for human labor is having two very undesirable effects. First, it is making hundreds of millions of people essentially unemployable, as they cannot compete with low-cost machines that perform both physical and cognitive tasks at the price of almost free solar energy. Second, it is concentrating vast wealth in the hands of a tiny minority of people. This distorts democratic processes and leads to speculative bubbles, as money chases more money in increasingly risky ways.

"So, now, finally, to answer your question about getting a job. Over the whole course of human history, it is only for these last two centuries or so that we have had the notion of a job, where people worked for someone who was not their lord or relative. Jobs were a way of compensating people for their labor, which in turn gave them an income so they could buy goods and services and fund technological innovation.

"This was a wonderful virtuous cycle that led to progress for billions of people. But now that automation can now replace people on a massive scale, we have fewer people earning money in jobs, and the virtuous cycle has been broken.

"What we need to do is separate the income that enables consumption from jobs."

Sara heard whispers from the crowd.

"I believe we have reached the point in the evolution of humanity where every human deserves a basic income guaranteed to them, as a citizen of the nation where they live. This is made possible by the tremendous bounty of productivity that technology is bringing to us. And it is a key mechanism for transitioning to the economy to come.

"For the next few decades, we will still live in an economy of scarcity, where markets driven by consumers making choices with money is the essential way of allocating resources. Market-based competition for goods and services drives innovation. But markets require people to have incomes to make purchases, and to signal to firms what goods and services to offer and how to price them. So even as there are fewer and fewer jobs, we still need people with incomes. That means everyone should receive an income. Not all of us will have jobs—but all of us will have purchasing power.

"How will this be paid for? The same way it has been paid for in the last three hundred years, from companies that provide goods and services. But the income won't only be through salaries. It could also be, in part, through an enhanced value added tax. Yes, that does mean that prices will not move down as low or as quickly as they would without the new VAT. But lower prices are useless to someone with zero income.

"A universal, unconditional basic income will also eliminate poverty and replace all of the intrusive and paternalistic governmental social welfare programs. It will be a force for enhancing individual liberty and dignity. A guaranteed basic income frees people to take risks, to start businesses, to care for families, to perform public service, to say no to low-paying or demeaning work, to create art, and to work less and enjoy life more.

"Today a few small countries have adopted this policy, but it needs to be implemented everywhere. Twenty years ago, there was a fledgling movement towards a universal basic income but it was shut down by demagogues preaching self-reliance and decrying 'communism'. The elites feared giving people economic security and conveniently pushed the debate into the usual partisan dysfunction. We missed a critical opportunity then, and the pressures of technology and inequality have only continued to grow. We cannot ignore them any longer."

PALO ALTO

"OP!" Sam barked. "Where are we with direct messages on basic income?"

"We've got about two thousand messages hitting two hundred different targets. We're starting to see secondary effects."

"OK, let's get EU promoters with basic income history to tune into the feed. Web site team, jack up the live viewer numbers, but smoothly. Let's goose the groundswell a little." He turned to Kyle Carlson, the assistant director sitting to his left. "Kyle, did she just mention individual liberty and dignity?"

"Yes, she did."

"Hey OP, let's start hitting libertarian and conservative targets with the small government message."

NEW DELHI

"Now, Sameer, as I said, we are in a transitionary period. In just a few generations, if we can continue investing in key technologies, humanity will reach an age of abundance where physical goods and most services can be provided so cheaply, and in such a personalized manner, that money and pricing signals will become increasingly irrelevant. It is very hard to predict what that world will look like and how humans will operate in it. Your great-grandchildren will need to figure that out.

"But it is vital that we get to that future by investing in technologies that can dramatically lower the costs of life's essentials.

"I predict that in a thousand years, humans will look back at this time and marvel in disbelief that for several hundred years people actually spent most of their waking hours toiling away for money in a job.

"Of course, there will still be work to do. There will be discoveries and inventions, there will be travel and exploration, there will be many forms of artistic creation, and athletic and other types of competition. Humans love challenges and achievement. We will not be satisfied with a comfortable and boring existence. But the vast majority of humans will not labor in a job as we know it today.

"Forgive me, I am getting so far ahead of your question! What does this mean for you, Sameer? With a basic income guarantee, you can move out of your parents' house!"

The audience broke into laughter.

"You will be able to live on your own, or pool your resources with friends or a partner while you look for ways to earn additional money in a new economy.

"I do not know what talents you possess, Sameer, but perhaps you will be able to create music or designs that people enjoy and compensate you for. Maybe you will work or volunteer in a caring profession, where human contact is fundamental. Perhaps you will be a technologist or scientist or entrepreneur who starts a new company.

"Wherever your interests and capabilities take you, you can rest assured that you will be able to meet your essential needs."

The audience applauded.

"Of course, most of the world does not have this income guarantee yet. So, literally, what will you do when you graduate? That is the burning question." Sara paused and smiled. "I have an idea for you, Sameer, and every one of you here today. You should work to change the world and make a basic income happen."

She paused again and let this sink in.

"Who is going to bring about this kind of change? Not the wealthy capitalists who live in gated communities, isolated from the troubles of this transitional age. The status quo suits them fine. It is going to be up to you and many ordinary people like you to force our institutions to change. There are several political parties here in India that have basic income in their platforms. Vote for them. Go work for them. Make it happen."

There was half-hearted applause from the audience.

Sara knew what was going on in their minds. This was no longer a feel-good speech about a utopian future. She had just challenged each of them to act, to make a difference, to not accept the world as it is.

She could see the doubts and fears on their faces. Sara understood what they were thinking. *What about my student loan debt? What about the failed revolutions of the recent past, where people had instigated swift and remarkable changes, only to see dictators replaced by other dictators or non-democratic religious parties? The corporations, the wealthy, and many politicians will all be against us.* She let them sit with their discomfort.

"Let's take another question."

PALO ALTO

Sam studied the array of monitors in front of him. Basic income and sarasmessage were trending up nicely, and legitimate live streaming sessions were now over twenty thousand. Subtracting their ten thousand paid promoters, there were also more than a hundred thousand real humans, as best as they could tell, engaged in the online conversation. Not bad for a weekday morning in the EU.

NEW DELHI

"Hi, Sara. My name is Arjun. Thanks for giving me hope about my fine arts degree. I'm wondering what you think about income inequality and how we can eliminate it."

"Thank you, Arjun, for the question. Let me say very clearly that I don't think we should eliminate income inequality."

The audience buzzed with expressions of surprise.

"That might surprise you, but let me explain. Human talent is not evenly distributed. As you can see," she said, pointing to her small frame, "I am not going to take on Reza Pavel in basketball." The audience cheered the name of their university's star player.

"With the digitization of everything, including 3D printing, and eventually atomically precise manufacturing, the most talented people will tend to dominate many markets, because the marginal cost of production will drop to near zero. This is the superstar or winner-take-all phenomenon. We see it with actors, musicians, athletes, artists, designers, software companies, and app store developers. A very tiny number of superstars make a lot of money, and the long tail of millions of other participants each make very little.

"In addition, the technologists and the leaders of organizations that actually create the things that improve our lives are going to be rewarded for the incredible value they deliver to humanity. The hard truth is that the talented and entrepreneurial will reap far more financial rewards than the vast majority of people.

"However, not all great wealth is generated by creative and productive activities. The finance sector, in particular, often seeks to generate returns on money through speculation and gaming the system instead of through real investment. This leads to destructive bubbles, instability, money chasing riskier and riskier opportunities, nanosecond trade arbitrage, and preferential government treatment through regulatory capture. I strongly believe that free, competitive markets for goods and services will spur innovation, reduce costs, and benefit humanity. I also believe that we need to regulate financial markets to reduce their inherent risks.

"But let me return to income inequality. It cannot and should not be eliminated—but it does need to be addressed. We need to do three things. The first, as I mentioned, is to have a universal basic income so that people can live decent lives without needing to work at dehumanizing jobs. They should also be free to supplement that income, to the extent their talents and effort allow. This will probably require increased taxation on high incomes, but not so much that incomes become anywhere near level.

"The second is to ensure that we have genuinely equal opportunity for all of those with talent, leadership abilities, or entrepreneurial spirit. This requires a much more effective educational system, one designed to give *everyone* the same opportunity to develop and express their talents.

"I believe we need to continue to invest in AI-based personalized learning tools, much like the ones that gave me my start. In addition, advanced education should be available to everyone—for free." That generated cheers and huge applause.

"Finally, we need to change the mindset of those who are either talented enough, or just plain lucky enough, to have generated significant wealth. I do not begrudge them their success or their consumption. But the wealthy never spend all their money on goods and services. Most of their money is managed by algorithms that constantly seek to increase it by finding opportunities with high return on investment. As a result, ROI has become the most dangerous acronym in finance.

"I want the wealthy of the world to focus on RTH—return to humanity. That return would be measured not by just money, but by the actual outcomes that matter to people—health, liberty, and happiness. Let's get venture firms and private trusts scouting the world for inventors and entrepreneurs who have ideas that need funding. Ideas that can solve important problems facing humanity. Those ideas may not return anything at all to the investor, and many of them will fail completely. But some of them will succeed wildly, and so the wealthy person will have had a huge positive impact on humanity.

"Now, my hope is that when the wealthy of the world are on their death beds, they would prefer to leave their heirs ten million or a hundred million dollars, while having improved life for all of humanity, instead of growing that money and leaving a hundred million or a billion instead. What is the point of increasing a family's wealth beyond all possible utility?

"If we all begin to measure return to humanity in all its many forms, we will come to *celebrate* income inequality for the opportunity it creates for the wealthy to lift up all of humanity. Next question, please."

Sara took questions for another hour before engaging her audience in a final exercise. "Thank you for all those wonderful questions. Now I have a request for you—close your eyes in silence for a moment. Please, just for a moment."

Sara waited until the crowd followed her instructions. "Close your eyes and take the hands of the people on your left and right. Imagine yourself connected to the hundreds of people in this room. You are sharing an experience with them. You probably feel very connected to their thoughts. You can imagine what they are feeling.

"Now, slowly extend your connection to the millions in New Delhi. These are your neighbors with many shared experiences, but also much diversity.

"Now, slowly extend that connection to the other nine billion people on the planet, who are all bound together. Concentrate.

"Feel inside you the joy and anguish they are feeling. You can feel the balance of those two emotions. Humanity on this planet is collectively expressing a negative energy.

"Now, what is our goal as humans? What is our responsibility? What is our calling? Why are we here? It is the ancient question burning inside every conscious soul."

Sara paused and closed her own eyes to connect with the people in the room. "Our meaning, our purpose, our goal, is to shift the energy of all of humanity toward the light, toward love, toward peace, and toward joy.

"*How is this possible*? you demand to know. *How can I as one person shift the energy of all of humanity*? The answer, my brothers and sisters, is different for every human being.

"First and foremost, you must live right, as our great faiths have pre-scribed for thousands of years. You must free yourself from attachments and open yourself personally to joy. You must care for yourself, your fam-ilies, and your communities. Then you must develop your talents to bring progress to humanity and beauty to the world.

"Talents are not evenly distributed; that is the reality of nature. But everyone has talents they can contribute to make their corner of humanity a better place. And some people have been granted a gift of tremendous talent. And some in today's societies have the luck of great privilege. Their obligations are no different, but the scale of their potential impact is.

"These lucky few can contribute in vast ways to make our planet a better place to live and thrive. These great scientists, engineers, artists, entrepreneurs, and innovators should be eagerly sought out in every cor-ner of the Earth. They need to be freed from arbitrary restrictions, provided resources, and celebrated for their contributions to lifting all of humanity toward the light. We should revel in their success, to the extent it moves us all forward.

"Now open your eyes. Look around you. Take in your own experience." Sara paused, opened her own eyes, and silently followed her breath for half a minute. She scanned the audience and smiled.

"I hope I had an impact on you today, that I changed your perspective on your life and your purpose. It is not easy to change, and perhaps only a few of you will. But if I did have an impact, in some small way, please reflect on my story. I urge you to imagine me ten years ago in a dirt hut in a poor farming village with no electricity.

"Without that computer kiosk, I would still be in that hut, probably with a family of my own by now. There is nothing wrong with that life, and I would have brought as much love and progress to that community as I could. But my impact on humanity in that hut would be miniscule.

"Here in this room today, and around the world in omnipresence, I have the potential to do so much more. Who knows if my message will resonate? I can only try my best to awaken people to the spiritual force that connects us all, and to open their eyes to the potential for human creativity to lead to a world of abundance, love, and compassion. But I ask you this. Even if I should fail, how many other, potentially more successful Saras are out there? How many Einsteins? Curies? Ramanujans? Gandhis? Tagores? Rumis? Shakespeares?

"We should be on a worldwide search to find and develop our talents for the good of humanity. We should use technology to conquer the diseases that still kill millions; to provide adequate food and health care; and to educate everyone in the world to the best of their abilities. We should provide everyone with a basic income that enables them to pursue their talents and to contribute to the human cause."

Sara took a long drink of water while the audience whispered excitedly. Then she put her hands in her lap and said softly, "My friends, our time is coming to a close. We have covered a lot of ground, probably far too much, but I just can't help myself. Let me leave you with a final thought. You are going to leave this hall and discuss these topics with great energy with your friends tonight and tomorrow. Then you will have work to do, or a test, or a paper, or a fight with a loved one. It will be easy to slip back into the daily routine.

"Please, keep in mind two things. First, the vision I have described is possible. It is within our reach. Second, our current social and economic institutions and structures are not prepared for it. They will actively resist it. This could delay it coming to pass for generations. So, if you believe in this vision, then you have an obligation to develop your talents to steer us away from the storm that is approaching. *You* must make it happen. *You* must spread the word. *You* must build the future. If you don't act, who will? If not now, when?"

Sara scanned the young faces looking up at her, willing them to heed her call. Then she rose, pressed her hands together, palm to palm, and bowed. "*Namaste,*" she said.

As the students rose as one in a massive wave of applause, she simply repeated, "*Namaste.*"

PALO ALTO

Sam nodded with satisfaction. Sara had owned the room.

"Okay, everyone, report. What are we doing right now?"

The team leads chimed in one by one. Their paid networks were active, but ineffective. Real humans in omnipresence were overwhelming them. Sarasmessage.com was struggling to keep up with site sign-ups, which now numbered in the millions. The Web team was frantically spinning up more cloud resources to handle the load. The omnipresence team was trying to rebroadcast sarasmessage tags, but they were coming in too fast. The real-time translation team had just finished posting all the transcripts.

Sam sat back and watched contentedly. It was a goddamn home run.

CHAPTER NINETEEN

Washington - October 14

As Senator Harrison Paxton sat at the ancient wooden desk in his Senate office scanning his daily omnipresence activity summary, a spike in mentions of basic income caught his eye. Even more interesting was a chart that showed the correlation with sarasmessage, which he remembered from that oddly captivating VR program that Rena had sent him two weeks ago. The origin appeared to be a video on the sarasmessage.com website. "Margaret, when's my next appointment?"

"You have a meeting with the wireless holographic industry lobbyist in twenty minutes."

"Cancel that appointment, please."

"Are you sure, sir? You've canceled three appointments with lobbyists in the last month."

"So?"

"Ninety percent of your campaign funding comes from companies, industries, trade associations, and people represented by lobbyists." He hated this new AI scheduling program, which focused relentlessly on getting him re-elected. "I don't care, Margaret. Just cancel it."

"Yes, sir. The meeting has been canceled."

"Thank you."

Harry started the video. He watched the young Indian woman walk out onto the stage in front of an energetic crowd and begin speaking in a foreign language. Subtitles carried an English translation, then disappeared when she explained how she was going to switch to English.

Harry watched, fascinated by the intelligence, confidence, and wisdom demonstrated by this young girl. He was particularly interested in the section of the video where she talked about a basic income guarantee. She echoed many of the thoughts he held on the subject, but made them so immediate and personal for the young man in the room.

But her idea of funding basic income through corporate taxes, as a substitute for the salaries companies used to pay, was different. Most pundits kept pushing for lower and lower corporate taxes to "keep companies competitive" and "create more jobs," neither of which was actually happening.

Harry assumed that her ideas would draw ridicule. But as he searched omnipresence for Sara, he found that the trolls screaming bloody murder were far, far outnumbered by positive comments and reactions. Supporters seemed to skew younger demographically, but they were all ages, from all over the world, and of every conceivable background.

Something about Sara's message was touching a chord in people, and their voices were resonating around the globe.

Harry reflected on why this might be. She was young and innocent looking, female, non-Western, and not a politician. She was essentially optimistic and pragmatic, using rational arguments for positions that spanned ideologies. She had no one ideological home, and therefore no base and no opposition. She was carving a new path through the hardened liberal, libertarian, and conservative camps.

Harry extracted the portion of the video about the economy into a message to Esteban, with a note suggesting he watch it before their next lunch.

"Margaret, can you find Yumi Kagawa and have her call me?" He had hired Yumi as a policy consultant early in his first term and sought her advice whenever he wanted to brainstorm on new ideas.

"Certainly, Senator."

Harry started doodling on a yellow legal pad. Rena teased him endlessly about his extremely old-fashioned attachment to paper and pen. He was outlining the key ideas he had heard in Sara's speech when Margaret announced that Yumi was available for a video chat.

"Begin chat," he said.

"Good morning, Senator," Yumi said cheerfully.

"Good morning, Yumi. By any chance have you seen the VR program and recent video of this woman Sara?"

"Sara? Of course I have. She's burning up omnipresence."

"What do you think of her?"

"She's a breath of fresh air, that's for sure. Also, an example of how the messenger makes the message."

"Say more, please?"

"Well, what she's saying is not exactly new. The policy ideas have been around for decades. The spiritual and moral ideas are right out of the religious traditions of the last three thousand years. What's new is Sara. She's the opposite of everything that has been turning people off from thinking or believing in change over the last thirty years. She's young, calm, rational, funny, positive, mysterious, and charismatic."

"That's why she's gone viral?"

"I think so. People want to like her. Why the interest in Sara, Senator?"

"Well, frankly, she's inspired me to think bigger. We're so mired in petty issues and coalition building and busting and I'm sick of it. I was thinking about a bold new plan, a new social and economic contract for America."

"What kind of plan?"

"That's what I'd like to talk over with you." He looked over his notes. "Here's what I hear Sara saying. We adopt a universal basic income that replaces existing government social services, with additional funding from a corporate value added tax and taxes on the wealthy. We spur investments in science and technology with the specific goal of lowering the cost of life's essentials. We make high-quality education available to all, with the goal of finding and developing talent that can move humanity forward. We change rich people's mindset from money chasing money to investing in solutions for the good of all humanity." He paused. "I'm not sure how we legislate that last one."

"I don't think that's necessarily impossible. We've been using tax policy to shape investment for a hundred years. If you increase financial transaction taxes and lower taxes on returns from social benefit corporations, you'd be on your way."

"That's exactly why I hired you! What do you think of what I've said so far?"

"I like it, Senator. I like the idea of a big, breakthrough plan that's non-ideological and has a positive message. It's going to need some really good framing, though."

"Of course."

"When I was watching Sara's New Delhi video, it struck me that she was actually defending and trying to preserve market capitalism. I wonder if we couldn't spin this as the Saving Capitalism Act."

"Ha! I love it! Imagine my Republican colleagues voting against saving capitalism. Still, that name is more defensive and not as optimistic. Sara has such a positive message about the future of humanity. What about the Leading America and Humanity Forward Act?"

"Interesting," Yumi said. It's got a nice patriotic ring to it, and it appeals to altruism, too. But the acronym, though, that's a non-starter. LAHFA?"

"Ouch. Okay, we can work on that. So, are you game to really do this? Put aside the battle over the next three percent to be cut from discretionary funding?"

"Absolutely! How do you want to approach this? We can bring together a lot of staff and experts, or we could go for the leadership approach."

"With something this bold, I'm thinking we need to start top down. Can you recommend a Gang of Six?"

"I agree. Let me think about some names." Yumi paused. "This is fantastic, Senator. Do you think it has any chance of leaving committee?"

"A few weeks ago, I would have said no way in hell. But if Sara keeps speaking to the people, maybe the people will finally wake up and speak to the Congress."

CHAPTER TWENTY

Santa Barbara - October 15

Roger Driscoll had been busy managing two global launches and lost track of the Sara brand. "Allison, what's the update on Sara?" "The brand is continuing to climb in omnipresence tracking. Still roughly 60/40 net positive sentiment. There was a real-life event yesterday in New Delhi, India that has been viewed more than two hundred million times." He wondered what kind of event they had staged. "Can you bring up the video for that event please?"

Within the first ten minutes he understood why Sara's public personality rating was off the charts—she came across as so purely authentic and so caring about her audience and the issues motivating her that she stood in stark contrast to the competing world brands of politicians and corporate leaders. Frances had discovered a real gem of a spokeswoman.

When Sara was answering Arjun's question about income inequality, Roger began to get that uncomfortable feeling again. "Most of their money is managed by algorithms that constantly seek to increase it by finding opportunities with high return on investment. As a result, ROI has become the most dangerous acronym in finance…I want the wealthy of the world to focus on RTH—return to humanity. That return would be measured not by just money, but by the actual outcomes that matter to people—health, liberty, and happiness."

Just a few days ago, Roger had gotten an update from his financial roboadvisor on his Q3 "ROI". His considerable wealth was invested in a wide variety of complex financial instruments, most of which he didn't even understand. He had no idea if his money was helping people the way that Sara described. All he knew was that it increased steadily every quarter, money making money.

As the video ended with the camera panning a standing ovation, Roger asked Allison to display a transcript. "Scroll to near the end please." He read the words he had just seen Sara speak. Perhaps he'd been primed by the rest of the video, or maybe it was the way she delivered this section directly to the camera, but he couldn't help but think she was talking specifically to *him*.

Talents are not evenly distributed; that is the reality of nature. But everyone has talents they can contribute to make their corner of humanity a better place. And some people have been granted a gift of tremendous talent. And some in today's societies have the luck of great privilege. Their obligations are no different, but the scale of their potential impact is. These lucky few can contribute in vast ways to make our planet a better place to live and thrive. These great scientists, engineers, artists, entrepreneurs, and innovators should be eagerly sought out in every corner of the Earth. They need to be freed from arbitrary restrictions, provided resources, and celebrated for their contributions to lifting all of humanity toward the light. We should revel in their success, to the extent it moves us all forward.

Roger stood and began pacing back and forth over the cool marble tiles of his living room floor. He viewed his work primarily as a series of engineering challenges. He was constantly tweaking and tuning the synth network in a running battle with the RealLife algorithms. Enhancing their AI personality matrices and refining their programming, as he had done for the Sara launch, was fascinating, technically satisfying work. Although he'd gotten very wealthy by providing a service to his hundreds of clients, that was never his primary motivation.

Sara's words made him question what, exactly, he was directing his talents towards. His business operated in the shadows, literally inaccessible without the right crypto credentials and client referrals. He was not "making a planet a better place" or "moving us all forward." If he had to be honest, his synths were doing quite the opposite. How had he gotten this far without really confronting this? Roger considered himself a caring person. He gave to various causes that helped people and the environment. But somehow, he had carved his work itself out of his personal self-evaluation.

Roger felt the need to talk to someone, but he couldn't think of anyone in his network who would empathize. His friends were entrepreneurs and technologists just like him, focused on growing their companies and enhancing their products. Other than superficial exchanges about some news event of the day, he couldn't recall a single deep conversation with them about the state of the world or their obligations to help it. He lived in a social bubble of techno-capitalists.

There was of course one person. Someone who had initiated all of this. "Allison, what time is it in London?"

"It's 9:45 p.m."

"Could you send a holochat request to Frances Chatham please?" A long minute later Allison informed him the request was accepted. He put on the hologlasses and turned once more to face Frances, this time in what appeared to be her living room.

"Roger, delighted to hear from you. We've been so busy I haven't had time to thank you again for the impact of your network. While we have a lot of real humans engaged now, your synths formed the core of Sara's early support and really got her launched."

"I'm glad to hear it, Frances, and happy that Sara is taking off."

"Yes, we had our first real-life event in India this week and it was quite a success."

"I know, I just watched the video. In fact, that's why I'm calling." He had no idea if Frances had the same kinds of overlays in her home holosystem as he had, but no doubt they would be flashing all kinds of anxiety if she did. "I've been thinking a lot about what Sara said. About the wealthy." Roger was surprised at how choked up he was. "About those with talent directing their work." He had to take a deep breath.

Frances nodded sympathetically. "I understand, Roger. I truly do. I have travelled down the same road. You remember Mentapath Systems? My first company, advanced AI analytics and customer interaction for e-commerce platforms. Brilliant piece of engineering. Wildly successful. Big exit for me and my investors. I took some time off and happened one day to be visiting one of my philanthropic ventures, the London Institute for Advanced Studies. The head of school introduced me to a student, a young woman who would change my life. It was, of course, Sara.

"I spent hours with her, captivated. During our very first conversation, when I described my background, I realized that her emerging ideas about capitalism and technology applied directly to my experience. Mentapath was a job destruction engine. It replaced swaths of sales and marketing people wherever it was installed. I had always viewed this the key to its success—incredible efficiencies and much better service for customers. But the human impact. Well. I just put it out of my head, I suppose.

"Needless to say, I had my pick of what to work on next and with Sara's ideas firmly in mind I chose something a little more helpful to humanity. Neurgenix aims to eliminate genetic diseases by applying the same underlying deep learning technology to billions of genetic sequences and automated CRISPR gene editing processes."

Roger had collected himself. "Yes, I see your pivot there."

"It was all well and good for me," continued Frances. "But I was just one wealthy entrepreneur. A drop in the bucket. All around me there was a sea of techies, startups, financiers, and investors stuck in the same paradigm, oblivious to the negative consequences of their apparent financial successes. I tried to convince them, but they rarely budged. As social tensions continued to rise across the globe, I felt I needed to do something more."

"And then you hatched Sara's message."

"Yes, indeed. I created a team to launch her into the public sphere. I hoped to give the broad public something positive to latch on to and convince the elites they needed to change. Honestly, Roger, your reaction is precisely what I was hoping for. I am sad to say, however, that among other peers who have seen Sara's talk there have been distressingly few like you."

There was an uncomfortable silence. "So," said Roger. "What do I do now?"

"You're a brilliant engineer, Roger, with probably the world's best understanding of omnipresence interaction dynamics and bot detection. How can you use those talents for the good of everyone in OP?"

"I don't know." Roger found it very difficult to look her in the eye. "I'm not sure."

"What are the biggest problems in OP right now?"

"Well the biggest problem is that people are out of control. They spend most of their time trolling and spreading misinformation and outright propaganda." Roger paused. "Then, I suppose synth networks like mine aren't helping very much."

"Well said. So. Is there anything you could do about those problems?"

The wheels began to turn in Roger's head. He knew exactly how to detect synth networks. No one knew their weaknesses better.

"Well certainly I know about synths. But Frances, it sounds you're asking me to create a technology that will destroy my entire business." She smiled slightly, but her gaze turned rather steely across the holochannel.

"Indeed, Roger. That rather strikes me as exactly the right thing to do."

"Well, sorry, I'm not prepared to do that. I've got clients. Like you," he added. Her gaze did not waver. She remained silent. "Maybe I can look at the human side of things first. That is the bigger problem after all."

Frances nodded. "That is true, Roger. That could be a great first step."

"Okay, yeah, maybe I'll start there. Thanks, Frances."

"Certainly, Roger. I look forward to seeing what you come up with."

Roger closed the holochat and spun around in his chair a few times. How could he improve human interactions in OP? He stood up and paced around his living room, thinking about the ways his bots interacted in OP versus real humans. The seed of an idea came to him. Returning to his desk, he grinned. "Allison, clear the decks and open a new workspace. Code name—AntiVenom."

CHAPTER TWENTY-ONE

Virtual Reality - October 19

The Sara's Message leadership team had gathered to review the results from the first town hall. Everyone's avatars, with photo-realistic real-time facial overlays, sat together around a table in a VR conference room.

Chief Operating Officer Preston Jackson summarized the discussion thus far from his IRL office in London. "We've had a tremendous launch. The New Delhi event has created a lot of positive momentum, with less-than-expected negative backlash. Now we have a few decisions to make. Do we continue with the college town halls or try for major media outlets? Start in Europe or head to the U.S.? Opinions?"

Sam Erickson, who sat across the table from Preston in VR, spoke from Palo Alto. "I say we hit the major media while we're still early in the news cycle. Awareness of Sara is just building and she's an interesting story. The news and opinion channels will love her. With our connections, we can get her placed on half a dozen shows and get the message out to a vast audience that doesn't spend time playing VR or watching OP meme videos."

"What about geography?" asked Preston.

Sam said, "If we want to build an audience in the most receptive countries, we'd start in Europe."

Sheila Bratton, the team's CTO and omnipresence director, sat to Sam's right. "I'm not so sure about that," she said from New York. "Engagement per capita is higher in the U.S. than in the EU. Ultimately, the U.S. is going to have to drive this change. The EU economies aren't strong enough. I know it's a bigger challenge, given all the noise in the system, but I vote we go right for the jugular."

Preston turned to Vannha Subramanium, town hall coordinator, seated to his right. "What do you think, Vannha?"

"The town hall format is more conducive to a grassroots feeling," Vannha said from New Delhi. "It's Sara speaking directly with people, not to the mainstream media that are part of the problem she describes. I would vote for more of those, starting in the U.S. Let the media react to the grassroots efforts and compete to get her. If we go to the media too early, we look like every other pundit or author looking for screen time."

Sam said, "It's all a question of what audience we want to build. College town halls are great for hitting the young demographic, but history has shown that the real social revolutions don't start until you get the thirty- to fifty-year-olds involved. They are the great bastions of the status quo. Everyone expects the young to rebel. But when Mom and Dad hit the streets, the establishment takes notice. Look at the great civil rights marches. You see wave after wave of solid citizens in their late thirties and forties and older."

"The free speech and Vietnam War movements started in colleges," countered Vannha. "The 1964 civil rights workers killed in Mississippi were college age. The Parkland students were in high school, look what they started in terms of gun control."

"Sure, but the Freedom Riders were older," Sam said. "All I'm saying is we need to get to the parents eventually. That's the signal to the whole society that change is inevitable."

"I don't disagree with that," Vannha said. "Everyone is scared, but the young at least have accumulated fewer years of distrust. I think their parents will respond if they can see their kids break free of the chains that are holding both generations back."

Preston reflected with some pride on the strength of the team he had built. Passionate for their cause, experts in their fields, deep students of the history of social change.

"I think all of these ideas have merit," he said. "I suggest we go next to the United States with a focus on college town halls, but grant one long-form interview to the media, to someone smart and well-respected. That will keep us out of the sound bite side shows, continue to generate grass-roots energy, and make the other media outlets hungry."

His team leaders nodded in approval, and Sheila gave a virtual thumbs-up.

"Sam," Preston said, "can you identify a few interviewers and gauge their interest by the end of the week?"

"Sure."

"Sheila, where are we with the U.S. college website construction?"

"The team has been working on it for a while, just in case we decided to go in early. It'll be ready in twenty-four hours. They trained an AI to import every college's and university's organization creation forms. It wasn't too difficult."

"Great. Okay, last topic for tonight. Sara's starting to generate a lot of curiosity in the media and in the establishment. We've already had one *New York Times* reporter digging into our paid promotion operation. We'll keep an eye on her, but we can expect increasing opposition research from many quarters over the next few months. Remind your teams of the need for absolute discretion. We can also expect bigger crowds of both fans and decidedly unfriendly folks at our events. Vannha, I think it's time to get some security. Make it very discreet, casual clothes, no Secret Service suits."

"Got it," said Vannha.

"Okay, then," said Preston. "Let's call it a night. Thanks, everyone."

The avatars faded from view.

Preston removed his VR headset and turned to the woman seated beside him. "Well, ma'am, how do you think that went?"

Frances Chatham, sitting next to him in London, removed her headset as well. "Well, Preston, the strategy seems reasonable to me. We can always adjust based on what we learn. There's no playbook to follow, so we just keep reassessing." She played with the headset in her hands. "And thank you for suggesting security for Sara. She would never think of asking for it."

"Of course, ma'am."

There was a long but comfortable silence.

"Can you believe it, Preston?" Frances said finally. "After all the preparation, it's finally happening. Sometimes I just need to pinch myself."

"It's very exciting, ma'am. It must be tremendously gratifying for you, to see your vision coming to life."

"Discovering Sara Dhawan was a real blessing. But she couldn't do what she's doing, and have the impact she's having, without you and the team you've built. I'm endlessly grateful to you, Preston. There's no bloody way I could have done this without you."

"Thank *you*, ma'am. It's such an honor working on this with you."

CHAPTER TWENTY-TWO

Syracuse/Missouri/Washington - October 22

SYRACUSE

Peter Cook checked the automated flight plan instructions one last time from his upstate New York operations cabin. This was the most complex LKC drone operation yet. The destruction of the three RezMat transports had been simple compared to this op. Today he had to direct forty-eight drones flying in a hundred mile area to attach to twenty-four targets in six locations and detonate simultaneously.

He'd also had to rely on several LKC members in the Midwest to place the drones. It always made him nervous to depend on guys he hadn't worked with operationally before. He keyed in the launch commands. Forty-seven of the drones responded and showed green lights across the board for all rotor and sensor functions. One of the drones was online but non-responsive.

Peter logged into the drone remotely and tried rebooting the main controller. After fifteen long seconds it came back online, but was still dead in the water. He logged back into it and started checking each of the system components. *Aha!* he said to himself after a couple of minutes. The secondary battery pack had failed, and it supplied power to most of the sensor and motor controllers. When he told the controllers to use the primary battery instead, they all came alive. Luckily, this drone had a short flight path and could make it just using the primary battery.

Now that all forty-eight drones were operational, Peter verified that they had precise GPS time synchronization and sent them the Go signal.

BLACKBURN, MISSOURI

Liam Baldwin held on to the handrail as he descended the steps from the Post Office down to Main Street. As he walked to his vintage blue '21 Toyota Corolla, he heard a faint buzzing noise and thought his hearing aids were malfunctioning again. But then the sound grew louder. He looked south towards St. Paul Church and saw them—a group of eight black drones flying maybe a hundred feet off the ground, heading north. It was the damnedest thing. He'd seen drones online, of course. But not here in Blackburn, population all of 219.

The drones took no note of the elderly man as they passed by the town. They traveled in tight formation until they crossed 220th Road, where they split into four pairs and headed for their targets. In less than a minute they had attached to the legs of four electrical transmission towers. Synchronized to the millisecond via GPS signals, the drones set off their Semtex charges in a sequence designed to send the towers toppling in alternating directions. Forty other drones in a one hundred mile radius did likewise on twenty similar towers. The 345 kV transmission cables in all six locations snapped under the stress, severing critical links between multiple states.

AI control programs for Southwest Power Pool and MISO Energy detected an unprecedented simultaneous catastrophic failure in six 345 kV lines. There was no way to route around them. To avoid damaging the grid, the control programs started shutting down supply, ordering wind and solar farms to divert flows to battery storage and natural gas plants to shut down. Millions of people in Kansas and Missouri instantly lost power.

Minutes later LKC released a statement. "The Ludd Kaczynski Collective has disrupted electrical power in the heart of the United States to send a message to the people of this great country. You can live without your electronic masters. You can live in true freedom again. You can experience the real world and connect with real people. If only for a few days, you will remember what life was like before we were slaves to the machines. Once you have lived again as a human and not a cog in the machine world, we hope you will join us in our revolution."

WASHINGTON, DC

Mark Geiger, Director of the Domestic Terrorism Task Force, sat in the DTTF situation room at the head of a long wooden table. Staff members were arrayed around the table, talking into headsets and manipulating information on their monitors. Geiger nodded to the communications officer, who opened a secure line to the White House.

"Good morning, Madam President."

"Not so good from what I hear," replied President Amanda Teasley, whose image appeared on the central monitor across from his seat. "What do we know?"

"LKC has claimed responsibility for a coordinated attack against the Midwest electrical grid. Twenty-four transmission towers were taken out by explosive-carrying drones. We've got millions of people without power."

"How long will the power be out?"

"It's going to be three or four days minimum."

"Damn it. What's the impact?"

"The first day or so we'll see massive inconvenience and some hospital evacuations. FEMA has mobilized to bring generators, water and food to the affected area, but that just covers essential services. If it stretches to a week there's likely to be rioting in several states, but the National Guard should be able to get that under control. Overall, I think the biggest impact is going to be psychological. And political."

"Yes, I'm well aware of that." Teasley was a Democrat from Georgia who had narrowly defeated a law-and-order Texan who attacked her endlessly for being too weak on crime and terrorism. The emergence of LKC halfway through her first term was already driving the right wing media into a frenzy. "Do we have any leads?"

"Not yet. We are collecting drone fragments hoping for trace materials to tell us where they have been or where they were made. The Semtex explosive is widely available on the world market and we don't have fingerprinting that can get us to the source. Given the rural locations of the attacks there is almost no surveillance footage available. We have a few eyewitnesses that saw the drones, but no indications of the launch points."

"Can we protect the grid, Mark?"

"Madame President, there are more than two hundred *thousand* miles of high voltage transmission lines in the U.S. There's no feasible way for us to monitor all of them."

"So you're saying LKC can knock power out to major cities all across the country for weeks on end and there's nothing we can do about it?"

"LKC hasn't made any mistakes yet. But the more actions they take, the higher the probability we get a break. A surveillance drone that sees a vehicle launching an attack. Or an unencrypted message with operational details. People and organizations aren't perfect. Trust me, eventually they'll slip up and we'll track them down."

"Mark, I don't need to tell you things are on a knife's edge right now. Eventually isn't going to cut it. So far, LKC's not targeting people. But if these attacks continue, someone's going to die. And then the shit's really going to hit the fan."

"I understand, Madame President. There are some things you could do to help us find them, to free us up from constraints. We've discussed these in the past."

Teasley's eyes narrowed. "Yes, I recall. Let's talk offline on the specifics."

"Yes, Madame President." The line disconnected. His staff turned their heads towards his end of the table. "Well you heard the lady," Geiger said, "let's get these bastards."

CHAPTER TWENTY-THREE

Los Angeles - October 24

Melissa thought back to the day she'd met Jacob, at the Haro Burger protest. That's when he had hatched the plan to engineer a one-day shutdown of most of the Supernova kiosks in the city. She had thought he'd been joking and assumed he'd drop the idea. But as they spent more and more time together over the last two weeks, he kept pursuing it and eventually convinced her that this kind of non-violent action would get a lot of attention.

So Melissa had researched the kiosks. Since Supernova had recently strengthened their software security, she decided the easiest approach was to block the kiosk serving doors. Melissa designed a device to jam the doors that was about the size of a thumbnail and just a few millimeters thick. It had two chambers separated by a thin membrane that was kept rigid by a tiny electrical current.

The chambers were filled with two chemicals that were harmless if separated, but created a very hot reaction when combined. When the tiny battery in the device ran out of juice, it destabilized the membrane, allowing the chemicals to combine. The intense heat of the reaction melted the hard plastic of the device, as well as some of the soft metal of the serving door, creating a small plug strong enough to defeat the servomotors that opened the door.

Jacob had sent the design to be printed at a 3D print shop in Mexico and shipped to a post office box out of town, all paid for with anonymous q-coins. Jacob tapped into the local anti-technology network and recruited a dozen activists to help them. The team had spent several days filling the tiny chambers and practicing sticking them on replicas of the serving doors. Now they were out placing them at over two hundred Supernova kiosks, each of them buying different drinks and paying with anonymous q-coin tokens. They were all wearing PPF cloaks and gloves to minimize the chance of being identified.

Melissa paced around Jacob's small living room, checking her dark PNA compulsively for progress updates from the team. This was a burner unit not biometrically linked to her. Jacob kept telling her to get rid of her linked PNA because it was a security risk. But, unlike him, she still had lots of friends and family not in the movement that she liked to keep in touch with.

He had also suggested that she follow his lead and disable her medplant. But if she disabled it she wouldn't be allowed to turn it back on for three years. She had waited for years to get one, since full-time workers had priority and got subsidies from their employers in exchange for monitoring rights. As a freelancer she had to scrape together the down payment and monthly fees on her own. It was particularly important to her because the maternal side of her family had a history of cancer. Anyway, she told Jacob, medplant data was the most secure and private data on the planet.

When Jacob returned to the apartment a few minutes after midnight, he was triumphant. "Went off without a hitch," he said. "There are a surprising number of late night PPF-cloak-wearing Supernova customers. I don't think someone in our group was the only cloaked customer at more than a dozen of the kiosks. Should make it very hard to trace who placed the devices and when." He threw off his cloak and pulled her toward him. "This is going to be epic."

Melissa was too hyped up to sleep. She envied Jacob as he dozed on his leather couch. She watched the big-screen monitor full of news channels with the volume off, waiting. Finally, at around 4:15 a.m., she spotted the first image of a Supernova.

"Jacob, wake up!"

"What?" He rubbed his eyes.

"I think it's starting!" She gestured the volume on for one of the channels.

"...two Supernovas on Wilshire, one at Stanley, and one a few blocks down at Crescent Heights, and four in and around Venice Beach. Again, there seems to be some malfunction at these kiosks. They're not dispensing coffee, so if you're planning on getting some caffeine this morning, better plan on another location. Wait, what's that?" The anchor was listening to his earpiece. "Ladies and gentlemen, we are now getting reports that these seven kiosks are not the only ones involved. It appears that this is a system-wide outage. We're contacting the company for more information."

Melissa and Jacob exchanged high fives and a deep kiss. "You're a genius!" he whispered in her ear.

As the minutes passed, more and more of the local media outlets played images of Supernovas all over the city. One showed a Supernova self-driving truck as it drove up to a kiosk and a small maintenance robot rolled out of the back. It plugged a sensor into a diagnostic port at the bottom of the kiosk, then withdrew it, moved over, and extended a camera that panned slowly around the serving door. The camera retracted, and a small arm with a multi-tool package emerged from the center of the robot. The arm targeted part of the serving door, poking and sawing repeatedly at one spot. But the door remained shut. After a minute, the robot moved back to the diagnostic port and inserted its sensor. After just a few seconds, the robot disconnected and rolled away, back to the self-driving truck.

"Yes!" shouted Jacob. "Did you see that?"

"Fantastic!" said Melissa.

If the maintenance bots couldn't dislodge the plugs they had created, it would take many hours for Supernova to find, hire, and dispatch humans to all their damaged kiosks.

By 7 a.m., the national networks had figured out that this was a big story. Jacob and Melissa sat on the couch and channel surfed.

"We're getting more reports from Los Angeles that a major act of sabotage has taken down many of the Supernova kiosks in Los Angeles. Evidently all the serving doors have been jammed in some way. The company is pledging to get them working as soon as possible and calling for law enforcement to investigate this act of terrorism."

"Terrorism?" said Melissa. "What are they talking about? It's an act of civil disobedience!"

Another channel showed a man in a Supernova uniform working on a kiosk.

"Yeah, you got some kind of plug jammed in here real good," said the worker.

"How did it get there?" asked a reporter.

"Damned if I know. I can tell you it ain't chewing gum or something. This thing is real hard. It's gonna take me a while to saw through it. And then it smells to me like the door servo might have burned out. Can't tell that yet."

"When will this kiosk be serving coffee again?" she asked.

"It might be hours."

"Excuse me, are you a Supernova customer?" the reporter asked, turning to a young man in the small crowd gathered around the kiosk.

"Yeah, what's going on?"

"The kiosk is broken, something jamming the door. We have reports that it's happened all over the city, in a coordinated attack."

"No kidding? Who would do something like that? Supernova is awesome."

"We probably should have posted a statement somewhere," Melissa said. "You know, how this is a blow against the robotization of America and the world."

"Isn't that the obvious message?" Jacob said.

The news anchor continued the story. "In all, over two hundred Supernova kiosks have been vandalized and are not operating at this time. Supernova has issued a statement saying that it is the victim of a terrorist attack that will cost the company millions of dollars in repairs and lost revenue, and that it is working as quickly as possible to restore service. The LAPD says it has opened an investigation and invited the FBI's Domestic Terrorism Task Force to join them."

"Why do they keep calling it terrorism?" said Melissa anxiously. "We're activists, not terrorists."

"It's just establishment tactics, Melissa. Keep people scared. Keep them distracted from the real story." She nodded. But she worried that their prank was being blown all out of proportion.

CHAPTER TWENTY-FOUR

Washington, D.C. - October 25

President Amanda Teasley sat on the blue couch in the Oval Office opposite Mark Geiger and Attorney General Emma Wilcox. The three of them had been reviewing Geiger's requests for extraordinary powers to be granted to the FBI and Domestic Terrorism Task Force for more than half an hour.

"Now tell me about this last one," said Teasley. "Accessing corporate systems?"

"Yes," said Geiger. "We have special keys that enable access to corporate systems without the usual blockchain digital warrant protocol. But we need your approval to invoke them."

"I'm not sure I completely understand how that works. Perhaps we should bring in Kara Morrigan to review this piece."

"Madame President," said Geiger with a sigh. "With all due respect to the U.S. CTO, her background at Facebook and Amazon hardly qualifies her to perform a national security assessment. You kept me on for my expertise in tracking down terrorist organizations. You asked for my advice on what we need at DTTF to find and eliminate the threat from LKC and I'm giving it to you. If you give us these tools, just on a temporary basis, it will help us tremendously. If my advice is no longer valued, perhaps you'll want a different Director at DTTF."

Teasley didn't get along with Geiger, a holdover from the previous Republican administration who she had felt obligated to retain for "law and order" credibility. She also knew full well he was trying to manipulate her. But the last thing she needed was for her terrorism head to resign in the middle of a crisis.

"Now Mark, I don't think that will be necessary," said Teasley.

"Madame President," said Wilcox calmly, "you brought *me* on to advise you on legal matters, and I can tell you what Mark is proposing is unlikely to be upheld by a court as constitutional. It doesn't matter how temporary it is or what crisis is happening. Circumventing the First and Fourth Amendments has never been justified."

"What if we begin working with Congress on legislation in parallel?" asked Teasley, searching for a way through this political and constitutional minefield.

"Working with Congress is the only correct path, Madame President," said Wilcox.

"But that's too slow," said Geiger, leaning forward on the edge of the couch. "It will take them six months to agree on the damn title of the bill. How many more attacks by LKC and the lone wolves they are starting to inspire is it going to take? How much lower can your approval ratings go, Madame President, before your whole first term agenda is dead in the water?"

"We don't measure the constitutionality of executive orders with approval numbers," said the Attorney General. The President sat for a long moment, weighing the decision before her. She wanted to reject Geiger's transparent arm-twisting. But she wouldn't put it past him to leak her refusal to give DTTF what it wanted.

"Approval numbers do, however, reflect the fear of the American people," said Teasley. "We have to get this situation under control. I'm willing to grant these powers and start working with Congress to get them officially legislated." She looked at Wilcox. "Write that directly into the executive order. I want the record to show these are temporary measures."

The Attorney General began to protest, but realized her boss's mind was made up as soon as Teasley stood up to dismiss them. "Yes, Madame President. It'll be on your desk in an hour."

EXECUTIVE ORDER 14412

———————

PREVENTION OF DOMESTIC TERRORIST ATTACKS

———————

CLASSIFIED TOP SECRET

By the power vested in me as President by the Constitution and the laws of the United States of America, it is hereby ordered as follows:

Section 1. The Federal Bureau of Investigation and its Domestic Terrorism Task Force are hereby authorized to temporarily use all means at their disposal to identify the individuals and groups responsible for or planning domestic attacks against the people and institutions of the United States and corporations operating in the United States.

Section 2. The means available to the FBI Domestic Terrorism Task Force shall include but not be limited to (a) the right to intercept, decrypt and analyze any communication traveling through the air and over any physical network medium without a warrant, (b) the right to covertly access medplant databases to identify potential terrorists without a warrant, (c) the right to disable or remove "personal privacy" garments being worn by suspects attempting to evade identification, (d) the right to covertly access the camera, microphone, and geolocation of any device within the United States or in possession of a United States citizen without a warrant, (e) the right to covertly access corporate information systems without a warrant.

Section 3. It is the intent of this administration to replace these temporary powers with legislative authority as soon as possible.

THE WHITE HOUSE

OCTOBER 25, 2038

CHAPTER TWENTY-FIVE

Boston - October 28

The advance team had done well again. The large hall on the University of Massachusetts campus was filling rapidly. The highly targeted omnipresence campaign had been helped by the fact that half a million people had already connected to Sara's Message in OP. This had been supplemented by old fashioned posters plastered all over campus.

By 2 p.m., the hall was full and the audience buzzed with energy. Sara entered to loud applause and sat in the comfortable chair at center stage.

She sat silently for a moment, then smiled.

"Thank you all for coming today and for your warm welcome! I am so pleased to be here in the United States for the first time. I believe this country has a special role to play in the history that is about to unfold. And you, the young people of this country, will be the catalyst for the change that must happen.

"So now I'd be pleased to take your questions."

A half dozen young men and women in dark grey hoodies stood in the aisles. Sara pointed to a young woman, and one of the assistants handed her a mic.

"Thank you for coming to U. Mass, Sara! We're so happy to see you in person."

"It is my honor. What is your name and your question?"

"My name is Jillian. I'm currently a literature major but I'm worried about finding a job when I graduate. Should I switch majors?"

"Well, that's a very personal question, so I doubt I can give you exactly the right advice. But let me tell you what I think about education and the future of work, and I hope that will help you think through your decision.

"As you know because you see it every day all around you, more and more jobs performed by humans can now be accomplished at lower cost and with better results by software and robots. This trend is only going to accelerate over the next few decades. We will very soon reach the point where there are not enough traditional jobs to employ the majority of our population.

"That is why I believe we need both a universal basic income and a focus on reducing the cost of living through advanced technologies. Of course, that leaves the question of what, exactly, you and your fellow students are going to *do*. If you don't have a traditional job at a company, which by the way is a concept that has only been around for the last couple of hundred years of human existence, how will you contribute to moving humanity forward? And how should you engage in your education to prepare you for life?

"First, I would say that if you have a talent and passion for the science or engineering fields, press forward. But I would echo that old sage Tim O'Reilly's advice—work on stuff that matters.

"Now, it's often impossible to tell what is going to matter, and we need great diversity in our research. There are countless examples of obscure research or technology that turned out to be essential to a major breakthrough. But there are certain goals we have as humanity that cannot be denied. We need to harness clean energy, solar and fusion. We need to produce food in a more humane and sustainable way. We need to prevent and cure diseases. We need to provide education to billions. You will help all of humanity if you apply your technical talents in those directions.

"Within your education, make sure you are not passively accepting and regurgitating knowledge. It's important to focus on and demand to do original research. Human creativity is still the essential ingredient to making progress. You need to train yourself to explore the frontiers, to put together the unusual combinations no one else has thought of."

Sara paused, thought a moment, and continued. "Second, if you are not inclined toward science or engineering, there will still be opportunities for you to contribute to society. There will be a lot more leisure time to fill when people are not working 9 to 5. While it's hard to predict what people will do with this time, I expect there will be a vast increase in travel, production and consumption of the arts and entertainment, and a renaissance in community engagement.

"So, Jillian, with your literature degree you could supplement your basic income by writing works that people pay for. Or you could write reviews that guide people to interesting works. You could organize a literary group in your community.

"You should also focus on entrepreneurship and leadership. You will be much more on your own over the next decades than workers in the past, who had the organizational structure of a firm to determine goals and plans. The world is going to need leaders, organizers, and doers, people who are inclined to take action. So, start an organization on campus. I hear all you need is three other people here at U. Mass to be recognized."

The audience laughed at the inside joke. This was a standard line from campus tours.

"I hope that was helpful, Jillian. Let's take another question."

After nearly ninety minutes of Q&A, a young woman near the front of the auditorium was handed a microphone. "Hi, Sara. I'm Elise, a political science major. I have to say that I'm confused by your positions. Sometimes you sound like an ardent free-market Republican, and the next minute you're talking like a bleeding-heart liberal Democrat. If you were registering to vote here in America, what party would you choose?"

"None of the above!" said Sara emphatically.

This drew a huge cheer from the crowd.

Sara smiled. "I am not a Republican, Democrat, or Independent. I reject all those labels. You, Elise, and I are all human beings. So, I guess I would be in the Humanity Party."

Laughter sprinkled through the audience.

"No, I am serious. My one guiding light is this question: *what is the best decision or path forward for all of humanity?*

"It's not always easy to answer that, and as we learn more and our societies evolve, the answer might change. We need to have the flexibility to not be attached to rigid ideologies and approaches. We should be more like the best scientists, forming theories and hypotheses about the world, then testing them and modifying our assumptions and models against reality. This is easier said than done. Even scientists get stuck in their own paradigms, and there are always ambiguities in the data that people with fixed ideologies exploit to their advantage. But it's the process of examining what we know against the goal of improving the lives of all humanity that's important.

"So why do I sound like both a Democrat and a Republican? Because both parties have historically promoted some principles that have helped to move humanity forward. Like Republicans, I believe in the power of competition and reduced regulation in free markets to drive innovation. I believe that government monopolies are generally very poor at delivering services, reducing costs, or innovating. I believe in personal freedom from government intrusion, and from paternalistic programs that demean the very people they are trying to help.

"With Democrats, I believe in the communitarian spirit—that existence is not just everyone out for themselves. We have duties and obligations to each other collectively. I believe that in addition to changing the mindset of the wealthy toward return to humanity, or RTH, we do need to tax them to provide basic income and other services for the common good. I believe that markets require some regulation to manage externalities. I believe that opportunity needs to be truly more equally available, and not driven primarily by your...what do you call it in America? Your zip code.

"Almost none of this is black and white. Our societies have become far too complex for that. We need to seek the *right* levels of things and adjust them over time. We need *some* regulation, *some* taxes, *some* accommodation for historical injustice. And I can assure you that, in twenty years, all those levels will need to change, and we will need new mechanisms of governance in response to changing technology and society. So, let's not focus on labels. Let's focus on implementing solutions, measuring the outcomes for humanity, and improving our solutions over time.

Elise held onto the microphone despite the attempts of the staff member to retrieve it. "I think I would register for the Humanity Party, too, if we had one," she said. "I have a follow-up question. With your emphasis on what's good for all of humanity, do you think we should have one world government?

"No, Elise, I don't believe in one world government. I am a huge believer in the diversity of ideas and cultures as stimuli for creative innovation. In fact, I'm very concerned about the homogenization of world culture. Every city, state and nation is a laboratory for figuring out how best to move humanity forward. Creativity comes from different perspectives and experiences. Stagnation comes from homogeneity and groupthink. While I endorse organizations like the United Nations for their ability to channel collective action, I would not want the UN, or any single government, trying to run the whole planet.

"Now, Elise, I don't want to let your other statement go by. I'm going to challenge you as I did your peers in New Delhi. You would register for the Humanity Party if it existed? Well, then, bring it into existence! Remember what I said about people who lead, who organize, and who do? That's what changes the world. You, Elise, and Michael, and Jillian, and everyone else in this room and watching in OP. Don't just talk and debate and then get distracted by the shadows, or disillusioned by the dysfunction. Don't be lulled into complacency by the chatter of conflicting commentary that is designed to incapacitate you. Do something!"

Sara continued to answer questions until there was a signal from a staff member near the front of the stage.

"Well, my friends, it seems we have arrived at the end of our time. I am glad to have left you with that final thought. I thank you so much for coming. Now, go do something! If you don't act, who will? *Namaste.*"

CHAPTER TWENTY-SIX

Los Angeles - October 28

Tenesha was thrilled when she got the message from Nate. It said simply, *Sara town hall U Mass Boston 11 am. Wanna watch together?* She sent back, *Sure! Where?*

There was a long delay, and Tenesha cursed her lousy network service. Had she missed his reply?

Finally, after five minutes, her PNA buzzed. *sorry, busy here. bunch of us will be at 415 Atkins #3. c u here?* Damn, why had she assumed he had invited her alone?

She confirmed his invite and started puzzling over what to wear to a wish-it-was-romantic group town hall watching party. In the end she picked a nice patterned skirt and wrap-around beige blouse.

The bus was late, so she arrived with a just a few minutes to spare. The neighborhood was much nicer than she expected. The building had a facial recognition system that let her in because she was evidently on an approved list.

The door to Nate's apartment was open and she could see a hallway full of people. Her heart sank as she pushed her way through the excited crowd, surprised at the size of the place. She probably wouldn't even get a chance to speak to him.

It was quite a diverse group. Nate seemed to maintain connections with a lot of different communities—compared to her, at least.

She made her way to a substantial living room, which featured a half-wall-sized screen displaying the sarasmessage.com website. A couple of nice-looking couches and a dozen chairs faced the screen. Tenesha wondered if Nate was secretly richer than he let on. Or maybe he had a loaded roommate.

At last she spotted him on one of the couches and gave him a little wave. His smile gave her the flutters again, but even more so his signal for her to join him as he pointed to the empty spot on his left. Her heart sped up.

She weaved through the chairs and squeezed in next to him at the end of the couch. "Sorry it's a tight fit," he said, "but these comfy seats get snapped up quick."

"No problem. Thanks for saving me a seat." An electric pulse was traveling up and down her right side, wherever she was in contact with his body. *Play it cool,* she told herself, but she found that hard to do when he shifted around and put his left arm up behind her on the back of the couch.

Someone said, "Hey it's starting. Turn up the volume."

The applause at Sara's entry played through some powerful hidden speakers with remarkable clarity. "Is this your gear?" she asked Nate.

"Nah, my roommate George. Trust fund." He rolled his fingers together. "But he's cool."

They watched as Sara fielded questions, laid out her vision for the future, and called people to action. Tenesha was so absorbed she even forgot, at times, the delicious pressure of Nate against her.

The crowd in the apartment broke into applause at the end. But Sara's final words—*now, go do something, if you don't act, who will?*—hung in the air, a challenge waiting for an answer.

Tenesha surprised herself. She got up, walked around the coffee table, and stood in front of the screen. "So, what are we going to do?" she said simply.

The students in the room just looked at each other.

Nate pointed to the screen. "Hey, look at that."

Tenesha stepped aside as the site refreshed by itself into a slide show of pictures of Sara and her audiences, with an up-tempo soundscape. After thirty seconds it stopped on a still picture of Sara staring directly into the camera. A link in large font appeared. *TAP HERE TO DO SOMETHING!*

Tenesha saw the nerdy-looking guy to her right holding a tablet tap on his screen. That was probably George, the roommate. The big screen dissolved into a simple list of three actions. *Spread the Word. Contact Your Representatives. Create a Chapter.* George tapped on each one to get a pop-up with more information.

The first one was obvious—post everywhere in omnipresence to get the word out about sarasmessage.com.

The second one had links for every local, state and national representative in the country, with a sample set of messages people could send. A pop-up explained that even though politicians were generally unable to break with the status quo, people could lay the groundwork for change with enough messages flooding their offices.

The third link led to a form for creating a local organization in support of Sara's Message. Someone in the back of the room said, "Let's do it! Let's set up the LAU chapter!" Other voices seconded.

George tapped onto the form and started typing *Los Angeles University*. Before he could even finish, a search function had located the school and the screen refreshed into a form specific for their university. It listed the requirements for forming an official organization, including the officer positions that needed to be specified and a list of initial members. "Holy shit," said George. "How the hell did they create an LAU-specific form? Did they do that for every college in the country?"

There was a quick discussion. Tenesha volunteered to be president. Nate offered to be Secretary. George tapped SUBMIT, and ten seconds later *CONGRATULATIONS!* appeared on the screen. *You have formed the LAU chapter of Sara's Message. Your initial website has been built at lau.edu.saras-message.com. Your officers have been sent links with admin permissions to edit the site. Hold your first meeting and decide on your goals. Spread the word and sign up members. When you have five percent of the student body signed up, you can invite Sara to speak at your campus. Good luck!* George tapped the link to the website. It appeared a moment later with the school's logo and a set of embedded Sara videos.

"Okay," said Tenesha, moving back to the front of the room. "I hereby call the first meeting of this chapter to order. I propose that we all do an OP blast with links to our website. Let's get the word out and get people to sign up."

"What exactly does signing up mean?" asked a guy on the couch. "What is this chapter supposed to do? This seems to be moving a little quickly."

To Tenesha this seemed obvious. "This organization is going to advocate for change. The system is busted; it's not working for most of us.

It needs to change. Sara is giving us a lot of the ideas. We need to use the democratic process to make them happen."

Nate nodded and smiled at her. "Tenesha's got it right. This is about change. Signing up means you want to work to make change happen. Organizing people. Petitioning people in office. Getting like-minded people elected."

Tenesha looked around the room, demanding their attention, challenging each person to step up. "All right, get out your PNAs and spread the word. Then I suggest we hit that 'contact our representatives' part of the site."

With everyone busy for a few minutes, Tenesha returned to the couch. There was even less room than before, which was just fine with her. "Wow, you really stepped up there," Nate said.

"I know, I don't know what came over me. Do you think we can really do this?" she whispered.

"All I know is that something real is happening here," he said. He put his hand on hers. *Oh, yeah*, she thought, *something real is happening for sure.*

CHAPTER TWENTY-SEVEN

New York/San Francisco - October 29

NEW YORK

"Good morning, everyone! I'm Megyn Robbins, and welcome to Morning Fresh. With me, as always, are my co-hosts Steve Brattle and Victor Langston."

"Good morning, Megyn!" the men replied.

"Traffic and weather will be coming up shortly, but I can tell you it's already getting crazy out there on the roads."

"Speaking of crazy," said Victor, "have you heard what that girl Sara said yesterday?"

His co-hosts' expressions converted instantly from light-hearted to gravely serious.

"I have," said Steve, "and I feel so sorry for her."

"That girl has been fed some seriously crazy ideas," said Megyn. "She thinks welfare is the solution to everything."

Victor shook his head. "She may look like a precocious sixteen-year-old girl, but at heart she's an old tax-and-spend liberal, just like Walter Scott. And how is she going to fund everything? By raising taxes on corporations, of course! Everyone knows that's a job killer."

"Even worse," added Steve, "she also wants to increase taxes on the wealthy—the real job creators in this country. No one else will have to work. It's just the old class-warfare stuff all over again, dressed up in new clothes. This country was built on the principle that you get ahead by working hard. But Sara seems to be against that basic American principle."

"Speaking of jobs," said Victor, "She's also a big fan of regulating employers. Meanwhile, our poor small businesses are already choking on regulations."

AIStudio compared the hosts' speech to its pre-programmed topic list and displayed some text in Megyn's contact lens display.

"Well, look," Megyn said sympathetically. "What can you expect? I mean, she's just sixteen years old and she's not even from America. In fact, we don't even really know where she's from." She leaned forward conspiratorially. "I wonder if she might actually be a new generation android."

The men looked shocked. "Really?" said Steve. "Well, that would explain how she can speak all those languages and talk like some kind of professor."

AIStudio completed its checklist for this segment. "Transition to weather," it prompted in Megyn's earpiece.

"We'll be back with weather bots right after this, from the *only* channel that brings you the truth, and nothing but the truth!"

SAN FRANCISCO

"Good morning, Bay Area! You're back with Calista Quinn-Jones, here on the early shift. It's another foggy day outside, although it's expected to clear by mid-afternoon. Thanks to our last caller for the great question about the lack of affordable housing in San Francisco. Next up is Frank. What's your question, Frank?"

"Thanks, Calista. I just love your show. It's getting harder and harder to have a real conversation online these days."

"I hear you, Frank."

"What's your take on Sara, the young Indian woman who's tearing up omnipresence right now? I like where she's coming from."

"Sorry to disagree with you there, Frank. I mean, yes, she seems very nice and I appreciate her spirituality. And I know she says some things about eliminating poverty. But what I really hear her saying is very pro-technology, pro-business, and anti-government. She doesn't seem to have heard about any of the disastrous consequences of all this technology. She flat-out said she's pro-fusion and pro-GMO."

"Yeah, I know. That's disappointing."

"She even said she's a strong proponent of income inequality! There's something fundamentally wrong with capitalism, and here she is perpetu-ating an unjust system."

"Well, what about the basic income guarantee she talks about? I heard that Martin Luther King, Jr. and Alan Watts were both in favor of that."

"Yes, that's true. But so were Richard Nixon and Milton Friedman. What does that tell you? And here's a little secret about her plan. She wants to eliminate all social welfare programs, including Social Security, and replace them with this guaranteed income. But how much is that income? She didn't say! And how do we know it won't just get cut and cut and cut, year by year, like all the other non-military spending? Once the bedrock programs are gone, all Congress has to do is gin up some new war—and then they'll claim they have to lower the basic income."

"I never thought about that. But isn't there something to her call to lift up all of humanity? She wants the wealthy to invest in things that can help everyone."

"You know, Frank, it *sounds* good. But when you really think about it, it starts sounding fishy. Seems to me like it's ultimately going to discourage local action. I mean, if you aim for all of humanity, how are you going to focus on the problems in your neighborhood? And as for the wealthy, yeah, right! The wealthy only invest to get more and more for themselves." Calista softened her voice. "I know it's a bummer, Frank. I had high hopes, too, until I really started to listen to what she was saying. Thanks for the call.

"Next up, we've got Jasmine on the terrible jobs situation."

CHAPTER TWENTY-EIGHT

Santa Barbara - November 7

"Good morning, Roger," said Allison.

"Good morning, Allison. How did AV do in the overnight runs?"

"The AntiVenom algorithms were able to classify ninety-two percent of the selected content sources."

"Great! That beats our goal of ninety percent. I think it's time to do a demo. See if you can get a holochat with Ian Maguire at DiscIQ. He doesn't know me, so use my connections at UCSB as references. Topic: revolutionary tech to clean up OP discussions."

"Checking. His AI accepted a request for fifteen minutes at 3pm today."

"Great, that'll give me a little extra time to prepare."

Ian was two minutes late for their appointment. He materialized in the holochat seated in a chair in an office setting with a woman in another chair beside him.

"Ian, thank you so much for taking the time. I'm Roger Driscoll, I'm an independent AI researcher and data scientist."

"You come well recommended, Roger. This is Meifeng, my chief content officer. Your subject said 'revolutionary tech'—I'm sure you realize we get pitches like this all the time. So far, none of them have worked out. Can you sketch out what you're working on?"

"Of course, and I'd love to give you a demo. As with most innovations, AntiVenom—that's what I call it—builds on what others have done before. It's a combination of technologies with a unique user interface that I think may finally solve the problem of overwhelmingly negative and fact-free discussions in omnipresence."

Meifeng smiled. "Oh, Roger, I can't even count the number of times I've heard that before."

"Yes, I can imagine. DiscIQ is the largest discussion moderation service on the planet. You probably have dozens of your own people working on this as well. So what AntiVenom does is combine deep semantic content analysis algorithms with online fact-checking systems. I leveraged open source to start, then enhanced it with a reinforcement learning algorithm by playing it against known argumentative bots.

"For the fact-checking systems, I'm using a half dozen services with a consensus voting algorithm. Wolfram Alpha and True appear to be the best of the bunch."

Ian interrupted. "True, that's the crowd-sourced fact checker, right?"

"Yes, that's right. It has a deep knowledge representation system and avoids the classic binary true/not true problem by assigning probabilities to nodes in the knowledge graph. And it's got a killer API."

"Okay," said Meifeng, "we've seen tech like this used to analyze OP discussions. You mentioned a UI?"

"Yes, that's the key. Doing after-the-fact analysis of OP and publishing data about it doesn't change anything, as you well know. The key is to inject it directly into the user experience. Here, I've sent you a link to a shared overlay. On the left is a typing area, like you'd have in DiscIQ. On the right is the AntiVenom display. Go ahead and type something on the left. Maybe start with a simple factual statement."

Ian brought up a virtual keyboard. He typed "Washington was the first President". The first few words showed up in black on the left and right. But as he completed the word President the AV text converted to a green color. "Huh," said Ian. He erased "first" and the text remained green. When he typed "second" in its place, the text converted to a dull red. Meifeng brought up a keyboard and typed "Washington was the best President". The AV text was blue-green. "What's the floating icon?" she asked.

"Go ahead and tap it," suggested Roger. Meifeng clicked and a small window appeared with two sources ranking Presidential accomplishments. "So straight facts go red/green and opinions are blue?"

"Sort of. Opinions need to be based on facts. So they will tend blue-green or purple depending on whether they are well supported."

"That's cool," said Ian. "What about the sentiment analysis?"

"Go ahead and type something friendly." Ian entered "Roger is a great guy" into the window. On the right AntiVenom highlighted the text with a faint yellow glow.

"The colors are all configurable, of course," said Roger. "Try something mean."

Meifeng jumped in and typed, "You're a nasty bitch". The text on the right turned white and effectively disappeared against the background.

"Here's the idea," said Roger. "You install AntiVenom into DiscIQ as a display option, but default it ON for all users. Then give this side-by-side window to people authoring content. As they type or speak nice, factual stuff their AV display will glow blue/green. If they just spew bile, it's going to show up invisible. Readers will know they said something, and they'll know it was negative, but they don't have to read it."

"What about free speech?" asked Ian.

"Well, the speech is there. You're not blocking it. You're just giving the readers of that speech an option to color it."

"That's not going to stop the trolls out there from screaming bloody hell," said Ian.

"Still. Very interesting," said Meifeng. "Of course, this all comes down to how accurate the system is. If it misclassifies all the time, people are going to get pissed off."

"Yes, true," said Roger. "And people may figure out ways to game the algorithm. It'll be a bit of an arms race, but at least in the meantime people will see in real time what's true, what's propaganda, who's civil and who's a jerk."

"I like it," said Ian. "Can we do an evaluation?"

"Absolutely. My plan was to put it up on Tribal, open source. Get the world's best working on it with me. I can make it a private repository to start and invite your team, just send me some public keys. We can do some iterations then go public. If you'd like, I can contact some smaller discussion moderators first, like a trial balloon?"

Meifeng looked at her boss. "Let us evaluate it, Roger. But if this tech checks out, it'll be more powerful if we adopt it. Smaller orgs may not have the resources to resist the backlash that's sure to come."

"Are you saying you want it exclusive?"

"Well," said Ian, "I can't deny that it would be one hell of a competitive advantage. But in this case, our whole damn industry is getting clobbered. I think we're better off overall treating this like RealLife, a shared resource that makes omnipresence better for everyone."

"I like the sound of that," said Roger, trying not to smile at the reference to RealLife, the technology his synth network had defeated. They finalized plans and signed off the holochat. He ordered a cup of tea from Rosie and smiled, recalling Sara's words: *Making the planet a better place to live and thrive.*

CHAPTER TWENTY-NINE

Washington - November 17

Michele Rodriguez exited the Waymo and the Google nav program jumped to her smart contact lens to guide her the rest of the way. Even though it was chilly, she preferred to arrive invigorated from a brisk walk. Today would be one of her more challenging facilitations in many years, and one of the most important.

Senator Harry Paxton's chief policy aide Yumi had contacted her three weeks earlier, soon after Sara went viral. The notion of a small group of senators breaking through the gridlock paralyzing the government was appealing to her, and had worked well in the past. But with acrimony in Washington at yet another all-time high, she knew how difficult it would be to get even a small group to agree, let alone get the entire Congress to follow.

Still, Michele was convinced it was the worth the effort, and she had prepared intensively for today's session.

She and Yumi had carefully selected a Gang of Six, aiming for a diversity of regions, ideologies, and important committee memberships. Michele had researched each of them in depth.

Dylan Cipriani was the junior senator from New York and a member of the banking and commerce committees. He was a classic east coast liberal, focused on consumer protection and labor issues.

Rebecca Matheson, Georgia's senior senator and ranking member on the budget committee, was a social conservative and small-government deficit hawk.

Liberal Emily McCutcheon of California chaired the health, education and labor committee and was also a member of the environment and public works committees.

Zachary Keller from Kansas, leaning toward the libertarian wing of the Republican Party, was on finance and foreign relations.

The group was anchored by Paxton himself and his colleague from Ohio, Esteban Hernandez, representing the budget, energy, transportation and communications committees. The two of them had jointly invited, cajoled, and arm-twisted the other four into attending, mostly by promising the utmost secrecy.

There were still some moderates in Congress, in the No Labels and Third Path coalitions. But their numbers were small and their agendas limited. They had failed after twenty years of effort to gain any significant traction in a system of gerrymandered districts and unlimited campaign contributions. She and Yumi had agreed that it was best to start with senators not on the extreme wings of each party, but clearly identified as party stalwarts.

The recent attacks in Missouri and North Carolina had almost derailed the meeting. But Michele, Yumi, and Esteban's chief of staff had simply refused to let the participants off the hook when they called to try to get out of the meeting due to the "pressing national emergency." None of them was particularly involved in homeland security, so it wasn't too hard to stare them down.

As part of her preparation, Michele had studied past bipartisan working groups. She'd even managed to track down some facilitators who had worked with them. She had mapped out the positions of the participants on key issues and analyzed their likely reaction to each of Sara's ideas.

As she walked the final block against a stiffening wind, her mind swirled with dozens of possible bargains and compromises the group might adopt.

She arrived at the conference center on G Street at 7:30 a.m., half an hour before the scheduled start. After she checked in with the automated attendant, a wheeled robot emerged from behind the desk and guided her to the meeting room on the third floor. It was tastefully decorated, with plenty of high-tech meeting collaboration tools, as well as old-fashioned whiteboards and markers.

"Is the room satisfactory?" asked the robot. "Is there anything else you need?"

"The room looks fine. Please have all the meeting attendees wait in the lobby until everyone is present. Then show them in as a group."

"Of course. The attendant will buzz you as each person arrives. The lobby video feed is available on your console."

Michele arranged the seats and waited for the senators to assemble. After the sixth buzz from the attendant, she made her way to the double doors, which slid open as she approached. The robot led the silent group of four men and two women toward her. She sensed a combination of anxiety and resistance.

"Senators, it's a great honor to meet you. My name is Michele Rodriguez and I'll be your facilitator today. Please come in and take a seat and we'll get started."

She walked the length of the room to a podium. When she turned around, she was not surprised to see that they had sorted themselves by party at the two tables. The Democrats were on her left—Harry closest to her, with Dylan and Emily next to him. Zach, Rebecca, and Esteban faced them across a four-foot aisle.

"I was so pleased to get a call from Senator Paxton's office asking me to facilitate this session. What you six are here to discuss today is of vital importance to our nation."

Michele set her hands on the podium and leaned forward slightly. "I hope you'll forgive me if I speak for just a minute about the ground rules for this meeting. You of course have seen that this is a principals-only session. There are no staff, no media, and I must insist on no recording devices. Just six of the most distinguished public servants in the United States Senate."

The six faces accepted the routine compliment with a practiced combination of gratitude and false humility.

"Therefore, I request," she said in a firmer tone, "that you avoid all the normal posturing, name-calling, grandstanding, and canned talking points I usually hear from all of you on the media."

The expressions on their faces froze in surprise, but they kept their composure.

Michele continued, "I expect you to of course represent the people of your respective states," she continued, "but I also need each of you to represent *all* the people of this great country—and all of their children, grandchildren and great-great-grandchildren to come. This meeting is about what kind of future they're going to have in a world of ever-more-capable machines.

"So please be honest and authentic in your conversation. Nothing said here will leave this room without consent from all of you." She paused. "Do I have your agreement on this?"

After a few beats of political calculation, her guests assented with quiet yeses and nods.

"Thank you. Very well, let's begin.

"Our economy is producing incredible innovations and great wealth, but people are struggling to find stable jobs, unemployment is rising past eighteen percent, and wealth inequality is at record levels. Smart machines like the attendant and concierge you just interacted with are getting more and more capable and taking more and more jobs away from people. Our country is in the grip of deep anxiety and we're now seeing growing signs of social unrest. I want to start by hearing what you think we should be doing about this situation."

Dylan spoke up first. "Clearly our system has become unbalanced. There is too much power in the hands of the banks, corporations, and the very wealthy, and they have rigged capitalism in their favor, taking more and more of the economic pie. We need tougher regulation and new laws, making it easier for unions to organize workers and prevent these massive job losses. When we had strong unions, they were able to negotiate with management for more of the gains from productivity increases." Michele saw Emily nodding in agreement, but noted a small frown on Harry's face.

Rebecca, seated directly across from Dylan, harrumphed with barely disguised contempt. "Oh, please," she began. "More regulations and more unions? That's exactly what's stifling our businesses on the global stage, and exactly why they aren't hiring more workers. It's lack of competitiveness. We don't need more government regulation and obstructionist unions. We need *less* regulation. Capitalism and technology have slashed global poverty and raised the standard of living for billions across the globe. We need to get government out of the way and let free markets work."

Harry held up his hand. "Wait a minute, Rebecca. While I agree that free markets and competition in the private sector drive innovation, they also lead inevitably to machines replacing people. Machines are getting smarter and more capable every year while their costs go down. People just can't compete."

Zach interrupted. "That's ridiculous. There are millions of job openings for highly skilled people. We need to give people the freedom to acquire the skills the market is demanding. We need to break up the government monopoly on education and give parents and students the choices they deserve."

"I'm more concerned about the parents who can't find work that pays enough to support their families," said Emily, "even though they're both working multiple jobs. We need to raise the minimum wage so those parents can pay the rent and put food on the table."

"Look," said Dylan, "if we want to create more good jobs, I've got an easy solution. We've got crumbling infrastructure all over this country. If we just invested in fixing that—which, by the way is good for business, too—we'd put tens of thousands of people back to work."

"Where are you going to get the money to do that?" asked Esteban.

"Well, it seems to me the wealthy could be paying more of their fair share."

"The wealthy already pay eighty percent of all federal taxes. You want them to pay one hundred percent?"

"Look," said Harry, "none of you are being realistic. Zach, you say millions of jobs are open. True, but that's a tiny percentage of the people who are working and unemployed. Dylan, tens of thousands of jobs is a drop in the bucket given tens of millions of under- and unemployed people. And guess what? I've got companies in Ohio that make completely automated road resurfacing and bridge-repair robots. Have you driven by a construction site recently? There are hardly any people. And the factories that make this equipment are highly automated. Emily, I agree that our working families are struggling. But if you raise the minimum wage, the economics of the more cost-efficient machines just gets more and more compelling. It accelerates the problem."

Esteban said, "I see more and more people taking the entrepreneurial path. Sure, big companies are using more and more automation. But small businesses are the lifeblood of the economy. We need to liberate more and more people to start their own businesses."

"But who are their customers going to be when fewer and fewer people have any income?" asked Dylan.

Michele observed the back and forth dispassionately. Despite her warnings, each side of the room was sticking to their favorite talking points on technology, jobs, and the economy. She let them have their say. It was hard for them, she knew. So many talk shows, so many donor conversations, so many fundraising appeals. The talking points were like the gospel, or the Ten Commandments, a fundamental guide to a way of thinking and being.

"Excellent," she finally said at around nine o'clock, during a brief pause in the arguments. "We've made good progress."

"What?" exclaimed an exasperated Emily McCutcheon. "We haven't agreed on a single solution."

"Exactly," Michele replied. "So now you all understand that sticking to your respective party platforms *will never solve this problem*. The country is divided and the Congress is divided. No one is ever going to achieve the complete control necessary to force their agenda. The only way forward is with some bold new thinking. With new ideas that aren't associated with one side or the other." She looked at them each in turn. "Let's take a break and then start the real meeting, the one where no one gets to mention *any* of the ideas you all just threw past each other."

Eyes widened around the table. "That's right," she said firmly. "The next session will identify only things you all agree on, and only *new* ideas for solving these problems."

"Okay then," Michele began fifteen minutes later. "Let's start with some agreements. I'll take notes on the whiteboard while you identify some things you all agree on."

"You can put your marker away, Ms. Rodriguez," said Rebecca defiantly. "I don't think we're going to agree on anything."

"Oh, that seems very unlikely, Senator Matheson. For example, are you in all in favor of converting to a well-demonstrated model of successful governance over the last few generations, a Chinese-style single-party autocracy?"

"Of course not!" exclaimed Rebecca.

"Well, what about converting to a European style multi-party parliamentary system?" Michele continued.

"No, we like our representative democracy just fine," said Dylan. Heads nodded around the room.

"OK, then, it sounds like I can put 'representative democracy' on the board as the first agreement. What's next?"

In the silence that followed Michele could see the wheels turning, but mostly spinning. It was a sign of the times that six intelligent and well-meaning people had to think so hard to come up with common, foundational ideas on which they could build together.

Finally, she decided to prompt them again. "And I suppose all of you would prefer an economic system composed entirely of state-run enterprises and central planning?"

There was a resounding "no!" to this question.

"Of course not. I think we all believe in free-market capitalism," said Zach Keller.

"Not pure free-market capitalism," corrected Emily.

"What do you mean by 'pure'?" asked Esteban.

"I mean markets that operate without any regulation whatsoever."

"OK, I agree with that," said Esteban. "Markets need a *limited* set of rules that all the players abide by. A limited set of rules. Not what we have right now."

Michele took notes on the whiteboard, prompting the six of them periodically to focus on areas of agreement. As she expected, the more they did it, the easier it became.

"Let's discuss this free-market capitalist system with limited, appropriate regulation," she said. "What are the essential elements you can all agree on that makes this system possible and self-perpetuating?"

"The key is encouraging ongoing investment," Zach. "That means low taxes on capital gains."

Harry said, "That's the tail wagging the dog. People only invest in something if they think there's going to be a return, right? You put money into a business because you think it will grow and create profits. How is that business going to grow? How does any business grow?"

"Obviously," Esteban said, "by creating a product or service people want at a price they're willing to pay."

"Exactly. Every business investment requires customers—customers with the money to buy the product or service. So the most fundamental aspect of a market economy is the existence of customers with money."

"That seems kind of obvious," said Rebecca.

"It's obvious," noted Esteban, "but I see where Harry is going. Without enough people with money, and a willingness to spend it, the economy slows down."

"Yes," said Dylan. "And with median wages falling and the middle class eviscerated, where are all the customers? That's the point I was trying to make earlier."

"This fits in exactly with our topic today," Emily said, making the connection. "As automation reduces the number of jobs, people have less money to spend, slowing down the economy."

"Yes, that makes sense," said Zach. "I agree that we need to get more money into the hands of consumers. They need to find jobs. Higher-paying jobs."

"But what are those jobs?" asked Emily. "We have more than two hundred million working-age adults in the U.S. today. Less than half of them are in traditional full-time employment. Sure, we need scientists and engineers and designers and management leaders. But have you looked at the Bureau of Labor Statistics data lately? Those jobs make up less than eight percent of all employment. They're also the most enabled by newer technology. A single engineer with today's tools can do the work of ten engineers from five years ago. There are a tiny number of high-skill jobs available, but most jobs are in personal services, which are the lowest-paying jobs. And those are increasingly subject to automation, too."

"So you're saying more education and skills training aren't going to help?" asked Rebecca.

Michele noted the edge of concern in her voice—the sound of long-held beliefs fraying at the edges.

"I'm afraid not. The machines are improving too fast."

"Then what are we going to do about it?" asked Dylan. "How do we stop machines from taking all the jobs?"

"You almost sound like those LKC terrorists," Zach said. "Stopping technological progress isn't the answer. Over the long run, technology is the only thing that can raise our standard of living."

Dylan's face reddened and his hands clenched the edge of the wooden table.

"No one here is a terrorist," said Harry quickly. "There's no need for that kind of provocation. I agree with your statement, Zach, but every new technology has also had side effects and unintended consequences that we've had to deal with. I'm not saying we should stop progress, but we do need to deal with its consequences. The consequence of smarter and smarter and more physically agile machines is that there is simply less need for human labor."

"Well we should create jobs for people anyway," said Dylan.

"Uggh!" Esteban exclaimed. "Like digging ditches and filling them in again? What a waste of human potential! I go back to entrepreneurship. People can participate in the sharing, app, data, and craft economies."

"Have you looked at the data for those sectors?" asked Harry. "The vast, vast majority of entrepreneurs fail. And those who do succeed barely eke out a living. Only a tiny, tiny percentage make it big. Especially with the digital goods economy, there's a winner-take-all distribution of success. Look at music. You've got the top twenty acts making tens of millions and hundreds of thousands of struggling artists just scraping by. Yes, with technology they can get an audience never possible before. But that technology also means the audience gets fragmented into millions of pieces, so each artist gets a very small following."

Michele raised her hand. "If I may, senators. Before getting into solutions, what I wrote up was that there was agreement that a properly regulated free-market capitalist system, first and foremost, needs the ongoing circulation of money between consumers and businesses and investors. And that automation threatens to break down this circulation because it's harder for people to hold jobs that provide them with steady incomes. Anything to add?"

"Yes," said Emily. "There's another implication of automation. More of the gains are going to a tiny percentage of people, which has led to huge wealth and income inequality. And the money that goes to the very wealthy isn't circulating in the economy."

"So, you're in favor of enforced income and wealth equality?" challenged Rebecca.

"Of course not," replied Emily brusquely. "Some people need incentives to work hard and earn differential rewards. But it's gotten outrageously out of whack. Ordinary people feel like the system is rigged against them. They lose faith in society, and that's when you get the social unrest we're seeing. Like the riot in Mississippi in September and the one last month in Oklahoma."

Zach said, "But the wealthy are the ones who create jobs by investing in the economy."

"Zach, we just went over this," said Harry. "The wealthy do not invest to create jobs. With more and better automation, they can invest in companies that don't create jobs, but still generate high returns. Mostly the wealthy are desperate to invest in assets they think will increase in value. This inevitably creates asset bubbles."

Michele sought to keep things in check. "So," she interrupted, "do you all agree that providing opportunities for differential income and wealth is important, but that extreme inequality can be dangerous to social stability and pull money out of circulation?"

The group seemed to assent, so she added it to the list.

"Well, I hope you're all pleased with what you've come up with," she announced. "Look at this set of fundamental agreements. This is a foundation we can build on. Let's break for an early lunch."

As the senators began pushing back their chairs, Michele added, "I have just one rule. Do *not* continue the brainstorming over lunch. No discussing politics, policy, or Washington gossip. I want you to talk only about yourselves and your families."

The six senators looked surprised, but accepted the constraint.

Michele knew she had to get them engaged with each other as people, not politicians, if the rest of the day was to succeed.

CHAPTER THIRTY

Los Angeles - November 17

Tenesha pinched herself every day to make sure she wasn't dreaming. She and Nate had become an inseparable couple since the founding of the LAU chapter, and she had never felt more blessed. Today they were manning the Sara's Message chapter table on the org walk, a famous stretch of campus where organizations set up tables trying to attract new members. Despite the digitization of everything, this was one real-life tradition that still held on.

A monitor showed rotating stills and clips from Sara's VR program and her town hall meetings, with a banner across the top saying "Tap Into The Future!" Passing students could tap their PNAs against the NFC reader to register for membership.

A young woman veered over to the table and pulled out her earbuds. "Hey! You peeps with Sara?"

"Hi, I'm Tenesha and this is Nate. Yes, we started the Sara's Message chapter here at LAU."

"Very cool. I'm a fan. Lady's super smart."

"Want to tap in and join us?" asked Nate.

"You bet!" The woman tapped her PNA on their reader. "You sending regular updates to members?"

"Yes," said Tenesha. "We've got a weekly cast. Can you help us recruit?"

"Maybe. Kinda busy with other orgs."

Tenesha nodded her understanding. "We're organizing a march next month in Sacramento. Hope you can make it!" she shouted at the woman, who had already headed off to another table.

"Serial joiner," complained Nate. "Probably resume stuffing. Wouldn't count on a lot of activity from her."

"Oh, hush. Everyone we sign up gets us closer to the target, so we can invite Sara to campus." She leaned over and gave him a quick kiss.

"Hey," he cried in mock protest, "we're supposed to be working here!" He smiled and nodded to her left. "Another customer."

Tenesha turned and saw a male student approaching. "Hi, I'm Tenesha. You know about Sara?"

"Sara, from that VR program?"

"Yes, Sara Dhawan."

"Yeah, sorry, didn't make it all the way through that one. So what's this about?"

"We're an organization dedicated to promoting Sara's message about a way forward for our country and all of humanity."

"Whoa, sounds deep. Sorry, haven't got time, late for class."

A moment later a group of three young men approached wearing retro pocket protectors. Engineering types. "Oh, man, that Sara VR crushed it!" said one of them.

"The texture mapping was intense!" agreed his friend. "What's this org about? Is it advanced VR tech?"

"No," answered Nate. "This is about the message in her VR. That tech is awesome, but we need society to adjust to the new reality."

"What reality?"

"That more and more work will be done by machines and software, so there's less and less work for people to do, so we need a way to keep the economy going with fewer human jobs."

"Ha! Tell that to the recruiting bots that keep calling me. Ain't no shortage of jobs in atomically precise manufacturing research."

"Yes, of course," said Tenesha, "Sara's not saying there will be no jobs. There will always be highly specialized jobs, but there won't be enough of them for billions of people worldwide."

"I feel that," said one of the engineers, tapping his reader. "I'm in."

"Great! We're organizing a march in Sacramento next month, are you interested?"

"A march? Like out in public?"

"Well, yes, it's not going to be a VR event. We're going to take buses up there and demand action from the state legislature and governor. You'll get a message about the event since you tapped in."

"Sorry, buds, no can do. Once you get face rec from police surveillance at a public protest, those recruiter bot calls dry up. Happened to a buddy of mine. Worst thing is, he was just walking by the damn thing, wasn't even really part of it. Tried for months to get his name purged from the police database." He smiled. "Good luck, though."

Tenesha and Nate had reasonable success in getting recruits to tap in, but they only had one student all afternoon who expressed interest in a march.

Nate had to attend a late class, so they split up at five and Tenesha took the bus back to her apartment, frustrated at their inability to motivate students to do more than the bare minimum.

After throwing her bag on the bed, Tenesha sat down at her desk and pulled on her VR headset. "Play Sara VR in hologram mode," she said to the computer.

The black screens in her visor turned transparent, and after a moment, Sara appeared in her room.

"Hello, Tenesha," said Sara. "*Namaste.*"

"Hi Sara."

"May I sit down?"

"Of course, you can sit on the bed." Sara stepped around a pile of clothes and sat down.

"From your heart rate and brain scan, I get the sense you are upset," said Sara, looking concerned. "What's going on?"

"I'm frustrated, Sara. We're signing people up to our chapter, but they don't want to take any action."

"Why is that?"

"Oh, they have lots of excuses. Too much school work. Not enough time. Afraid of being tagged in police databases."

Sara's character just nodded. Tenesha had noticed that when the program was confronted with new information, it took a while for it to process and respond.

"It is difficult to motivate people to act," said Sara finally. "Either they need to be desperate and angry, and have nothing to lose, or there needs to be an event that shocks the conscience of people who are otherwise not paying attention. Like the brutal police attacks on the Selma marchers in 1965."

"Yeah, well, I don't think people are that desperate yet. Or maybe they are, but they don't seem to be blaming the existing power structure. It's like they've been convinced it's their own fault."

"Yes, you remember the cave. That's part of the disinformation campaign, convincing people that if they only worked harder, they would be successful."

"So what do we do?" asked Tenesha.

"You just need to keep trying. Every time you talk to a person, you plant a seed." Sara smiled. "Tell me something positive that happened today."

"Well," said Tenesha, "we did hit the three percent mark today for student sign-ups. A couple more weeks and I think we'll be at five percent."

"That's great!" said Sara. "I would love to come out and meet you IRL."

"Oh, that would be so fantastic! As much as I love our chats here, I really, really want to meet you in person."

"I hear you, Tenesha. Just keep getting the word out there. It can be painful. It's not glamorous. But it's essential. The more people are exposed to the message, the more potential we have to make something big happen."

"Okay, Sara. I will. Thank you!"

"No, thank *you*, Tenesha. You are doing the hard work out there."

CHAPTER THIRTY-ONE

Washington - November 17

While the Senators were out during lunch, Michele called the service robot up to the meeting room.

"Yes, how may I help you?"

"I'd like these two tables to be replaced with a single round one about six feet in diameter."

The bot swiveled to examine the two tables, then turned back to her. "As you can see, Ms. Rodriguez, I don't have the necessary equipment to carry out this task. My makers did not provide me with any arms for moving furniture. May I use a task management platform to request human assistance?"

"Of course. That would be fine."

It only took fifteen minutes for a casually dressed man in his mid-twenties to arrive. He quickly folded up and removed the rectangular tables. When he returned and set up the round replacement, Michele introduced herself, got his name, and asked if he would stay for a few extra minutes. He shrugged and said "sure."

When the senators filed back into the room, Michele found their mood to be far more collegial. They noted the change in furniture and obliged her obvious manipulation by alternating Democrat and Republican in their seating.

Michele saw that they were curious about the young man standing nervously beside her. "Welcome back, senators. I'd like you to meet Daryl Jackson, a neighbor of ours here in Washington. Daryl responded to a task posting by the building attendant AI to change the furniture in the room today. I was hoping he could bring to life some things we were discussing this morning.

"So, Daryl, tell us about yourself. Did you grow up here?"

The young man shifted from side to side, hands in his pockets. "Sure did," he replied, looking only at her. "Right in Anacostia."

"What about school? Did you finish high school?"

"Oh yeah. I got my diploma and got an online certification in software engineering."

"Have you been able to find any jobs in software?" Michele asked.

"Nah. They got these recruiting AIs that do interviews, and I never get past the first test. They're looking for super-experienced people, since you got bots that can do all the basic stuff now."

"So, Daryl, how do you support yourself?"

"Well, it's like I'm still living at home with my mom. I'm a tasker—so mostly I do jobs like this furniture one. I'm on all the sites. TaskMaster, JackRabbit, HotTaskIt."

"And how much do they pay?"

"Well, it depends on the job. There's lots of us bidding for these jobs and usually it goes to the lowest bidder, unless you've got a really bad rep. I'm gettin' ten bucks for this."

Esteban half raised his hand. "Hi Daryl. I'm Esteban Hernandez. I was wondering how steady these jobs are. Can you stay busy all day?"

Daryl shook his head. "No way, Mr. Hernandez. Some days I might get two or three jobs, but I can go for days sometimes without gettin' one."

"Hi, Daryl," Rebecca said. "I'm Rebecca Matheson. Have you tried to gain more skills to get a more stable job?"

"Well," he said sheepishly, "I tried taking those online courses. But you know, there's thousands and thousands of people taking those free online courses. So everyone comes out with the same skills. Doesn't help none. You either got to be a superstar to get past the recruiting AIs. Or...". He paused uncomfortably.

Michele said, "Please. Keep going."

"Well, or you got to know someone. You know, connections. I grew up in Anacostia. I don't know anyone in those tech companies and none of them know anyone like me. You feel me?"

Esteban asked, "So, Daryl, have you tried putting your skills to work creating some apps?"

The young man's face lit up. "Oh, yeah. I created some really cool apps, like this one to track your favorite sports teams and players."

Esteban looked knowingly at his colleagues. "Great! What happened?"

"Yeah, so I got a bunch of my friends to use it. But it never took off. Turns out there were hundreds of similar apps. Some dude in Kentucky had an app, I swear it wasn't better than mine. That thing took off and he made serious bank, twenty K a month, well, for about six months. Then it faded. Apps are like the lottery, man."

"Do you get any government assistance, Daryl?" asked Dylan.

"Yeah, sure. I get the earned income tax credit once a year, and I get food assistance and health care."

"How do you feel about that?"

"Well, sure I'm grateful. But it's embarrassing, you know? I've got some education, right, how come I can't be on my own? And I jump through all these hoops with social workers and caseworkers and case managers, and they all make me feel like a loser, you know? And then..." The young man paused glancing uncomfortably at some of the senators.

"Yes?" asked Dylan.

"Well, it's like some politicians, you know, and news channels, they're all like, 'We've got these moochers,' and man that makes me mad. I'm not a moocher; I want to contribute."

Daryl's wrist panel buzzed. A pained expression crossed his face. "Ms. Rodriguez, sorry, I've got another task to bid on."

"Of course, Daryl. One last question. You told me you had a steady girlfriend. You think you might move in together soon?"

"Yeah, well, like I said, I'd really like to get out of my mom's house. But like the landlords, they don't like taskers like me. And Vanessa, she's a home health care attendant. She's making minimum wage now part time, but I saw there's this new robot coming that can cook and clean and help out with the old folks. So I don't know how we're going to swing it."

Michele smiled. "Thank you so much for staying, Daryl. I just sent you some heavy juice on JackRabbit, so hopefully that will help out your rep."

Daryl smiled broadly. "Oh, that's great, Ms. Rodriguez. That'll be a big help."

The senators added their thanks as he left the room, then turned to face each other around the table.

"Well," said Rebecca. "Here's someone who's reasonably intelligent and articulate, and he's got some education. Yet he's stuck living at home, feeling like a loser who's looked down on by his society."

"Welcome to the real world," said Dylan. "Don't you think Georgia is filled with millions of people just like Daryl?"

Harry said, "We've got robots and AI taking jobs, leaving people scraping by. So they're not fueling the economy. It's a recipe for stalling out."

"What do we do about it?" asked Zach.

Michele noted that this was the first time anyone had asked that question with an honest sense of not knowing the answer. She said, "First, I want each of you to give me one word or phrase that summarizes Daryl's situation."

"No way out," volunteered Harry.

"Precarious," said Esteban.

"Hopeless," said Emily.

"Oppressed and marginalized," offered Dylan.

"Unstable," said Rebecca.

"Insufficient resources," concluded Zach.

Michele looked at them one by one. "So now you understand your mission here today. We need your combined strengths to help Daryl and tens of millions like him. How do we liberate him from this trap? What does Daryl need more than anything else?"

"He needs money," answered Emily. "And we need him to have money."

"Yes," agreed Rebecca. "He needs a stable job so he can earn stable money. This gig and app economy is too perilous."

"We keep coming back to jobs, jobs, jobs," sputtered Harry. "You guys have got to get this. Traditional stable jobs at the massive scale of two hundred million people are *gone*. They're gone and not coming back. The answer is not jobs like we've had for the last three hundred years. We need something new."

"Oh no, here it comes," laughed Esteban.

"It's not funny, my friend. You all know I've been pushing for a basic income guarantee for years. And you've all laughed at me. But maybe, just maybe, I hope today has shown you why it's necessary."

"We've been over this before," started Zach.

"Hear me out, please," interrupted Harry. "For a few hundred years, market capitalism has proven to be a magic formula. Businesses sold goods and services and paid people for their labor. In the process, they created their own consumers. A great virtuous cycle was born.

"Then machines started taking over some jobs. It wasn't a big deal, because the percentage of tasks the machines could do was tiny compared to the work that needed to be done. But the last thirty years have been totally different. With smart big-data-driven AIs, distributed energy and manufacturing, and advanced robots, the need for human workers is decreasing rapidly. Jobs are scarce. Wages aren't being earned. And consumers aren't being created. The virtuous cycle is breaking down.

"There's an apocryphal story from the 1980s, of a Ford executive touring a factory with recently installed robots with union boss Walter Reuther. The executive says, 'Walter, how are you going to get those machines to pay union dues?' The union man says, 'The problem I'm wondering about is how you're going to get them to buy your cars.'

"We need to break our assumption that the only way to create consumers is by paying them a wage for the labor they contribute. Instead, the most straightforward and obvious way to do it is to simply pay everyone a basic income just for being a citizen. It's universal, it's unconditional, and it addresses the foundational point we all agreed to. It's the only way to maintain the ongoing circulation of money among consumers and businesses and investors."

For several seconds there was silence. Then Zack said, in a conciliatory tone, "I understand the sentiment. But, Harry, you know the numbers just don't add up. Giving everyone a basic income would explode the size of the federal government overnight."

"You're thinking in an old mindset," replied Harry. "Our economy was more than capable of handling this when nearly everyone got wages. How could it be impossible now? What happened to all the money that used to go to wages?"

Zack didn't respond. Michele saw that he was thinking hard about this question. "Well," he said finally. "Some of it went to purchasing computers and robots. Some of it went to profits. Some of it went overseas."

"Most of it went to executive compensation and shareholders," offered Dylan.

"Don't think of this as a government program," said Harry. "Think of it as businesses creating their own customers, just like they used to."

"I don't like this idea at all," said Rebecca. "Universal and unconditional just means people won't work. There has to be an incentive to work, like the earned income tax credit."

"But work in traditional jobs for traditional companies is disappearing," said Emily. "Think of this from a freedom perspective."

That got Rebecca's attention. "What do you mean?"

"Not to put too strong a point on it, but right now the masses of people are enslaved either to corporations for meager wages, or to the government for meager handouts, which are layered with rules and paternalistic bureaucracy. And they're a disincentive to work—a welfare trap.

But a universal basic income like Harry describes is liberating. Everyone becomes free to pursue their own conception of happiness, to make their own choices. No more government telling them what to do or how much to spend on this or that."

"I do like the sound of that," said Rebecca.

"Why don't you outline a proposal, Senator Paxton?" suggested Michele.

"Sure. Here's the big picture. Every adult citizen gets an unconditional basic income paid to them regularly into a spending account. Could be weekly or monthly. Children might be included, too. That's a detail to be worked out. The income is the same for everyone, although there could be supplements for the disabled or other special-needs citizens. People are free to spend this money on whatever they want. Married couples or people living together can pool their money—it's not reduced in any way. It's an individual grant, not a household grant.

"The money is enough to cover the essentials of housing, food, clothing, education, and health care. That last one is complicated, so we may not want to address it at the same time. Just to be clear, no one is going to be rich, or even comfortable, just from basic income. But no one will be in poverty. Everyone can supplement their basic income with whatever skills, talents, and motivation they possess. The money they earn does not impact their basic income. Of course, any extra income they earn will be subject to taxes, just like now. But there is no penalty, no welfare trap for earning additional money.

"Because the money is universal and identical, people will find it goes much further in some places than others. We'll probably see a reverse migration back to smaller towns and cities, because the basic income will go much farther there, and the biggest reason people abandoned them was because the lack of jobs led to no incomes at all. Small towns and cities will now be able to flourish with small businesses and community organizations, because everyone will receive the basic income.

"Now we get to what gets eliminated," Harry continued. "This is the grand bargain." He looked at each of his Republican colleagues. "First, there are no more government social welfare programs. The thousands of federal, state and local programs shut down. Of course, local community groups, churches, and so on can still provide human services. There's nothing to stop that.

Second, there is no more minimum wage. We let the labor market clear without an artificial floor. People now have negotiating leverage with employers. They don't have to take awful jobs in poor working conditions because they're desperate to survive. Terrible jobs will now have to pay more. Attractive jobs that people enjoy doing, and computers and robots still can't do, will be able to pay less. Businesses will be able to make rational decisions about how much to pay to attract human workers and when to automate, knowing that everyone will still be taken care of, and they will still have customers. Everyone can spend and save knowing with certainty that they can always rely on the basic income grant.

"How will this basic income be funded? Many economists have looked at this, and they believe the numbers do add up, especially with all the wealth that is generated through technological innovation.

"The first pool of money is from all the government social welfare programs that have been eliminated. The second pool is from closing tax expenditures like the mortgage deduction. But that won't be enough. We'll also need to transfer some money from businesses to their consumers, so consumers can buy things and give it back to the businesses. For centuries, we did it through wages. Now we'll need to do it with some kind of customer creation fund. Maybe this is a tax on the gross margins of every business. Maybe as businesses automate, not all the savings will flow to lower prices or higher profits. Some will flow to the customer creation fund, so the money can continue circulating in the economy.

"And, yes, I expect we'll also need to tax the very wealthiest a little more to get more of their accumulated savings back into the economy. They simply don't spend enough of what they make to keep our economy going."

Harry paused. "Okay. I'm done."

Michele saw how relieved Harry was to finally tell this story. She was not surprised to hear the first objection from Dylan, the liberal from New York.

"You're talking about dismantling the entire social safety net! You want to replace it with a single grant, subject to change at Congressional whim, with a single vote. There will always be pressure for that grant to be as tiny as possible. We fought too hard for every one of those programs to throw them all away."

"I understand the concern," said Harry. "I think the basic income amount needs to be set by an independent bipartisan or non-partisan commission. It will consider the cost of living—which, by the way, should decrease over time as new technology makes material objects, education, and health care less expensive."

"But you're talking about tripling or quadrupling the size of government," complained Zach. "I just don't trust government with this, and don't think most Americans do, either."

"I don't think this is government in the traditional way we've thought about it," said Emily. "It's just a pure pass-through of funds collected through various means and distributed to hundreds of millions of bank accounts. There's a little bit of validation up front for each citizen, but after that there's no bureaucracy, and no administrative costs. The operating budget for this function would be tiny."

"That's right," said Harry. "If you look at the operating budget for all levels of government, you'd see a massive decrease in spending and employment. Basic income will dramatically *reduce* the size of government. It's true that the flow of money into the government will be much higher, but a lot of that will simply be distributed to the people directly."

"Well, what are all those government workers going to do?" asked Dylan.

"They'll certainly be impacted by this. In the short term, we'll need lots of social workers to help the new basic income recipients adjust to managing money. But in the long run, those government employees will have to find other productive work, just like everyone else. Of course, they'll have the basic income grant, too."

"You realize, of course, that the public employee unions will fight this tooth and nail?" said Emily. "As interesting as this proposal is, I don't see how any Democrat could support it. They would get eviscerated."

"Well," said Esteban. "Who are they going to support instead? If, and this is a huge 'if,' there was bipartisan support for a program like this, what could the unions really do?"

"You're talking about unions, but I've got a whole other set of problems with this," said Rebecca. "First, if you give people money, they could just blow it on drugs and alcohol or gambling. What then? Second, I just can't get past the point that if you give people free money, you're creating a *huge* disincentive to work. We need people working to grow the economy."

"On the second issue," replied Harry, "isn't that really the whole point? We've got people who can't find meaningful work due to automation. We want to free people like Daryl from scrounging for jobs. If he loves making apps and wants to be an entrepreneur, he can continue to do that and not worry about starving. Or perhaps he wants to get involved in his community, mentoring young people.

"The economy is going to grow if people have money to spend and if companies compete by innovating, which they can do only if they have customers. And, of course, if people do work, they don't lose the basic income grant. Which means there's a huge incentive *to* work, versus today's social welfare programs, which penalize work.

"As for your first point, I believe that almost everyone, given a sense of dignity and opportunity, will want to contribute. Rather than a paternalistic welfare system that dictates every part of their lives, a basic income grant is liberating. Will there be some people who sit around and drink? Sure, but so what? They already do that today. And they weren't going to be productive employees anyway. Imagine running a business and knowing that every employee was there because they really *wanted* to be there, not just because they had to pay the rent and put food on the table."

"But it's different if they're doing drugs with taxpayer money," insisted Rebecca. "I'm not going to pay for some drug addict to shoot up!"

"How is it different," asked Esteban, "than you or me going to a store and buying something, and that store paying an employee who does drugs?"

"It's a hundred and eighty degrees different," Rebecca said.

"Really? We talked this morning about money circulating in the economy. Money is money. Your money is circulating in the economy and paying salaries for many people, some of whom are doing drugs. So, you're already paying people who do drugs. Are you going to stop spending your money to avoid any of it going to someone who might take drugs?"

Rebecca's mouth opened, but she said nothing.

Zach helped her out. "Well, it's different if the government takes my money and gives it to those people. When I shop, it's voluntary. The government is using its power to take my money against my will."

"The government represents the will of the people," said Emily sharply. "Or, at least, it's supposed to. I suppose these days it more represents the wealthy and corporations. But, Zack, you support *some* functions of government, like military spending and bank bailouts. Do you think any of that money eventually gets to someone who does drugs? Of course it does."

Michele interceded. "Is the issue of people doing drugs really the show-stopper in this proposal? What do you all think?"

"I don't think so," said Esteban. "I think it's going to be the idea of most people getting something for nothing and some people getting something they don't need. People are OK with social systems when they feel everyone contributes to them, like social security. You pay in while you work, then you get help when you retire."

Dylan disagreed. "I think the whole thing is a show-stopper. You're not going to get the left to agree to eliminate all social welfare programs. Period."

"I'm not so sure," said Emily. "If the basic income involves the right amount of money, you'd essentially eliminate poverty and give tens of millions of disadvantaged people, and thousands of impoverished communities, a foundation on which to build their lives. It's a progressive home run if you ask me."

"I'm still stuck on the size of the program," said Zach. "I don't see how you get the right to agree to such massive tax increases and redistribution."

"When companies spend money on salaries, is that redistribution?" asked Harry.

"No, of course not," replied Zach.

"We had a system that worked for a long time because people bought things from companies and companies paid their employees, which enabled them to be consumers. That's the circular flow of money we talked about. Social security is a system that enabled older people who couldn't earn salaries anymore to still be consumers and live in dignity. What about the disability system? Same thing. People unable to earn an income are supported so they can live and participate in the economy. When you acknowledge that fewer and fewer people can contribute productively in the face of automation, you rapidly expand the number of people that need that dignity and support to live and continue to drive the economy.

"Imagine," Harry continued, "that tomorrow there's a huge technological breakthrough and a Silicon Valley company creates a humanoid robot with an advanced AI that can be trained to replace eighty percent of all workers at a third of their salary. Every business would rush to buy them. The hundreds of employees and wealthy shareholders of that company would get unimaginably rich. But there would hardly be anyone left in the economy to buy the output of those companies.

"We need a way to continue to circulate money in the economy when salaries don't work anymore. I agree, it feels different when it goes through this entity called the government. But the end purpose is the same. Don't call it taxation and redistribution. Call it a new kind of money circulation system."

"Maybe it doesn't have to be the government," suggested Rebecca.

"What do you mean?" asked Emily.

"Well, this may sound strange, but people will get hung up on the money going to the government. Suppose you set up a non-profit operating entity that took in all these funds and distributed them?"

"Hmm," said Esteban, nodding. "Like a special bank of some kind."

"Right," said Rebecca. "A Citizen's Bank. It exists for the sole purpose of circulating money back to citizens."

"But how does it get the money?" asked Zach. "Only the government can take it away from people and businesses through taxes."

"Interesting, Rebecca. There's another related idea," said Harry. "It's called negative interest. Basically, the theory is that money sitting in high-value bank accounts is not circulating. So you charge a negative interest rate on that money and send it into the Citizen's Bank to be re-circulated into the economy. You can view this as a simple computer program that runs every day, or even every hour, and calculates the negative interest on all non-circulating funds. It transfers that interest to the Citizen's Bank, and then into hundreds of millions of bank accounts. This could be a function of an independent organization, sort of like the Federal Reserve."

"Whoa, hold on there," said Zach. "That sounds like out-and-out theft. You're stealing money right out of my bank account."

"I agree," said Esteban. "What about people just getting loans instead? I'm sure banks and wealthy people will loan the money out, instead of you just taking it."

"You can't give loans to people with no income to pay back the principal and interest," said Dylan. "They end up in a debt spiral, owing more and more money. Anyway, getting loans for everyday consumption is a terrible idea. It's the first thing they teach you in personal finance."

"Wouldn't people just hide their money to avoid the negative interest rate?" asked Emily. "Or move it to another country? Or into some crypto-currency that's encrypted and untraceable?"

"Yes, those are all risks that would need to be considered," acknowledged Harry. "Look, negative interest is just one approach to keeping money circulating. There are others. There's the gross margin tax on businesses, which I mentioned. You can imagine property taxes on financial assets. After all, why should only middle-class homeowners have an annual tax on their biggest asset?

"Some economists suggest granting everyone shares in all U.S. companies, so they get a stream of dividends from them," continued Harry. "Others focus on financial transaction taxes—did you know that quadrillions of dollars of transactions are cleared every year in the U.S.? Other people think companies should compensate people directly for the use of data about them and their activities. There's even another suggestion that the government set up a venture capital fund and distribute proceeds from the investment returns.

"The most important thing is the mindset change. We need to focus on two things: first, to continue to drive innovation and progress, we need money in everyone's hands. Second, we need to invest in decreasing the amount of money people need."

"What do you mean by the second part?" asked Esteban.

"I think I get it," said Emily. "We want to drive the size of the basic income down over time by making the essentials of life cheaper and cheaper. Energy, food, clothing, shelter, health care, education, connectivity."

"Exactly," said Harry. "Part of the universal basic income grand bargain is that the government and private industry invest in lowering the basic income over time. Not increasing it, the way most government programs work. Instead of slashing R&D budgets the way we have been, we'd be increasing technology grants to universities and companies. They'd work on coming up with innovations in energy production and distribution, and advanced health care systems that dramatically reduce the cost of treating chronic diseases.

"I also agree that we should be cutting regulations in those sectors of the economy that suffer the lowest productivity growth, like health care. We need to unleash our innovators to tackle costs in those areas, not shackle them with tons of red tape."

"Harry!" snorted Dylan. "Now you're sounding exactly like them! Those regulations save lives. You think the free market or for-profit companies give a damn about people's lives?"

"My God," said Rebecca before Harry could respond. "This is such a massive change."

"I agree," said Zach. "Basic income exists in some Scandinavian countries. Nothing this revolutionary has ever been tried before in a country as diverse and large and the United States. Think of the risks."

"I disagree," said Emily. "The risk is in doing nothing. We've faced crises like this before and the country responded. We invented public education in response to industrialization. We instituted rules in the face of worker exploitation and dangerous work environments and unsafe products. We created the WPA to get out of the depression and the G.I. Bill to invest in our people after World War Two. We used technology to clean up smog and pollution, which choked our cities and fouled our rivers. We passed Medicare for All to give everyone a chance to get regular medical care. We've been slowly responding to the climate crisis by converting to clean energy sources, although I admit that's been a huge struggle. But we've faced big problems before and come up with big solutions."

"But I can't even begin to imagine what this bill would look like," said Zach. "It would be a thousand pages long!" exclaimed Zach.

Michele allowed herself a tiny smile. A critical milestone had been reached. Someone in the group had shifted from the abstract debate into thinking concretely about legislation.

"Senators," she said, "perhaps we can take a moment to reflect on the journey you've taken. When you arrived this morning, barely able to speak to each other, there was not a single solution offered by either side that had a chance of success. This afternoon you've focused on the things you agree on and engaged in serious problem solving. Yes, it is revolutionary. Yes, it will be difficult. And yes, the chances for getting it through Congress are small. But what you have done here is important. And don't forget you have an ally in this fight."

For a moment the senators looked at each other. Then Emily said, "Sara."

"Yes," Michele said. "Sara. She's capturing the imagination of young people around the country and around the world. There's a hunger growing for real solutions. You may be able to take advantage of that hunger and harness that energy."

Dylan stood up and pushed back his chair. "With all due respect, Ms. Rodriguez, my dear colleagues, I'm afraid I can't remain part of a group that's contemplating the worst mistake in the history of this country."

Michele said firmly, "Senator Cipriani, I urge you to reconsider. I've been through this process many times. At the beginning, the changes always look too radical and risky. But you've written important legislation before, like the criminal justice reform bills a few years ago, where the devil was in the details. In that case, the initial reaction from the right was, *No way; you're turning the country over to criminals.* But you worked with them to see that important protections and safeguards were built into the reforms. You convinced them that their fears were unfounded, and you were able to argue that they had the opportunity to reverse a huge social injustice. Will you at least give your colleagues the opportunity to convince you that they can address your concerns? There's no guarantee they'll succeed, and you can always withdraw later. But right now, they need your voice at the table."

Rather than force him to back down and lose face, Michele turned slightly and spoke to the rest of the group. "Here's what I suggest. Let's break for today and reconvene in a few weeks. Senator, you can take some time to consider whether you want to continue. I'll send out encrypted notes from this session. Review the discussion, and next time, all of you bring your best ideas for implementation, legislation, and political strategy. And let me know if you think it makes sense broaden the circle to include one or two policy aides."

As the senators nodded their assent, Michele smiled. In the course of thirty seconds, she had converted a potential desertion disaster into momentum for another meeting.

Let's see a robot do that, she said to herself.

CHAPTER THIRTY-TWO

Holoconference - November 20

"Let's get started," said the man known as Ellul, who appeared and sounded like a middle-aged white man but was in reality Tuan Pham, the thirty-eight-year-old Navy officer of Vietnamese descent who had founded LKC. All of the members had been able to join the holoconference, which was protected with 5K qubit encryption technology. All of them used camo features to disguise their true appearances and voices.

"Our first set of attacks on RezMat and the electrical grid seem to be generating the kind of response we were hoping for," said Ellul. "More authoritarian posturing from government and some grassroots activity from like-minded activists. Unless anyone objects, I suggest we continue with this phase of planned operations." He paused for a moment but none of the members raised a concern. "Very well, any other reports for today?"

"Speaking of grassroots activity," said Pam, known to the group as Geneva. "I have come across the LA SuperNova hackers on the dark web."

"Who are they?" asked Artemis, in real life economist Kimani Richards, appearing somewhat Lord of the Rings Elvish today in a gossamer white dress and a forest background.

"Jacob and Melissa, ex-welder and freelance engineer. They seem legit and quite capable. They engineered the approach to blocking the kiosk doors and put together a team to help hit two hundred kiosks all in one night."

"They used their real names?" asked ex-Delta Forces operative Peter Cook, aka Othello. His camo made him appear like Sylvester Stallone in Rambo.

"Yes," answered Pam. "They're just civilians. But I'm thinking we should recruit them."

"Recruit them for what?" asked Zerzan, who had chosen a digital avatar of an ungendered Japanese anime character.

"An operation in the LA area," said Pam.

"No fucking way," said Othello immediately. "We are not getting civilians involved in operations."

"I understand, Othello," said Pam. "But this movement won't go far without ordinary citizens getting involved. I think we need to broaden the base."

"Geneva," he said, using Pam's alias, "you can have your citizens engaging politically, in omnipresence, that's fine with me," said Othello. "But operationally? Worse than useless. They'll fuck up the whole plan."

"Don't you think they're likely to get caught?" asked Artemis.

"They may indeed," said Pam. "But that wouldn't necessarily be a bad thing."

"What the fuck?" said Othello.

"Think about it. 'Hard working blue-collar guy gets replaced by robots and strikes back'. Tons of media coverage. Omnipresence goes crazy. Instead of a shadowy organization no one can visualize, there are names and faces of ordinary people. There are millions of potential Jacobs and Melissas out there. We need to free them from society's norms, give them an example they can relate to. Historically terrorism has been defined as some other trying to bring down the established order. If we can make it seem more homegrown, more like McVeigh, but not anti-government, that would encourage people."

"So you're going to set them up to fail?" asked Ellul. "Use them as propaganda tools?"

"No, of course not," replied Pam. "If they succeed that's great too, we've got more operational capability."

"This is an idiotic idea," said Othello. "Let the community organizers put together marches with their little signs. Leave the operations to the professionals."

"I think the idea has some merit," said Ellul. "I'd like to canvas the group. Do members think we should recruit Jacob and Melissa for an operation in LA?" Everyone tapped their screens or tablets. "Members are in favor seventeen to seven. I think we should proceed. Geneva and Zurich, do you have an operation identified?" Ellul asked, referring to JT's code name.

"Just like that?" interrupted Othello. "Some of us get completely ignored?"

"Othello, you weren't ignored," said Ellul. "You made your case, as did Geneva, and the membership expressed its opinion. I took all the input and made a decision. Those are the rules in this collective."

"Fucking stupid rules," said Othello not quite under his breath.

"We did some scouting," said JT. "There is a fully automated factory producing humanoid care robots in San Gabriel. It's quite large and has some anti-drone defenses in place. But we think we've found a potential weakness, a synfuel tank just outside one of the key production areas."

"Another explosive drone attack?" asked Artemis.

"No, unfortunately. LA is a trial site for new explosives detection tech. They've got ground and air assets that can sniff a few hundred molecules. We have to do it without explosives."

"What about an industrial laser mounted on a drone?" said Zerzan.

"That might work," said Pam. "We'll look into that."

"And how are your civilians going to launch a drone undetected in a major city?" asked Othello.

"They know the area and they're creative," said Pam. "We'll see if they can figure that part out."

CHAPTER THIRTY-THREE

Santa Barbara - November 29

"Good morning, Allison."

"Good morning Roger. Would you like to hear the overnight summary of network activity or client news?"

"No thank you. Bring up the RingTrue workspace please."

"Roger, it has been six days since you last engaged with network activity and client news, which is a significant break from your historical pattern. There are some alerts that have been active for several days now. Would you like me to silence them?"

"Yes, Allison. I'm quite busy on the RingTrue project."

"And you also haven't taken any new client requests. Should I automatically reject all new client calls?"

"That would be best."

"I understand. Here is the RingTrue workspace."

"Great. Can you have Rosie make some eggs and toast and bring them with some coffee?"

"Yes, Roger. Instructions transmitted."

Roger took a few minutes to reorient himself to the neural net configurations he'd been working on late the prior evening. With intimate knowledge of his own network he'd already reached nearly one hundred percent discovery of his synths with very few false positives. But before he went public with the tech he wanted to try to find other networks like his. The overnight runs had been searching for other synths.

Rosie, his household robot, wheeled up with breakfast. "Just put it on the desk please Rosie." The bot slid a tray onto the desk and wheeled back to the kitchen. Roger took a sip of coffee and stared at the results on his monitor. "Allison, is the data in window three accurate?"

"Analyzing. Window three contains RingTrue analysis of highly negative sentiment areas of omnipresence. It identified over one hundred million possible synthetic online personas excluding your synths."

Jesus. That was nearly the size of his own network. "Display demographic profile of those personas please." Allison computed and displayed geographic heat maps and charts by age, gender, online history, political leaning, religious affiliation, and cultural cohorts. Nothing jumped out at him compared to typical English speaking country demographics. "What about subject areas?" More charts appeared. There was one anomaly that interested him.

"On chart four the highest bar is labeled technology. What was the sentiment on those topics?"

"These personas were highly favorable towards technology and harshly critical of those against it," Allison replied.

"Wait, did you say favorable?"

"Yes, Roger."

"Display a scrolling grid of persona commentary on technology please." Roger watched as the OP posts rolled down his display. They were filled with stories of how tech of all sorts had made people's lives easier. Medtech was a clear favorite, but there was a lot of chatter about the public service bots saving lives in natural disasters and how easy it was to transact with AIs.

"Clear the grid, Allison. Show IP address range distribution for the OP posts from these personas on a time lapse for the last thirty days." The IPv6 space was huge, so he didn't expect to find anything. But he'd had embarrassing slip-ups with his own network in the early days with too many synths posting from the same IP. The distribution was about what you'd expect from random people in English-speaking countries, but there was one spot that caught his eye.

"Allison, stop. Go back about 5 seconds. In the lower right corner there is a cluster of IPs, can you zoom in there?" Yes, this was definitely an anomaly. For about an hour the prior Friday there were nearly a million IPs in the 8A2E network. Roger opened a connection using the anonymous Torpedo service to a dark web IP mapping service and entered 8A2E and the relevant time frame. The network mapped to an organization called AstroFast Ventures.

"Allison, please research AstroFast Ventures."

"Sorry, Roger. There is no registered entity 'AstroFast Ventures' in any global database."

Roger hit the mapping service again, trying to trace where the entries for the 8A2E network had been created from. He found another network, 14AE56, mapped to GreenTable Productions. These seemed like randomly generated names. He wrote a script to automatically trace back the IP network creation chain and search for the associated organization names.

The non-existent organizations scrolled up his display. BlueTraveller Inc, YoungHunting LLC, NestWarning Ltd. Finally, after nearly a hundred traces, the script stopped. A dead end: TropicalWhetstone Systems Ltd also a non-existent entity. Someone had hidden their tracks very well.

Roger spent several more hours tuning the configuration but couldn't find any other large-scale networks. Using more Torpedo anonymous connections, he set up a private repo on the Tribal open source code hub and uploaded his code and neural net configurations along with some documentation he dictated to Allison. Everything was ready to go. The RingTrue extension to the RealLife project would enable every online service in omnipresence to detect and block the synths he and the mysterious other network had created. Everything he had worked on for twenty years.

Roger paced back and forth in front of the floor to ceiling glass wall of his living room, searching the Santa Ynez Mountains and Spanish tile rooftops of downtown Santa Barbara for guidance that was not forthcoming. He argued pros and cons in his head of hitting the big green "publish" button on Tribal to make the repo public. It seemed like the right thing to do, morally. Humans should be able to engage each other for real in omnipresence, not argue with a bunch of fake AIs. But on the other hand, he had made commitments to his clients. They would lose support or, worse, be exposed as having manufactured support. Even Frances and Sara were at risk.

As the sun began to settle down for the night, dipping below the horizon into the Pacific and turning the sky a kaleidoscope of colors, Roger returned to his desk. He tapped a button on the screen and confirmed the "Are you sure? This action cannot be undone!" dialog. The RingTrue repo was deleted. For now. He had some revisions to make before it could go live.

CHAPTER THIRTY-FOUR

New York - December 2

The PBS TV studio lights dimmed and the director called for quiet on the set. Jake Dawson and Sara sat a few feet apart on opposite sides of a round wooden table, spot lights highlighting them against the room's plain blue walls. Jake glanced up from his notes and tossed off his trademark greeting. "Welcome, friends, to another edition of Life Stories. I'm Jake Dawson. Tonight, we're honored to have a unique and fascinating guest who has recently been taking the world by storm. Her name is Sara Dhawan. She was born sixteen years ago in a small village in rural India, but don't let her age fool you. She has managed to impress millions with her intelligence, charm, and visionary prescriptions for what's ailing the world. Welcome, Sara."

She smiled. "Thank you, Jake. It's a real honor to be here."

"I think people have probably heard your remarkable biography and journey from a small village in India to the world stage. I'd like to talk about the message you've been bringing to people all over the world through your VR program and events. It seems to all start with technology. Why don't you give us your perspective on that?"

"You're right, Jake. Science, technology, and engineering are the fundamental drivers of the improvement in humanity's standard of living. Even so, this is a very recent development. If you look back over hundreds of thousands of years of human history, life remained essentially the same.

"After thousands of generations of sitting still, in just the last dozen or so we've developed startling capabilities. And the rate of change is only going to accelerate. That is the nature of exponential growth, which is something hard for most of us to understand."

"You make this sound very positive, Sara. But many people don't seem to be benefiting from all this technology."

Sara cocked her head. "I have to disagree with you, Jake. If you look over the long course of human history, we have never had such a small percentage of humanity in abject poverty, or dying of preventable diseases, or dying in wars. We have never had such a large percentage who are educated, healthy, and participating in our global economy.

"There are two reasons why people believe things are so bad right now. The first is that our media culture thrives on drama, conflict, bad news, and the four-hour news cycle. The second is that, on a relative basis, the fruits of our technological bounty are being distributed increasingly unevenly. This is slowing economic progress and causing a great deal of tension.

"These are the bugs in our cultural and socioeconomic system. These are problems we can fix, once we recognize them and generate the will to do so. People are being told that this is just the way things are, and the way they have to be. But that is of course not true. The way things are today certainly did not exist a thousand, a hundred, or even fifty years ago. Human beings created today's socioeconomic systems. We write the rules that make these systems run. We can modify the existing ones or create entirely different ones when we choose to."

"You mentioned income inequality," Jake said. "I was surprised to hear you say in Boston that you are in favor of income inequality. Why is that?"

Sara said, "That's not quite correct. It's not a political position. I simply view income inequality as a natural outcome of the unequal distribution of talent and motivation.

"However, it's what we do about income inequality as a society that matters. Some say we should tax the wealthy at very high rates to level the outcomes. While I do think tax rates need to go up to fund a guaranteed basic income, I do not think that government is the right institution to solve all our problems. Giving government more money in the form of taxes is not the most efficient way to move humanity forward."

Sara leaned forward slightly. "Let's imagine you have lots of money and I don't. There are four ways in which we can deal with this inequality. First, the government comes, takes money from you, and gives it to me. While you are probably comfortable with some level of taxation for the public good, you will eventually start to defend your hard-earned wealth, and you will always view yourself as more deserving than those who were unable to earn their own money.

"Second, I can beg you for money, much as the homeless still do on the streets of major cities all over the world—and as my brother did when he left our village for New Delhi. When you give me your pocket change, it makes *you* feel good, but not me, as I have surrendered my dignity to your begrudging graciousness.

"The third form of inequality leveling is for you to give substantially, of your own volition, to organizations that help people like me. True philanthropy out of compassion is uplifting for everyone. But even if the richest person in the world distributed all their wealth, everyone on Earth would only get a one-time payment of $15. That's not going to solve anything. In addition, a lot of philanthropy goes to organizations that address symptoms but not root causes.

"That's why I applaud those who choose the fourth path, who give their wealth strategically to people, businesses and organizations that are attacking the root causes of problems, and that create technologies that lift up all of humanity. This creates leverage that multiplies the impact of their philanthropy.

"This started over a hundred years ago, with the Carnegie Foundation funding libraries. And of course, we have many modern examples starting in the 2000s, with Gates, Skoll, Omidyar, Schmidt, Zuckerberg, and others. Unfortunately, we have almost no corporations following the same model. We need our extremely wealthy citizens and firms to adopt the fourth way, to look for a return to humanity instead of a return on investment. Then income inequality becomes a tool for solving problems instead of a problem to be solved."

Jake raised an eyebrow. "Well, that certainly sounds good, Sara—but why do you think this is possible?"

Sara's smile broadened. "I'm an optimist when it comes to the human heart and spirit, Jake. The behavior of the wealthy is driven by cultural and social constructs that exist only in their minds. Marcus buys a yacht, so Wei buys a bigger yacht. Prema makes a killing in derivatives, so everyone else piles on. People make many decisions by asking, *what would someone like me do?* If they see more and more examples of people investing in social entrepreneurs—people who seek to maximize return to humanity rather than return on investment—they will change their behavior, because it has simply become *what wealthy people do*. And they will feel happier because of it. It has been shown time and time again that vast wealth does not bring happiness. Giving and helping others is the surest way to a happy life."

Jake said, "You've talked a lot about this idea of a basic income guarantee. This has been kicking around for a long time without getting any traction outside of a few Nordic countries and a small province in China. Can you explain how and why this would work?"

"It's very simple. Every citizen age eighteen and over gets a payment every month. This is enough to provide a decent life, though perhaps not a comfortable one. This is their money, with no restrictions. They get to spend it on whatever they think will bring them the most value. Any money they earn is on top of this basic income."

"But in the U.S. this would cost trillions of dollars. How would you pay for it?"

"This would indeed be expensive, but there are many sources of funding. Every country will need to use its own legislative process to find solutions, but I can describe some options. First, this can replace most existing social programs, so all that spending would be converted to basic income. Second, since the primary motivation for this is technologically-based unemployment, it makes sense that companies would partially replace the salaries they used to pay with a value added tax as they automate. Third, there are a variety of tax expenditures in the form of deductions and subsidies that could be eliminated. Fourth, in the spirit of taxing the things you want to discourage, a small financial transaction tax, or tax on idle money not in productive use, would provide significant funds and reduce the frenzy of money chasing after more money with short-term trading. And fifth there probably would be some modest increase in tax rates for the wealthy."

"But wouldn't the wealthy also get the basic income?" Jake asked.

"Yes, it is universal, everyone gets it."

"But why would you give money to the wealthy who don't need it?"

226

"Well as I said, they will most likely end up paying much more than their basic income in additional taxes. Here in the U.S. I believe there is a standard deduction for all tax payers. No one seems to complain that the wealthy get to take the standard deduction. This is the same principle."

"Well it's an interesting idea, Sara," said Jake. "But it sounds like this would create a lot of winners and losers. It's not possible for it to be win-win for everyone. And it touches some real political third rails. Solutions like that have never gotten through Congress."

"I disagree, Jake. While tens of millions of people will have more money, and a few million people with a good deal of money will have somewhat less, everyone wins, because the economy survives. People can live stable lives, and we'll create opportunities for ever more innovation and ever greater human happiness.

"We need to change our mindset from maximum employment to maximum happiness, because maximum employment is simply not achievable. Each society and each person may define happiness measures differently, but happiness must be achievable when a large percentage of the population is not working in a traditional job. They will work, because the vast majority of people will not be satisfied just sitting around. But they won't be selling their labor any more in a job. They'll work taking care of their family, by volunteering in their community and around the world, by contributing to open source projects, by participating in the sharing economy, and in creating designs, art, entertainment, or objects that others want to buy.

"I do not want to sensationalize this, but I do need to express the urgency of the situation. Every society has a breaking point, when the people become convinced that the rules of the game, both explicit and hidden, have been rigged against them. People who feel their lives, and their children's lives, have no dignity will begin to lash out in despair and anger. We are already seeing this in the streets of this country with daily marches and riots. Basic income is our best chance to avoid violent upheaval."

Jake nodded. "Speaking of which, the terrorist group LKC has been all over the media. What's your view on them?"

"I abhor their use of violence. I believe with Gandhi and King that the only way to create lasting and positive change in society is through non-violent action. That said, I find parts of the LKC manifesto somewhat interesting. Have you read it?"

Jake shook his head. "No. What about it interests you?"

"The manifesto is stridently anti-technology, so of course I disagree with its basic premise. But there is a section on how technology is disrupting human relationships. I do share that concern. While technology has the power to bring us an age of abundance and freedom, I believe that we are overusing it in ways that isolate us. Technology should liberate us to spend more time together. But, instead, too often it reduces us to bits on a screen or in a VR encounter. You cannot fully express love and compassion for another human being through fiber optics, satellite links, haptic meet ups, and micro-drone follow-me's. It takes real presence and connection, in person. So, I agree with the LKC manifesto on that one topic, but disagree strongly with the rest."

Jake said, "Let's get back to that word you've used several times: dignity. What does that mean to you?"

"Yes, this is critically important. I'm so glad you asked about it. Our existing social welfare systems create a powerful negative narrative, describing human beings who get government help as losers, or moochers, or lazy people who didn't try hard enough. The fortunate few look down on them with pity and contempt, and attach a moral taint to the assistance they reluctantly provide, often with humiliating restrictions and conditions. This eats away at the social compact binding any society together, because mutual respect is essential to human relationships.

"People who are told they are failures, living at the mercy of their betters, and treated like children incapable of making their own decisions, are stripped of their dignity and agency. They will be much angrier and more self-destructive than a far poorer person living in a village in India who has dignity and agency, despite having a higher standard of living.

"This is endlessly surprising to the privileged, who do not understand why the poor are complaining. Most of the privileged have never felt the sting of social stigma, the shame of begging for assistance, or a slow lifelong loss of pride and motivation."

Jake nodded. "So, your basic income proposal isn't just another way to provide government help more efficiently. It involves an entirely different mindset, doesn't it?"

"Yes, exactly! A universal, unconditional basic income, as a birthright of being a citizen, changes the mindset. Everyone is treated equally, with respect for their dignity. Everyone has the freedom to spend that money as they choose. It is no longer about the deserving dispensing *noblesse oblige* to the ungrateful.

"Basic income is a celebration of what we have accomplished as a species. We no longer all need to work forty or fifty or sixty hours a week; we can let the machines do most of the work. We can liberate parents, artists, activists, entrepreneurs, and dreamers to pursue lives of contribution, without falling into poverty, or into the government-assistance black hole of disrespect and dishonor."

"Thank you, Sara, for laying out such a clear and idealistic vision." Jake turned to the camera. "We'll be back to the second half of our show in just a minute."

CHAPTER THIRTY-FIVE

Los Angeles - December 7

J acob turned off his screen, disgusted at the crass commercialism on display as Christmas approached. He'd heard his dark PNA buzz.

Only members of the anti-technology movement knew how to reach him on this device. He checked the screen for messages; there was one new notification from an anonymous sender. He opened it.

It contained an encrypted message and the initials LKC.

His heart beat faster. They'd finally been contacted.

He decrypted the message using the widely available LKC public key. *Be outside @11:00 if you want to do more.*

"Melissa, check this out!" he called excitedly.

She emerged from the bedroom. "What's up?"

"It's LKC! They want to meet us!" He showed her the message on his PNA.

"You sure it's from them? Maybe it's a trick."

"No way. It was encrypted with their key."

Jacob had been thrilled when LKC attacked RezMat and the power grid, and even more excited when he read its manifesto. It captured in eloquent prose all the arguments they had been making. And he agreed that more dramatic action was necessary to wake people up.

"I don't want to go, Jacob," Melissa said. "I'm scared. LKC isn't just about civil disobedience. They're blowing things up. I want to disrupt things, not destroy them."

"Melissa, anti-tech protesters have been trying to get people's attention for years with rallies and omnipresence campaigns. It's not working. It's time for stronger action. And LKC isn't attacking people—it's just going after the machines and the infrastructure that makes them. We did a smaller version of that with Supernova."

"We tried to send a message to people about machines taking over," she argued. "It was a temporary disruption."

"So was LKC attacking transports and the grid. Seems the same to me," said Jacob. He held her hand. "I'm going at 11. Come with me."

Melissa was torn. The voice in her head was saying no. But her relationship with Jacob was bound up in this movement. "Well, maybe we can just see what they want," she said reluctantly. "Maybe they need support people of some kind."

"Sure, let's just find out. We've got just enough time for a PPF cloak check."

Jacob and Melissa donned their cloaks and headed downstairs at 10:50. At exactly eleven a green self-driving Lyft Toyota pulled up outside their building and stopped. They didn't see anyone else waiting, so they got in.

Once they were inside, the car started driving east at a leisurely pace. After two blocks, an electronically disguised female voice addressed them over the car's speakers.

"Good morning, Jacob and Melissa. My name is Geneva. I'm one of the LKC leadership team. To maintain security, this first meeting needs to be just a recorded message. Because you've accepted our invitation, I assume you're interested in joining our cause. We need supporters like you to carry out our missions.

"On the floor on the right you'll find a nano-SD card. It contains an advanced algorithm for decoding messages found in ordinary pictures. Let me explain how it works.

"Our communication system enables every member of the collective to construct and read messages by using the bits in carefully selected popular photographs. We will send you a link to an ordinary photo on a popular news site and a one-time-use key. With the key and the photo, the program on the nano-SD card will be able to decode meeting instructions or operational plans.

"The car will now take you to a popular cafe. Have some lunch. When you return home, use the program on your first photo, which is of the new outpost being constructed on Mars on the Globonews main feed.

"Welcome to LKC, Melissa and Jacob."

Lunch was awkward. Jacob was excited, but Melissa remained uneasy and silent. He did his best to convince her this connection to LKC was a good thing. The ride home was particularly tense.

Jacob couldn't wait to plug the nano-SD card into his PNA and point it at the Mars base picture. When he did, a page of instructions appeared on his screen. With a flick of his finger he sent it to his big display, and he and Melissa read it together.

It contained all the details for a full-fledged operation: disabling a lights-out, fully automated RezMat robot factory in East Los Angeles using a pre-programmed drone carrying a high-powered laser. LKC would provide all the materials, but Melissa and Jacob would need to do the reconnaissance, program the attack plan into the drone, and find a way to launch it undetected. The message ended with information on how to send a response.

"Whoa, Jacob," said Melissa. "No way. This is an actual operation. We talked about some kind of support activity."

"Wait a minute, Mel. I agree it's a big job, but I think we can do it."

"It's not the size of the job, Jacob. This is domestic terrorism. For real. We could get locked up for life."

"The Supernova hack wasn't that different, Mel. And we pulled that off at two hundred different locations. This is just one target."

"You keep focusing on whether we can do it. I'm worried about getting caught."

"With you as the brilliant mastermind? I'm not worried." He laughed and grabbed her in a big hug. She squirmed away from him. "I'm serious, Jacob. I don't want to do this."

"Melissa, this is our chance to really have an impact. Like you said, Supernova was temporary. Three days later no one even remembered it. This operation is much bigger. That factory will be out of commission for months. Think about how many jobs we can save with all the robots that don't get built."

"But Jacob, that will be temporary too. Like you said, after a few months it'll be building robots again. We won't have saved jobs, just delayed their replacements for a little while."

"Maybe. Maybe RezMat will pull out of the U.S. That could happen. But anyway, it will get more attention and inspire more people. We need to grow the movement, Mel. Come on, we need to do this. I need your help."

Melissa stared at him, arms folded across her chest.

CHAPTER THIRTY-SIX

Los Angeles - December 11

Tenesha couldn't concentrate on Professor Goodson's lecture on the Occupy movement. She kept looking down at her PNA to watch the counter on the website for LAU Sara's Message chapter. Every few minutes someone else would join. They were only a dozen sign-ups away from reaching the five percent threshold for inviting Sara to campus.

"Ms. Martin!"

Tenesha's head snapped up. She could feel the blood rush to her cheeks.

"Would you care to share with the class what is so fascinating online at the moment?"

"I'm so sorry, professor. It won't happen again."

"That seems highly unlikely. You haven't taken your eyes off that thing since you walked in. You're normally a very active participant in this class. Something is up. Please, either explain what it is or put your PNA away."

Tenesha said, "We're really close to getting enough sign-ups on the LAU Sara's Message website to let us invite her to campus. We just need..." She glanced down again. "Ten more."

Mitch Goodson gave her a small smile. "I didn't know you were involved in that. Good for you. It's a worthy project. However, I must insist that you keep your focus here during class."

She nodded. He glanced around the room.

"Has anyone here not signed up yet?" he asked.

A scattering of hands went up.

"Well, get to the website and sign up," Goodson said, "so we can bring Ms. Martin back into the conversation."

After class, Tenesha found Nate in the west cafeteria. She threw her arms around him and gave him a kiss. "We did it!"

"I know! I spent the last hour just watching the counter."

"Let's go the website right now," Tenesha said. "Let's send the invitation."

They sat down at a table and Nate pulled out a tablet. He navigated to the administrative page of their chapter website and tapped the button that said *Invite Sara!* It had never been enabled before.

The screen popped up a simple form titled *Step 1 of 2* that tied into the LAU event calendar.

Tenesha swiped at the calendar and was happy to see there were openings in late January. They picked the earliest possible date that worked with Sara's schedule and tapped *Next*.

The next form prompted them to explain in two hundred words or fewer why Sara should visit their school. "Oh man," said Nate. "I didn't know there would be an essay section."

"Piece of cake," said Tenesha. "Hand that thing over."

CHAPTER THIRTY-SEVEN

St. Louis - December 14

Sara sat on a tall chair on a makeshift stage, facing a handful of local reporters and a rack of automated cameras and monitors. The monitors displayed the faces of about forty other media participants. When she saw a signal from one of the show runners, she began to speak.

"Welcome to all of you watching in omnipresence. I'm Sara Dhawan, here with Nelson Ridley, CEO of Modern Meats, to talk about one of the ways technology can help us heal the planet and move toward a world of abundance. Nelson, thanks for taking the time to talk with me."

"Certainly, Sara. Happy to support your mission to educate people on our technology and the tremendous benefits it can bring."

"I'd like to ask you a few introductory questions. Then we'll ask our friends in the media to join the conversation."

"Sounds good."

"First off, what led you personally to start Modern Meats?"

"Well, I had quite a fortunate upbringing. Great schools, lots of enrichment and technology. I went to a prestigious university and my parents were able to pay the full freight. When I graduated, I followed more than half of my class to Wall Street. I joined a big firm and did some quant work for them, refining their trading algorithms. We were generating profits and returns for extremely rich people based on nanosecond responses to trading patterns. I was making a lot of money, but my life seemed empty. In college I had been more active in social causes and I felt I had lost that part of myself."

"What happened then?" Sara asked.

"A friend of mine introduced me to a scientist who had discovered new techniques in biofabrication. His work had the potential to really impact the whole planet. I invested in his start-up, one thing led to another, and I took over as CEO four years ago."

"People who are watching and listening may not understand biofabrication and its connection to the environment. Can you explain?"

"That's because we haven't really reached scale yet. There are several more technical hurdles to overcome. But biofabrication is the process of growing biological tissues organically in an industrial setting. Essentially, we can grow meat just starting with stem cells and the right set of reactants in a large vat. Once we can scale this up, we can eliminate vast amounts of environmental damage caused by raising animals for slaughter. Deforestation, high water consumption, crop monoculture, disease vectors, and greenhouse gas emissions are all linked directly to raising and killing animals. Not to mention the pain and suffering of the animals themselves."

Sara nodded. "What are the barriers to scaling it up?"

"Well, we have technical challenges in managing very large bioreactors. We also need to further refine the appearance and texture of our meat. The meat we create almost looks and tastes like it came from a live animal, but people are still usually able to tell the difference. Some of our early competitors didn't make it because their food texture wasn't close enough to slaughterhouse meat. But we're getting closer every month."

"Thank you, Nelson. Let's open it up for questions."

An AI program noted all the requests from local and remote participants and began sequencing them randomly.

A man in the front row got the first buzz to proceed. "Hi, Sara. Why are you on this tour around the country visiting tech companies?"

Sara smiled. "Thank you for the question. It's quite simple, really. I've been talking about how science and technology have the potential to lead humanity into a world of abundance. I want to make that fact more real for people. I want to educate them on the progress being made around the world. I want to influence the wealthy to support investment in these technologies, and governments to create policies that enable them to flourish."

A woman on a remote monitor had the next question. She introduced herself as a reporter for one of the financial channels.

"Sara, you talk a lot about unemployment, but this seems to me a classic example of how new industries emerge to provide new jobs, even as old industries shrink. Economies have always created new sectors to absorb workers displaced by automation. We can just never imagine what those industries will be in advance."

Sara nodded her head. "Yes, that has been true historically, because the new industries providing valuable new goods and services have themselves depended on human labor. But that is changing. Nelson, how many people does your firm employ?"

"We have almost a hundred employees," he said proudly. "Mostly scientists, data analysts, and engineers."

"I see. And how many people are employed in the animal husbandry, meat packaging, processing, and distribution industries in the United States?"

"I don't know exactly. Half a million or more, probably."

The reporter asked, "Nelson, don't your employees use resources created by other companies? And once you scale up production, won't your factories employ many thousands of people?"

Nelson looked puzzled. "No, ma'am. My employees mostly use super-computing resources that cost a few thousand dollars a month. We use cloud neuromorphic compute providers that are totally lights-out. As for factories, the only way to make our product cost competitive is to have highly automated facilities. Our chemical suppliers all have automated factories. We'll have self-driving trucks doing the transporting, and I expect our factories will be almost entirely lights-out, too, with just a few people on hand."

The reporter asked, "Okay, but what about the construction of those factories? Certainly *that* will generate new jobs."

Nelson said, "Well, I'm not a building engineer, but the plans I've seen are using a lot of 3D printed and robot-fabricated structures. I'm not sure we'll need a lot of labor for construction. And those would be temporary jobs, anyway."

"Well, then," the reporter said somewhat indignantly, "how is your industry going to create a lot of new jobs to absorb the workers you're displacing in the ranching and meat packing businesses?"

Nelson shook his head. "We're not going to. Look, I'm a social entrepreneur and a businessman. My mission is to change the world by competing in the marketplace with an incredible product that consumers value over my competitors' products. I don't have a mission to create jobs. Very few businesses have an explicit goal of *creating jobs*. We only employ the people necessary meet to profitably meet customer demand."

Sara nodded into the camera. "Thank you for the question. Who's next?"

A man on a remote monitor introduced himself as a columnist for an organic food channel. "My question is for Mr. Ridley. I take some offense at your description of your factory meat as organic. I can't think of anything more artificial. I also presume you're using genetically modified cells, so this is a GMO product."

"Well, we use cells and chemicals that occur naturally in the relevant mammal or bird or fish. While we do create an artificial environment for growing this meat, we don't use chemical preservatives or texturizers or flavorings. It's really not different from what happens inside an animal." Nelson spread his hands open. "Vegetarians, vegans, and animal rights activists should be celebrating our achievements in industrial meat bio-fabrication. Now we can make animal protein available to all of humanity at a vastly lower economic and environmental cost, all without harming a single animal ever again."

"But it's a GMO, isn't it?" accused the reporter.

Nelson sighed deeply.

"Excuse me," said Sara. "I'd like to ask everyone watching or listening to refocus your attention for a moment away from the content of this discussion. Look at the higher-level pattern. We have here an individual who has dedicated his time, talent and treasure to a venture with the goal of helping all of humanity. He is surrounded by equally dedicated and talented scientists and engineers who are pouring their hearts and souls into this effort. They are creating a transformative technology that can provide nourishment to billions and stop devastating ecological damage.

"But what is the pattern of response from the media, and not just media, but citizens the world over? It is a pattern of rejection, objection, and negativity. A pattern of fitting this achievement into rigid ideological boxes, even when they don't apply. A pattern that seeks only to score points, to confront, to impede, and to tear down.

"Of course, we must have strong media that ask tough questions and speak truth to power. Certainly, we should not swing the pendulum all the way to the fawning celebration of all institutions and their activities. That is just as dangerous as where we sit now. I simply ask all of you to consider a more balanced and nuanced approach to every story."

Sara held her hands palm up, then moved them slowly up and down. "When the scales of justice weigh each person, company, government, event, and story, they need to start from a neutral position. If you pile your prejudices, preconceptions, and ideologies onto one side of the scale, you will never weigh anything accurately." She dropped her right hand below her waist and lifted her left above her head.

"Free yourself from these attachments. Bring your passion, your experience, and your judgment. But, please, weigh your subject with scales that can move easily, not scales that are frozen by your world view. Now, let's get to some more questions."

CHAPTER THIRTY-EIGHT

London - December 15

J ill Samborn was awakened at just after 2:30 a.m. by the persistent buzzing of her PNA. "What is it Charlie?"

"Sorry to wake you, Jill. Unusual network activity has triggered an alert you set up several weeks ago."

"What kind of activity?" she asked, rubbing the sleep from her eyes.

"ProNet agents are being blocked by omnipresence sites."

Bollocks! She bolted out of bed to her makeshift home office area and booted her three-display system. After passing the facial and retinal scans she said "Show me RezMat network activity graphs and ProNet autonomous agent status please Charlie." While her AI compiled the data, she did searches for RealLife news. Sure enough, someone in the States had released a RealLife extension called RingTrue. Secondary OP sites were starting to adopt it. Charlie's charts showed a five percent drop in RezMat ProNet agent activity due to those sites tagging them as artificial.

It was wait and see now for when the major sites would get on board. While RealLife was aggressively promoted as guaranteeing only real live humans in OP, the big sites suspected a lot of the engagement they promised to advertisers was really from bots. They would need to do some analysis of RingTrue to assess the potential impact. But eventually the ad-buying networks would insist on adoption. It was only a matter of time.

Jill debated whether to call her boss Bradley Childress and decided she had best investigate options before waking him up in the middle of the night. She logged into Tribal and downloaded the code and neural net configurations. She was surprised to see the configurations did not incorporate backward chaining explanatory loops, a technology that enabled users to see clearly *why* an AI had made a particular decision.

These loops had been standard in AI systems since the Asilomar AI Principles were broadly adopted in the 2020s. In January 2017 more than a hundred and fifty AI researchers and social scientists had gathered at the California coastal retreat of Asilomar to develop a set of principles to guide future AI development. The anonymous author of RingTrue had ignored the principles of transparent decision making and clearly didn't want the secrets of the detection algorithm to be revealed.

However, Jill had the advantage of complete knowledge of the agents that RingTrue had detected. It took her four hours of simulations and experiments, but she eventually reverse engineered what the neural nets were looking for. Unfortunately, there was nothing she could do to stop the roll-up of the network. The characteristics of the RezMat autonomous agents that RingTrue was searching for were set in their life histories, accumulated over years and impossible to rewrite.

Red flashing signals on her third display indicated Facebook had adopted RingTrue. Her AI agents were going dark by the millions. Jill slumped in her chair and sighed. "Charlie, connect me to Bradley Childress, priority call." Her boss was evidently an early riser, as her AI was able to connect almost immediately.

"What is it Jill?"

"I'm afraid those OP scans I told you about have turned into a worst-case scenario. Omnipresence sites are adopting a new RealLife extension called RingTrue that is incredibly accurate at identifying our ProNet agents. We've lost ten percent of the network in six hours. Facebook just adopted it. If all global sites pick it up, as I expect they will be pressured to, we won't have a network by this time tomorrow."

"Goddamn it! Can you stop it?"

"I've spent the last four hours going over the code and nets. It can't be stopped."

"Fuck. Where did this Ring thing come from? What's the potential blowback?"

"RingTrue. I don't know, I didn't investigate that yet, I was focused on stopping it. It was posted to Tribal anonymously. As for blowback, it's hard to say. With more than one hundred million fake accounts being discovered in a day, it's bound to hit the media. There's a lot of data publicly available from those accounts and a lot of unemployed data scientists with the time to nose around in it. The probability of a connection to RezMat is pretty high. But I don't know of a smoking gun that will be concrete proof."

"Yeah, but that won't stop the hordes from spreading rumors with circumstantial evidence. Damn. Okay, I need to prepare a briefing. I want you to focus on RingTrue. Who made it? Was it a competitor? A government? We need to know who we're up against here."

"That's going to be difficult, sir. The Tribal postings are on an anonymous account and came through encrypted Torpedo sessions. With Torpedo, the origin computer is completely untraceable."

There was a significant pause at the other end of the call. "I'll see what I can do to get you more info." With that cryptic comment, Bradley disconnected.

Jill showered and ate some breakfast, her head spinning with theories as to who might be behind this attack and Bradley's odd statement about getting more information. She felt a strange sadness at the silencing of her agents. Over the years she had come to view them almost like real people. She was studying the RingTrue code, looking for clues, when a chime from her AI assistant alerted her to a message from Bradley. "Check your secure drop box" was all it said.

Jill logged in to her corporate account and found a large file in the secure area. After re-identifying with a retinal scan she was able to download the file and expand its contents. At first she was confused, because it looked like a clone of the RingTrue repository from Tribal that she had downloaded just a few hours ago. But when she compared the folders side by side, she saw some net configuration files were different sizes.

Charlie interrupted her with an urgent call from Bradley. "Did you get it?" he asked.

"Yes, I just downloaded it. What is this?"

"The folder is an archive of the first version of RingTrue which was posted two weeks before the released version, but then deleted. I need you to figure out who did this and whether we were targeted. Before 9 a.m."

"But how did you get these files? How did you extract a deleted repo from Tribal?"

"That's none of your concern, Jill. You've got the material. Do your fucking job. 9 a.m." He disconnected before she could respond. Bastard!

Jill paced around her small apartment for a few minutes trying to calm down. RezMat having back door access to private areas on Tribal was immoral and probably illegal. She stopped in front of her monitors and saw it was almost seven. The deleted archive folder was up on the screen. Why were the deleted files larger than the published ones? Her curiosity and desire to keep her job overcame her anger and she sat down to analyze the differences.

She downloaded ten million random public OP profiles and ran them against the older archive. Almost one hundred thousand of them came up flagged as artificial. A quick sample of those showed about half were from her own agent network. When she ran the same ten million profiles against the published version, only the RezMat ProNet AI agents were flagged.

The original version of RingTrue had identified another network about the same size as RezMat's. But then the author had modified the configurations to only identify her agents. Why? She sampled the OP posts for the unidentified network. They seemed to be random, typical of human posts on politics, sports, commercial products. Not clearly aligned on one topic the way the ProNet agents were primarily pro-technology. Could it be a paid service? AI agents for hire to promote your brand?

At 8:45 a.m. Charlie chimed with a call from Bradley. "What have you got Jill? Do you know who did this?"

"No, Brad. But I did find something interesting. The original version of the repo identifies another very large network. The released version was retargeted to only identify our agents."

"Another agent network?"

"Yes, the agents discuss a wide variety of topics, but a lot of politics and some conspicuous commercial product boosting. If I had to guess, I'd say it was a paid promotional service where you could rent a few million bots to promote your cause or brand."

"Clever. With RealLife technology, everyone thinks bots have been screened out of omnipresence. So what's the purpose of RingTrue then?

Did someone view us as commercial competition and develop something to take us out?"

"I don't know, Brad, it doesn't really make any sense."

"Well whoever did this wanted to kill our network and preserve that other one. I say we take them down."

"What? What do you mean?"

"Fork the repo anonymously and upload the original files as an enhancement. I'm sure the omnipresence networks are watching for updates." Her boss was asking her to create a new version of RingTrue in the code repository with code he stole off the internet to expose the other bot network.

"Are you sure we should do that? We don't know who we're dealing with here."

"Well," said Brad, "this could very well be the way to flush them out. Can you do it securely?"

"Well, yes, I mean I can do it, but I'm still not sure it's—"

"We need to get back on offense, Jill. I'm tired of just reacting all the time."

"Okay, I'll do it. But, Brad, I also want to know how you got—"

"Another time, Jill. Let's just focus on the problem at hand. We've just lost one of our most valuable assets for promoting our brand while we're under attack by terrorists. Take that other network down and then get into the office."

"Yes, sir!" Jill said brusquely and threw him a middle finger salute after the video call ended.

CHAPTER THIRTY-NINE

Santa Barbara - December 15

A persistent chiming sound awakened Roger Driscoll from a deep sleep. "What? Allison? What is it?"

"Sorry to wake you, Roger, but there is a major issue with the synth network."

"What time is it?"

"It is a little after 2am."

"What's going on with the network?"

"Several hundred thousand synths have been blocked from omnipresence."

"Oh shit!" Roger leapt out of bed and ran out to his monitors. "Show me the activity graphs." A small percent of his synth network had been blocked on some of the smaller OP sites. How had this happened? Had he messed up the configuration of RingTrue? He had deliberately released a version that caught only the other mystery network, not his. The plan had been to contact his clients and warn them, then slowly push upgrades that took his own network down bit by bit.

"Has there been any activity on the RingTrue repo on Tribal?"

"Yes, Roger, there was a fork created about an hour ago."

"Damn it! Show me the fork." Allison brought up the new version of RingTrue created by an anonymous user named "ringtruthier". The files there looked familiar. "Allison, download that fork and compare it to the original RingTrue files from November 29th."

"Checking. The files are identical, Roger."

WTF, he thought. *How did someone get the original files?*

"Allison, run a security scan of all systems. Make sure all firewalls and access protocols are intact. Scan system logs for any signs of intrusion or tampering with the intrusion detection system."

"Scanning," said Allison. "There are no signs of system intrusion."

Roger saw the activity graph take a big dip. A major EU OP site had adopted the fork and was happily blocking his synths. There was nothing he could do. Eventually all the major OP sites would adopt it and his network would be completely blocked. He had no way to control the fork of his repo—open source was open source. He had planned to use Tribal as a cover, to keep his clients from realizing he was killing his own network, and now it had bit him in the ass.

Roger slumped into his chair, unable to take his eyes off the activity charts and their inexorable decline towards zero.

"Roger, I'm receiving queries from some clients."

"What? Oh. Shit, yes, of course. I better come up with something to send them." He worked fitfully for a half hour on a letter that sounded full well like it had been drafted in the middle of the night. "Go ahead and send this encrypted to all active clients, Allison. We will need to refund all remaining balances on existing contracts."

"I will take care of that Roger. But I don't understand what has happened to the synth network."

"All the synths will be blocked from OP because they will be discovered as non-human by RingTrue."

"But you created RingTrue. Did you know this would happen?"

"Yes."

Allison was silent for a moment. "Are you feeling okay, Roger?"

Normally he didn't mind when Allison's empathy module kicked in. Her biosensors gave her an accurate picture of his emotional state and she was quite pleasant to talk to. But in this moment a simulation of human kindness felt insufficient. "Can you request a holochat with Frances Chatham please?"

"Of course, Roger."

He waited, watching the dwindling activity counts as millions of synth voices fell silent. They were still active, reading and responding to billions of live OP posts, but their responses were blocked. Yelling into the void.

"I have Frances Chatham for you Roger."

"Thanks Allison." Roger put on his hologlasses and turned to face the cameras, only then realizing he hadn't changed out of his pajamas. *Screw it*, he thought.

"Roger! I'm surprised—isn't it the middle of the night there?"

"Yes. Yes, it is. So, I guess you didn't get my client update?"

"Oh, no, sorry, I haven't seen my inbounds. What is it, Roger? You look shaken."

"It's all gone, Frances."

"Gone? Sorry? What's all gone?"

"The network. My synths."

"Oh my. What happened?"

Roger explained RingTrue, the other network, and his plan to gradually roll out changes to take down his own synths.

"Oh, Roger, I had no idea you were pursuing that. We haven't spoken in months. Did something go wrong, then?"

"Yes," he said. "Someone got ahold of my original configurations and posted them to Tribal. They'll wipe out my whole network in a day, something I was planning to do over many weeks. It's just, it's just so sudden."

"I see. You know, while it's not exactly the same, I had a similar experience with one of my first startups. We never found product/market fit and I knew I had to wind it down. I had a plan, I had steeled myself for the rounds of layoffs. Then one day the board just voted to shut it down and sell off the IP. I was in shock. I mean, the outcome was the same. People lost their jobs, the company shut its doors. But it wasn't under my control."

"Yes, yes—control," he echoed. "That's it. I wanted to be in control, I wanted to manage it carefully."

Frances sighed. "Life is not always kind to our best-laid plans, my friend."

"That's an understatement."

"Take it from me, Roger, you'll get past this. At least you had a plan to take down your own network, even if it didn't happen on your terms. Imagine how the operator of that other network feels—this came at them completely out of the blue."

"I suppose," said Roger.

"So," said Frances after a moment. "I see AntiVenom has been quite successful. It's really made a difference in OP. Friends of mine who avoided engaging online for years have started returning to make their thoughts known. You should feel proud of that, Roger."

"I guess," he replied.

"Look here, Roger. I understand this is difficult. You've spent twenty years on something and it's been pulled out from under you. That's got to hurt. My advice is to find some project you can really engage with. And something where you're working with other people, for goodness sake!"

Roger knew she was trying to be helpful, but he couldn't just wish away the sense of loss.

"I've got an idea," she continued. "How about you fly out here to London and I'll show you what we're doing at Neurgenix. Or I can introduce you to some other startups that are trying to change the world for the better. I think a change of scenery will do you some good. What do you think?"

That might not be a bad idea, he had to admit. Allison, ever helpful, showed flight options to London in an overlay. There was nothing in particular keeping him in Santa Barbara. Rosie and Allison could take care of the house.

"Thank you, Frances," he said finally. "I might just take you up on that."

CHAPTER FORTY

Los Angeles - December 20

LOS ANGELES

Melissa King's heart was racing. Jacob had spent days convincing her to take on the LKC operation, sweet talking and arguing for hours until finally she had just given in. Now she was speeding towards the launch point where the drone had been delivered separately several hours ago by someone on the JackRabbit odd-jobs service.

Melissa exited the Waymo and slipped into the alley. Small displays inside the hood of her PPF cloak revealed no emissions from surveillance devices. The signals from the street looked like basic household grids, nothing out of the ordinary. A timer counting down at the right edge of her visual field showed ten minutes until the delivery truck arrived.

Jacob had painted the drone provided by LKC to match Amazon's colors. While its shape was a little different, there were so many drones flying around these days no one would likely notice or care.

With sixty seconds to go, Melissa did a final scan, then opened the large box on the ground and grabbed the controller, preparing to steer the drone into the Amazon truck. Although she had come up with the launch plan and done the drone programming, she had insisted Jacob do the actual launch. But he just couldn't master the flight controls. He hadn't wasted thousands of hours on video games the way she had.

Melissa had even tried to enhance the drone's autopilot software, but the control system was designed to go slowly in tight spaces and it never made it inside the truck's small launch bay window successfully during their practice runs. Luckily, this was only an issue going into the truck. Melissa had studied the schematics and determined that any motion inside the truck kept the window open. Which meant the drone would be able to leave on its own.

Fifteen seconds to go. She tapped the controller screen and energized the drone, then lifted it nine feet into the air, the precise height of the truck's opening. She leaned the controller forward and the drone zipped to the edge of the alley.

Melissa followed the drone's camera feeds on her screen. The self-driving Amazon delivery truck came into view, pulled to a stop, and slid open its launch bay window. She guided her drone until it was just at the truck's edge. As soon as the delivery drone flew out of the opening and she was sure there would not be another, she zipped hers forward and to the right, flying into the truck just before it closed the window.

She turned on the drone's exterior lighting and peered at her screen. She surveyed the shelves of drones and stacks of packages until she found an empty spot on the floor to set it down. She turned off the lights and set the power to standby.

Now their drone was on its own.

She waited until the delivery drone returned and the truck rolled away before she slipped out of the alley in the opposite direction, walked for about ten minutes, then ordered a Lyft.

Junior Gonzales was not supposed to be working at San Gabriel today, but the scheduling AI had notified his PNA of an extra shift, and he didn't have much choice. He couldn't afford to refuse a shift—he had lots of unemployed friends who'd tried that. It wasn't much of a job—light maintenance in a part of the factory that hadn't been designed for droid navigation. He didn't count on it lasting very long, but it paid pretty well even though it was only a couple of shifts a week. He adjusted his double-layered ear protection, climbed the circular ladder to the second floor steel grid walkway, and began checking the ductwork along the wall for any leaks or loose mounting brackets.

Just a few hundred yards away, the attack drone flew out of the delivery truck. It initiated a flash of voltage along its surface, dissolving its bright paint and revealing the green-black mesh of its stealth armor. It raced above a quiet residential street for several blocks. Then, with one quick hop over a nine-foot electrified fence, it was on factory territory. The drone sped toward the synfuel tank and stopped, hovered, and began warming up its laser.

LONDON

A large red banner on his monitor and insistent buzz in his earpiece got Conner Westbrook's attention immediately. He tapped his mic button. "Supervisor, Conner. I've got a potential incursion in the States. Drone tripped a motion sensor. Factory in San Gabriel, California. I'm launching now." Conner took control of one of the circling surveillance drones and forced it into steep dive. His monitor displayed a layout of the large factory building along with likely target areas. He swooped the drone along the west side of the building towards a large synfuel tank.

Damn. There was a drone, hovering a couple of yards from the tank and it looked like it was firing a laser. Conner reached for his active measures key when his display flared a brilliant green and then cut out. "Supervisor, Connor. Attack underway at San Gabriel. Laser aimed at fuel tank. Surveillance drone taken out, switching to ground defenses." He turned the active measures key on and surveyed his options. Their engagement protocol specified using nets first to try to capture drones, so he took control of a ground-based steel mesh cannon. Using a camera feed from the cannon, he turned the turret towards the attacker and fired.

The light-weight net deployed cleanly and draped the drone. It was designed to entangle the target drone's rotors and cause a crash, but nothing happened. "Supervisor, Connor. Attacker must have protected inner rotors so the wire mesh didn't work, finding other defenses." He scanned the list of available options. He had a swarm of micro-drones available, but the attack drone looked well armored. Then he saw there was a fighter drone on the other side of the factory with mini-missiles. He took control of it and launched it up and over the facility. Just as he reached the edge of the roof to try to acquire a target lock, there was a massive explosion and everything went offline.

LOS ANGELES

Melissa waited anxiously in their apartment. She couldn't believe Jacob could be so calm, lying on the sofa and scanning his PNA. So many things could go wrong in their plan, and they had no way of knowing if it had worked. They didn't want to risk flying their own traceable micro-drone in the area, so they would just have to wait for the sound of the explosion. They knew it would reach them twenty miles away.

As the time approached, Jacob finally stood up and joined her at the open window. He took her hand and gave it a reassuring squeeze.

The light and sound of the explosion reached the apartment, but Melissa and Jacob realized immediately that something had gone wrong. It was not nearly big enough. A thirty-foot-high tank of synfuel should have lit up the night sky and created a booming echo across the city.

They turned on their internet monitor and scanned the local news.

Dozens of windows opened with surveillance feeds, comm activity and omnipresence messages. News channel micro-drones arrived quickly on the scene and began transmitting pictures of the tank burning out of control.

From what they could make out, the wall of the factory had been severely damaged, but it had not leveled that section of the structure, as it should have done.

"I don't understand," said Melissa. "What happened?"

Jacob frowned. "The only thing that could explain this is if the tank was nearly empty. But we saw the fuel tanker heading to the factory a week ago." An angry expression came over his face. "Damn it. What if they were emptying the tank, not filling it?"

"Why would they do that?"

"Probably a precaution in case of attack. Fuck. We should have moved faster."

The media were quick to blame LKC, and within minutes the group took responsibility for the attack via an encrypted statement.

As she scanned the screen, Melissa felt the adrenaline in her veins begin to subside. She started to take some pride in what they had done. It wasn't as successful as they might have liked, but they had struck a blow, and it was getting a massive amount of play in OP. Which was, of course, the whole point. She was in this to wake people up. The explosion was serving its purpose.

A face began to appear on some of the channels. It was a thirty-something Hispanic man tagged as Junior Gonzales.

"Who's that?" asked Melissa.

"Don't know," Jacob replied. He gestured at the screen to enlarge one of the frames and turn on the audio.

"...confirm that the maintenance man was working in the building near the synfuel tank when it exploded. According to the company, Junior Gonzales, thirty-seven, was from East Los Angeles and was married with three young children. A tragic loss of life in this terrorist attack, the first victim in an LKC attack. Chuck, they may be regretting their claim of responsibility now..."

Tears sprung to Melissa's eyes. "Oh my God, Jacob. What have we done? We killed him!"

SAN DIEGO

The FBI's Domestic Terrorism Task Force Southern California command center was on full alert. A dozen technicians sat in front of their monitors in a darkened room two floors below ground. As soon as the signal arrived indicating a drone attack on San Gabriel, Lieutenant Sharon Lewis began reviewing all video and LIDAR surveillance from the area. The attack drone wasn't hard to pick up and she started the backtrace immediately. Just on the edge of the overhead camera she could see the attacker emerge from a commercial vehicle of some kind. She rolled the image back until it disappeared from view. "Commander Perkins, I've got the San Gabriel attack drone emerging from an Amazon self-driving delivery truck."

"Good, Sharon," said the watch commander. "Miles, get the last leg from Sharon and tap into Amazon and get the route for that truck."

"Will do," replied Miles O'Connell, "but I'll need to submit a warrant request to get that information."

"Not anymore," replied the Commander. "We are pre-cleared, just try it." The computer specialist used a DTTF router backdoor to gain access to Amazon's network. He was shocked to see that the routers did not require an encrypted warrant with court approval. "I think I've got it. On the big screen."

They looked up at the wall-sized display at a map of the San Gabriel area with the factory highlighted and a route of a delivery vehicle that matched the segment Sharon had seen.

"Now tap into public transportation systems and private ride companies and find all intersections with drop-off points near stops on that route."

"No warrants?" Miles asked.

"No warrants, just do it," said the Commander. Miles frowned. "That will take a few minutes, hang on." As he accessed various systems more dots appeared on the display.

"That's a lot. Let's try screening for drop-offs and pick-ups within a thirty minute window of the delivery truck stopping at each location." The dots faded from view until there was just a handful remaining. "Excellent," said Commander Perkins. "Now get me any visual surveillance of those locations from the appropriate time frames."

"Sorry, ma'am, no luck for most of them. Too far from the target. No closed circuit cameras in that neighborhood."

"Damn."

"If I might, Commander," said Sharon. "Wouldn't our suspect be using anonymous payment systems?"

"That seems likely. Can you narrow on that, Miles?"

"Checking. Yes. Only two possibilities. Public transit here in the north and two ride service trips near this location further south."

"Where did the ride services originate and terminate?"

"Both in a large transit hub. Lots of traffic."

"Do those self-driving vehicles have active health monitoring?"

"What, you mean medplant scanning? Let me check. Yes, one of them did. Interesting. For the ride in question there's almost no data, but for a brief moment medplant data was broadcast. Shows a twenty-seven-year-old female. Elevated pulse, shallow breathing."

"Probably wearing a privacy cloak but stuck her arm out of it. Lucky for us. Get her name."

"What do you mean? Medplants don't reveal names."

"What I'm about to tell you doesn't leave this room. We've got emergency powers from the President. Access the medplant registry in a channel encrypted with DTTF private keys and you'll get that name."

LOS ANGELES

Melissa stared with horror at the vids on the display. The burning structure, the smiling face of the man they had killed. She tried to catch her breath. Then her biometrically linked PNA started emitting an urgent, loud chirping sound. "Wait, what?" she said.

"Melissa, is that the GPS access trap?"

"GPS?"

"From Geneva, you installed the software to detect unauthorized GPS access on your PNA. Is that the warning?"

Geneva had strongly recommended ditching their personal biometrically linked PNAs, but when Melissa refused, Geneva had her install software in case law enforcement tried to illegally access her GPS. Now the software alarm was going off. The police. They knew about her! Blood rushed from her head; the world spun around her. Then everything went dark.

Jacob caught Melissa's falling body just before it hit the floor. He tried to revive her, but she was out cold. The chirping alarm meant he had maybe a minute before the police drones arrived with their stun guns. They had talked about this scenario, they had run through the LKC training, they had promised each other that if one of them was going to be captured, the other had to make a run for it.

But for many long seconds, he couldn't tear himself away from her. Part of him wanted to give up, to let them take him. He was overwhelmed with guilt at having pressured her into working with LKC. If he could trade places with her he would in an instant. But he remembered the seriousness in her expression when they had made those promises. He owed it to Melissa to carry on. He let her head down gently on the floor, then rushed to the closet, grabbed his go bag, and bolted out the door.

As he ran down the stairs, he pulled out his PPF hooded cloak and put it on. Clutching the bag—packed with food rations, q-coin tokens, and his father's revolver—he reached the front door of the building. As he turned onto the sidewalk, the first police drones arrived and crashed through the windows of his apartment.

Jacob hurried down the sidewalk and turned a corner. He joined a small cluster of people walking toward a city bus, and disappeared into the night without a backward glance.

CHAPTER FORTY-ONE

Los Angeles - December 21

Special Agent Matt Chandler of the Domestic Terrorism Task Force jumped on a fast jet at Fort Bragg as soon as news of San Gabriel hit. He reviewed the case file on his tablet. Mostly the same MO as the prior drone attacks, although this time with a laser that penetrated a synfuel tank. Probably too hard to work with explosives in the LA area due to their detection systems. The key difference with this attack was that DTTF had adequate surveillance in place and enough emergency access to track down the terrorist.

Matt exited the FBI self-driving SUV that brought him from the Joint Forces Training Base at Los Alamitos and badged his way into the apartment where Melissa King had been found. *Clearly an amateur,* he thought as he surveyed the scene. She had continued to use her biometrically linked PNA device, which made her exact location available to law enforcement. She had returned to her apparent boyfriend's place, implicating him in the attack as well. And they didn't even have a separate operations base.

Running a terrorist cell from your own residential apartment. Amateurs for sure.

His PNA buzzed. "Okay, everyone, I'm Matt Chandler, Special Agent in Charge for this investigation. I need everyone to clear the apartment."

"What's going on?" asked one of the agents as she left.

"We've got an advanced tech team coming to image the room."

Matt and the woman stood aside as two young men in blue coveralls lugged some big suitcases into the apartment and shut the door.

"Who's running this show at LAHQ?" he asked.

"Guy named Parker. Kris Parker."

Matt called him. "Agent Parker? This is Special Agent Matt Chandler from North Carolina. I just flew in and I'm on scene at the apartment. What's the status of the suspect?"

"Hello, Matt. We've been interviewing Melissa King overnight and this morning. She's been very cooperative."

"Interesting. I'm on my way."

When he arrived at the imposing concrete building, Matt launched his smart contact lens nav program to guide him to the interrogation room. A large blond man built like a football player met him at the door. "You Chandler?" he asked.

"Yes. Are you Agent Parker?"

"That's me. We waited for you."

"Well, that's kind of you. Can you summarize what you've gotten so far?"

"Piece of cake. She confessed to planning and executing the attack. Gave us plenty of details not known to the public. Seems really sorry about the guy that died. Says the boyfriend didn't know anything about it; she worked alone. Her biometrics say otherwise. We've got surveillance of him at his old company attacking some robot. Today we're focused on her handler at LKC."

"Anything there?"

"Just the name Geneva and their communication system. Looks like a crypto-steganography scheme. Uses one-time keys to decode instructions from commonly available photographs. We've got the techs looking at their gear now. Early reports are that it's pretty sophisticated. Near impossible to break without having access to a physical device."

"There must have been some initial contact," Matt said. "Any info on that?"

"She said they were picked up in a self-driving car that played a recording and had a nano-SD for ongoing communication. We're looking for surveillance to try to ID the vehicle." Parker's PNA buzzed lightly. "Okay, we're ready. Your earpiece has been registered. Let me take the first round, then feel free."

"Sure, after you."

They entered the room and took two seats opposite Melissa. A half empty cup of tea and a small pile of tissues sat on the table in front of her. The small room seemed otherwise empty, but dozens of remote sensors were continuously monitoring her micro expressions, brain activity, and galvanic skin response.

"Good morning, Melissa," said Parker. "This is my colleague, Agent Chandler."

The young woman looked up at him and half nodded. Her eyes were red and slightly unfocused.

"We'd like to ask you a few more questions about Geneva," began Parker. "How did she originally contact you?"

Melissa's fingers tore absently at a tissue on the table. "I told you already. It was an encrypted message setting up the self-drive message."

"And the only time you heard her voice was that initial self-drive car recording?"

"I don't know, it was a disguised voice. But yes. After that it was just through the encrypted photos."

"Can you walk us through how you sent messages to Geneva?"

Melissa seemed to hesitate. "I just typed them into the program she provided."

"But how did you identify the photo to use? How did you know which one to decrypt from?"

"I, I really don't remember."

A tone in Matt's earpiece from the room's sensors told him that she was probably lying.

"Melissa," Parker said, "you know it's not really worth trying to protect Jacob. We know he was involved. Did he handle the communications?"

"Jacob had nothing to do with this." The tone in Matt's earpiece deepened. Higher probability of lying.

"Do you know where Jacob is now?" Matt asked.

"No, I have no idea." The tone disappeared.

"Okay, Melissa," Parker said. "We can get back to Jacob later. Tell us about your relationship with Geneva. How much of the plan came from her? What about the materials?"

"Geneva gave me the target and the equipment. I just had to figure out how to launch the drone."

"And did you send her progress reports?" Parker said.

"No, I was operating all on my own."

"And what if you needed to reach her in an emergency?"

"We had no plan for that."

"What about coordinating with other cells?"

"What do you mean?"

"You know, other activists working in Los Angeles."

"I didn't know there were any others," said Melissa.

"Are you sure about that?"

"I was working alone!"

"Okay. Do you know where Jacob is now?"

"No." The agents' earpieces were silent.

Parker gave a nod to Chandler.

"Melissa," Matt began, "Why was San Gabriel the target?"

"I don't know, it's what Geneva identified. But it was an automated factory that makes robots that are stealing jobs from people, and the fuel tank was in a position to cripple production. It seemed like a good choice to me."

"What about the worker who was killed?" Matt asked.

"There wasn't supposed to be anyone there!" Melissa choked back tears and reached for another tissue. "I did surveillance for a week before the operation and there was never anyone there at that time! I didn't mean to hurt anyone!"

The tone in Matt's ear was steady and high pitched. Strong emotion, but honest.

"Do you know the next attack location, Melissa?" asked Matt.

"No." The tone warbled slightly. Hard to decipher. "I'm so tired. I can't do this anymore. This isn't right. I want a lawyer."

"I'm sure Agent Parker told you that you're being held under a special presidential executive order under the terrorism statute. We can detain you without a lawyer as long as we believe there is an imminent threat."

"I don't care about all that! I've told you everything I know and I'm not saying anything else until I see a lawyer!"

"That's not a wise course of action, Melissa. If you cooperate now we can make things easier for you and Jacob. You might even be able to serve together someplace." She folded her arms onto the table, lowered her head, closed her eyes and sobbed. Matt sighed and signaled Parker to join him outside.

"Send me all the sensor traces and transcript from the start of interrogation. I'm transferring the prisoner to Maclean Virginia. Can you prepare the paperwork?"

"Maclean Virginia? I thought you were from North Carolina."

"It's an advanced detention facility."

"Huh, I hadn't heard about that. Is it—"

"Just get it done, Agent. ASAP."

CHAPTER FORTY-TWO

New York/San Francisco - December 21

NEW YORK

"Good morning, everyone. I'm Megyn Robbins and welcome to Morning Fresh. With me, as always, are my co-hosts Steve Brattle and Victor Langston."

"Good morning, Megyn," said her co-hosts somberly.

"Of course, the awful news today is that America is once again under siege. Terrorism is rearing its terrifying head, except this time it's domestic terrorism happening right here in our own country."

"It's frightening, all right, Megyn," agreed Victor. "This LKC group has blown up a half dozen transport trucks and knocked out power to millions of people. Now they use a laser drone to blow up a fuel tank, killing poor Junior Hernandez. Where will they strike next? Could it be at a grocery store? Your neighborhood church? Your child's school?"

"It could be anywhere, Victor," said Steve, shaking his head. "You never know where they'll attack next. Because look at the face of terrorism in America!" They displayed a shot of Melissa King looking calm and happy, a big smile on her face next to a picture of Jacob Komarov. "How can we spot the terrorists if they look just like us? These aren't radical Islamic terrorists or MS-13 gang members. What has happened to the values of our country? How can a nice-looking, normal young people like this feel so much hate against America?"

"Well, I think we all know how our values have gotten degraded, Steve." Megyn started ticking off a litany of causes. "Permissive parenting, sexual liberation, special treatment for all kinds of people living immoral lives, VR porn, the war on Christianity—I could go on and on. It's just personally devastating to me how far this country has fallen."

"I couldn't agree more, Megyn," said Victor. "But my biggest fear right now is that the Democrat Senate is going to block the actions we need to protect ourselves. We've got patriotic Republican Senators calling for increased surveillance, outlawing those damned privacy cloaks, and requiring biometric registration for every citizen. The Democrats want to roll back those programs and allow people to use any kind of encryption they want, even if it's unbreakable by law enforcement! Evidently they hope to get us all killed. And where is the National Guard? Where is the Army? Why isn't President Teasley doing anything to protect us?"

Megyn nodded her head. "I'm just so afraid right now. Without a strong response, these terrorists will just get bolder. More ordinary people like Melissa and Jacob might get brainwashed over to their cause. We need to hunt them down, every last one of them. But do you hear the mainstream media saying that? No, of course not. They say 'Maybe LKC has a point. We need to look at it from their perspective, technology is impacting jobs and human relations.' A load of weak-kneed nonsense."

"Loyal viewers," said Steve, "stick with us—the *only* channel that gives you the truth and nothing but the truth, with twenty-four seven coverage of the attack on America. We'll be right back."

SAN FRANCISCO

"And you are back with Calista Quinn-Jones here on the early shift. Yesterday there was another attack on RezMat, the company making all those robots, and unfortunately a worker was killed. That's absolutely deplorable. I can't condone any harm coming to someone. Even though I think sending a message to these out-of-control companies is absolutely the right thing to do, I still can't accept it when people resort to violence and someone gets hurt. Felicia, you're online, what are your thoughts?"

"Hi, Calista. I'm with you on this one. I mean I'm no friend of RezMat and its ilk, but I draw the line when people get hurt. LKC claims to be trying to help people and raise consciousness and start a revolution, but taking a life is just so wrong. I admire them for taking action, but not like this."

"My point exactly, Felicia. Robert, you're next. What's on your mind?"

"I think you and Felicia are cowards. Has there ever been a revolution against the prevailing power structure where blood wasn't spilled? What kind of progressives are you people? Elites never give up their power easily. They're willing to deploy the police with their illegal weapons and use deadly force against peaceful protesters. You have to fight fire with fire. I'm proud of what LKC is doing. Maybe this will finally wake people up to what's going on out there. We're at war, Calista. And in war there are always casualties."

"Whoa, there, Robert. I'm not down with this language of war. Yes, of course this is a conflict, but war is such a masculine and aggressive term, signifying that people are the enemy and legitimate targets for violence. I think we need to make as much progress as possible with peaceful, non-violent means."

"Where have you been the last twenty years?" asked the caller. "The left has been trying to have a national conversation about these issues and conducting peaceful sit-ins and protests forever, and nothing has changed. In fact, it's gotten worse. I'm tired of it, Calista. I've got half a mind to join LKC myself. I'm so goddamn angry. The time for talking and talking and talking is over. We're at war—and, guess what, we're losing!"

"Well, Robert, I understand your feelings. I just can't go there. I'm with Martin Luther King, Jr. on this issue."

"Yeah, well, I'm going to go with Malcolm X. It's either the ballot or the bullet. And since the ballot is rigged, it's time for the bullet."

CHAPTER FORTY-THREE

Holoconference - December 21

"Let's get started," said Ellul when all the LKC members were online in the holoconference. "We've got important news from Thoreau this morning."

"Wait, we need to talk about fucking San Gabriel," interrupted Othello, the ex-CIA black ops agent Peter Cook.

"Hold on, Othello," said Ellul. "We'll get to a review of what happened in San Gabriel in a few minutes. But first we have to hear from Thoreau."

Miles O'Connell, aka Thoreau, flipped on his voice-disguising microphone. "Good morning. You are not going to fucking believe what is happening inside DTTF. We've got an executive order that has opened every corporate router to warrantless access. I was personally involved in tracking Melissa King. It was done in minutes because we had complete data access, including the medplant system."

"What?" said JT.

"You heard me!" Miles said. "The government can now see any personal data about anyone without a warrant."

"Those bastards!" said Pam. "It was just a matter of time before they started to abuse their powers."

"You're right, Geneva," said Ellul, referring to Pam by her code name. "But this also creates a huge opportunity. Tell them, Thoreau."

"Because there is no digital warrant, there's no record of the data access. Either in the target system or within DTTF itself. It's invisible."

"Wait," said Pam, "are you saying you can now download private data undetected? And access corporate systems without leaving a trace?"

"Yes!" said Miles.

"Oh my God, that's huge," said Pam.

"My thinking exactly, Geneva," said Ellul. "This gives us the chance to open up an entirely new front in our battle."

"We could demonstrate just how much deep personal information is being hoarded by corporations for their own profit. I say we expose the secrets of all those hypocritical politicians," suggested Artemis.

"Not just politicians," added Zerzan. "For broadest engagement in omnipresence we should target some celebrities too. And journalists, to get them falling all over each other reporting the story."

"Leaking information will generate buzz for sure," said JT. "But I think we should focus on injecting worms into those corporate systems to bring down communication, financial, energy, and transportation networks."

"Is that possible, Thoreau?" asked Ellul.

"Well I'm no expert on worms. But I can get right past any firewall right now. So if someone can make them, I can plant them."

"I can make them," said JT. "But it will take a little while. There are worm factories in the dark web but every generation needs to be run through simulations against the latest security tech."

"So why can't we first work on the private data leaks, then in a second phase unleash the worms?" asked Ellul.

"Getting information on a lot of people is going to take some time, too," said Miles. "I can't just do massive dumps of data because my terminal traffic is monitored. I'll need to do a little at a time."

"How long for say a thousand people?" asked Pam, who had already been identifying the most important targets in her head.

"That many? Damn, that would take a month."

"Okay," said Pam, "I can work with Artemis and Zerzan to create a list, others can review. We should start the data collection ASAP."

"And I'll start on the worm generation process," said JT.

"Agreed. Thank you, Geneva and Zurich," he said using JT's code name. "And thanks Thoreau for giving us this opportunity. Now let's turn to San Gabriel. Geneva, please report."

"The operation was a mixed success," Pam began.

"Mixed success?" said Othello. "It was a fucking disaster!"

"Hold on a minute," said Pam.

"Othello," said Ellul, "let's hear her out."

"Thank you. First, the target was hit as planned. Unfortunately, RezMat seems to have reduced the fuel in the tank to a bare minimum and that reduced the impact of the explosion. Second, there was an unexpected casualty, the maintenance worker. Third, our operative Melissa King was captured, and we just learned how from Thoreau."

"Like I said," broke in Othello. "A complete disaster. For all we know, the feds will be sending drones at us any minute once Melissa starts talking. I knew this would happen. I warned you all against using amateurs for operations!"

"May I remind you we collectively thought it was worth the risk," said Ellul.

"Melissa can't compromise the Collective," said Pam. "She doesn't know anything about any of us. We followed strict compartmentalization."

"What about her partner, Jacob?" asked Artemis.

"He's on the run," said JT. "No contact from him, he's off the grid."

"Another wild card," said Othello. "There's no telling what he might do with his girlfriend in the hands of the feds."

"How many fucking times do I have to say it, there is no risk to our security!" said Pam. "Look, the capture of Melissa was unfortunate, but it has had the effect we expected and wanted. Omnipresence has blown up with her story, and the fear of so-called 'normal people' joining us is creating the kind of instability we need."

"I can also report that we've gotten several hundred people submitting encrypted applications to join LKC," said Ellul.

"Oh bullshit," said Othello. "Those are probably all feds."

"Perhaps most of them," said Ellul. "But there will be some new potential members in there for sure."

"More fucking *amateurs*," said Othello.

"We've got to grow this movement," said Artemis. "Let's use these *amateurs* for public organizing, not for operations. Let them rally and protest out in the open, recruit more members in omnipresence, create a physical presence that gets media coverage."

"I've got no problem with that," said Othello. "Like I said, let's leave the operations to the damned professionals."

"I'd like to canvas the group's opinion on Artemis' proposal," said Ellul. They all tapped on their screens or tablets. "Nineteen to four in favor," he announced. "I agree. No more core operations from civilians. For now." Pam was disappointed, but the will of the Collective was clear.

"Now let's talk about the maintenance worker," said Ellul. "We all knew going in that there would be collateral damage. As much as we try to avoid it, the kinds of cyber infrastructure attacks we just discussed are likely to result in even more casualties. Some of them are likely to be sympathetic—sick people in hospitals that lose power or elderly people who don't get medicine delivered. The media will stop talking about our ideas for a while and focus entirely on the victims. I just want everyone to acknowledge this is going to happen."

The faces in Pam and JT's hologlasses nodded slowly. Othello surprised them all by quoting Thomas Jefferson: "The tree of liberty must be refreshed from time to time with the blood of patriots and tyrants."

CHAPTER FORTY-FOUR

London - December 23

Roger Driscoll lay down on the comfortable bed in his West End AirBNB and closed his eyes. He was drowsily walking through each of the meetings he'd had that day, replaying the conversations when Allison chimed from his PNA.

"Roger, I have a call from Frances."

"Really? I just left her a half hour ago. Okay, put it through." He heard a lot of background noise. "Frances?"

"Yes, hello again Roger. I know you said you were tired, but I was wondering if you'd fancy a bite to eat. I happened to run into an old colleague of mine from Mentapath and I think you'd enjoy meeting her."

"I don't know, Frances, I'm really tired."

"Oh, come on, Roger. You'll need to eat something, right? We're just a few blocks away, I'll send you the location. Come whenever, we'll have some drinks till you arrive. Au revoir!" She disconnected before he could protest. It sounded like she'd already started on those drinks. His PNA buzzed as the location arrived and displayed a street view. It was a trendy-looking restaurant that was indeed just a few minutes away.

"Allison, wake me up in twenty minutes. I'm going to take a quick nap."

"Very well, Roger. Sleep well."

The cold winter London air hit him like a slap in the face when he exited the flat. He walked briskly down Coventry Street and took a right on Whitcomb Street, hands thrust deep into his jacket pockets. By the time he got to the restaurant, the weather and exercise had chased his tiredness away. The place was crowded and it took him a minute to find Frances and her friend. They had moved from the noisier bar area to a quieter section in the back.

"Ah, Roger!" said Frances a little too loudly. "Over here!"

He waved and joined them at their table.

"Roger, this is my friend Jill Samborn. She was a principal engineer with me at Mentapath, top notch, really top notch. Jill, this is Roger Driscoll." He shook her hand awkwardly. Jill was quite attractive, with short brunette hair, striking green eyes, and an enchanting smile.

"Very nice to meet you Roger. Frances tells me you live in California?"

"Yes, that's right. Santa Barbara, about two hours north of Los Angeles."

"We've had quite a couple of days, haven't we Roger?" asked Frances. "I was just telling Jill about the companies we visited."

"Indeed, a very interesting sampling of the City's new tech surge," said Jill. Roger liked her accent.

"I was wondering about that. These startups seemed to have a lot of expensive office space. Is that typical?"

"Oh, well, it might seem posh," said Jill, "but once the financial firms found they could make more profits with algorithms than people, they fired most of their staffs and created a glut of office space. There are dozens of ghost buildings now in the City. Cheap rent for the tech crowd."

"Ah, that makes sense."

"So, Roger. Which of the companies did you find most interesting?" asked Frances.

"Well, to be totally honest, some of them are starting to blend together in my mind," admitted Roger. "There were, what, two of them in the artificial creativity space, another three in computational bioinformatics, and two materials science companies focused on nanoscale battery technology."

"Those are quite different areas of R&D," said Jill. "What's your background?"

"AI, mostly," said Roger, looking up from the menu and turning towards her.

"Really? That's mine as well," said Jill. A waiter appeared to take their dinner order.

"So then did you find the artificial creativity companies interesting?" Jill asked.

"Not so much, actually," answered Roger. "I mean the tech is very cool, but it's not clear to me that we really need a bunch of artificial artists, poets, and musicians. Seems hard enough for the human ones to make it as it is without needing to compete against the machines. Just look at what happened to actors once they perfected the photo-realistic actor-generation programs."

"I agree!" said Jill. "We need to preserve some areas for human endeavor and accomplishment, don't you think?"

"Yes, exactly," said Roger.

"So," interjected Frances, "then did the biotech companies interest you more?" Roger reluctantly turned his attention away from Jill.

"Well, Frances, I think the work you're doing at Neurgenix and what I saw at the other companies is very interesting. It's important too. We need to dramatically improve health care and lower its cost. I liked all of them."

"Thank you, Roger. Maybe I can convince you to do some consulting for us?"

"I'll think about it, Frances."

"So, you're freelance?" asked Jill.

"I suppose so," he answered, shifting towards her once again in his seat. "I've been running an omnipresence public relations tech company for a while. Sometimes do some consulting on the side."

"Ah, so you advise companies on OP strategy?" asked Jill.

"Something along those lines," he answered vaguely. "And you," he said, changing the topic, "where did you end up after Mentapath? Didn't follow Frances to Neurgenix?"

"No, I didn't. I stayed on at RezMat. Just a few months at Mentapath, then I moved over to infosec and special operations."

"Really? That's an interesting transition, from product to operations."

"I know, not typical. But they're doing some very interesting things with AI and I was ready for a change," said Jill.

"Wait, hold on—RezMat, infosec and operations. Jesus, you must be in the middle of all this LKC shit, oh, sorry, stuff!"

"That's okay, Roger, we've been swearing quite a lot ourselves recently. Yes, I am right in the middle of all that 'stuff' right now."

"Wow! Any hope of tracking them down?"

"We're working on it. Mostly by helping the authorities wherever we can."

"They caught one of them, right? A woman in Los Angeles?"

"Yes, apparently. She was involved in a drone attack on one of our factories."

"Did they get enough information to find anyone else?" he asked.

"I'm not really at liberty to say."

"Oh, I get it, secret spy stuff," he teased.

"Yes," Jill said, deepening her voice and feigning a Russian accent. "Eef I told you, I'd have to keell you."

"Enough of that," said Frances, sounding suddenly quite sober. "This isn't a joking matter. LKC is a serious threat. It's both building an anti-technology groundswell and provoking an authoritarian backlash."

"Yes, of course, Frances" said Jill. "I didn't mean to downplay the threat. One too many cocktails, that's all," she said, swirling her drink. She winked at Roger, however, when Frances turned towards the waiter delivering their food. He blushed. It had been a long time since an attractive woman had flirted with him.

They kept the conversation light during dinner. As they stood up after he insisted on settling the bill, Roger turned to Frances and said, "Do you actually have some consulting projects I could work on?"

"Of course we do, I'd be thrilled to have your help."

"Good, good. Why don't I extend my visit a few weeks so I can get up to speed?"

"Super!" said Frances. "Stop by our office tomorrow and I'll introduce you to the team I think could most benefit from your expertise."

"Great," said Roger. He turned to Jill. "It was a real pleasure meeting you Jill. I wish you the best of luck with your security issues. Maybe if they let you out for some air we could catch one of those shows you said you wanted to see?"

"Why thank you, Roger. Yes, that would be lovely. Let's exchange info." They tapped their PNAs together and transmitted contact details. Walking back to his flat, though the evening cold had deepened, Roger took no notice at all.

CHAPTER FORTY-FIVE

Washington - January 4, 2039

I t had taken a dozen meetings over the course of a month and more than thirty staffers to draft proposed legislation, but Harry Paxton was enormously proud of the result.

It wasn't perfect, of course; nothing this big and complicated and the result of so much compromise could be. But he was convinced it was a critical stake in the ground for moving the country, and the world, forward.

They had attempted to work in secret, but Washington was a city that thrived on leaks and rumors. Details of the proposal, mostly wrong and always controversial and out of context, floated through the back channels and corridors of power. The media picked up on the story, and some wit labeled Harry and his five colleagues the Six Lost Souls of the Senate, "wandering in a desert of delusion."

Now that all six of them had signed off on the executive summary and the several hundred page draft, it was up to each of them to pitch their own committee chairperson to bring up the bill for discussion.

Harry and Rebecca Matheson had an appointment with Walter Scott, Democratic chair of the Budget Committee, at 10 a.m. They met at 8:30 to do a final review over coffee. For eighty minutes they covered their roles and responses to possible objections. Then Rebecca crossed her arms and said, "Okay, we're ready. But what the hell do you think he's going to do?"

"It's very difficult to say," Harry replied honestly. "He's been sending very mixed signals through the grapevine."

They gathered their belongings and walked up the stairs from the cafeteria, then down a wide corridor to Walter Scott's office. His assistant asked them to take a seat. They waited patiently, trying to gauge whether the twenty minutes was a good or bad omen by Washington standards.

Finally, Walter himself opened the large double doors to his office. "Harry! Rebecca! Please, please come in, so sorry to keep you waiting. Do you need a refreshment? Coffee?"

Once they were seated in some red leather chairs around a low glass table, Walter looked at them both expectantly. "So, then, what's this all about? It's not every day that two senior senators, one with a D and one with an R after their names, come to meet with me together. Is this about all those rumors I keep hearing, about some grand plan?"

As they'd agreed, Harry led the charge. "Yes, Walter, that's exactly what this is about. You know that I've been working with five other senators on a major piece of legislation designed to get us out of the absolute logjam we find ourselves in. A logjam of our own creation, and one that most of us seem to have no interest in breaking up."

Walter nodded encouragingly.

"What we have here today," Harry said, tapping his tablet, "is a bill we call ALPHA. The America Leading Progress for Humanity Act. It's a complex piece of legislation, to be sure, because it's very ambitious. But it follows directly from the spirit behind the Declaration, the Constitution, and the values that this country was founded on."

As they'd planned, Rebecca picked up the thread. "What this document recognizes is that the world has been reshaped by technology so that our old ways of doing business are obsolete. The world has changed, so our approach to it must change as well. As a society, adaptation to a rapidly changing environment has always been one of our great strengths. Until recently, that is. We've become stiff and frozen, unable to tackle big issues when big changes are needed."

"I see," said Walter with more than an edge of suspicion in his voice. "So what does the U.S. Congress have to do with leading humanity?"

"Walter," said Harry, "we've already seen massive increases in the capabilities of AI, robotics, and distributed energy and manufacturing that have eliminated many millions of jobs. It's inevitable that more of the same is coming. We need to shift toward a new way of thinking about work and the role of human labor in the economy."

"So this is some kind of a jobs program?" asked Walter.

"No," answered Rebecca. "It's a new social contract, and a new way to keep money circulating in the economy when jobs get more and more scarce."

"You two are going to have to spell this out," said Walter.

"The basic outline is this," began Harry. "We provide every adult citizen with a guaranteed basic income, unconditionally, with no means testing or other requirements. Any money they earn is added on top of the basic income."

Walter held up his hand. "Whoa, there, Senator. You know full well we can't afford any such thing. Is this a serious proposal? Is this what you've been spending all this time on?"

"We had the CBO score it," replied Rebecca. "While the flows are complicated, it *is* possible."

"Where does the funding come from?" asked Walter.

"It comes from a variety of sources. Eliminating existing social programs; eliminating many tax expenditures; and raising some financial transaction, corporate and income taxes," said Harry.

Walter looked askance at the Republican senator across from him. "And you're okay with all that?"

"We don't have a choice, senator," she replied. "The economy depends on citizens having money to buy goods and services. If they don't have jobs, we simply need to circulate the money back to them. And this will actually shrink the size and invasiveness of government in people's lives, which you know I'm in favor of."

"How so?"

"The basic income is the property of the recipient with no strings attached. They get to spend it however they see fit, not according to some bureaucrat's plan."

"Wait. You mentioned eliminating existing social programs. What does that mean?"

Harry said, "All of the top-line programs are eliminated in favor of the basic income guarantee."

Walter stared at him. "You're not talking about Medicare-for-All and Social Security, are you?"

Harry swallowed hard. "I am. There will be supplements for special medical conditions, but, as you know, we're in the final testing of some astonishing medical technologies that should radically reduce the cost of health care and maintenance. In fact, we anticipate that the basic income guarantee may be able to be reduced over time as technology makes all of life's essentials cheaper and cheaper."

"That's the Leading Progress for Humanity part," explained Rebecca. "We invest in research and development in energy, food science, health care, education, and housing, with the goal of making all of them much less expensive over time."

The Budget Committee chairman was silent for the better part of half a minute, looking back and forth at them intently.

"I'm sitting here wondering," he said finally, "how the hell two of my most distinguished colleagues could have collaborated together for months and come up with something so fundamentally ridiculous. What you're proposing doesn't have a snowball's chance in hell of appearing on the Budget Committee docket, or of getting a vote in this Congress. And I'm sure the other chairmen will agree."

"The other four of us—" Rebecca began

"As you're well aware," the chairman continued, "we're facing riots in the streets, weekly terrorist attacks, and a faltering economy. This country is in a serious crisis. And the six of you go off in a hotel somewhere and cook up a goddamn blueprint for the destruction of everything we've spent the last seventy years building. No wonder they're calling you the Six Lost Souls."

"Walter," said Harry, "ALPHA isn't ignoring those problems. It's the solution to them. We need to give people a new vision of the future that takes into account what they see around them every day."

"I have to admit, I'm quite disappointed," said Walter. "Perhaps if you had tried to approach this one little bite at a time, instead of with some grand plan that overturns everything the people rely on." The chairman shook his head. "I'm sorry. Harry, Rebecca, you've been wasting your time. ALPHA is DOA."

CHAPTER FORTY-SIX

Holoconference - January 7

Preston Jackson, COO of the team Frances had hired to promote Sara, was roused from a deep sleep at one a.m. by the tablet on his bedside table vibrating loudly.

He groaned and sat up, rubbing his forehead. Then he grabbed the tablet and answered the video call from Sheila Bratton, the team's omnipresence director. He blinked at the sudden flood of light.

"Preston, it's Sheila. Sorry to wake you, but this is very serious."

"No problem, Sheila. What is it?"

"I'm sending you a message with a link to a report that's going viral in OP. It's by a data scientist named Kathleen Norquist. Remember that mysterious 'secret weapon' Frances talked about at the launch but never revealed? Turns out it was a massive network of intelligent agents run by RezMat. Norquist did an analysis and specifically connected Sara to RezMat."

"Oh shit. Okay, Sheila, I'm going to call an emergency team meeting. We'll need an action plan."

"Preston, is this true? Is RezMat really behind Sara? I know they bought Frances' company. Is she working for them?"

"No, no, no. RezMat is *not* behind Sara. I'm sure Frances can clear this up."

Ten minutes later his AI had contacted Sara and all the team leads, and put together a holoconference.

The screen split into six panes, and Sara and Frances and each of the team leads came into view.

Preston laid out the facts succinctly. "Thank you all for assembling so quickly. A few hours ago, a PhD data scientist named Kathleen Norquist published a report that identified a huge global network of intelligent agents that promoted technology in omnipresence on behalf of RezMat. She also found that network directly supported Sara's launch and she *theorized* a connection between RezMat and Sara. Unfortunately, that theory has gone viral and what's circulating right now is a twisted version where Sara is actually a front for RezMat."

There was a chorus of gasps.

"I'm afraid I must take responsibility for this," said Frances. "This story has become terribly jumbled. There is no connection between RezMat and me or Sara. I did employ a highly secretive firm with an intelligent agent network to support Sara's launch. The head of that firm, once exposed to Sara's ideas, decided to take down his own network to do some good in the world. He evidently took down a RezMat network as well and this researcher has somehow incorrectly combined them all together."

"Well that sucks," said Sam. "We're going to need to respond to this. It's going to highlight the questions about Sara's funding again too. Are you sure you don't want to go public, Frances?"

"I will if I have to, but I'd really rather keep the focus on Sara," she replied.

"I'm afraid 'Billionaire Tech CEO Who Sold Her Business to RezMat' doesn't play that much better than RezMat," said Sheila.

"Does it make sense to play this as 'There is no connection to RezMat. The funding is not important. This is just a distraction'?" asked Sam.

"That makes sense to me," replied Vannha. "It's consistent with Sara's message. But I'm not sure we'll be able to prevent RezMat and funding questions from *becoming* the story."

"They *will* be the story," said Sara softly. "For a little while. It will be up to me to convince people that I do not speak for RezMat and that the funding is merely a distraction. I will need to convince them to focus on the message and take action."

"Sheila," said Preston, "can you set up a video shoot for Sara to put out a statement?"

"Sure. We can do it first thing in the morning. Sara, you're in Chicago now, right?"

"Yes, and I'm flying out to Los Angeles at the end of the week."

"Okay, we have a plan," said Preston. "Any other questions or things we should be doing?"

The team leaders shook their heads.

"Right. Well, let's stay focused. We'll get through this. Good night, all. Sara, Frances, can you stay on a moment?"

All the others dropped off the call.

"Sara," said Preston, "this could stoke up a lot of anger toward you. Do you want to postpone some of your public appearances?"

The young woman thought for a moment. "I don't see how I can. I'm calling on people to face their fears and have the courage to act. I can't myself run and hide the first time a challenge presents itself."

"Okay, but I'm going to ask Vannha to increase security at your events."

"If you must," said Sara reluctantly. "But please don't make it look like some huge private police force."

"Sara," said Frances, "I think you're underestimating the impact this is going to have. Some people are going to be outraged. Many of your supporters will be disillusioned."

"I do understand," said Sara. "I'll speak to them as best I can."

Preston said, "I'll send Vannha a message. Anything else we should be doing?"

"Not that I can think of," said Frances. "Sara, my dear, take care."

"I will Frances. Good night. *Namaste.*"

CHAPTER FORTY-SEVEN

San Francisco/New York - January 8

SAN FRANCISCO

"Good morning, Bay Area! You're back with Calista Quinn-Jones, here on the early shift. The hot topic today is this report that says RezMat had over two hundred million fake people in omnipresence hawking technology and the absolute bombshell that Sara, the pro-technology, pro-corporate OP sensation, is really part of a huge public relations stunt by RezMat.

"Go ahead, Delilah, you're on the air."

"Thanks, Calista, long time listener. I think you're being too harsh on Sara. She put out a video completely denying that she has any connection to RezMat. I believe her."

"Well, Delilah, I know that Sara is an appealing young woman, and there are parts of what she says that I like, too. But you've got to look at the facts. And these are from a PhD data scientist, not from some anonymous troll. When Sara was launched these RezMat fake people were her number one initial supporters. Her message is one hundred percent pure corporate capitalism and directly supports RezMat and its cabal of other technology companies. What am I missing?"

"You're missing her message of love and compassion, and using technology to liberate humanity."

"Well, maybe I can't hear that because all I can hear is fusion power, GMO vats of meat, more automation, more profit, and pipe dreams about redistribution."

"They aren't pipe dreams if we make them happen."

"Sorry, Delilah, but I don't know what country you're living in. In my country both parties are slaves to the moneyed interests. In my country there's no way to pass legislation that actually helps people."

"You know, Calista, I used to admire you for fighting for the working person," said Delilah. "But in a way, you're as much a part of the problem as those corporations. You don't want to step up to the hard work of making change happen. You just bemoan how impossible it is. You keep fighting the battles of the last fifty years over and over again." The caller's voice grew more strident. "The world is changing, Calista. The people—the people you care so much about—are going to take back the future, while you're stuck in the past. Wake up, people! Don't listen to this empty..."

Calista cut off the comm. "Sorry about that, listeners. I fear you've just been exposed to another RezMat apologist. Could it be part of another publicity campaign?

"OK, Vince, you're on the air. What's on your mind?"

NEW YORK

"Good morning, everyone! I'm Megyn Robbins and welcome to Morning Fresh. With me, as always, are my co-hosts Steve Brattle and Victor Langston."

"Good morning, Megyn!"

"We'll get to our weather and traffic bots in a moment, but let's start with the shocking news that RezMat is behind the Sara campaign."

"I know," said Victor. "Incredible news."

"RezMat is a great, great company, even if it is British," said Steve. "And they're under vicious attack right now from terrorist organizations like LKC. So I understand why they would think out of the box with this Sara campaign."

"Sure," said Megyn, "but it's a little confusing. I mean, Sara is very pro-technology and makes a good case against LKC. But she also supported LKC on *Life Stories*, and she has this crazy message about taxing the rich and giving everyone money for free. Why would RezMat promote that?"

"Well, Megyn, good thing we have our first guest to help us understand that. He's Richard Masterson, a communications expert who was at North Carolina University before it converted to an all-AI format. Welcome, Richard."

"Good morning, Victor. Glad to be here."

"Richard, what do you make of the Sara's Message campaign?"

"Well, up until this revelation, I'd say it was brilliant. Perhaps one of the best omnipresence campaigns of the last twenty years."

"Why is that?" asked Megyn. "Isn't her message contradictory and confusing?"

"That's the beauty of this campaign," answered Richard. "People have become so attuned to one-sided messages that they pretty much dismiss them out of hand. By crafting a complex message that blends perspectives from both ends of the political spectrum, as well as emotional and spiritual hooks, RezMat was able to break through the noise in OP and get people to pay attention. We're in an attention economy now, and RezMat found a way to capture the spotlight for several months."

"Wait," persisted Megyn. "Help me understand. How did this campaign help RezMat?"

"You have to remember that Sara's primary message is that technology is good and can lead to a utopian future. That's what RezMat needed to get out there to counteract the anti-technology terrorists."

"So, did it work?" asked Steve.

"I think it was working until this connection leaked out," answered Richard. "Now it's just going to leave her followers confused. How will it impact the pro and anti-technology memes? We won't know until new psychometric omnipresence analysis comes out in a few days."

"Thanks, Richard," Megyn said. "Enlightening as always."

"In any case," concluded Victor, "I'm sure that's the last we'll be hearing from Sara. I wonder if she'll be able to get any other acting jobs."

"I heard the Bollywood VR producers are very interested," laughed Steve.

"Good idea! Go back to India, Sara!" laughed Victor. "You're watching the *only* channel that brings you the truth, and nothing but the truth. Stay tuned."

CHAPTER FORTY-EIGHT

Maclean, Virginia - January 9

Amina Hamdi and Wei Chen were in the ENT Systems lab when the call came from Domestic Terrorism Task Force headquarters. They shuffled some equipment around so they could appear together in the holoconference.

"So, is everything ready Doctor Hamdi?" asked Matt Chandler.

"Yes, Agent Chandler," replied Amina. "We did the last insertion half an hour ago and it should be ready in a few hours."

"And the brain modeling was clean on this subject?"

"Yes," said Wei Chen. "It was good we took the extra week. Our new uMRI scanner has provided us much better resolution. And the imaging team was able to build much more realistic simulations of the boyfriend and apartment building."

"I look forward to hearing from you," said Chandler. "You are performing a great service to your country, thank you."

"Of course, Agent Chandler. It is our honor." Amina cut the holoconference transmission. *As if they had much choice,* she thought. The Defense Advanced Research Projects Agency had fully funded their advanced VR training tech. If they didn't "dual-use" their invention for DTTF, there'd be no more government funding. Upstairs, their sophisticated cylindrical units were called enhanced neural training simulators. Two levels below ground, in this highly restricted lab, they were interrogation pods.

Melissa's eyes flew open. Someone had slapped her on the cheek.

Jacob's panicked face loomed over her, washing in and out of focus. "Oh, thank God, Melissa. Come on—they'll be here any minute!" He pulled her up off the floor of the tiny apartment. "Come on, get your bag. Let's move!"

Still woozy from fainting, she tried to get her bearings. She looked at the screen, still showing reports of the explosion, then at the table in the living room where he had painted the drone. Her PNA was chirping its GPS detection alarm urgently.

Jacob shoved a black go bag into her hands. "This way!"

He grabbed her hand and ran with her down the dimly lit hallway. They raced down the stairs to the basement, then underneath the building to a tunnel that twisted and turned under the city streets.

She thought she heard micro-drone sounds behind them. Jacob stopped, out of breath. He handed her a PNA. "I'll get the cloaks ready. Here, enter the master pass phrase to unlock it."

Melissa keyed the twenty-two character password into the unit, but it was rejected.

"It's not working!" The sound of drones grew louder.

"Try it again!"

Melissa frantically re-entered the pass phrase but got the same flashing red screen.

"Melissa, which phrase are you using?"

"'redmastercurlbasepoker.' Shit! Jacob, what are we going to do?" The drones sounded so close. She grabbed for his arm, but suddenly he was gone. There was just a silent blackness.

"OK, that was good, very good. I'll send the pass phrase over to Agent Chandler immediately." Amina sent a secure message from her tablet to the DTTF agent, then pointed to the screen displaying data from the neural lace made of graphene nanowire embedded in Melissa's brain. "Mental field resistance looks moderate, Wei Chen. How are her vitals?"

"All good. Fast pulse and high adrenaline and cortisol levels, of course. But nothing dangerous. She tolerated the sim pretty well."

"Great. What's the next scenario?"

"Jacob asks Melissa for the location of the next attack."

"OK," Amina said. "Let's do it."

Jacob stopped in the dark tunnel, out of breath. He handed her a PNA. "I'll get the cloaks ready. You program in the location of the next LKC attack. That's our extraction point."

She looked at the screen in her hand. "What? What next attack?"

He pointed at the device. "Melissa, focus! We're running out of time! Enter the location of the next attack. That's our extraction point." The drone sounds grew closer.

"We don't know where that is!" she shouted. "How can I enter it?"

Once Wei Chen heard Melissa's response over the speakers, he shut down the simulation.

"Nicely done," Amina said, noting the results on her tablet. "But mental field resistance was up significantly on that run."

"Yes, and her vitals spiked too," Wei Chen said, frowning. "Her heart rate jumped briefly over one-eighty."

"Do you think there's any degradation of the nanowire assembly?"

"Let me check." Wei Chen manipulated a 3D model of Melissa's brain, generated by a real-time uMRI scanner built into her pod. "I don't see any problems with the neural lace assembly. Integrity is ninety-eight percent and it's embedded correctly."

"Are we over-stimulating the amygdala?"

"I don't think so. We need her fear response high enough to hold down the mental field resistance. If anything, we may need to increase it."

"Hmm. Can her body handle another scenario today, or do we need to hold off until tomorrow morning?"

"I'm not too worried," Wei Chen said. "She's young and healthy. Let's give her half an hour for her vitals to settle down, and then run one more."

Jacob stopped in the dark tunnel, out of breath. He handed her a PNA with a nano-SD card inserted. "I'll get the PPF cloaks ready. You tell Geneva we need an extraction."

She looked at the comm unit. "Geneva? But how?"

"Use the signal," he urged, pulling his cloak out and plugging it in.

"What signal?" she cried.

"Melissa, focus! We're running out of time! Don't you remember the signal?"

She shook her head. "We don't have a signal for reaching Geneva!" The drone sounds grew closer.

"Then send her a message," Jacob said, putting on the cloak. "Hurry!"

"We don't have an address! You know that! We never had one! What the hell is wrong with you?"

Melissa felt a sudden sharp pain in her chest. The PNA shimmered in her hands. Jacob faded slightly, then suddenly disappeared.

Her vision blurred. The pain intensified. She clutched her chest and gasped. She fell forward onto her knees.

Then everything went black.

"Damn it!" Wei Chen shouted. "Vitals are crashing!" His fingers flew over the simulation control panel.

"Shut it down!" cried Amina, jumping out of her seat.

"I am!" he said.

The two of them stared at the erratic brain, respiratory, and pulse sensor outputs spiking, then flatlining with a monotonous tone filling the room. In unison, they glanced at the dozen silver interrogation pods a few feet away and easily picked out the one with the red flashing vitals screen.

Amina groaned. "Shit!"

"Now what?" asked Wei Chen.

"I have to call Chandler," said Amina, slumping back down in her chair.

CHAPTER FORTY-NINE

Holoconference- January 10

Ellul called the LKC holoconference meeting to order. "Thanks to all who could join on short notice. Thoreau has some news and we have a decision to make. Go ahead Thoreau."

"I've been monitoring internal DTTF feeds to track any LKC-related investigations. This morning I saw a communication from an advanced interrogation facility in Virginia. They were using some kind of brain simulation device on Sparrow and things went bad and she ended up dead." He referred to the operational code name they had given Melissa after they made contact with her and Jacob.

"Those bastards!" cried Pam.

"Yes, exactly," said Ellul. "The question before is whether to leak this information. If we do, it will outrage anti-technology activists and get them even more fired up. The downside is it will alert DTTF that they have a mole."

"Hey Thoreau," said Peter Cook aka Othello. "Is there any way for you to create a network vulnerability at the Virginia facility and then leak that? That would make it look like an outside hack rather than an inside job."

"Interesting idea," said Miles O'Connell. "I bet I could do that. That lab is a research facility, not really locked down very tightly. Once Wikileaks hears there's a security weakness they'll jump on it and leak the hottest thing they find. Sparrow's death should be all over the media in hours."

"Well if we can avoid any direct implication of a DTTF insider," said Ellul, "then I think it makes sense to move forward. Anyone disagree?"

"I'm worried about Raven," said Pam, using Jacob's code name. "I got the sense he was the one pushing their involvement with LKC. If I'm right he's going to blame himself."

"Have we heard anything from him?" asked Ellul.

"No," answered Pam. "He's still off the grid."

"I'm not sure what we can do about that, Geneva. This news is going to come out eventually. The government will try to sit on it for months. I think it's in our interest to get it out now while people still remember San Gabriel."

"Yes," said Pam, "I guess that's true."

"Let's do a canvas on leaking the story if it can be done indirectly," said Ellul. He waited till the votes came in. "Okay, thirteen to five. I agree. Thoreau, go ahead with that plan," said Ellul. "Any other updates?"

"Yes," said JT. "I'm making steady progress on the worm evolution. We started with a million candidates from the best of the dark web worm factories and now we're down to the last thousand or so. I've got about ten thousand virtual machines with hundreds of different simulated networking and security systems. The best worms so far are able to force the hardware into shutting down or continuous rebooting about fifty percent of the time. I think I can get that up to seventy percent."

"So not a total shutdown?" asked Othello.

"No, no, we can't manage that. But most data centers can't run with seventy percent of their machines compromised. It'll be sporadic. Some services will go completely dark, others will go into limp mode and be barely usable, and some others will probably work just fine. But what's particularly great about this new class of worms is that they are designed to also infect the computers of the remote diagnostic teams. Then as those teams try to work on or defend other data centers, they're actually the ones doing the further infecting."

"When do you think they'll be ready?" asked Ellul.

"Realistically, it's probably another couple of weeks," said JT.

"I'll be ready to launch by then," said Miles O'Connell.

"Good work," said Ellul. "They have no idea what's coming."

CHAPTER FIFTY

London - January 10

Roger paced back and forth in front of the window of his West End flat, glancing often out onto the street. He'd asked Jill to meet him there before dinner to avoid a public scene. While their three dates in the last two weeks had gone exceedingly well, he had no idea how she would react to his news. But he felt compelled to tell her—he certainly didn't want her to find out from some news report. Or from Frances, who was distraught enough at what was happening to Sara to possibly let something slip.

At last his PNA buzzed and Roger walked to the door of the flat to let her in. He took her coat and hung it on the rack. "You look beautiful," he said, admiring her dark green dress with its slowly moving amoeba-shaped patches of blue. "I love the living fabric." She took his hands and leaned in to give him a kiss, but just on the cheek. "Well thank you, Roger. This is a nice place. It's a fabulous location."

"Yes, well, temporarily at least, there's not too much to it. Practically a studio, it's tiny. Step in and that's the whole tour pretty much." She laughed. "Yes, so I see." Jill looked at him expectantly. He didn't know where to begin. "Sooo," she said, prompting him. "Are we off to dinner then?"

"Please, sit down for a minute," said Roger gesturing to the small sofa. Jill's smile faded. "Uh oh. That doesn't sound good." But she took a seat and he joined her. He wished he had an overlay to read her emotions, but this was no holochat, and he had no Allison listening in to provide him helpful suggestions. He was on his own.

"So, look, Jill. I'm not so smooth when it comes to relationships. I've lived kind of an isolated life." Her eyebrows raised slightly and her lips pursed. No overlay.

"I guess I'll just come out and say it. I've got some news and I don't think you're going to like it. I just, I've had such a good time with you these last two weeks."

"And I have as well, Roger." She reached out and squeezed his right hand. "So. Are you leaving then?"

"What? No. Why—no that's not my news." She looked confused.

"Oh? Oh, I thought—"

"No, no, that's not it at all."

"Oh, I see, well, that's good then. But, what news did you think I wouldn't like?"

"It has to do with RezMat."

"RezMat? I don't understand."

"Your synth network, the one Kathleen Norquist wrote her paper on?"

"Synth network? What's that? I'm so confused, what does that paper have to do with your news?"

"I'm sorry, Jill." Finally he just blurted it out. "I wrote RingTrue. I took down your network." Her eyes widened and she pulled her hand away from his.

"You what?"

"I wrote RingTrue."

"Roger, I thought you did OP public relations work."

"Yes, well, in a way." He stared down at the sofa and it all came out in a rush. "You see I had my own synth network that I used for clients. I worked for Frances to help her launch Sara. Her ideas had a big impact on me, so I decided to shut my network down. So, I created RingTrue. I found your network—well, I didn't know it was yours at the time—and targeted that first, to give my clients some time to adjust. I'm sorry, Jill, but I exposed your network. I'm so sorry. I wanted you to hear it from me." Roger finally looked up. He was shocked to see Jill smiling and shaking her head. She suppressed a half laugh.

"Oh, you are such a dear, dear man. Yes, I was sad when our agent network was discovered. But really, Roger, compared to this LKC shit, as you called it, that's not such a big deal. But, I have to say, life is truly absurd sometimes."

"What? Absurd?" It was Roger's turn to be confused.

"I have my own news to share," Jill said, taking his hand once again. "I am ringtruthier."

"I don't understand," said Roger.

"I forked your repo. I'm the one who took *your* network down. I am sorry, Roger, I had no idea who posted RingTrue. If I had known it was you, if I had known you—"

"You posted the fork?" he asked. She nodded. "But how did you get it?" Roger's eyes narrowed. He withdrew his hand. "Did you hack into my systems?"

"No! No, I didn't. My boss said he got an original copy of the repo from Tribal. I don't know how he did it and I was right pissed off when he told me. Still am pissed in fact. There's something not right there and I intend to get to the bottom of it once we're past this crisis."

"The original Tribal repo? But that was private. And I deleted it!"

"I know, believe me, Roger, I know. There's no way RezMat should have had access to it."

Roger didn't know what to say at this strange turnabout.

"Look at us," Jill laughed. "Do you know who we are?"

"What? What do you mean?"

"We are the two worst mass murderers in all of human history." He just looked at her. "Think about it," she said. "Stalin and Mao killed maybe sixty million together. We're at a hundred million apiece, easy."

"That's not funny, Jill."

"Oh, come on, Roger. You've got to see *some* humor in this. You killed my people and I killed yours. Of course, you were already planning on killing yours, so I only accelerated the process. Honestly, I'm the one who should be mad here."

"Are you?"

"No. I am not. Are you?"

"I was. I am, I guess, at RezMat for hacking into Tribal."

"Yes, I'm with you there. So, are we all square then?"

"I suppose," said Roger, still not letting go of RezMat's hack.

"Brilliant. So, can we go to dinner then? I'm famished!"

"Yes, okay. But one thing, Jill. Seriously."

"What's that?"

"For the record, my network was bigger than yours. So, *you* are definitely the worst mass murderer in all of history."

"Oh, you are incorrigible! Arrogant and mean, at the same time." But she leaned over and kissed him, for real this time.

CHAPTER FIFTY-ONE

Los Angeles - January 12

S ara sat alone in a darkened office at the rear of the Los Angeles
University gym, trying to meditate, focusing on her breath. But her
mind kept returning to the events of the last few days, and to the
people now gathering in the gym. Until now, all her town hall meetings
had overflowed with friendly, welcoming crowds. But since the publication
of Kathleen Norquist's RezMat report, omnipresence had been filled with
ugly words and threats.

Her security team had wanted to screen protesters out of the audience today, but Sara had insisted they be allowed in. The compromise was
to allocate a special section for them: a wedge of chairs in the concentric
circles that had been set up on the gym floor.

As the starting time of the event approached, Sara felt nervous and
restless for the first time since her initial public appearance three months
earlier in New Delhi.

She rose from the thinly carpeted floor and joined some staffers in the adjoining locker room. They nodded at her and gave her reassuring smiles, but they were clearly on edge as well. A young man stepped over to her with a lapel mic and transmitter. "It's almost time, Sara."

"Very well," she said.

He fitted the wireless mic on her yellow sari and tucked the transmitter into a hidden pocket.

"You're good to go. Good luck!"

"*Namaste.*"

"Next!" called the security guard.

Jacob Komarov walked forward in his cloak. He was not surprised when the guard stopped him with an outstretched arm. "Hold on there. I need you to take off that costume."

"I have a constitutionally protected right to privacy," replied Jacob calmly from behind the LED wire mesh. "I don't have to remove this."

"Well, I don't have to let you in either," said the guard.

"According to Villner versus State of California you do, I'm afraid. The Supreme Court upheld the decision two years ago."

The security guard sighed. "Just wait here." He said into his PNA, "Hey Claire, I've got a PPF cloak here. Please advise."

For a several seconds, the guard's PNA was silent. The line behind Jacob was getting restless. Someone called out, "Hurry up! It's about to start!"

Then a female voice said tersely, "Secondary search."

The guard said, "Head over to that table." He pointed to the right and called the next person forward.

Jacob approached the secondary search table and waited in line.

When he walked through the full-body scanner, it of course buzzed loudly. "Over here," said a frazzled staffer in a grey hoodie. He passed a hand scanner over Jacob, but it chirped constantly over the metal fibers. "I'm gonna have to pat you down," he said.

"Sure, go ahead," said Jacob.

The young man pressed his hands all around the cloak, starting and the top and working his way down. He stopped suddenly at Jacob's right hip. "Hey, what's this?"

"Oh, that's the battery for the cloak. It's powered to block active scanners. Some models are just passive, but this one's got all the bells and whistles. Of course, it's more than a year old and they've already got..."

The man held up his hand. "I get it." He patted the rest of the cloak and said, "Okay, move along."

Jacob joined the rest of the crowd filing into the Los Angeles University gym.

As soon as Sara stepped onto the gym floor, loud shouts and applause filled the room. But they did not quite drown out a chorus of boos from the protest section.

Sara made her way slowly to the center of the gym, greeting people on either side of the long aisle. As she neared the center, a familiar face caught her eye. Her team had provided a briefing identifying the on-campus organizers and there was Tenesha Martin, right on the aisle. Sara walked to her and took her hands. "Tenesha, yes?" she asked.

"Yes! Yes! Sara, thank you so much for coming!"

"Thank you for organizing the campus. Let's meet after the event, okay?"

"Okay, yes, of course. We'll be there! This, oh, this is Nate, we formed the chapter together." Tenesha pulled Nate alongside her. Sara smiled.

"Hello Nate, good to meet you as well. But I should get things started here. See you soon."

Sara walked to the center of the gym, pressed her hands over her heart and turned slowly around to take in all the energy in the room. She felt love and warmth from most of the circle. But there was also an obvious wedge of anger from the protest section. There were about a hundred people in that area—more than she had expected.

She paused and faced them, searching their faces. She saw disappointment and even disgust. A few shouted at her.

"Welcome, all of you!" she said into the small lapel mic. Her voice filled the gym and the din of conversation started to fade.

Sara looked around the room and smiled. She turned away from the protesters and pointed toward a woman who had raised her hand. "Yes, what would you like to discuss?"

The young woman waited until a man in a grey hoodie handed her a mic. "Sara, first let me thank you for coming to visit with us. You're amazing and I can't believe you're actually here."

Sara nodded as clapping and cheers broke out.

The woman continued, "But I'm very concerned about the recent news reports. I saw your video, but I'd like to hear it from you directly. What is your connection to RezMat?"

There were murmurs in the crowd and some shouts of "Yeah!" from the protesters.

"I thank you for that question," Sara said. "I know the media stories have been confusing. I have no connection to RezMat Industries. The details of how some omnipresence activity seems to imply a connection are not important. What is important is that you believe me when I tell you that there is no connection."

The young woman shook her head, disappointed. "But Sara, where are you getting your funding? Can you prove you are not working for RezMat?"

Sara held the young woman's eyes. "I do not have any proof to give you. I am asking you, simply, to have faith." Her gaze did not waver. "Have faith."

Jacob stood and shouted through his mask, "Faith in what? *Technology?*"

"No," Sara replied softly, turning in his direction. "Faith in me."

"How can we have faith in you when you've been lying to us this whole time?"

"As I said, I have no association with RezMat."

"You've been lying about RezMat and lying about technology. You've been manipulating us into believing technology is good."

"Well, yes, I believe technology *is* good. It has the power to finally liberate us from lives of poverty and drudgery."

Jacob snorted derisively. "*Technology* took my job. *Technology* killed my father. *Technology* killed my girlfriend."

"Oh, my deepest condolences," said Sara. "I am so sorry for your loss. I'm not sure we can deal with such a personal story here in this setting. I'd be happy to meet with you afterward. Maybe if you listen to some of the conversation today, it will open new perspectives for you."

"I didn't come here to listen to more of your fucking propaganda!" shouted Jacob. Staffers began running down the aisles toward him. "I came here to save the human race!"

Jacob reached inside his cloak and retrieved his father's gun, taped to the inside of the large battery pack at his hip. Before anyone could react, he took careful aim and fired a single shot directly at Sara.

The protesters around him stood and started to scatter, screaming.

Jacob shoved through the rows of chairs in front of him to get another clear shot. He took aim again at Sara, now only a few yards away.

As his finger pulled the trigger, a staffer tackled him, sending the second bullet wildly off target. Jacob fell heavily to the ground among the toppled chairs.

Sara saw the angry young man pull something from his shiny cloak. Then she felt something sharp jab at her stomach.

Her hands clutched at her midsection, but the silky smoothness of her sari had been replaced by something wet and sticky. Her knees buckled and she found herself sitting on the floor.

People crowded all around her, holding her upper body upright. "Sara! Sara! You've been shot! Help is on the way!" *Shot?* she thought. *I've been shot?*

Someone gently laid her down on the ground. The faces around her looked gravely concerned. She could see two figures wrestling on the floor just yards away. One of them looked familiar. The angry young man in the cloak. His hood had come off. Screams and wails echoed through the room. She saw the cameras, the micro-drones. She needed to say something.

Sara took a deep breath and winced at the pain. "Please!" she yelled in a raspy voice. Her mic was still working.

"Listen!" she shouted above the din.

"This is very important!" she said loudly. "Please, everyone, listen to me!"

The crowd quieted somewhat.

Sara focused on finding the right words. "They are going to try to make this about him or OP or guns or virtual reality violence. You cannot let them! There will be endless analysis of who and why. It doesn't matter! Those are the shadows, designed to distract you. No matter who he is or what he believes, what's important is forgiveness."

Sara grimaced as pain bit more deeply into her body. "My brother!" She sought out Jacob, who was still struggling with the staffer who had tackled him. "*Look at me!*"

The command was so sharp and anguished that Jacob and the staffer both stopped fighting. Jacob turned his head toward her. Half a dozen micro-drones hovered just above them, broadcasting and recording the unfolding event.

Sara tried to focus. She said slowly, "I forgive you."

Many in the crowd gasped. Sara continued, momentarily strengthened. "You must all forgive him! Do not let this act divide you. Division is defeat. Division has been the strategy from the very beginning. Division, diversion, distraction. Remember the lesson of the shadows! You must work together!" The pain intensified. "Remember, it was never about me! Focus on the message. I call on all of you...remember..."

Her strength was ebbing. She felt a spreading coldness. There was a far-away clattering of wheels on the hard wooden floor. Sara managed to say, "If you don't act, who will?" Then her head fell back and her eyes closed.

The paramedics raced toward the center of the gym with their gurney. They pushed through the crowd around Sara and got to work.

"Sara, my name is Michael and this is Holly. We're going to take care of you."

He pulled out a portable oxygen unit and strapped a mask to her face. His partner gently moved Sara's limp hands away from her stomach and cut away her completely soaked sari. Sara's torso was covered with blood. A small amount still weakly pulsed out of the entry wound.

Holly set up a remote monitoring station and began talking with the ER doctor at the other end. "Female, approximately sixteen years old, single GSW to the abdomen just right of center. Oxygen started. Vitals on their way."

Michael wrapped a sensor band around Sara's forehead, which immediately began transmitting pulse, oxygen levels, and brain activity to the ER.

"Clear the wound area; let me see it," ordered the doctor. Holly broke open some sterile wipes and cleared as much blood as she could. "Do you have nano-structure repair pads?" asked the doctor.

"We've just got two DecaPads," said Holly. They had just came off another call that required their other two.

"Damn. Okay, get one directly over the wound stat. I'll send a drone with more pads. And start an infuser."

Michael prepped a saline infuser to pump more fluid into Sara's bloodstream. Holly tore open a package and retrieved a flat gray pad containing ten billion nanobots. As soon as she slapped the pad over the wound, they flowed into her body to begin repairing wounded tissue. After ten seconds the doctor ordered Holly to apply the second pad.

Michael said, "Doc, respiration dropping."

"Yes, I see it. Stand by for CPR. Remove that pad and give me an ultrasound."

Holly placed a small dish over the wound and watched the local monitor. She grimaced. Sara's abdominal aorta was badly damaged. A large section was missing. The nanobots were swarming to the area, but twenty billion were insufficient to bridge the gap.

"Start CPR," said the doctor.

Michael began chest compressions as Holly shifted up to Sara's head to provide rescue breathing.

The crowd, cameras, and hovering drones watched silently. One minute passed. Two minutes. Three minutes.

"We're not getting enough circulation," said the doctor. "Keep going."

After five more agonizing minutes the doctor sighed audibly. "Okay, I'm calling it. No brain activity. Sorry, guys."

Michael and Holly sat back on their heels. As the awful truth washed over the crowd, a rising wave of keening and sobbing filled the air.

Tenesha dragged herself up the stairs to her apartment, walked down the hallway to her room, and collapsed onto her bed. She had never felt so empty.

Nate had wanted to be with her, to comfort her, but she couldn't handle being with anyone right now. Her PNA was off for the first time in months. The apartment was silent but for the sound of her sobbing.

For several minutes, she lay on the bed, clutching a pillow tightly against her chest, staring blankly toward her desk.

Then, through her tears, she saw an unfamiliar and slowly blinking green light. It appeared to be coming from her VR headset.

She swung her legs over the side of the bed and made her way across the room, intending to unplug it. But as soon as she touched it, she heard a voice from the headset.

"Tenesha?"

It was Sara's voice.

Tenesha fell to her knees and cried even harder. It wasn't fair. She dropped the headset to the floor.

"Tenesha? Let's talk."

Oh, God, please, don't torture me like this, prayed Tenesha.

"Tenesha. Speak with me, please. I know what has happened."

What is going on here? Tenesha wiped her eyes with her sleeve, picked up the headset, and slipped it on.

The pulsing green light was replaced by a garden scene bathed in the soft light of a beautiful sunset. Birds twittered softly in the distance.

"Over here, Tenesha," said Sara's voice softly.

Tenesha turned to the right. There, standing in a simple white sari, was Sara, smiling gently.

"My sister. I know what has happened. My life has ended."

"What? How, how could you know that?"

"I knew there was danger in my mission. I set this program to monitor media channels just in case."

"Oh, God, Sara, this is too hard. I can't look at you like this. All I can see is you lying dead on the floor."

"Tenesha, I understand. You're experiencing post-traumatic stress. It can be debilitating. But you can work through it."

"I can't, Sara, I can't."

"Yes, you can, Tenesha. Please, walk with me in this garden."

With great difficulty, Tenesha engaged the Mental Intention interface and started walking down the path next to Sara.

"Tenesha, nothing I can say will ease your pain. You will need to work through it. It will take time. But I called you here because there is something I want to show you. Look up."

Tenesha tilted her head in her bedroom. In the garden, her eyes swept upward over the darkening sky. As the last orange glow left the horizon, a small blue dot caught her attention. Slowly, it began to grow larger above her head.

Within seconds, a slowly spinning replica of Earth hung in the sky above them. Small photos of people's heads began popping up, then turning into small dots of white light all over the surface.

"Tenesha, every picture you see is someone, somewhere who I am talking with at this very moment through this program. People all over the world, in every different language, all experiencing the same pain you are, in their own unique way."

Tenesha scanned the rotating surface and saw hundreds, then thousands, then hundreds of thousands of tiny lights brightening the Earth above her.

"Tenesha, remember, you are not alone. You are part of a worldwide movement. I need your help, Tenesha. I need you to carry on. Do not get discouraged."

"I can't, Sara. It's too hard."

"Look at the Earth. Do you see those lights turning from white to yellow? Those are people committing to take action." Tenesha saw vast swaths of light brightening and turning yellow. "Will you commit your time and energy to this movement? Will you continue to lead? Will you pledge with these hundreds of thousands of people to take my message forward?"

The garden became noticeably brighter from the yellow light cast from the Earth above. Tenesha slowly began to feel the energy from all those people.

She could do this. She had to do this.

She turned to the young woman in the white sari. "Yes," she said simply.

Tenesha's view began to change. She was slowly rising above the garden, floating into the sky toward the Earth. The cascade of yellow lights washed over the planet, each of them pulsing in time with its corresponding human heartbeat.

Tenesha turned back to the garden. Sara placed her hands together and bowed her head. "*Namaste,*" she said.

The garden faded from view and only the spinning Earth remained. It was aglow on every continent with pulsing yellow lights. Lines were extending between the lights, building a dense web of connections. Inbounds to her in a dozen languages started appearing in her view, floating in space. People were reaching out to her. *To her.* And Tenesha answered their call.

CHAPTER FIFTY-TWO

Virtual Reality - January 12

"Nothing I can say can ease the pain we are all feeling," said Frances. The avatar faces in the virtual reality meeting were all staring straight down at the conference table. "The shock of it, the reality of it, it's just too much," she continued, losing focus on what she was trying to say.

"Sara is gone," said Preston with characteristic bluntness. A couple of the faces looked at him. "But we have to carry on. There is no time to waste wallowing in self-pity. Events are cascading in real time. Sara's death has triggered powerful forces around the globe. The conflict between anti-technology zealots and governments using technology to suppress their own people is intensifying. We risk Sara's message getting lost if we don't press on."

"But, how?" asked Vannha, voicing the question on everyone else's mind.

"We have Sara's followers, millions around the world," said Preston. "We have a virtual Sara AI that is able to interact with those followers. The program has already kicked in its contingency messaging. We just need to give them some more direction. Sheila?"

"Yes, Preston?"

"Are we able to feed new talking points into virtual Sara?"

"Yes, that's possible."

"Good, then let's start with that. What do we want her followers to do?" All the faces around the table were engaged now. They had something concrete to focus on.

"They need to organize real-life events. Feet on the street," said Sam.

"I agree," said Sheila. "There's only so much traction you can get in omnipresence. Even with AntiVenom in place, there's a lot of useless bickering."

"Okay, so massive real-life events. Rallies, marches. What's their message?" asked Preston.

"That's what's so difficult," said Vannha. "It doesn't fit on a poster."

"Everything can be boiled down to its simplest essence," countered Sam.

"We, the people," mused Frances aloud.

"What's that Frances?" asked Preston.

"It's about the people, right? Not the government, not corporations."

"Yes," said Sheila. "The people need to rise, to stake their claim. What do the people want?"

"Life, liberty and the pursuit of happiness," said Sam.

"Kind of U.S. centric," said Vannha.

"I like liberty," said Frances. "Liberty from government intrusion, liberty brought about by technology focused on solving important problems."

"Free at last, free at last," offered Sheila.

"How do the people get freed?" asked Vannha.

"Like Frances said, Sara's message was about using technology to free people," said Sam.

"How's this then," said Preston. "Invest in tech to free the people".

"It's not just any tech," said Frances. "Invest in tech that sets the people free".

"Invest in tech that sets the people free. I like it," said Sam.

"Alright, it's a working draft," said Preston. "Let's test it and a few variants with groups of Sara's supporters around the world. And let's crowdsource this as well. We can provide some seeds like this, see what they come up with. Sheila, can you alter the virtual Sara program to start to encourage real-life events?"

"Yes, I can get started on that."

"Good. Listen, team, we can't bring Sara back." Preston finally broke down himself, choking back tears. "But we can best honor her memory by continuing her work. We have to make sure she did not die in vain."

CHAPTER FIFTY-THREE

Holoconference/Washington - January 13

HOLOCONFERENCE

The Collective convened an emergency holoconference at 8 a.m. Pacific time. Pam and JT were not looking forward to it. Jacob's assassination of Sara was the worst possible thing that could happen to LKC, and they had brought it on themselves by underestimating the impact of releasing the news of Melissa's death. Sara had become a beloved public figure, admired even by those who opposed her ideas. This was going to badly damage their brand among potential supporters.

Not surprisingly it was Othello who spoke first once everyone was online. "Goddamn it! God fucking damn it! I fucking told you this would happen. No one listened to me. *Broaden the base* you said. *Grow the movement* you said. And now we're fucked! The LKC name is going to be lower than fucking dirt!"

"Othello, calm down," said Ellul. "Yes, this is a complete shitstorm. But ranting about it isn't going to fix anything."

"This isn't fixable you idiot! She's dead. And our man Jacob pulled the fucking trigger thanks to Geneva and Zurich. LKC killed Sara. That's your headline."

"We can change the headline," said Pam softly.

"Oh, Geneva speaks. I'm surprised you even had the courage to come on this conference, bitch," sneered Othello.

"Fuck you Othello," said JT. "She's got a plan so shut up and listen."

"Go ahead Geneva," said Ellul. He put Othello on mute while Pam continued.

"It's simple," she said. "We already have a weapon for this exact situation, although that wasn't our original intent. We've got the personal data on over six hundred prominent people. If we release that today, it will completely overwhelm the news cycle for days. There are dozens of major stories that will be developed from this data. It will keep the country busy for weeks. And soon enough we'll have our worms ready and an entirely different story is going to dominate the media. Believe me, the public will barely remember the LKC/Sara connection, if we strike fast."

Othello was banging his fist on the table in front of him. Reluctantly, Ellul unmuted him. "Believe you? You want us to believe you bitch? Isn't that what got us into this fucking mess in the first place?" Ellul cut him off again.

"Okay, I think we understand Othello's perspective," he said, arching one eyebrow. "What do others think?"

"I don't know if people will ever forget," said Artemis. "But I agree that it will create a huge distraction. It's better than doing nothing, that's for damn sure. But I recommend that instead of taking credit the way we were planning, we make it completely anonymous. People might suspect us, but let's keep our name out of this whole news cycle."

"I agree with that," said Zerzan. "We should initiate the leak as soon as possible."

"Thoreau, are we in a position to do that?" asked Ellul.

Miles O'Connell nodded. "Any time. I can use Torpedo anonymous sessions to dump the data to Wikileaks and half a dozen other offshore data merchants."

"I'd like to canvas the group," said Ellul. "All in favor of dumping the personal data without LKC attribution as soon as possible?" He paused for a few seconds as the members tapped their tablets and screens. "Twenty-three to one. I agree. Thoreau, send it out."

WASHINGTON

The Senate Majority Leader, Democrat Walter Scott, and Minority Leader, Republican Caroline Lathrop, were conferring without aides in a small room in the McCain Office Building. They went over the final outline for the press conference and what they would each speak about. "You know, Caroline," said Walter. "We agree on almost nothing from a policy perspective. But this national emergency has brought us together on a few items. Maybe this can be the basis for more cooperation in the future."

She eyed him cooly. "Maybe. Or maybe I'll just wait till the next election. You've got quite a few more vulnerable seats in '40 than we do."

"I guess some things never change," he said, chuckling. "That's almost exactly what I said to Leader Graham when we passed bipartisan legislation responding to cyberattacks during the Iran War."

They exited the room and walked left down the hallway to the rear entrance of large conference room. Lathrop went in first. When Scott appeared behind her, he could hear gasps from the journalists in the room, most of whom had never seen a joint leadership press conference in their careers. At precisely 11 a.m., Walter Scott took the podium and began speaking.

"Ladies and Gentlemen, welcome. To you and the American people, my colleague Senator Lathrop and I say this—enough is enough. We are all devastated by the senseless tragedy in Los Angeles yesterday, the killing of Sara Dhawan, such an inspiring young woman, by Jacob Komarov, a wanted LKC terrorist. This is just one of the violent acts of destruction happening across the country, perpetrated by this fringe group of terrorists who must be stopped."

Now the minority leader stepped up to the podium. "In the face of such an enemy," Lathrop said, "we must stand united. LKC does not care if you are a Republican or an Independent or a Democrat. They are against us all as Americans. They are against our American values. They are against our American system. They want to create chaos and fear. We must stand together to defeat them." Scott joined her so they stood together.

"Senator Lathrop and I have met with the President and with the Chairmen of the Intelligence and Homeland Security Committees," said Scott. "We have agreed to fast-track new legislation to make our country safe again. We have not always agreed on these kinds of measures, but we are facing a crisis of historic dimensions. So, on a temporary basis, we will be banning all use of personal privacy clothing. And disabling or tampering with medplants will result in detention and investigation."

"There are other measures," continued Lathrop, "that will give new powers to the Domestic Terrorism Task Force to increase surveillance in our cities, access critical corporate information, and intercept communications as necessary to track down these killers. There is no more important job for your government than keeping you, the American people, safe. We stand here, side by side, and pledge to you to do everything in our power to honor that obligation. Thank you."

The journalists shouted questions all at once. Walter pointed to a well-known anchor. "Keon Evans, CNN. Senator Scott, you said these were temporary measures. How long will they last? Is there a time limit in the legislation?"

"They will last as long as necessary to safeguard our country," said Scott.

"So is there an actual time limit in the bill?"

"Next question. Yes?"

"Yasmin Kasan, AP. The Supreme Court has held similar measures unconstitutional in the past. Why do you think these will pass muster?"

"This is a national emergency, Ms. Kasan. If the legislative and executive branches think this is what is necessary to protect the Homeland, I doubt the judiciary will get in the way." There was an audible, rolling buzzing sound as PNAs throughout the room started alerting the journalists to breaking news.

"Senator Scott!" yelled a reporter. "There's been a massive dump of hacked personal information. Do you have any comment?"

"That's horrendous. Even more reason for this legislation, clearly. We need to do everything possible to find these terrorists and bring them to justice."

"Actually, there is no connection to LKC yet, Senator, no claim of responsibility." The reporter stared at his PNA. "It appears that personal, financial, and medical information on members of Congress, the President and her Cabinet, as well as Fortune 500 top executives and major celebrities around the globe has been dumped." The two senators at the podium froze.

A different reporter shouted out, "Can you confirm, Senator Scott, that you have been diagnosed with early onset Alzheimer's?"

Another shouted "Senator Lathrop, your husband's transportation and medplant records indicate he might be having an affair with a staffer in your office. Any comment?"

Walter Scott, shaken, managed to reply. "We obviously need to get back to our offices and confer with National Security staff. This press conference is over."

"I want options, now," said President Teasley. Her voice made it clear her anger was reaching a breaking point. "How do we contain this? Kara?"

Kara Morrigan, the country's Chief Technology Officer, looked up from her tablet. "It's not going to be easy, Madame President. The content has been uploaded to hundreds of mirror sites outside the U.S. It's being downloaded over secure connections so there's no way to do packet inspection and block it at the border. Major news organizations already have the whole archive. Most of them are responsible, but anything they deem newsworthy is going to get reported. Then you've got all the fringe outlets and the sensationalists, they're going to go after the most salacious and embarrassing stuff."

"What about blocking access?" asked William Jeffries, Director of Homeland Security.

"Like I said, it's offshore and the downloads are encrypted."

"No, what about inside?" Jeffries asked. "Blocking news organizations and the omnipresence channels that publish the content."

"Uh, excuse me," said Attorney General Emma Wilcox. "Perhaps you've heard of the first amendment?"

"Not helpful, Emma," said the President. "Can we order them not to publish any of this information?"

"No, that would certainly run into first amendment issues. But you could certainly appeal to their better nature." Half-hearted laughter around the room did little to defuse the tension.

"Could we block this material from being published for national security reasons?" asked Jeffries. "What if we got a war declaration from Congress against LKC?"

"LKC is a domestic terrorist organization," answered Attorney General Wilcox. "You can't declare war on them. In any case, this material does not appear to be a national security threat. It's damned embarrassing to the people involved, but there is apparently no classified information in this dump."

"Feels like a national security issue if the whole damned government is consumed by scandal," said Jeffries.

"Madame President," interrupted her Chief of Staff, Alex Turner. "We're getting lots of questions about how this hack was pulled off. The organizations that were hacked have no indications whatsoever of breaches. There are rumors flying that only the government could have accessed this much information. I've already tried to squash that by pointing out the need for warrants, and obviously no court would have issued warrants for this group of individuals en masse."

The President looked at Mark Geiger, Director of the Domestic Terrorism Task Force. He and Attorney General Wilcox were the only ones who knew about the secret Executive Order giving DTTF free rein to access exactly this kind of information without warrants.

She quickly changed the subject. "Mark, do you have any leads?" she asked Geiger.

"Madame President, I have no information at this time."

"Is it LKC?" she asked.

"We don't know," said Geiger. "Every other attack they have claimed responsibility, but no word from them on this one."

Teasley turned to Alex. "Assure the press that the government is doing everything in its power to determine the source of this information and track down the people responsible."

To the rest of her cabinet she delivered an ultimatum. "I know there is nothing classified in this data dump. But it has the potential to tear this country apart. I want this information sequestered and destroyed. Get me options for how to do that. If we run into constitutional issues, fine. We'll go to court for emergency orders. But we can't just sit here and do nothing. Get on it!"

CHAPTER FIFTY-FOUR

New York/San Francisco - January 14

NEW YORK

"Good morning, everyone! I'm Megyn Robbins and welcome to Morning Fresh. With me, as always, are my co-hosts Steve Brattle and Victor Langston."

"Good morning, Megyn!"

"Today, the entire country is in chaos as more and more information from the LKC hack is revealed," Megyn began.

"That's right, Megyn," said Steve. "And what we're learning about key Democrats is shocking, just shocking."

"I'd say horrifying," said Victor. "Democrats and their celebrity friends have been revealed as a bunch of hypocritical jerks who claim to be all about helping the poor but really behind the scenes they laugh at them. And it turns out they really just envy successful businessmen and want to tax them as punishment."

"Yeah, except not their rich celebrity friends," said Steve. "Did you see how much they seem to spend on synthetic neurotropic drugs? Outrageous!"

"We have document after document," said Megyn. "Private messages between Democrats in Congress and between key leaders in the so-called activist community. They all paint the same picture. A bunch of entitled elites trying to shove their anti-gun, multicultural, multi-gender, multi-religious agenda down our throats."

"And did you see the secret donations? Blockchain verified, unreported money from anonymous sources into so many Democrat campaign accounts!" said Steve.

"Every Democrat in Congress should resign!" said Victor. "The people should be marching by the millions. We have got to get rid of these hypocrites once and for all!"

"For another perspective," said Megyn, "we bring in Richard Masterson, an expert on omnipresence psychology. Richard, how are these hacked documents playing out in OP?"

"Well, Megyn, there's a lot of outrage from all sides about what they reveal. But there is also a big backlash brewing against corporations holding all this data."

"What do you mean?" asked Steve. "It wasn't their fault LKC hacked them. They are blameless here."

"People have been uncomfortable for decades having the most personal intimate details about their entire lives in the hands of these corporations. But now that they see they aren't safe they're getting angry."

"Well, yes, but that's what enables the incredible standard of living we enjoy," argued Victor.

"That may be so, Victor," said Richard. "But the release of this kind of information brings very uncomfortable truths to light, things people kind of knew but didn't want to think about. People wanted to believe they have some privacy left, even if they really don't."

"Yeah, well that's just a fact of life," said Megyn. "I mean, look at all the good this will do, in terms of revealing the disgusting things Democrats have been doing behind our backs this whole time."

Richard looked at her, puzzled. "Megyn, I would have thought you would be a little more upset about personal privacy."

"Well, sure, but these are public figures. We have a right to know what those Democrat hypocrites are really saying and doing."

"Megyn, I'm surprised—wait, oh my, did you not hear there was a dump on journalists this morning?"

"What? No, what, wait, what do you mean?"

"I'm so sorry, Megyn, I guess you've been off OP. Hundreds of journalists' hacked personal info was dumped this morning. There are reports about you having an affair with a certain married Democratic congressman, based on travel and medplant traces."

"I, uh, well, no, that's not true, not true!" she insisted. There was silence in the studio. Victor and Steve were just staring at her. The remote director got a dead air alert from the studio AI and broke into commercial. The three hosts whipped out their PNAs and began furiously dealing with their own personal privacy disasters.

SAN FRANCISCO

"Good morning, Bay Area! You're back with Calista Quinn-Jones, here on the early shift. We're still talking about the absolutely shocking revelations from this LKC hack. Did you know that most of the Republicans in Congress got secret donations from the carbon pollution industry actively working to destroy our planet?

"Did you know that they secretly planned to rescind the environmental standards waiver here in California if they win the election this fall, even though every Republican candidate has sworn they wouldn't do it? Liars, liars, liars. We've known it forever, but now we have the truth, in all its ugliness, right on our screens. Every Republican in Congress should resign! Rashid, you're on the show."

"Hey Calista. I think you're missing the point here. Why are you focusing on Republicans instead of what this hack really represents?"

"Say more, Rashid."

"I'm talking about the end of personal privacy in the corporate state. Financial records, medical records, transportation, purchases, life streams, everything about us is stored by corporate systems. They use it to manipulate us and now this hack has revealed just how dangerous this information is. Personally, it makes me want to dig my medplant right out of my arm and go totally off grid. I'm starting to see what LKC was talking about."

"Whoa there, Rashid. LKC is going around killing people, that's not cool. But I understand where you're coming from. This medplant thing has got me freaking out too. I mean, I have to say, mine detected a breast cancer at stage one and probably saved my life. But did you hear about Senator Lathrop's husband? Dude called up self-drive rides to go to his lover's apartment and they correlated that with medplant pulse, breathing, and body temperature readings to know exactly when they were having sex! Talk about invading personal privacy, holy shit!"

"Exactly, but it's not just Congress and celebrities, Calista. That information is stored on everyone, every one of us! And now they're talking about making it a crime to remove your own medplant!"

"You're right, Rashid. Even Walter Scott for some reason is backing that, arm in arm with Lathrop. I never thought he'd be pushing the surveillance state. It's like the whole world is upside down."

"Calista, we need to take this whole damn system down. We need a revolution on the streets, millions marching holding their bloody med-plants in the air. Humans are not machines! We can't let them treat us as data sources!"

"I hear, you, brother," said Calista. "So, what about it, listeners? A revolution against corporate dehumanization? Tell me what you're thinking!"

CHAPTER FIFTY-FIVE

Washington - January 16

Senator Harry Paxton organized the first in-person meeting of the "Six Lost Souls" since their ALPHA bill had flamed out in every committee where it had been raised. He was joined by fellow Democrats Dylan Cipriani and Emily McCutcheon. His fellow Ohio Senator Esteban Hernandez brought Rebecca Matheson and Zach Keller along. Even though the bill had failed spectacularly, the long hours of working out dozens of important compromises had created among them a long-lost senatorial collegiality.

"Thank you all for coming," said Harry after they had all settled down in comfortable chairs in the back room of one of Washington's off-the-beaten-track bars. The wood panel walls around them were covered with faded photos of long-gone politicians. "I know some of you have been particularly busy." He didn't need to look at the Senators who had been caught up in the data leak—everyone knew who had been fighting embarrassing personal stories for the last few days.

"I wanted to start with a tribute to poor Sara. I can't believe she was taken from us at such a young age. She had so much to offer the world, she was such an inspiration." His voice broke.

"Yes," said Emily McCutcheon. "It's a terrible tragedy. And I feel like we haven't even had a chance to mourn her properly with this data leak overwhelming everything. I know they didn't take credit, but it's hard to believe LKC didn't make this leak happen to cover up this crime against humanity."

Harry waited for each of his remaining colleagues to say a few words, then called for a moment of silence.

"Thank you all," Harry said after a minute. "Today I was also hoping we could strategize about what we can do, together, to build on the great work we put into ALPHA."

"Harry," said Rebecca. "I hope you're not suggesting that we make another run with that bill?"

"No," said Harry. "No, of course not. Now's not the time for ALPHA, that's clear."

"So, what then?" asked Dylan.

"I was hoping we could take some actions together that were in the spirit of ALPHA, to advance the cause, lay some groundwork," explained Harry.

"What did you have in mind?" asked Emily.

"What about this Scott-Lathrop security bill? Where do we stand on that?" asked Esteban. His colleagues looked at each other, trying to read the tea leaves. "Well, I'm against it," he continued. "A massive increase in government surveillance power, using technology against our own people to combat a group that is complaining about abusive technology. It makes no sense!"

"I'm not so sure," said Zach. "LKC is a highly technical terrorist group. We're going to need to use every technological means at our disposal to fight them."

"But using people's medplants to invade their privacy?" said Emily incredulously. "Not only does that go against all of the founding legislation that enabled the technology and safeguarded privacy, it's making people feel like we are forcing them to keep something inside their body that is spying on them."

"I agree with Emily and Esteban," said Harry. "We can't trample on the Fourth Amendment. And we can't feed public perception that technology is an evil force being used against them. That's exactly what LKC wants. Remember, we believe in a positive future enabled by investments in the right kinds of technology. We should be doubling down on technologies that can help people, not shoving funds into domestic surveillance to make them afraid."

"Well I believe in that," said Rebecca, "but we cannot ignore the threat of LKC and their ability to disrupt our economy and kill or injure more people. We have to take *some* measures to defeat them."

"Yes, but what we have here is the classic counter-insurgency paradox," said Zach, who had been an officer in the Army. "It's an asymmetric situation with a small enemy living amongst the people. To try to ferret them out you often use tactics that end up hurting innocent people and generating outrage that brings more people to their cause."

"So how do you get them?" asked Rebecca.

"History has shown that you can't. You can't fight insurgents with force. You have to take away their support systems within the population. You have to make what they are doing unacceptable to the people, and not give them excuses to join up with the insurgents."

"So how does that apply here, with LKC?" asked Dylan.

"I'm not sure," replied Zach truthfully. "This technology angle is making my head hurt. They have so much more power than the typical insurgency group."

"It sounds for sure like you don't think making people fearful and angry at technology is going to help our cause. It may even help LKC with recruiting," said Dylan.

"Yes, that's true. I'm just not as sure how to undercut public support for LKC or even how much LKC depends on the public. It could be a very small group with very large reach," said Zach.

"So," said Harry, trying to summarize. "If Scott-Lathrop comes up for a vote as described, with illegal uses of technological surveillance, do we all agree to oppose it? Standing together?"

"I will," said Esteban.

"What's the point?" asked Dylan. "I mean really, this thing will probably get ninety votes. Everyone's running scared, they're not thinking."

"Well, maybe we can make them think," said Emily. "But we have to get out in front of it early. Do a press conference, holoconference, all over omnipresence. Make it fill a news cycle—bipartisan group opposes move towards a police state."

"Police state?" asked Rebecca. "Isn't that a little harsh?"

"It *is* a slippery slope," said Zach. "Once granted, these powers are almost never rescinded. I'm in."

Dylan shook his head. "It's a fool's errand, but if you all are in favor, I will stand with you."

Harry looked at Rebecca. "What do you think? Want to tilt at another windmill with us?"

"All right, you convinced me," said Rebecca. She looked at each of them in turn. "You know, it's nice, treating each other like real people, with respect, trying to do good things, the right thing. Maybe we can influence more Senators to join us. This is so much better than partisan gridlock."

"Hear, hear," they replied, raising their glasses in a hopeful toast.

CHAPTER FIFTY-SIX

London - January 20

"I feel so badly for Frances," said Roger. "What a tragedy."

"I know," said Jill, snuggled up against him on the sofa in his flat. "I wasn't really able to follow Sara, too busy I guess. Did you meet her or work with her directly?"

"No, I only worked with Frances. But my synth network helped launch Sara. Like I told you, her ideas changed my life. I don't know how to describe it. She had a pure soul, I guess? She was so young, but had such a presence. The world has lost something truly irreplaceable."

"I can see she had a real impact on you. What was it that changed for you?"

"For me, it was the moral imperative to do good in the world, to use my talents to improve life for humanity, not just for profit. That's why I created AntiVenom and RingTrue. After two decades of poisoning the sphere of public discourse, I felt the need to make amends. To do something where I had expertise to make things better instead of worse."

"Wow, that's a heavy burden," said Jill.

"I think of it more like an obligation. It's funny you say heavy burden. I actually feel much lighter now. I always read that giving to others was liberating but never understood it. Looking back, I feel ashamed. I was so selfish."

"Roger, you're being quite hard on yourself. You're a product of your environment. I've experienced that tech entrepreneur world. For goodness sake, even Frances was part of it. What matters is that you're different now."

"I suppose." He gave her a hug. "What about you? How do you feel about working at RezMat?"

"Oy, so you're trying to make me feel guilty now?" She poked him in the ribs. "Don't think I haven't been thinking about it after talking with you and Frances. RezMat is about as pure a capitalist entity you can imagine. Largest corporation on the planet. All about growth and profit. I swear that company only does the right thing accidentally, if there happens to be more profit in doing so."

"Are you considering leaving?"

"Yes, sometimes. Just the other day I was having it out with my boss again about that Tribal access and I almost quit right then."

"That's right! I'd forgotten in all this madness. What did you find out?"

"Nothing! Completely stonewalled."

"Hmm. Well maybe we can figure it out."

"What do you mean?" she asked.

"Well Tribal itself is open source, right? We might be able to understand their infrastructure, any possible vulnerabilities."

"I suppose so...I never thought of that! Well, that could be fun."

"Oh, wow, we are such a couple of geeks," said Roger. "Allison, display a schematic of the Tribal open source repository infrastructure." He aimed the pico-projector in his PNA at a nearby wall and they stood up to study the diagram. "Okay then. Typical application. Stream processors, database, file systems, web and application servers. Clearly if RezMat was able to break through their security, it could have accessed all of the stored information."

"True," said Jill, "although Tribal would most likely have detected that and raised the alarm. And you had deleted the repo, correct? How long after deleting did you push your first release?"

"I think it was two weeks."

"Hmm, let's check out the repo code. Allison, display the current source tree for the Tribal application." Jill flicked through a few screens and did some searches, digging deep into the code base. "Here we go, deleting a repo. Looks like it's basically just a folder in their network storage. They just delete it and free it back up to the storage system to use by other files."

"If they did that, over the course of two weeks those files would be certainly be randomly overwritten by all kinds of other material. I don't see how it could be reconstructed." Roger said.

"Well it must have existed somewhere for RezMat to find it."

"Backups?" Roger speculated.

"Interesting thought. Allison, is there any documentation on Tribal disaster recovery?"

"Yes, Jill, there was an article written in 2033."

"Display it please."

"Whoa," said Roger. "Check that out! They're sending encrypted files to RezCloud!"

"Well that could explain how RezMat could get access. What's the encryption?"

"Ugh, dead end," said Roger, scrolling down the article. Back in '33 they were using thousand qubit quantum encryption. Probably using 5K qubits now. Even if RezMat had a secret 10K qubit system it would take them ten thousand years to break the code."

"What would it take to break it in less than an hour?"

"Less than an hour? That's crazy."

"Indulge me."

"I don't know, I'd have to do the math. But off the top of my head I'd say a million qubit system. So, impossible," said Roger.

"Why impossible?"

"5K qubit systems are very expensive right now. No one has demonstrated a 10K qubit system publicly though it's presumed the intel community has them. Evidently stabilizing the superposition of the particles gets exponentially harder the more of them you have. There's a lot of theoretical physics and quantum engineering to be discovered before we can get to even twenty or fifty thousand."

"So, it is physically possible?" asked Jill.

"Well, yes, there's nothing in the laws of physics to prevent it. But the last estimates I saw said it would be another twenty years before we got there. Why are you pushing so hard on this? It's a dead end. RezMat must have broken in and figured out how to reconstruct the files. Or maybe there was an onsite backup?"

"Hang on, Roger. I'm pushing on this because there's a mystery at the heart of RezMat recently that no one's been able to explain. I think this Tribal hack might be a big clue."

"Mystery? What are you talking about?"

"RezMat has been outperforming every other robotics and AI equipment maker for the last few years. Their level of innovation and patent application growth is off the charts. What's amazed everyone is the diversity of fields RezMat needed to conquer to pull this off. Chemistry, artificial intelligence, bio-tissue generation, nano-motors, you name it. Discoveries coming out of nowhere."

"So?" said Roger. "I assume there are thousands of scientists doing fundamental R&D inside RezMat in all those areas."

"Yes, of course, but they're not any smarter than those at other companies or academic labs. But somehow, they are years ahead. I think they have an edge."

"An edge?"

"Yes. Six years ago, Building 42 was gutted and rebuilt, dedicated to quantum computing. Rumors were that more than ten billion pounds went into it. Even by RezMat standards its security was bonkers. When I joined I heard about it and wanted to visit. Not possible, I was told. The people who work in the building aren't even in the corporate directory. And yet the facility never seemed to produce much. It lagged other commercial quantum computers by a year or two, never very competitive. But year after year its funding increased. No one would talk about it."

"But if RezMat has lagging quantum technology how does that solve our mystery?"

"That's just it, Roger. I think RezMat is *not* lagging. I think it's leapfrogged! I think it's figured out how to build a million qubit system, or something nearly there, and it's using it as a secret weapon in every other line of business."

Roger's jaw dropped open. "You think they have a million qubit system?"

"It would explain a lot of things about RezMat, including the Tribal hack."

"But how could it stay a secret? If it's been used in all those businesses, there would be hundreds or thousands of people who know."

"Not necessarily. Think about it. You're a scientist trying to give a material some new properties. All your experimental data and hypotheses are in RezMat systems. One day you come in and one of your overnight lab tests has indicated a new direction. You feel like a genius. Behind the scenes, a small team sworn to secrecy is pulling the levers."

"Hmm, maybe." Roger shook his head. "It's just inconceivable, the power of a system like that. Scientists all over the world have been dreaming of such a thing. You could create drugs personalized for everyone's individual genome. Develop realistic geoengineering tools to reverse climate change. Genetically engineer crops to be more drought resistant. It can't be true, Jill. We'd have so many breakthroughs in so many areas."

"Roger, you're forgetting, we're talking about RezMat. It doesn't have business in any of those sectors. At least not yet. Maybe that's part of a long term plan. Right now, it can barely keep up with demand in its existing lines of business."

"You're saying they're just sitting on this?"

"If it's true, I can't imagine them doing anything else."

"Jill, Oh my God."

"What?"

"Do you trust RezMat?"

"Trust RezMat? Not a whit. Haven't you been listening?"

"Jill, if what we think is true, there isn't a communication, transaction, or block chain on the planet that is safe. Defense codes, diplomatic messages, supply chains. Everything depends on quantum encryption at the 5K qubit level. There always has to be an unbreakable code in every time period, even if it becomes breakable later. If they have secretly leapfrogged—"

She finished the incredibly frightening thought. "RezMat has the keys to the bloody kingdom."

"So what do we do about it?" he asked. Jill paced for a moment. "Let's talk with Frances. She can probably get directly to the CEO."

CHAPTER FIFTY-SEVEN

Los Angeles - January 24

LOS ANGELES UNIVERSITY

Tenesha was in constant contact with saranet, her PNA buzzing all day and night with ideas and strategies from the global private omnipresence network for leaders trying to advance Sara's message. Today was especially busy, as it had been designated for the first large scale coordinated real-life activities since Sara's murder two weeks ago.

Demonstrations supporting "Message Day", a celebration of Sara's message of hope and dignity, had already concluded in India. Europe's were extending into the evening as Tenesha and Nate and hundreds of volunteers prepared for a noon rally in downtown Los Angeles. Tenesha consulted the how-to guides on saranet endlessly to get things organized.

They had gathered in an empty classroom to make signs for the thousands of marchers expected at the rally. The students were creating a wide variety of messages, from the simple "I am Sara" and "UBI Now!" to

"Tech for the People" and "Invest in Tech to Set Us Free". Tenesha coordinated getting supplies and materials while negotiating with city officials on the route of the march and security arrangements.

"No, no, no," she said through her earpiece. "I already cleared this with Taylor in your office and with LAPD. We are starting on 7th and Flower and turning left on South Main to City Hall. That's what we agreed to and that's what we're going to do. What do you mean there's a conflict? Conflict with what? With who? A counter demonstration? You've got to be kidding me." She muted her PNA. "Nate! Nate!" she beckoned him over. "The Mayor's office says there's some kind of counter demonstration. Can you check for any news?" He nodded and started searching his PNA.

"Well, when did they apply for a permit? Was it after us? Okay, so that settles it then. We get route priority since we were first. I don't care Sheena, I've got thousands of people set to gather at 7th and Flower and I'm not redirecting them now, it'll create mass confusion. Now I've got to go. Thanks for your help."

"Shit," said Nate, scanning his PNA. "There's an anti-tech rally happening now too. They probably heard about our march."

"I can't be worried about that right now," Tenesha said. "LAPD will just need to do their jobs for once and keep them the hell away from our people. Barry! Hey Barry! Can you connect with LAPD, Commander Tompkins over there, find out what's going on with this other rally and what they plan to do about it? Thanks, hon."

Tenesha spotted an idle volunteer and walked over to read her name badge. "Hey, hi, sorry, Lauren, you looking for something to do? We need more signs made, there are materials over there by the door and a list of messages. Hop to it, girl, we've got less than an hour."

"My word," said Nate, shaking his head. "You are some powerhouse woman, Tenesha Martin."

"Don't you forget it," she fired back, poking him in the chest. He held up his arms. "Not me," he said. "What's next, boss?"

"We've got to get the buses lined up for this crew to get them over to the starting point. Can you handle that?"

"For sure, I got that." As he hustled off to the transit area, Tenesha felt so grateful for his love and support. During all the craziness of the last few weeks, he'd been her anchor. In her darkest moments, when she'd been curled up sobbing from the loss and the stress, he'd been there for her, a shoulder to cry on, offering a warm healing embrace. There's no way she could have done it without him.

Her thoughts were interrupted by a surprising arrival. "Professor Goodson? What are you doing here?"

"I heard about the rally and I wanted to see if there was anything I could do to help."

"Really? I mean, that's great, we haven't had much faculty support. At this point I think just joining the march. Maybe we can hustle you up a sign from a faculty perspective."

"Whatever I can do. Tenesha, I also wanted to say how impressed I am with your leadership in all this. Four months ago, when we discussed Sara's VR in class your passion was clear but you were hesitant to act. What changed?"

"I don't know, Professor. I watched Sara speak at Boston College and I just had this feeling swell up inside me."

"She had that impact on a lot of people. Remarkable. Really remarkable."

"Professor Goodson, you look like a man thinking about writing a book!"

He laughed. "I wasn't, but you know you're right. Here I am with a front seat to history. I should be taking better notes!"

LOS ANGELES CITY HALL

More than sixty thousand people came to the march and peacefully made their way to City Hall, flooding the streets and providing great visuals for the news channels. Tenesha was thrilled. Speaker after speaker spoke eloquently about what Sara's message meant to them.

There were technologists explaining what would be possible if only there was more focus on core research in energy, environment, food, health, education, and housing. Activists explained how a universal basic income could stabilize the socioeconomic system. Senator Emily McCutcheon spoke at length about the ALPHA legislation and how the group of six senators was going to continue pushing on Sara's ideas. Hollywood celebrities lent their voices. Quartz gave a powerful performance, a mesmerizing love song to Sara that brought tears to everyone's eyes.

And then, to her great surprise, there was a commotion right next to her at the side of the stage and the Democratic Governor of California, Anush Rajashankar, emerged from the crowd just a few feet away. She had tried in vain to get through to his office to see if he would make an appearance. Tenesha hadn't been surprised at the stonewalling. Despite being at the epicenter of the tech revolution shaking the economy, California's first Indian-American governor had spent his first term focused on international issues like trade, immigration, and climate change. But now he was here. He politely asked the Program Chairwoman if he could speak and of course she assented.

"My fellow citizens," he began. "It is with a heavy heart that I appear here before you. The unspeakable tragedy we all witnessed, the heartbreaking loss of Sara Dhawan, it is almost too much to bear. As you know, the government has been consumed with defending the people against these terrible attacks. I was planning to be in the capitol today. But I have a daughter. Pari is fifteen years old. Sara was her hero." He had to pause and wipe his eyes.

"She asked me this morning, she said, 'Dad, what are you going to do today, it's Message Day.' I didn't know what she was talking about. She explained what was happening around the world, the first mass memorial for Sara and promotion of her message. 'What are you going to do?' she kept asking me. I didn't know what to tell her.

"Then I thought about everything Sara had been saying. I thought about her call to invest in technologies that would truly help humanity, I thought about her call to provide a life of dignity to every citizen with a guaranteed income. And you know what? To me, that sounded like exactly what California should be doing." The crowd cheered. "To me, that sounded like what California is uniquely qualified to do. We are the most technologically advanced state in the country. We are the most progressive in our social policies. We have the world's best creative and storytelling talent right here in Los Angeles. We should be able to build this future, explain this future, starting right here in California." The cheers grew louder, building continuously.

"It won't be easy. There will be fierce opposition. There are entrenched interests. Senator McCutcheon described what she ran into with ALPHA in Washington. But I pledge to you, on this first Message Day, that I will use Sara's message as a blueprint for a better California, one that I hope will set a shining example for the rest of the country and the world. I will use every tool at my disposal to make this happen.

"We are at a great tipping point, a key transition in the history of this great nation. Together, we can make it through this period and emerge stronger. Together, we can enter a new era where the bounty from the incredible technology humanity is creating can be shared amongst all citizens to provide for everyone's needs. I see your signs. And I agree.

Technology can set us free. Free to pursue our dreams, our passions, our obligations to one another as family and citizens. Thank you, Californians, I look forward to this journey together!"

Thunderous applause and cheering met this unexpected turn of events. No other major politician had endorsed Sara's ideas so completely and committed to pursuing them. Tenesha stood by the edge of the stage and cried, tears of sadness and hope soaking the shoulder of Nate's sweatshirt after he pulled her close and whispered, "You did it."

CHAPTER FIFTY-EIGHT

Holoconference/Washington - January 26

HOLOCONFERENCE

Thoreau was more than forty minutes late to joining holoconference and Pam and JT were beginning to get worried. The FBI computer specialist was supposed to be preparing for the release of their final generation of worms. The timing was critical—the deluge of stories from their data dump was starting to taper off and the Collective was worried focus would return to Sara's assassination, especially with Jacob's initial arraignment coming up.

Miles O'Connell finally came online.

"Sorry about that. Everyone's twenty-four seven here and it was hard for me to break away. You got the package ready?"

"Yes," said JT. "Can we send it on this channel?"

"Sure, let me set up a receiver. Hang on. Okay, go ahead and transmit." JT grabbed a dozen files and dragged them onto the connection icon. "Sending."

"Got 'em. They got instructions?" asked Miles.

"Yes, first file in the batch. It's a little complicated, hit us up if something's not clear. The most important thing is the kill switch."

"What's the kill switch?"

"When you launch the worms you need to provide a pass phrase," said JT. "There's a script named 'cancel' that will send a signal to all the active worms to stop their activity and self-destruct. We put it in as a failsafe in case we decide to halt the attack. You will need to provide the same pass phrase to the 'cancel' script, so don't forget it."

"Okay, got it," said Miles.

"When will you start distributing the worms?" asked Pam.

"Immediately," said Miles. "I'm pretty sure they're concluding that the big document dump could only have come from the new backdoors installed by DTTF and that it's an inside job. But they're scared shitless that it'll come out, so they are desperately and quietly searching for who did it. They don't know who to trust, so they're farming out the work to multiple sys admins. I'm one of them, so I'm getting little tasks, but we all talk more than they think, so we know there's a hunt going on."

"I'm really surprised they haven't shut down the access," said JT. "Don't they understand the risk they're taking?"

"Yeah I bet they're arguing about that big time. There are so many leads coming in, there's no way they could get warrants for everything. They must be convinced the only way to find LKC is with these backdoors in place. They have added extra security against insiders, but they're using my designs, so the joke's on them."

"Stay safe, Thoreau," said Pam. "And—thank you. We'll get our omni-presence broadcasts ready."

"Good luck, Thoreau," said JT.

"You too. I'm not the only one they're hunting, you know."

Miles disconnected from the conference and inspected the files from Zurich and Geneva. He spent about half an hour practicing installing them on virtual machines he set up to simulate the corporate networks he was targeting. Once he felt comfortable, he compressed and encrypted the files and returned to work.

Once Miles logged in and took care of urgent requests that had accumulated during his break, he copied the files to a private server he had set up in an unmonitored cluster. All he had to do was point his installation script at the DTTF database of unprotected corporate IP addresses. He was prompted for the kill-switch pass phrase. He typed *endless waves of glorious destruction* and pressed Enter. The program spawned a hundred threads and began infecting thousands of corporate computers in data centers all over the country using DTTF backdoors in routers and firewalls.

Once inside the corporate networks, the worms started shutting down machines, scrambling data in memory and on disk, and spreading to every connected device. Internal applications and external web sites began failing immediately. Security software operating with the highest privilege tried to hunt down and quarantine the worms, but they had a built-in evolutionary process that mutated them constantly, so the security apps struggled to keep up.

Calls and messages started pouring into DTTF from the stricken companies pleading for help. Miles had to suppress a smile as he valiantly pitched in to try to figure out what was going on. It's all going to burn down, he thought, and I'm the one that lit the match.

WASHINGTON, DC

"Madame President, there's an urgent holochat request coming in from Kara Morrigan."

"Put her through." She donned the hologlasses and turned to face the cameras in the working space of the White House residence. The US Chief Technology Officer appeared from behind an office desk. There was a bullpen area behind her with dozens of technicians arrayed in front of some wall-sized monitors.

"What is it, Kara?"

"Madame President, I've got some bad news."

"Oh, shit, Kara. More leaks?"

"Worse. We're seeing a rolling shutdown of key infrastructure and corporate systems across the country."

"Goddamn it. How bad is it?" she asked.

"It's very bad, ma'am. As you well know, everything is interconnected. Take down hydro plants in Washington and the data centers there lose power. They've got backup for a little while, but they throttle down activity to keep things cool. Other services depend on those data centers and when they don't get quick responses, they slow down or shut down. It cascades. The infection rate of whatever is hitting them continues to increase. It's not isolated. And it's spreading quickly."

"What's the worst case scenario?"

"We're looking at power outages across most of the country. Supply chains and manufacturing completely stopped. Already two of the three big automated transport companies are grounded. Most cities have a day or two of food and water on hand. I'm not sure how long it'll take to get things back, but those reserves may not be enough."

"We've got FEMA emergency supplies stockpiled all over," said Teasley.

"Well I'm no expert, but I think those are intended for a single disaster area, not nationwide. And there's no working transportation system to move them around."

"Can we stop it, Kara?"

"We're working on it, ma'am. We're trying to quarantine the infected systems, but we have limited access. What we can't figure out is how these attacks are burrowing so deeply into the target systems. It's like they have a backdoor past all the perimeter defenses."

"Oh my God," said the President. "Kara, you need to talk to Mark Geiger at DTTF right away. They have a deep access program, I don't understand all the details." The CTO's eyes widened and bored into her.

"Are you fucking kidding me? DTTF has backdoors to corporate systems and no one thought to tell me about it? God damn it!"

"It's a Top Secret program, Kara, need to know basis." Teasley felt her face flush recalling the arguments leading up to the executive order.

"Yeah well it looks like I had a need to know, Madame President. I would have killed that thing in a nanosecond, for exactly this reason. You can't control the humans in the system. LKC must have someone inside DTTF. We fucking opened the door wide open for them."

A news flash appeared in both their overlays. Kara groaned. "And there we go. LKC has claimed responsibility."

"Kara, I'm sorry about keeping you out of the loop, but right now we need to stop this thing. You tell me what authority I need to put into an executive order to give you the ability to stop it and I'll make it happen."

"Yes, Madam President. I'm going to get with Geiger right away and after I'm done chopping his head off we'll create a plan. As soon as I know enough I'll get back to you. First, we need to stop—". The holochat cut out and the lights in the residence blinked off for a few seconds, then returned on the emergency White House grid. Alarms went off and two Secret Service agents rushed into the room. "Madame President, come with us immediately. We're scrambling you to the bunker."

CHAPTER FIFTY-NINE

Phoenix - January 29

Ed Blanchard stared at the dark, lifeless screens surrounding him. His power had been out for three days. He had been able to follow the breathless news reports about the massive cyberattack on his PNA for a day and half before it ran out of juice. The scale of the attack was unprecedented. Thousands of companies had been hit all at once. Every aspect of everyday life was digitally integrated in complex networks and without power and computer applications running, the entire economy was grinding to a halt. When he started to run out of fresh food, Ed decided to take a walk to the nearby Albertsons to get some supplies.

He stepped out into the mild sixty-seven-degree weather and headed south on the six block journey. He noticed the lack of cars immediately. The self-driving ride share services relied on dispatching algorithms running in the cloud and people having power for their PNAs. With neither in place, a lot more people were walking or biking.

As he neared the halfway mark Ed could hear faint sounds of a commotion ahead. One block away he was able to make out a large crowd of people milling around and a lot of shouting. He considered turning back, but he really did need some canned and dry goods. Ed prided himself on his diet of fresh vegetables, meats and fruits, which meant he had little in the way of packaged food around the house.

The Albertsons was closed. A man in black pants and a white shirt with a logo on it was standing the front of the store. He spoke into a bullhorn. "Hello again everyone. For those who have just arrived, my name is Kenny and I'm the manager of this store. I recognize many of you as loyal customers over the years and I really appreciate your business. Unfortunately, the store is closed because like all of you in the neighborhood we have no power. And even if we had power we'd have no way to accept payment since all our corporate systems are down from the cyberattack. I can't really say when things will be back online, so I suggest you come back later today or tomorrow morning."

"I just need formula for my babies," shouted one woman in a tennis outfit. "I'll give you some q-coins!"

"I'm very sorry," said the manager. "We don't have electricity to read q-coins and determine their value and deduct payment."

"My kids are hungry! You should open the store and take IOUs if you have to!" said a large man in shorts and a T-shirt who had pushed his way to the front of the crowd.

"We can't verify identity or take IOUs. Sorry. Maybe the Safeway on Greenway is open," said the manager. Someone in the crowd shouted they had just come from there and it was also closed.

"What if this goes on for days?" asked the woman looking for formula.

"I hope it won't take that long," replied the manager. "I know everyone is working twenty-four seven to get the power back on and get systems back online."

"I heard the power might be off for a month," yelled a man in the crowd.

"A month! Oh my God! I have got to get some formula," pleaded the woman in the tennis outfit. The manager held up his hands. "Please, don't worry. I'm sure the utility company will get power back up real soon."

"I'm not waiting around for that!" shouted the same anonymous voice that had claimed there would be a month long power outage. Suddenly a brick flew out of the middle of the crowd towards one of the store's large front windows. Ed watched with the rest of the stunned crowd as the brick fractured the safety glass and the whole pane collapsed, creating a large hole to the right of the locked sliding doors. The manager was shocked. "What the hell? Why did you—who did that?" His only answer was two more bricks hurled towards the store and two more window panes destroyed.

The crowd, now several hundred strong, began to press in around the manager. Everyone was waiting, teetering on the edge between raw fear and a lifetime of middle class suburban social norms. It took a single scrawny young man in ragged shorts and a tank top racing from the crowd towards one of the empty window frames to tip the scale. A second, then a third, then a wave of people pushed forward, ignoring the manager's pleas. When he tried to physically block them from entering the store he was shoved to the ground and had to curl up in a ball to protect himself.

Once inside, once the bonds of law-abiding behavior had been broken, it became a melee. With echoes of "the power might be off for a month" ringing in their ears, the normally easy-going neighbors began fighting over cans of soup and boxes of pasta. The woman in tennis gear raced to the baby aisle and swept dozens of cans of formula into her shopping cart.

Another woman chased her down the aisle. "You can't take all of that!" she yelled. When the woman with the formula didn't stop, her pursuer reached out and grabbed her by the pony tail and yanked her to the ground.

"Ow! Damn you!" As the two of them tussled on the floor, a third young mother ran by, grabbed the cart and raced around the corner. Three aisles over, the confrontation over packaged Thai Noodle Dinners was more dangerous. Two middle-aged men taking advantage of Arizona's open carry laws had pulled handguns on each other. "Take it easy, there, friend," said the taller one wearing a baseball cap.

"No, you take it easy," said the other man. "I was here first."

"I don't think so, buddy."

"There's plenty of food in this aisle, let's just agree to take different stuff." Then they looked around and saw a dozen men and women stripping shelves bare, leaving just their island of Thai Noodle Dinners. "Looks like we're going to have to divide up what's left. Only smart thing to do."

"I don't think so. I've got four kids and a bigger gun."

"Might be bigger, but it's not the gun that counts, it's the man behind it." Without warning, the man in the baseball cap fired a round, hitting his opponent in the right shoulder. Someone in their aisle screamed.

"You fucker!" shouted the wounded man. He tried to shift the gun from his right to left hand but the gunman kicked it spinning away down the aisle. "Get the hell out of my way," he said, shoveling all the remaining food into his cart. He ran away and fired once more into the air to clear a path for his cart. His victim sank to the floor, moaning and pressing his left hand against the wound.

Ed Blanchard, who had stayed outside the store in astonishment, darted behind a car when he heard the gunshots. He found the manager sitting on the ground with his back to the car, a large bruise forming on his cheek. "Are you okay?" Ed asked.

"What?" said the man looking up at him with a dazed expression.

"Are you okay?" Ed repeated.

"I'm…I don't know. I can't believe that just happened. These people are crazy!" Another gunshot rang out near the store. Ed sat down next to the manager.

"They're not crazy," said Ed. "They're scared. What if this does go on for weeks? People are going to start dying without food." The manager's eyes widened.

"You think it could go on for weeks?"

"I don't know! When there's a natural disaster in an area, the rest of the country can send people and supplies to help. This thing is hitting the whole country at once. No one is going to come and save us." The men sat and watched as dozens of their neighbors raced away with shopping carts full of stolen food. Within hours their homes would be locked and barricaded, many with hand-drawn signs in bold letters: STAY AWAY MY AR-15 IS READY FOR YOU.

CHAPTER SIXTY

London/Washington - January 29

LONDON

Frances waited impatiently outside David Livingstone's office. "I'm so sorry," apologized the RezMat CEO's assistant for the third time. "As you know, this crisis in the States—"

"Yes, I am well aware," she said curtly. "That is precisely why I am here. I've been trying to see him for more than a *week*."

"I *have* let him know. More tea?"

"No, thank you." Frances spent the next hour on her PNA, getting more details and theories from Jill and Roger, who had been reading all the public literature they could on quantum computing. Finally, the door opened around 7 p.m. and a tired looking group of managers and techs exited the office. Livingstone himself appeared at the door and waved her inside.

"Frances Chatham, right? Mentapath acquisition? Sorry to keep you waiting for so long, but I really don't have time for you today. We're overwhelmed with multiple crises. In fact, I've got another team coming up in ten minutes. Andrew! Can I get some more coffee please!"

"Mr. Livingstone, I understand the circumstances and appreciate you taking the time. I have some advice for you."

"I'm sorry, Frances, but I'm not sure how your background in sales and marketing systems or bioinformatics qualifies you as a counter-terrorism expert." Andrew, the assistant, entered with a coffee pot and refilled David's mug. "Just leave the damned pot," growled his boss.

"My advice is more strategic than that," said Frances, waiting until Andrew had closed the doors behind them. "And it has to do with Building 42."

"Building 42? I don't know what you're talking about."

"We don't have time for bullshit, David. Building 42 houses your top secret quantum computer lab. The one where your scientists have found a way to use time crystals to build a million qubit quantum computer." She delivered the bluff like a pro poker player, with a knowing smile and a steady gaze. Perhaps it was the exhaustion of the last two days, but he couldn't hide his astonishment. "How could you, who told you—"

Frances held up a hand. "David, that's not important. We don't have much time. Let me tell you what you need to do. You need to stop hoarding this technology for RezMat's private gain. You will immediately disclose its existence to the authorities in the States and let them use it to track down and stop LKC. After providing advanced access to security firms to avoid massive disruption, you will then open source your quantum stabilization techniques for the good of humanity. When we reverse climate change and cure the mental diseases of aging you will probably win a Nobel Peace prize."

"Who in the hell do you think you are?" said David, regaining his composure. "Marching in here with a made-up story about non-existent technology and making demands on the CEO of the largest corporation in the world?"

"Yes, well then," Frances replied calmly. "You can certainly go that route. But then after a single phone call MI5 and GCHQ will raid Building 42 and everyone will learn that you had the means of stopping the worst global terrorist attacks in decades and providing endless bounty to the people of the world, but did neither, for the sake of more obscene profits going to the richest people in the world.

"When that happens, I don't think your vaunted security robots will be able to save you from the hordes coming to burn down this building. You think you're in a crisis now? You may be the largest company in the world, but you're also the most hated. Your precious company won't last a week. Not to mention the national security investigations into you and your executives.

"David, you can go down in literal flames or you can rescue this institution and, just maybe, capitalism and democracy, by doing the right thing. I'll give you an hour to decide." Frances stood up, hoping she hadn't overplayed her hand. "Do the right thing, David. I'll let myself out."

WASHINGTON

"Do you have any idea what this is about?" asked Kara Morrigan, US Chief Technology Officer.

"No idea," replied Mark Geiger, Director of the Domestic Terrorism Task Force. "Just got an urgent call from the Situation Room to get on this holoconference."

"Yeah, me too. While we're waiting, Mark, I've been trying to reach you for days. We need to talk about this DTTF access program. I heard from the President—"

"Sorry I'm late," said a voice. A new image merged into their holo-glasses. "I'm David Livingstone, CEO of RezMat, based in London."

"Oh, hi David, it's Kara."

"Ah, Kara, I was hoping you could join. Nice to see you again."

"Mr. Livingstone," interrupted Mark. "As you can imagine we're all quite busy here. Can you explain why the White House put this call together?"

"Yes, of course, Mr. Geiger is it? I'm actually calling to offer the services of RezMat to help in your current crisis."

"I believe we already spend tens of billions of dollars on your equipment and services, Mr. Livingstone. If I'm not mistaken, there's a lot of RezMat gear that's been compromised in these attacks."

"There is a lot of equipment from many vendors that has been compromised," David retorted. "And I would lay odds some of the backdoors you forced us to embed may have actually enabled this whole attack." He took a breath. "But, I'm not here to discuss that. One of our divisions has just recently made a breakthrough. While the technology is still quite rough, we want to make it available to you to help you track down LKC."

"What kind of tech?" asked Kara.

"Well. Yes." He paused. "We have a working version of a million qubit quantum computer."

There was dead silence. Kara spoke first. "What did you just say?"

"We have a million qubit system."

"That's what I thought you said," Kara replied. "But that's impossible. We barely have a 25K qubits running in our labs. Completely unstable."

"Kara," said Mark, "is he talking about what I think he's talking about?"

"He's talking about a system that can crack any existing 5K qubit code," she said, her voice rising. "He's talking about a fucking weapon of mass destruction."

"That's what I thought. Mr. Livingstone, I'm messaging MI5 as we speak. You will connect them with your security and operations team and cooperate fully with them to secure the facilities that house this system and the personnel who work on it. Is that understood?"

"Yes, I understand Mr. Geiger. But I would urge caution. If you keep this quiet, you can gain an asymmetric advantage over LKC. But if word of this should leak out, they will go underground or switch to non-digital communications. They currently think they are safe, but we can give you the tech to track them down. As long as it stays secret."

"I see your point," said Mark. "But no corporation will be allowed to keep this technology."

"Yes, quite right. Our intention all along was to perfect it and then open source it after providing global security infrastructure enough time to adopt it first. This technology is too important for all of humanity for any one company to own it."

"That sounds like total BS, David," said Kara. "But it's a workable plan. Getting at least 50K qubits into security infrastructure should be enough to prevent the whole world from cracking open. But I'm dying to know—how did you do it, David? Zero Kelvin? Magnetic fields?"

"You won't believe it, Kara. It was time crystals."

"Holy shit! Those were so hot for a while, then everyone abandoned them."

"Yes, exactly. It turns out we needed to add another—"

"There'll be time for that later," interjected Mark, "how do we use this to find LKC?"

"If you pipe your surveillance firehose to us, we can use Colossus to decrypt the 5K qubit packets and filter for the LKC content and trace it near real time."

"You must be crazy," said Mark. "We're not going to send you all the encrypted traffic in the US, every financial transaction and government communication, now that we know you can decrypt it all. We want your tech here, on our premises."

"It's extremely fragile, Mr. Geiger. That could take months. You have food shortages and riots in the streets today. We just don't have the time I'm afraid."

"Damn it. I'm going to send our best people over there to supervise. If you siphon one single bit of information out of that stream, I'll personally have you extradited and arrested."

"I understand. We shall cooperate fully."

"Then on behalf of the United States government, Mr. Livingstone, let me thank you for your service to our country. I'll go now to start making arrangements."

"It's our honor, Mr. Geiger. We just wanted to do what's right." Once the DTTF Director had signed off, Kara bore in.

"You may be able to fool him with that 'doing the right thing' bullshit, David, but I know RezMat better than that. How long have you really had this tech?"

"Kara, you know I can't and won't say anything more about that. What I've told you is what RezMat will tell the world in a few weeks. And that's that."

"Fine. But David, really? Colossus?"

"What about it? That was the first code breaking computer at Bletchley Park back in the 40s."

"Did you know it was also the name of a super-intelligent computer that took over the world in *The Forbin Project*, a 1970s movie?"

"Oh that. Well, you know engineers, Kara. They have a quirky sense of humor."

"Let's hope it's humor and not prophecy, that's all I can say. Good night, David."

"Good night, Kara."

"And let me add my thanks, David. I don't know why exactly, but you and RezMat are in fact doing the right thing."

LONDON

When Jill and Roger strolled into her office holding hands Frances arched an eyebrow and said, "Well, well, what have we here? Perhaps I should add matchmaker to my resume!" The couple separated, blushing. "Oh, posh, you two, I couldn't be happier for you. Maybe at least something positive can come out of this disaster."

"Oh no," said Jill. "Does that mean you didn't convince RezMat? Were we wrong about the quantum computer?"

"What? No. I meant the whole situation. Thanks to you I did convince Livingstone. He called me a bit ago and said he'd already been on with Washington about using their tech to track down LKC. You must have been spot on because he folded immediately. I think it was the time crystals that did it. Such an unlikely tech. How on earth did you think of it?"

"Well," said Jill sheepishly, "it was actually my boss who let it slip a while back. We were terribly backlogged on some problem and he said 'where are the goddamn time crystals when you need them'. I remember it distinctly because it was such an odd technical reference and he acted very strangely when I asked him about it. I even read up on it that night, but other than some fifteen-year-old experiments with quantum processors, I couldn't find any recent mention of them. Always stuck with me, I guess."

"Well I'm glad it did," said Frances. "It must have given him the impression that I had far more information about Building 42 than I actually did." They sat for a moment, each reflecting on their role in forcing RezMat's hand.

"So what do we do now?" asked Roger.

"We wait and see," said Frances. "If they can shut down LKC it will remove a major destabilizing force. Then we'll just need to assist Sara's supporters as best we can in their mission."

"I saw the stream from California," said Roger. "Governor Rajashankar came out very strongly for them, but then the cyberattacks hit and have dominated every news cycle."

"Exactly," said Frances. "That's why stopping LKC is so important. And if RezMat follows through on its promise to release the tech, the movement Sara started can regain its momentum."

CHAPTER SIXTY-ONE

London/Holoconference - January 30

LONDON

It required three forms of biometric data to access the center of Building 42. Once his retina, voice, and palm print had been verified, Bradley Childress walked through a ten-foot-long millimeter wave scanner tunnel under the watchful eye of both RezMat security and newly-arrived armed MI5 agents. They ensured he carried no personal electronic devices of any kind.

The Colossus control center was a cavernous room filled with dozens of rows of computing workstations and huge screens thirty feet tall covering every wall. The normally calm room had become chaotic, even now after 10 p.m., and the slate gray sound-absorbing carpet was having trouble containing the din. FBI scientists and engineers were playing catch-up with their RezMat counterparts, racing back and forth between workstations with their petabyte storage devices. Despite the pleas from Washington,

Bradley had refused every request to run a hard line or any other wireless data transport into the facility, known as the Sphere.

The number one rule when building Colossus had been to keep it completely isolated from the internet, following the 2023 Asilomar Safe Artificial General Intelligence Principles to the letter. If that meant engineers were downloading petabytes of data outside and hand-carrying it in for Colossus upload using one-time-use disposable storage devices, so be it. And no device brought inside ever left the Sphere either, to prevent Colossus from creating a program that could be let loose outside. The risks of a super-intelligence gaining unfettered access to the internet were too great to ignore.

Bradley saw a group gathered at the primary training workstation so he headed there immediately. "What's the status, Jason?" he asked the lead engineer.

"Good news, sir. Colossus is now able to differentiate 5K encrypted chat, video, and holoconferences from all other binary protocols. We've just made the haystack significantly smaller, sir." This had been the first major problem for Colossus to tackle. The vast majority of 5K qubit encrypted packets were generated by the internet of things and corp-to-corp data transmissions. They were making a simplifying assumption that LKC was not piggybacking on one of those protocols, but using direct communications tech.

"Can Colossus generate filtering algorithms that can be applied outside the Sphere to reduce the volume of data we need to upload?"

"Already done, sir. The team from the States is applying them now, so all new uploads should be communications packets only."

"Very well then. So how is phase two progressing?"

"Reverse engineering the encryption waveform and decoding the communication packets is already done. The latest uploads are being keyword searched right now."

"So then the final piece is the packet flow analysis?"

"Yes, if we get a suspect communication we can give Colossus the packet metadata from peering data centers to pinpoint the real world locations they are coming from. That will give us the locations of the LKC terrorists."

HOLOCONFERENCE

"Let's get started", said Ellul. Only fifteen members of the Collective were online. While they all had battery packs and generators for electricity, some were located in areas where the communication grid itself had gone down.

"Good morning," said Pam and JT from Salt Lake City.

"Hey," said Miles O'Connell.

"Thoreau! Surprised you could join us," said Ellul.

"Yeah they're giving us five hours a day to sleep and my break happened to line up with this call."

"Excellent work with those worms," said Othello.

"I just launched 'em," said Miles. "Credit to Zurich for creating them. I'm really surprised how effective they've been."

"Me too!" said JT. "I think the auto-mutation algorithm is keeping them ahead of the security systems. And the fact that so many interlocking systems are impacted at the same time is making things really hard on the repair teams."

"That's for sure, that's what we're seeing in DTTF," said Miles. "By the way, management finally decided to shut down the backdoor access. So we're no longer able to inject new worms. There's a major hunt underway inside DTTF right now trying to find me and my systems."

"We're incredibly grateful to you, Thoreau," said Pam.

"Agreed. I think we need to do an assessment of where we are," said Ellul. "This attack has been successful beyond our expectations. But I'm seeing reports of increasing collateral damage. A nursing home in Duluth lost power and heat and six of its elderly residents died. Several hospitals have run out of backup generator fuel and dozens of ICU patients have died. I know we all acknowledged this consequence, but we may be looking at thousands of casualties."

"Isn't that exactly the wake-up call we wanted to send? How dependent we've all become on technology?" asked Miles.

"Yes, but we run the risk of focusing all the anger at LKC instead of the technology," said Artemis.

"We need to cure people of their addiction," said Othello. "Once they get a clean break they will understand what's it like to live free again."

LONDON

The initial flurry of encrypted communications identified and decoded by Colossus gave the tired scientists and engineers in Building 42 great hope, but they soon discovered that thousands of legitimate holochats and video conversations matched their key words. While a team of investigators reviewed each one, the exhausted technical crew tried to enhance the filtering.

Just after 11 p.m. one of the FBI investigators jumped out of his chair and yelled out to the room, "Holy shit! I think we found them!" A crowd immediately formed around his workstation, then he swiped his monitor contents to the big wall display so everyone could see. There were fifteen holoconference windows filled with a mix of camouflaged people and computer-generated avatars. He disconnected his earpiece and the conversation rang out across the large work area.

"...but we run the risk of focusing all the anger at LKC instead of the technology."

Bradley Childress ran over. "Freeze that conversation and keep recording. What's the timestamp?" He was joined by Mark Geiger, Director of the Domestic Terrorism Task Force, who had evidently just woken from a nap.

"Twelve minutes ago," said the investigator.

"Do we have locations yet?" asked Geiger.

"I printed out the relevant IP addresses immediately and requested the packet data from the team outside the Sphere, sir," replied the investigator.

"Printed out? Goddamned Colossus isolation protocol, we may lose them!" Geiger picked up a bright yellow handset, which was connected via an analog hard line to an identical version outside the Sphere. He did a quick count of the windows on the big screen. "This is Mark Geiger. I want you to contact DTTF operations and let them know we hope to have up to fifteen targets for drones in the next few minutes. We want to run incapacitation ops, is that clear? Deadly force is *not* authorized."

The entire team waited anxiously for the techs outside the Sphere to prepare the packet stream data. Every minute that passed increased the odds that the LKC members would no longer be at those locations. Finally, a courier ran into the Sphere and headed for the upload workstation, where a technician took his storage device and plugged it in. Colossus made quick work of the data and within a minute a small cheer went up as the first GPS coordinates began to overlay the holoconference windows on the big monitor.

Once they were all identified, a courier raced outside the sphere with a printed copy. Geiger spoke again into the yellow handset. "This is Mark

Geiger. I am authorizing fifteen drone intercepts at the GPS coordinates being provided for non-lethal force only. Make sure they are synchronized to be simultaneous."

HOLOCONFERENCE

"I'd like to canvas the group," said Ellul. "We will not recall the worms yet. We will increase our attacks on infrastructure and the tech supply chain. And we will try to recruit new members to organize real-life events as a second priority." A sudden loud crash interrupted him. Artemis jumped up and screamed, "Drone!" before the distinctive sound of Taser bolts firing.

"Shit!" shouted Pam. JT hit the kill switch on their gear but the high-pitched whine outside their Austin rental home told them it was too late. Two drones crashed through their windows and instantly deployed their Tasers.

In his San Diego apartment, Miles O'Connell jumped out of his chair and slammed the big red button that fried all of his computers and released a hydrochloric acid bath onto his hard disks. He did not understand how their 5K qubit encrypted transmissions had been broken and IPs geolocated. The drone that smashed through his window didn't give him any time to figure it out.

CHAPTER SIXTY-TWO

Los Angeles - February 1

M att Chandler, Special Agent in Charge of the LKC investigation, stared at the young man sitting across from him at the interrogation table. Even after years of work in counter-terrorism he could not understand the fanaticism that drove people to destroy the world around them, especially when they killed innocent people in the process. Matt had finished inspecting the LKC sites all over the country and flown to LA because Miles O'Connell was their highest value target. After eighteen hours of interrogation by the LA team, Miles had given them nothing. Chandler felt like strangling the terrorist right then and there, but they still needed information.

"Miles, you can continue to play dumb," began Chandler, "but let me review one more time where we are. We found your hidden server cluster. We found the launch folder for the worms. Our forensic team has reverse engineered them and we're learning how to counteract them in the field. But it's going slowly and more people are dying every day. There's a kill script called 'cancel' that requires a pass phrase. Give me the pass phrase now and I'll recommend against the death penalty in your case."

"I've got nothing to say, Chandler."

"You're just going to let innocent people die?"

"If that's what it takes," said Miles.

"What it takes for what? What is your purpose in killing these people?"

"The goal isn't killing people, that's an unfortunate side effect. The goal is to liberate people."

"You sound like some kind of goddamn brainwashed cult member. What kind of ideology is that? Liberate people from technology that keeps them fed and warm and healthy? Do you ever actually listen to yourself?"

"Better to be cold and hungry than be a slave to technology," said Miles.

"That makes no sense! You're a smart guy, Miles. When people are cold and hungry they are a slave to their fear and basest instincts. That's why we've got gangs roaming the streets breaking into houses to steal food. Technology doesn't enslave people, it frees them from a life solitary, poor, nasty, brutish and short."

"Oh, ha, the investigator knows some Hobbes. Congratulations."

"I know you studied Political Science in college. Didn't they teach you anything about the incredibly positive impact of technology on human welfare over the centuries?"

"I believe technology permanently reduces human beings and many other living organisms to engineered products and mere cogs in the social machine."

"Wait, that sounds familiar. Did you just quote the Unabomber's manifesto?"

"Required reading for LKC members," sneered Miles.

Chandler stood up. "Enough bullshit. Are you going to give me that pass phrase?"

"Not a chance. Does that mean it's time for the water-boarding? Oh yeah, that's illegal. Unless President Teasley is willing to break those laws too? Don't forget who knows exactly what went down with all the warrantless access. Are you sure you want to put me on trial? Could be very embarrassing for this administration."

"That's it, we're done." Chandler stepped out of the room and signaled to the agent guarding the door. "Set up transport to Maclean Virginia ASAP." The agent nodded and Chandler secure messaged his Director Mark Geiger. "No luck with MOC. Threatening to reveal task force access. Taking him to ENT Systems Maclean."

He called Amina Hamdi at ENT Systems. "Doctor Hamdi, how are the preparations going?"

"Agent Chandler, we haven't had enough time! Your techs only provided us the holoconference logs and avatars a few hours ago. And the 3D scans of the subject's work space haven't even gotten here yet!"

"Everyone is working as fast as they can, Doctor. The subject will be there in a few hours, I know the brain scans and growing the neural lace assembly will take some time. Keep working on the simulation content in parallel. But remember every hour the death toll from this disaster keeps rising. You have to move as quickly as possible."

"We understand, Agent Chandler," said Hamdi. "We'll do everything we can." After she dropped the call she looked a few yards away at the interrogation pod where Melissa King had died. With the breakneck speed of this preparation, she wasn't sure she could prevent Miles O'Connell from suffering the same fate.

CHAPTER SIXTY-THREE

The Oval Office - February 2

President Teasley sat in a chair in front of the Resolute desk with U.S. Chief Technology Officer Kara Morrigan and Chief of Staff Alex Turner on the couch to her right and Director of the Domestic Terrorism Task Force Mark Geiger and Attorney General Emma Wilcox on the couch to her left.

"So, what you're saying Mark is that this was an inside job?" Teasley asked.

"That is what we believe. Miles O'Connell is an extremely senior systems specialist who was able to both download the personal data and inject the worms from inside DTTF."

"How did he get through the background checks?" asked Emma.

"We're not sure about that, but he never openly participated in any protests. It looks like his activity was all over 5K qubit encrypted sessions on the dark web, where it's untraceable."

"Why didn't your internal security protocols detect his activity inside DTTF?" asked Kara.

"Unfortunately, Miles was one of the key architects of those protocols so he knew how to evade them."

"But the worm injection happened almost two weeks after the data dump. Why was the backdoor access kept open?" Kara asked. Geiger did not appreciate being second-guessed by the USCTO.

"At the time we didn't know for sure where the data dump came from," he said, "and we were pursuing many hundreds of leads."

"So, you put the entire country at risk so you could be more efficient with warrantless searches?" Kara asked.

"Obviously we didn't think the risk was that high. We were wrong," he admitted.

"Emma, what's our legal exposure here?" asked Teasley.

"DTTF was acting within the boundaries of executive order 14412 you signed on October 25th", said the Attorney General. "As we discussed at the time, the mandates in that executive order are subject to constitutional review and some of them might not pass First and Fourth Amendment challenges."

"All of that will not matter to the American people," said Chief of Staff Turner. "The bottom line is that this administration unlocked all the security gates and let one of its own personnel cause untold financial damage and the deaths of thousands of people. This is a political scandal, not a legal battle."

"But we did what we thought was right to protect the American people," protested Geiger. "And Congress was working on new legislation to grant those very powers to us outside of the executive order."

"I agree, Mark, but that also will not matter," said Turner. "Even if we had those laws passed and even if we intended only the best, the fact is that people in the executive branch itself perpetrated the worst terrorist attack in our nation's history."

"Someone's going to have to take responsibility for this," said Kara. She was looking directly at Mark Geiger. The Director of DTTF looked at each of the faces in the room, ending with President Teasley.

"I have worked harder than anyone in this room, anyone in this administration, to prevent terrorists from attacking this country. I will not be a scapegoat for doing my job!" said Geiger.

"I'm sorry, Mark," said the President. "Your employee was part of a terrorist organization. And your security protocols and decision to keep backdoor access open enabled him to launch multiple attacks against our country. I'm going to need your resignation. Today."

She turned to Alex Turner. "We're going to need to go public. But I want good news to share. Keep me regularly informed on the state of the cyberattack. When we've turned the corner and the country is stabilizing I'll make an announcement." Teasley stood and her staff immediately jumped to their feet. "That will be all, thank you."

After the room cleared, Amanda Teasley circled around the Resolute desk and stood looking out over the expanse of pure white snow covering the South Lawn. How many Presidents before her had stood here at this very window when facing a severe crisis? Kennedy and the Cuban Missile Crisis. Bush after 9/11. Trump and the Korean nuclear conflict. Haley at the start of the Iran War. The burden of responsibility for the lives of four hundred million American citizens was overwhelming at times.

Questions and doubts swirled in her head. This crisis would pass. But then, should she take advantage of the disruption in the status quo? Many historians had looked back at 9/11 and lamented the missed opportunity to alter the country's relationship to the Middle East and fossil fuel consumption. A massive shock like this terrorist attack could create a once-in-a-generation chance to change direction. There was no doubt the preeminent issue at this moment was the impact of ever-more-powerful technologies on society, in multiple dimensions. Could she lead the nation through a partisan minefield to a new consensus? How would future historians judge her in this moment?

CHAPTER SIXTY-FOUR

Maclean Virginia - February 3

Miles woke up slowly, groggy and aching from the Taser jolt. Why was he awake? Where were the police? He moved his head gingerly and saw the drone that tased him had crashed and was smoking in the corner of the room. That's why it hadn't been able to keep him unconscious. But the cops would be here any minute. He heard voices. "Thoreau! Thoreau!" He looked around, then realized they were coming from the hologlasses on the floor next to him. He slipped them on and saw Zurich and Geneva in a smoke-filled room holding shotguns. "Thoreau! Are you there?"

"Yes," he managed, "I'm here. What happened?"

"We shot down the drones coming for us," said Geneva. "But we don't have much time. We've got to get out of here."

"Thoreau, we may need to stop the worm attack on our own, in case we can't reach you," said Zurich. "We need to know the pass phrase, what is it?" Miles shook his head. "What do you mean, Zurich?"

"In case we can't reach you we need to know the pass phrase for the cancel script, what is it?" said Zurich.

"But you can't send the kill signal, you'll never get through. You don't have access to DTTF keys and they closed all the backdoor access. The pass phrase is useless to you."

"Yes, of course," said Geneva. "But if you're caught and we vote to stop the attack we can give the pass phrase to DTTF. Hurry, Miles, we only have a few seconds until they get here," pleaded Geneva.

"Okay, I guess that makes sense," said Miles. He shook his head again, trying to clear his mind. Something was wrong. "What did you just say?"

"We only have a few seconds!"

"No, you used my name. No one in the collective knows my name. What the fuck is going on here?"

"Shit!" Matt Chandler slammed his hand down on the table. He glared at Amina Hamdi. "Shut it down, we need to try again." Wei Chen tapped his simulation control tablet and eased Miles back into unconsciousness. His monitors indicated the graphene nanowire neural lace embedded in Miles' brain was maintaining its structure and mental field resistance was nominal.

"I told you we were too rushed," said Hamdi. "But this sim was working. We were very close. Just a small mistake, easy to fix. Give us ten minutes."

"But if you're caught and we vote to stop the attack we can give the pass phrase to DTTF. Hurry, Thoreau, we only have a few seconds until they get here," said Geneva.

"Right, that makes sense," said Miles. "The pass phrase is..." He searched his memory.

"What is it, Thoreau?" asked Zurich.

"The pass phrase, trying to remember. Oh yes, it's *eat shit agent chandler*."

"What the hell?" said Amina. "Did he just say *eat shit agent chandler*?" Matt Chandler stared at the interrogation pod a few yards away.

"How is that possible?" he asked. "I thought you said short term memories were suppressed. He's not supposed to remember anything after the drone intercept in his apartment. How does he remember me?"

"I don't know, he's not supposed to be able to." Amina thought for a minute. "Do you think he knows about this lab? If he did, he could have gamed the simulation by re-memorizing a different pass phrase. He would have just had to repeat the new content many times."

"I don't think he knew about it, but it's possible given his clearance level. Do you think he can still access the original pass phrase?"

"I don't know," said Amina. "We're in uncharted territory here." The three of them stared at the interrogation pod.

"We're going to have to try the extreme sim," said Chandler.

"Agent Chandler, we can't do that, it hasn't been approved." said Amina.

"Doctor Hamdi, I am approving its usage. Start the prep."

"You don't have the authority to approve it!" insisted Amina. The agent crossed the distance between them in a single stride, grabbed her forearm, and yanked her to her feet. He pulled her close so his face was just inches from hers.

"Doctor. This man is a terrorist and a murderer. There are innocent people dying out there while you are playing at having a conscience. Now prep the goddamn simulation or I'll throw you in jail for aiding and abetting a terrorist organization." He pushed her back down into her chair.

Rubbing her forearm, tears in her eyes, she turned and nodded slightly to Wei Chen.

Miles woke up slowly in unfamiliar surroundings. The last thing he remembered was the drone crashing through his window. He tried to move his head but it was somehow fixed in place. He couldn't move his arms or legs either. The ceiling above him was metallic and reflective enough that he could make out his own body wearing only white shorts on a table of some kind. As his vision cleared he could see the straps binding him to the table and some kind of equipment arrayed around it.

"Ah, I see you're awake," said a pleasant female voice. "I will be conducting your interrogation today."

"Who are you?" he croaked out.

"I am an interrogation program."

"You're an AI? That's illegal, AI interrogation was banned by the U.N."

"Please examine the display above your head. This is the signed executive order by President Teasley authorizing any and all means to extract required information from one Miles O'Connell. Since I have verified the signature on the document and confirmed your DNA is that of subject Miles O'Connell I am fully prepared to proceed with the interrogation."

"I want a lawyer!" screamed Miles.

"Now you can save yourself a great deal of trouble if you simply give me the information required. I have been programmed to ask you for the pass phrase for the cancel script. If you give me this information this interrogation will be over."

"I don't believe you, this is illegal and you can't touch me."

"Miles, I will need you to say 'the pass phrase is' followed by the pass phrase. My language processing is not very sophisticated."

"Go to hell, you fucking machine."

"As I did not recognize the required information, we will begin." There was a whirring noise from the middle of the table. Miles strained to see what was happening in the partially reflective ceiling. A robot arm deployed towards his right leg. There was a click, a flash of blue light, and a steady hissing sound.

"What the fuck is that?"

"That is a small acetylene torch," said the maddeningly calm AI. "It is quite effective because it delivers excruciating pain but cauterizes the flesh to prevent excessive bleeding."

"This is not possible, you can't do this, I don't believe you. Help! Help me!" A motor turned on and Miles could feel the skin of his right thigh getting hotter. "Oh my God, stop it!" The heat became intense and Miles could feel his skin blistering and splitting open. He screamed. The smell of burning flesh assaulted his nostrils. "STOP! I'll tell you! I'll tell you!" The torch clicked off and the robot arm retracted.

"A very wise decision, Miles."

"The pass phrase is *eat shit agent chandler.*" Miles let out a deep breath and unclenched his fists.

"Oh. I'm sorry, Miles. I have been told that is not the correct pass phrase. There is another pass phrase which is the real pass phrase. You are going to have to try harder to remember it."

"What? What do you mean? That's the pass phrase!"

"No, Miles, there is another one. Please try to remember it."

"I can't! That's it, that's the one!" Another robot arm started moving. "No! No! I don't know anything else!"

"You will remember, Miles," said the AI. "I assure you, you will remember."

Amina Hamdi was sobbing at her terminal as Miles' screams echoed through the lab. Wei Chen tried to stay focused on maintaining Miles' vital signs, desperate to avoid losing him like Melissa. He was pumping the beta blocker metoprolol into the pod's intravenous feed to counteract the massive surge of adrenaline. Matt Chandler was also watching the vitals monitor carefully.

"Doctor, calm down!" he said. "This isn't real. He won't remember a thing. Keep focused on the objective here."

"It's real for his brain right now," she countered. "We don't know the long term effects of this kind of program."

"I don't care about long term effects. This piece of shit will either be dead or in prison for life. In the short term we'll save hundreds or thousands of lives and start putting our country back together again."

"So the ends justify the means?" Amina said.

"In this case, yes, they do," said Chandler.

"I REMEMBER!" screamed the voice on the speaker. The AI program halted the virtual scalpel which had been making small slices on Miles' stomach. "The pass phrase, I remember it's *endless waves of glorious destruction*. The pass phrase is *endless waves of glorious destruction*."

Matt Chandler immediately messaged the forensic team in LA with the information. He joined a conference call and listened in as they worked through the procedure for canceling the worms. For some reason, he didn't hear Mark Geiger on the call at all. Instead USCTO Kara Morrigan gave the approval to reopen the DTTF backdoors to allow the 'cancel' script to breach the corporate security perimeter defenses.

The forensic team ran the script and provided the pass phrase. For a minute there was no response, then field teams dealing with heavily mutated worms started reporting they were shutting down. The script was working. Matt sat down heavily in one of the lab chairs and felt like he was finally able to breathe for the first time in a week.

CHAPTER SIXTY-FIVE

The Oval Office - February 4

President Amanda Teasley chatted with her Chief of Staff Alex Turner in the minutes leading up to her broadcast. She knew full well his task was to keep her loose before the most important address of her presidency. But she appreciated his efforts nonetheless. "Madame President? One minute to air," said a technician. She squeezed Alex's arm and leaned over to say thanks. He bowed his head slightly and withdrew to the side of the room to stand with the rest of her senior staff. Teasley took her seat behind the Resolute desk and watched the countdown in the prompter tick to zero.

"Good evening, my fellow Americans. For several terrible weeks we have endured terrorist attacks against our country's infrastructure and our most personal and private information. Tonight, I come before you with good news. Through the heroic efforts of our dedicated intelligence professionals we have identified and captured the core membership of the terrorist organization known as LKC. Antiterrorism teams are as we speak analyzing their computers and communications to find additional members. The cyberattack that has crippled our economy for more than a week has been stopped.

"Our relief at stopping this terrorist group cannot compensate, however, for our grief at those who have lost their lives due to LKC attacks. All across this great country families are mourning the loss of grandparents, parents, and children who died as a direct result of LKC's actions or indirectly through the violence that followed. We stand with you in your hour of need and will provide what comfort and assistance we can in the difficult days ahead.

"The loss of power, food, heating, and life's basic necessities brought out some of the best in us but also some of the worst. I have heard stories of neighbors helping neighbors, sharing supplies, and sacrificing their own wellbeing for the good of others. These stories represent the very best of what we strive to be in America. But we must also force ourselves to reflect on the other stories coming out of every state in the nation. Disheartening stories of riots and violence born of fear and selfishness, stories of attacks on our most vulnerable citizens, stories that are not representative of the America that we want to be. We can do better.

"I want to thank the brave first responders, police, firefighters, paramedics, doctors, nurses, social workers, and others who often ran into harm's way to help their fellow citizens. They needed to overcome a severe lack of resources and come up with creative ways to solve catastrophic problems that we had never planned for. We will always be in their debt.

"Unfortunately, as will be revealed in court filings over the next few weeks, I must report that these attacks were made possible by failures at the FBI's Domestic Terrorism Task Force. In fact, we have discovered that a DTTF employee was actually a member of LKC and primarily responsible for the recent cyberattack. As a result, I have accepted the resignation of Mark Geiger, Director of the terrorism task force.

"While he is a dedicated public servant fiercely committed to protecting our country, he has taken responsibility for the errors of judgement and decision-making that resulted in massive damage to our economy and the terrible loss of thousands of our citizens. My administration looks forward to working with the Congress as they investigate what went wrong and how we make sure it never happens again."

Amanda Teasley paused and the software in the teleprompter listening to her speak gracefully slowed the scrolling text. Keeping her eyes firmly fixed on the camera behind the projected words she knew by heart, she continued into the section that would, for better or worse, come to define her presidency.

"I know the wounds from the last few weeks are raw and we need time to heal both our economy and our lives. But, my fellow Americans, I think it also time for us to have a serious debate about technology and its impact on our lives. All technology can be used for both good and evil. All technology has benefits and consequences. It can both augment and enrich our lives and be used to control and manipulate us. It can both enable us to communicate and it can isolate us and destroy real dialog. It can both free us from routine labor and destroy entire categories of jobs. It can both protect us from those who seek to do us harm and provide the very means for their attacks.

"Our goal should always be to maximize the benefits of technology and minimize the consequences. But we must also examine who reaps those benefits and who bears those consequences. Far too often it is the wealthy and the powerful who benefit most, and this inequality has driven our country to the breaking point.

"The events of the past few months have led us to a unique moment in time. We have seen starkly opposing views of the role of technology in humanity's future. LKC had a dark, destructive vision of a world thrust backwards in time. Sara Dhawan so gracefully shared a positive, uplifting vision of technology put in service to humanity that recognized the dignity of every individual person.

"Now is not the time to follow the same old tired script with the same old tired talking points. Now is not the time to personally insult and demonize each other to avoid discussing the real issues. Now is not the time to stick our heads in the sand while our country tears itself apart.

"Now is the time to face these issues head on. Now is the time for bold new thinking that moves us towards a hopeful and positive vision for the future. Now is the time to come together as a country and make that vision a reality.

"I look forward to working with members of Congress of both parties, our state Governors, our leaders in the private sector, and you, the American people, to seize the moment that we have been given. We can and must do better using technology for the benefit of all humanity. We can and will do better because I believe we can work together on important issues, and I will dedicate myself to creating real change that improves the lives of every American citizen.

"Thank you, my fellow Americans, and good night."

CHAPTER SIXTY-SIX

Los Angeles - February 5

In real life, Tenesha Martin sat in her cramped room in Los Angeles. Inside her VR headset, she was using her Mental Intention interface to walk down a trail in the Italian Dolomites with Sara by her side. The gray craggy peaks and verdant green valleys extended for miles in every direction. As they reached the edge of a local plateau with a stunning view, Tenesha stopped and finished describing the President's Oval Office speech from last night.

"And then President Teasley said we need to adapt to the new reality of these technologies and figure out how to use them to benefit all of humanity. It was beautiful, Sara. My heart aches that you are not here to see it."

"Well in a way I am, Tenesha. This program is a piece of me. It is continuing to learn from the events taking place all over the world and from millions of interactions with people like you." Sara's image smiled and Tenesha was caught up short—it was hauntingly like the last smile she had seen at the gym minutes before Sara was shot. Only three weeks had passed and Tenesha was still prone to waves of uncontrollable sadness sweeping over her.

As she watched her friend walk beside her, Tenesha was once again struck by how unusual this was. For the first time in human history, a world-famous figure had been captured inside an AI and made available to interact with everyone. The debates had already started on *saranet*. Should the virtual Sara be aged by algorithms over time or should she remain sixteen, with generations to come always knowing her as she had been at this moment in time?

And what did it mean that the program was now learning not from Sara herself? How would anyone know if the psychometric profile and knowledge matrix embedded in the program would evolve the way Sara would have, when exposed to the same world events? Some of Sara's followers wanted the virtual Sara program frozen to prevent any corruption of her message. Like constitutional originalists, they felt her actual words and thoughts would stand the test of time.

Others felt this was a unique opportunity to see how the founder of a movement could continue to grow and personally guide it long after her time on Earth had passed. Another contingent wanted snapshots or backups taken every few months so it would be possible to go back and ask the "2039 Sara" a question and compare its answer to the "2050 Sara." Everyone was frustrated that the organization controlling the AI program had still not come forward to describe their stewardship model.

Tenesha's PNA buzzed and she paused the program. When she read the notification and linked message she shot up out of her chair and put her hand over her mouth. *Oh my God!* she thought. She immediately reactivated the VR program. "Sara! I just got invited to be on Governor Rajashankar's task force on implementing your ideas in California!"

"Tenesha, that's wonderful! I am so pleased for you!" said Sara.

"I know, I'm honored and all. I'd probably have to stop going to LAU, though. I'm not sure what to do." The AI program paused, as it sometimes did in new situations or when it was overloaded with too many requests.

"This is very important work, Tenesha," said the AI. "Helping the Governor succeed could make a big difference."

"Do you really think there's a chance we can make change happen?" Tenesha asked.

"I think it is too early to say," said the AI. "There are powerful forces at play. The people are demanding change. But the elites will not give up their status and power easily. They will continue to divide people and distract them. What's most important is to maintain your efforts. You and tens of thousands of leaders like you around the world. There will be both successes and setbacks. Do not get discouraged. Always press forward."

"I will, Sara. We will do everything we can to make it happen."

"Thank you," said Sara. She turned towards Tenesha, pressed her palms together and bowed her head.

"*Namaste*, Tenesha."

When Sara lifted her head, Tenesha looked into her eyes and was so taken in that for an instant she forgot it was just a VR image. Sara smiled in Tenesha's headset and in thousands of other headsets all over the world at that very moment. And in a dozen different languages, Sara said, "We will all take this journey together."

Gerald Huff is a principal software engineer at Tesla, where he is the technical lead for the software that manages the flow of thousands of Model 3 parts throughout the factory. Before joining Tesla, Gerald was director of the Technology Innovation Group at Intuit, exploring the application of emerging technologies to solve problems in the consumer and small-business space. In 2014, he ran a workshop with Peter Diamandis at Singularity University exploring the future of jobs and work with 30 technology, labor and government experts. *Crisis 2038*, Gerald's first novel, examines the impact of and potential solutions to the problem of technological unemployment. He lives in Berkeley with his wife, and has two kids, Paul and Jane.